THE CADAVER

ALEXANDER LAING was born in Great Neck, Long Island, New York in 1903. He attended Dartmouth College, but dropped out before graduation to become the Technical Editor of *Radio News*. In 1926 he shipped as an ordinary seaman on the S.S. *Leviathan*, bound for Southampton, England, and spent two years at sea. He then returned to Dartmouth, becoming a tutorial advisor in the English Department in 1930. His first two books, volumes of poetry, were published in 1927 and 1928, and the following year he was awarded the Walt Whitman Prize for poetry. He turned to fiction in 1930 with *End of Roaming*, a fictionalized account of his own childhood and student life. Laing finally earned his degree in 1933 and remained close to Dartmouth for the remainder of his career, retiring in 1968 as Professor of Belles Lettres. Laing was best known for his seafaring tales, the most popular of which was *The Sea Witch* (1933), though he is remembered by horror connoisseurs as the author of *The Cadaver of Gideon Wyck* (1934), a bestseller that Karl Edward Wagner later cited as one of the all-time best science fiction horror novels. Laing died in 1976.

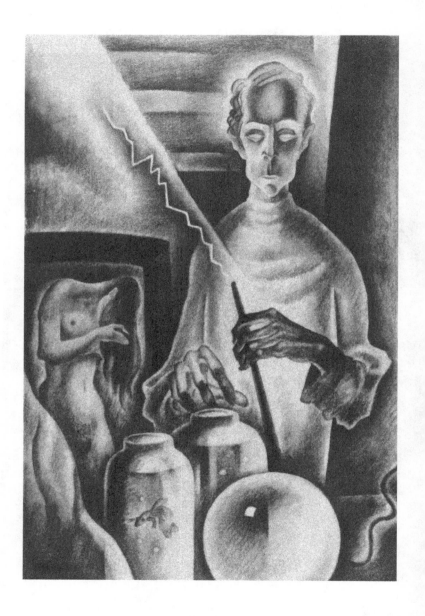

THE CADAVER OF GIDEON WYCK

by a Medical Student

EDITED BY
ALEXANDER LAING

VALANCOURT BOOKS

The Cadaver of Gideon Wyck by Alexander Laing
First published by Farrar & Rinehart, Inc., New York, 1934
This edition first published 2016

Published by Valancourt Books, Richmond, Virginia
http://www.valancourtbooks.com

ISBN 978-1-943910-49-6 (trade paperback)
Also available as an electronic book.

All Valancourt Books publications are printed on acid free paper that
meets all ANSI standards for archival quality paper.

Cover and frontispiece by Lynd Ward

The Publisher is grateful to Mark Terry of Facsimile Dust Jackets,
LLC for providing a scan of the dust jacket used for this reprint

Set in Dante MT

NOTE

Editors ought to keep their own personalities out of other men's books; so I have not presumed to tamper at all with the general, straightforward narrative of this one. Its conversations, however, were most unevenly presented, perhaps because some were taken down in shorthand and others reconstructed from memory. Consequently, I have chosen typical passages from what seems to have been the authentic speech of each character, for use as touchstones in imparting a similar colloquial ease to his other spoken words. Some incidents, originally related in long stilted speeches, I have reduced to a terser narrative form. The grammar of the expository parts called for so little revision that I have given it none. There were no chapter or "part" divisions in the Ms. but I was able to make them with trifling rearrangements of the text. For the name of the book, as well as for all subtitles and footnotes, I am responsible. There is no questioning the fact that this is the work of an anonymous but genuine medical student. Thomas Painter and Gertrude McClure, a teacher and a student of morphology, have verified all technical references, and have shared equally with me the task of preparing the book for the printer. The following "Explanation" accompanied the original Ms.

A. L.

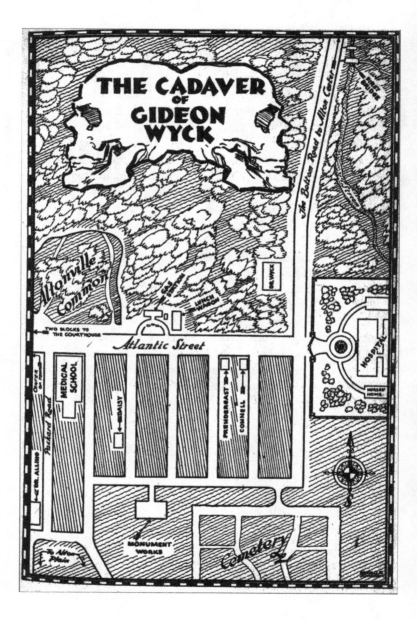

EXPLANATION

During the past year I have been drawn unwillingly into a series of grim events—and I have no assurance that their sequence is ended. The climax could yet be my own death. That is one reason for writing, but there are others. Sometimes the impartial application of just laws can work a particular injustice. I happen to be possessed of knowledge that ought to convict any one of three persons of a capital crime; yet I am morally convinced that all are innocent. This makes me reluctant to divulge what I, and I alone, have learnt.

Yet to conceal it, even briefly, may mean that it will die with me; and, since its partial discovery might work greater injustice, I intend to write down all I know. Then, as chance has put me in the way of information which I neither desired nor sought, I shall let chance decide whether it is to be known to the world as well. That seems the only fair way. I intend to describe these happenings in the strict order of their occurrence, starting with the first significant evening, a year ago tonight. Even though later events at times have erased the seeming importance of earlier ones, I shall try to show everything as it first appeared, for it may be that some item which I have thought trivial may be vital knowledge to another investigator. My shorthand diary will aid me, as will a great many shorthand notes taken in the course of duties which I shall presently explain. I shall alter the names of all persons, places, and institutions, and refer to the climate as that of Maine, with which I am familiar. There will be plenty of references through which anyone who is interested can locate the real town and school about which I am writing.

If at any point it seems unlikely that I can complete the story,
I shall mail what is done to a literary agent who knows nothing
of me.[1] Perhaps this will be considered a clever hoax to interest
a publisher; but even if that prevents publication, the Ms. is not
likely to be destroyed, so some day the truth will out. If it comes
too late to affect persons now living, that may be for the best.

[1] The story was received in two installments, the first of which, containing
everything but the material in Part III, was postmarked Chicago, the last
part, New Orleans. Both may have been remailed by the "readdressing" services.

THE CADAVER OF GIDEON WYCK

PART I

... WHICH CONCERNS ITSELF WITH OCCUR-
RENCES IN ALTONVILLE, MAINE, DURING
THE TWENTY-FOUR HOURS THAT PRECEDED
THE VANISHING OF GIDEON WYCK, M.D.

CHAPTER I

I room at the Connells', on Atlantic Street, four blocks east of the medical school. The hospital is about as far from us in the other direction, but most of the distance is not divided into blocks, because the main buildings are clustered in the middle of a private plat of forty acres, studded with pine groves and inclosed by a high iron fence. The hospital is quietly situated at the extreme eastern edge of the town of Altonville, the center of which is half a mile westward, beyond the Maine State College of Surgery.[1]

My rooms are in what used to be the garret of a one-story frame house. Biddy Connell, who did my washing during my first two years as a medic, let me fix them up with wall-board and promised me free use of them for the next two years. After I graduate (if I live long enough) she will be able to rent the place, which I have made habitable at no expense to her. You can stand only when near the middle line of the rooms, as the roof slopes both ways from its ridgepole. I am writing now in the front room, my study. The bedroom is in the rear. Between them opens the well of a steep stairway. I have got the habit of swinging into it, a hand on the floor on either side, and lowering myself by my arms. It is easier than turning my feet sidewise on the very narrow steps.

I mention this because the trick lets me leap out of bed, even in the dark, and be in the lower hall within a couple of seconds. It must have taken only a split second in the very early morning of the 3rd of April, 1932. I had gone to bed about one o'clock, and may have just fallen asleep when sharp, explosive shrieks brought me swinging down before I even knew what I was about. Dr. Wyck had told me to keep an eye on Biddy Connell's husband Mike, a truck driver, whose left arm had been amputated two weeks before. So far, despite the shock, and the need to get used to being a cripple, he had borne his misfortune without a whimper.

But I had been conscious of possible emergencies; so his

[1] The author has changed the name of whatever institution he may be actually referring to. There is of course no such institution in Maine.—ED.

shrieks brought me down in no time. The Connells insisted on sleeping with windows shut and door open. Consequently, as I groped for the hall light, I caught a glimpse of the scene on the bed when Biddy, pawing for the bulb that dangled above her, twisted the key so hastily that the light flashed on and off again, leaving against the black a bluish, momentary impression of Mike's features, stark with pain.

"For the love of God, Mike, what is it?" she yelled, her fingers knocking against the socket, aswing at its cord's end.

"The black one, wit' white eyes, Owoo! His nails are in me sowl, tearin' it out through me arm's end. Mother of Heaven! He's torn off me arm. Where is it? Where is it? Owoo! It's not here at all."

I found the hall light, which showed her the one over the bed. As I stepped in, Mike's right hand was clutching at nothing, just below the bandaged stump of his left arm.

"There, darlin'," she said, kissing his forehead, "'tis dreamin' ye were. 'Twill take time to get used to it, Mike. Oh, Mr. David, tell him it's all right."

Mike lay rigid, shivering, his breath painful and loud. Then the stump of his arm lifted and banged hard against the mattress, until he howled with agony. I held it still and tried to quiet him; but his right hand kept clutching spasmodically for the left forearm that was not there.

"Owoo! God, God, I can't stand it, Biddy, call the doctor."

"Here's Mr. David, come down to take care of ye," she crooned.

He shook his head and insisted upon having Dr. Wyck.

"Him? Not that one. Niver will I let him in here again."

Her husband nodded obstinately. "They're afraid of no one but him, I tell ye. He knows them all, and the names too. A black one it was, wit' white eyes, like in the hole in the hill."

I thought him delirious, until Biddy pressed hands to ears and cried, "Stop yer talkin' of such things. Ye niver had such ideas till ye took up with that old—divil, himself. He's the only—divil, in this town."

I could guess what was prompting this talk, but did not care to let myself believe it. Moreover, I was busy trying to account for Mike's symptoms. Under my hand I felt his heart behaving in an amazing fashion, beating more rapidly than seemed possible, only to pause periodically for a dangerous interval, give a terrific pound, and continue its rapid, steady pumping. For all my restraining strength, he suddenly sat upright, a noise of pain gasping in and out his throat, continuous, horrible.

"Oh, then, I'll call him," Biddy agreed. "But lie ye down."

She pulled on her pink wrapper and hastened into the hallway. It seemed a long while before anyone answered. Then came the faint sound of Marjorie Wyck's voice, evidently saying that her father, who was a night owl anyway, as usual had not come in yet.

"Oh, darlin', is it Miss Wyck speakin'? Sure, 'tis Biddy Connell. —Yes, sure, for Mike.—Yes, there's Mr. David here, but my Mike won't let a sowl but your fayther go near 'im, the thick mick. Oh, God forgive me, and him sufferin'."

It was too bad that it was night, because Daisy Towers, who had the switchboard daytimes, usually knew where anyone in town was to be found, and always prided herself on keeping accurate track of the doctors. As it was, Biddy had to make several calls before she got an answer to 190, the number of Prexy Alling's private laboratory at the medical school. Dr. Wyck proved to be there. He made violent objections, but Biddy implored, "Oh, he's altogether sure he's dyin', doctor. Yes. Quick, now."

I had stepped toward the door, from interest in the outcome of the call. We both turned to find Mike sitting up, pressing the stump into the pillow, his face twitching, his eyes wide and scared.

"Why do I feel it there, Biddy, like pokin' me arm through the bed? Look! I can feel the springs with me fingers, all twangy, like a harp. Listen to 'em. No, no. Me poor fingers—they ain't there."

"Does it still hurt so much, Mike, darlin'?" she asked.

"No. It stopped hurtin', sudden, a minute ago. Hurtin' that way. It always hurts. But it was like to kill me then—even after —the black one—let go."

"Stop yer blather. Lie down. I'll tell the doctor to niver mind," she said; but he became frantic, and she had to reassure him. "All right then. Lie down, now, while I talk a minute to Mr. David."

She led me to the far end of the hall, and whispered hoarsely,

"Look, ye know Miss Finch, the pretty nurse? Well, today she told me there was no more need to cut off his arm than to—to—fly. One of thim young interners looked after him, after the accident, till up comes that old divil Wyck, and says 'Call in all the students to—to look at an amputation.' And the nice young feller said he didn't think it was needed. And the old divil told him to shut up. They did it, then. And I promised meself I'd niver let that old divil come in here again, but I can't tell Mike why. Would it be true, d'ye think, Mr. David?"

"It's utter nonsense," I said at once; but my voice may have sounded too cocksure. I had witnessed the amputation, and had heard the whisper that the limb could have been saved by anyone less interested than Dr. Wyck in a chance to demonstrate the suturing of skin flaps. As a student, I was no competent judge, and naturally preferred to oppose so dangerous a rumor, in the absence of a positive opinion.

When we went back, there was a crafty, wild look on Mike's face. "I heard what ye said," he whispered. "I heard it. But there's nobody but him can make 'em go away. I know. I've seen him do it."

"Make what go away?" I asked, but Mike looked uneasy and refused to answer.

A few minutes later Dr. Wyck entered, growling, as usual. Biddy turned her back on him at once. His face, which I always remember as being ruddy and youthful, despite his years, seemed pale for some reason and wore a sardonic scowl. Here was one doctor who never cajoled his patients. He might tell them they were sicker than the diagnosis warranted, but not the opposite. That was why persons in Altonville used to choose other practitioners for the removal of tonsils; but it was also the reason why, when in danger of their lives, the braver ones called upon the passionless, machine-like skill of Gideon Wyck.

"Well," he asked gruffly, "what ails you?"

Mike looked uneasily at me and Biddy, and then whispered, "It was the black one, doctor, wit' white eyes. Oh, I was afraid he'd come, and he did. Tuggin' me sowl out, he was, here." He indicated a spot a few inches beyond the outthrust stump.

I held my breath, expecting a tirade of annoyance; but Dr.

Wyck seemed to catch hold of his temper. "Oh," he said, flashing at me a wink which I failed to understand, "the black one, eh? You mean my friend Beelzebub? Why didn't you twist his tail, like I told you to?"

"God! I couldn't move a finger. Frozen stiff, I was."

"And so you hauled me all the way over here because you dreamed you were being hurt. You fool, I'd——"

"Dreamed? Fool? Fool yerself! Shriekin', he was," protested Biddy. "He niver yelled before, iver. Wide awake, he was, and near dyin' with pain, long after. Ask Mr. David."

"I told you all he'd imagine he felt pains in his missing arm."

"You told us, but this was different," Mike insisted sullenly. "Pains? I felt thim all along. Pains in me fingers —where they ain't there—any more. This was ten times worse than iver it was."

"Poppycock."

"His heart was most abnormally affected, doctor," I put in.

"Humph. Any man can scare his heart to death if he tries hard enough."

"'Twas you that was scarin' 'im," Biddy blurted, "I heard ye, with all that talk about"—she sniffed, and hesitated, and spoke the word defiantly—"divils."

Gideon Wyck glanced menacingly at Mike, as if to rebuke him for having revealed a secret. I thought again that I sensed an outburst of temper about to break from Gideon Wyck, but again it was quelled, and I got another quick wink.

"That's all he needs to be scared of. The arm's all right. And I don't want any more night calls about grown-up babies."

"Babies? Yes," Mike said hoarsely, a wild glare in his eyes, "that's a nice way to speak to a feller that gave his own blood to keep ye alive, ye old ghost."

The doctor seemed to start, at that. Then he said quickly, "*Gave* your blood? We pay fifty dollars a pint from any donor, you included. More than a truck driver's blood's worth."

The dual storm of invective from Mike and his wife was stilled by a long ring of the telephone bell. Still sputtering with wrath, Biddy answered it and came back to say, "Yer poor sweet daughter, and she's a thousand times too good for the dirthy likes of ye, says ye're wanted at the hospital, quick. And it can't be too quick for ye to be gettin' out of here, after givin' us the paper-thing about the insurance."

"I haven't had time to write it, and I won't find time till you learn to be civil with your betters."

Mike, who had been fizzing with indignation, suddenly became panicky as Gideon Wyck left the room.

"Doctor," he called. "Oh, please—if he comes again, the black one—Ye didn't say what to do, instead. I can't git hold of him. I can't."

Dr. Wyck gave me a third wink, and said very solemnly, "I told you there's only two things to do. Either say the words I gave you forwards and backwards, or else twist his tail." With which, the attendant medico stalked from the house.

"You'll be all right, Mike," I assured him. "He just likes to kid people. If you stop biting, he won't have half so much fun."

Mike had closed his eyes, and seemed not to hear me. I gave Biddy's hand a squeeze, and told her to call me if anything else went wrong. Then, with the memory of her furious eyes to confront me, I climbed back to my garret.

But it was more than the memory of her eyes that kept me from sleeping. Anger, which I had suppressed in the presence of the doctor, now made me lie trembling with indignation. I was very fond of the Connells. Their blundering hospitality helped to compensate for my lack, since the age of twelve, of a home to call my own. They were simple, superstitious: the best reason why a doctor, of all people, ought not to scare them. Despite her show of disbelief, Biddy had been as frightened as Mike; and my denial of Muriel Finch's story about the amputation had not seemed to impress her.

What should I have done? It is easy enough to say now that I ought to have confided at once in some person of authority; and to anyone else who finds himself in a like situation, I say, *Speak up at once!* for, the longer you delay, the harder it is to explain why. It is especially difficult to acknowledge the blame for letting things occur that you perhaps could have prevented. Yet, even today, I am not sure that I should have spoken. It is not usual for a student either to rebuke his instructor or to bear tales about him. The idea was especially difficult in the case of Gideon Wyck. A lifetime of teaching at medical school had fostered certain deplorable traits that offset his technical excellence in surgery.

We medics and internes are notoriously a hard-boiled lot. We have to be, at first: mellowing comes later, after we have learnt Nietzsche's injunction *Be hard!* When your hand first holds a knife over living tissue, there is no room for sentimentality anywhere around you. That is why medical students choose strange idols, and seek to emulate teachers who are teaching for the very reason that they are not successful practitioners. Gideon Wyck was idolized by half his students for the very ruthlessness that made him a bad practitioner, but a superb scientist. Youngsters whose stomachs began to squirm in the operating room would think of the cool self-control of Gideon Wyck and get a grip on their urge to vomit. His professional anecdotes, often revoltingly cruel, were something you learnt to laugh at before feeling at ease over a dissection.

Quite as strong as the desire to emulate Wyck was the fear of his scalpel-like tongue, always ready to be thrust at a show of weakness. I can remember distinctly the first paracentesis I witnessed. It was on a middle-aged woman who had borne many children and served them until her frail physique began to fail. Her abdomen was fearfully distended with fluid which, slowly accumulating, was just as slowly killing her. Wyck performed the operation with consummate skill and necessarily without anæsthesia. As the trochar punctured the distended flesh there was a tympanitic pop and fluid gushed forth into a pail. The woman gave a low agonized moan and began to weep softly. I could feel the blood draining from my head, and my stomach began to contract. As I reached wildly for a stool to sit on, Wyck looked up. He smiled and then sneering contemptuously said, "Someone take the ninny outside; he's sick." Almost in a second my face flushed again, and still weak and nauseated I edged back into the row of students who lined the rail of the amphitheater.

The frequency of such episodes should explain why those who admired him immensely were balanced by as large a group of students who hated him heart and soul. His arbitrary whims no doubt balanced up. He was lenient with those whom he trusted, and far too severe with those of whom he chanced not to approve. A hundred times I have heard one medic begin to praise him, only to be cut short by bitter denunciation from another. I had contrived to be of neither group. While disliking him, I was determined to avoid his disfavor. That, however poorly, will have to excuse my irresolute conduct during his bullying of the Connells.

Vexation over my own cowardice made sleep impossible. I got out my diary and set down a shorthand account of what had happened, trying to remember the speeches verbatim, as a mental exercise to quiet my mind. Presently I heard Mike say,[1] "Where's the paper, wit' the words he wrote down, Biddy?"

"That nonsense?" she answered. "I burnt it. Now go to sleep."

"I could never get the memory of it anyhow. Oh, Biddy, I'm scared that he'll come for me again."

(I continued to record their conversation verbatim.)

"'Tis nonsense, I tell ye," she shrieked, "whativer it was that ould divil put in yer head, Mike Connell. Ye niver was like this before he came here, last week."

"'Twas longer than that," he said, biting off the sentence as if he had spoken it inadvertently. Then he went on, "Out of a book he read it, Biddy, an old, holy-lookin' book, wit' all the words to say at 'im, the black one. And he read some of it out of the Holy Bible."

"Holy Bible. Ye know what Fayther Dunn said, about listenin' to the Bible, except when the priest reads it. He's an old atheist, that Dr. Wyck. How do ye know he read it true?"

"He showed me. I read it over meself. All about the different colors of divils, it told, in the Bible."[2]

1 The preceding conversations all needed to be made colloquial. The ones in the remainder of the chapter I have left just as the author wrote them. Note that what he claims to have taken down directly has the aspect of genuine speech. What he tried to remember, lacked it.—ED.

2 I cannot find such a passage either in the Bible or in any standard work on demonology. Watt's *Bibliotheca Britannica* lists, under the date 1583, a book with the following title page: THE WORLDE POSSESSED WITH DEVILS, *conteyning three dialogues; 1. Of the Devil let loose; 2. Of Blacke Devils; 3. Of White Devils, and of the comminge of Jesus Christ to Judgment; a verie necessary and comfortable discourse for these miserable and daungerous dayes.* Perhaps this is the "old holy-lookin' book" referred to. Mike, having been shown both, may

She tried to change the subject. "Now, don't ye even think about it any more, Mike, darlin'. 'Tis all nonsense. And we'll git the insurance, and ye can spend all day fishin' wit' Charlie Michand, and I'll buy me an electric washtub, and we'll live in style, like the Glennons."

"He didn't give ye the insurance thing?"

"No. Three times I've been to git it, and he's always busy. Tomorrow! says he. He'd as lief we'd not get a penny of insurance, to save 'im the scribblin' of a note—the old—bastard."

"Ssh! Biddy."

" 'Tis all right to say it, of him. And 'tis himself that's sown a fine crop of thim, around this town, if the truth was told."

He did not answer. Exhaustion must have lured him to sleep. But for a long time I lay wakeful. Could people still be serious about the devils of our fathers? I remembered the witchcraft scandals of western[1] Pennsylvania, not many months before, as shocking proof that modern men could be driven to murder by such irrational beliefs. My diary shows that I was also pondering, even then, the meaning of Mike's remark about giving his blood "to keep ye alive, ye old ghost." Dr. Wyck had seemed startled by the accusation; yet I could not remember his being ill during my three years as a medic. Was it an old event? No, because the Connells had first settled in Altonville at about the time of my own arrival—and it was I myself who had suggested to Mike, when he was out of a job, that he might prove an acceptable blood donor.

I resolved to look up the record of transfusions at the hospital, to see whether Dr. Wyck actually had received blood from Mike Connell. The incident could have occurred during a vacation, and thus might have escaped my knowledge, even though I had spent most of my vacations in Altonville, for lack of any other place to go, and of money to go on. Hardly anything of interest occurred in the hospital that was not known to the generality of medics

---

have confused a passage from it with one from the Bible. I have been unable to consult the former book.—ED.

1 My editorial collaborator Mr. Painter, himself a native Pennsylvanian, says that the "hex doctors" are to be found more frequently in the southern part of the state. See New York *Times*, 7 Jan. '30, p. 24, col. 2.—ED.

within a few hours; but efforts were occasionally made to hush up certain cases. Wyck might have done this. It would have been in character with his customary desire to be thought an iron man. He never missed an opportunity to sneer at students who gave illness as an excuse for absenting themselves from the classroom. It was his boast that he had not been sick a single day in his life. "How can you expect to keep other people in health," he would snap out, "if you don't know how to stay healthy yourself? Doctors have no time to be sick, you idiot. You'd better go learn to be something else. Be a poet, why don't you? They're always dying of something or other. Pity they didn't die quicker, most of 'em."

Remembering this, it occurred to me that the old tyrant had not said anything of the sort in my hearing for some months. He had seemed unnaturally pale when he appeared at Mike's bedside. Perhaps he had recently required a transfusion, because of some ailment natural in one of advancing years. If so, it certainly had not interfered with his ordinary activities.

When at last I went to sleep, it was only to have a noisome dream in which the features of Dr. Wyck, pale as a ghost, confronted me. He raised a glass of blood to his lips and drank. The fluid pulsed wavelike across the wan face until it glowed crimson in the darkness—like an illuminated devil's mask on Hallowe'en.

CHAPTER II

When I mentioned, some pages back, that I could guess what might be prompting Mike's ravings about devils, I was thinking of the coincidence that his physician happened to be an authority on the literature of demonology. His interest in the subject was not entirely frivolous, by which I mean that he was not concerned merely with a study of the mistaken notions of past ages. Shortly after coming to Altonville for my first year I had read a paper contributed by Dr. Wyck to one of the psychiatric journals, offering modern diagnoses of the symptoms legally recorded in some of the old witchcraft trials. What I principally remember from the article was his citation of authenticated instances of the occurrence of extra nipples and breasts on bodies otherwise normal, and of the mental effects resulting from efforts to conceal these deformities from the world. He demonstrated, with what seemed to me to be perfect logic, that persons bearing such stigmata considered themselves set apart from mankind in general, were unusually susceptible to occult beliefs, and frequently expressed a grievance against their Creator for having failed to make them "in his own image." From this he argued that in more superstitious ages, when witches were universally believed in, persons so afflicted would not only be unusually susceptible to persecution as witches, but would have equally good reason for suspecting themselves of belonging in that category. He therefore argued that the frequent charges that condemned witches had been found to have "extra teats to suckle the devil" were not fictions invented by bigots, but actual facts. Moreover, the publicity from one such witch trial would have served to convince other poor wretches similarly deformed that they must be witches, and might as well make the most of their opportunities, if witches they were.[1]

1 See pp. 90-96, *The Witch-Cult in Western Europe, A Study in Anthropology*, by Margaret Alice Murray. Oxford: at the Clarendon Press, 1921. I quote excerpts: "The other form of the Devil's Mark was the 'little Teat.' It occurred on various parts of the body; was said to secrete milk and to give suck to the familiars, both human and animal; and was sometimes cut off by the witch before being searched. The descriptions of the 'teat' point to its being that natural phenomenon, the supernumerary nipple ... [which] occurs in both sexes; according to Bruce, 'of 315 individuals taken indiscriminately and in succession, 7.619 per cent. presented supernumerary nipple.' ... Alice Gooderidge and her mother, Elizabeth Wright, of Stapenhill near Burton-on-Trent, were tried in 1597: 'The old woman they stript, and found behind her right shoulder a thing much like the vdder of an ewe that giueth sucke with two teats, like vnto two great wartes, the one behinde vnder her armehole, the other a hand off towardes the top of her shoulder. Being demanded how long she had those teates, she aunswered she was borne so. Then did they search Alice Gooderidge, and found vpon her bely, a hole of the bignesse of two pence, fresh and bloudy, as though some great wart had beene cut off the place.'" Miss Murray notes that the removal of such a deformity is a simple operation, and states that an unskilled operator would be able to perform it with a sharp knife. Records of several witch trials show that this expedient had been resorted to by the terrified suspects, indicating

This reference to one of Dr. Wyck's chief interests is here made for reasons that will become apparent at a later point in my narrative. Perhaps I should also make it clear in advance that he was not the only person in town distinguished by special interests and abilities. Another of his colleagues, Dr. Kent, is accredited with being one of the foremost authorities in the country on the legal aspects of medicine, a subject in which he gives a regular course at the medical school. And Dr. Alling, the president of the local institution, is perhaps the world's most learned investigator into the causes of deviation from normal structure in the growth of the mentality as well as of the body in man. If you ask why such distinguished men should be sequestered in a small and comparatively out-of-the-way community, I can only ask in reply why the work of the Mayo brothers has been done in a town in Minnesota, rather than in the city of New York.

Altonville, as a matter of fact, is an ideal community in which to conduct researches in medicine. Aside from the Maine State College of Surgery, it contains the largest hospital but one in the whole state. The patients, drawn equally from the countryside, from villages, and from manufacturing towns, give perhaps a better cross-section of mankind and its ailments than could be got in any of the better-equipped hospitals of the world's great cities. I have been assured of this by Dr. Alling, who founded the college thirty years ago, under conditions which made it possible for him to choose a location with considerable freedom. He had private means; and his brilliant record as a research assistant to several of the foremost physicians of Germany had made it easy for him to get endowment funds from some of the newly established foundations. His strongly individualistic policies later estranged these sources of financial assistance; but Dr. Alling,

---

that they knew perfectly well what to expect. Miss Murray cites from Reginald Scot's *Discoverie of Witchcraft*, London, 1584, "that if the witch 'have anie privie marke under hir arme pokes, under hir haire, under hir lip, or in her buttocke, or in her privities; it is a presumption sufficient for the judge to proceed to give sentence of death upon her.'" I have not been able to find in the professional journals any paper that might correspond to the one mentioned at the beginning of this chapter by the anonymous author, as having presumably appeared in the latter 1920s; but my search was admittedly incomplete.—ED.

whose genius includes executive and administrative abilities of a high order, has been able to cajole the state legislature into making yearly grants to sustain the college. As a compensation, men who signify their intention of practicing medicine within the state itself, and who have been bona fide residents thereof, are required to pay only the nominal sum of $100 a year for tuition. Outsiders pay four times as much.

I hope the foregoing facts will make clear why it is that several men of the highest rank in their profession are to be found conducting an up-to-date medical school, and researches of a most advanced sort, in the midst of a largely decadent farming area; for it was only the coincidence of these apparently anomalous factors that made possible the events I am about to describe. Crime of an urban kind, with abstruse scientific ramifications, has been committed in a setting provided with only the primitive police facilities of the back country. That, I suppose, is the reason why I am now writing of a still unsolved mystery. If the same events had occurred in Boston or in New York, the culprit doubtless would have been apprehended long ago. At any rate, I myself should not have been allowed to blunder upon so much pertinent and horrible information, at present unknown to the authorities, without at least having become more of a suspect myself.

Before going on with my story, I ought to explain how it came about that I was able to discover so much concerning a matter which I from time to time have really tried to avoid. The crucial fact was my residence at the Connells', where everything started. Another entangling circumstance was my old habit of keeping a shorthand diary, which served to sustain interest in many little occurrences that would otherwise have been soon forgotten, but which proved, long after I wrote about them, to be mutually significant. The main factor, however, that caused me to be drawn into the very center of this mystery was my job as secretary to our "Prexy," Dr. Manfred Alling. The luck which prompted me to learn shorthand in high school, for no definite purpose except a scientific interest in getting things done in the most efficient manner, made it possible six years later to qualify for a position having many concurrent advantages.

My official rating as a member of the administrative staff

(even while I was registered as a student) gave me the privilege of attending all classes without paying any tuition whatever. Daily contact with the most brilliant worker in his field of course was an inestimable advantage to any student. The fact that he sometimes needed me at odd moments had the effect of freeing me from most of the curricular restraints, because I could always plead the privilege of official business. And my salary, though small, was sufficient to pay all my living expenses, since rent and tuition were free.

Last year my schedule of courses was such that I had arranged to take dictation from Prexy every morning for two hours, until it was time for the eleven o'clock lecture. At half past eight, after a troubled sleep and a hasty breakfast, I was on my way to Dr. Alling's house. My unpleasant reveries over the events that had occurred in the dark early hours of the morning were interrupted by the incisive noise of feminine heels behind me. It was Muriel Finch, walking stiffly, frowning. I paused in front of the medical school and waited for her to catch up, but she was not in a talkative mood.

"Regular morning grouch?" I asked.

"It's getting to be regular," she said. "That's the least you can expect, after an all-night shift."

"Why aren't you in the dorm, then, by now?"

"Didn't think I could sleep. I wanted some air—fresh air. I hate that smelly place. Oh, how I hate it!"

We had taken the left-hand turn, southward, onto Packard Road, the last house on which was my destination. Indeed, there was no other house on it, past the medical school itself. Prexy had located his home for solitude, when he wanted it. We walked for a little way without speaking. Then Muriel sobbed suddenly, and pushed knuckles into the corners of her eyes, crying, "I hate this whole damned town. I'll go crazy if I stay here another day. I will. I know I will."

When I patted her shoulder, she shrank from the touch, and then apologized. "I just can't help it. People are such muts. All of them. I don't mean—any one person." She looked up in a half-scared fashion and said, "You didn't think I meant anybody in particular?"

"Well, I hope you weren't meaning me," I admitted, and she tossed her head.

I thought I knew what was wrong with her. She went by the name of "the blond floozy" among the medical students, who had a theory that a unique impediment of speech made it very difficult for her to pronounce the word "no," especially when the moon was shining, with a jug of applejack near by. If I had not tested the theory myself, my restraint was due to no essentially puritanical notions, but rather to the fact that I had gone misogynistic, for the time being, over the lees of another affair. The young lady who was the light of my life at the university had recently decided that her idea of deathless love did not include the prospect of waiting for me to go through medical school and interneship before anything could be done about it in a legal way. But that is an episode all past and done with.

As regards Muriel, most of my classmates were vivid liars if the theory about her impediment of speech was not valid. In fact, we had all thought for a long time that she was due for dismissal from the hospital staff. There was a general tendency to be lenient about the private lives of nurses and of medics, so long as their affairs were managed with discretion and without impairment of duties and studies. But Muriel had several times been slated for lateness on the night shift, and for a fit or two of hysterics while in attendance upon critical operations. It was hard to understand why these derelictions, in her case, were being overlooked. As I did not learn the reason till later, I shall save it for its proper place in the narrative.

"Dave," she blurted suddenly, "do you think I could get a job somewhere else?"

I asked where she had worked last, and she said, "I came right here from the farm. Father died. There are four kids younger than me. They need what I can send, they and mom. She works her hands off. That's the only reason I've stayed through this last winter. But I'll go crazy if I have to stay any longer."

"Want to tell me what's the trouble?" I asked.

She looked quickly sidewise, as if in fear, and asked, "What are you thinking? What do you mean?"

"Nothing much. I'd just like to think that some of my friends are liars. Would it help any if I punched them on the snoot?"

She looked almost relieved, and then defiant. "Oh, that! I don't care about that—what they say about me. What of it? I guess I'm not much worse than the rest of the girls, am I? Just 'cause I'm a farm kid, I suppose. Lot of credit you get for it around here. All you read about—wicked cities, nice upright country folks. Oh yeah? If they knew what went on back of the barn on every farm I ever saw. That's the trouble, they do know, in a town like this. It's only those guys that write books in the cities that think how nice and sweet a farm is. Nice and innocent. I knew plenty about what it's all about, long before I ever came to this town."

She was talking shrilly, and hysterically. I did not interrupt.

"Don't worry, Dave. They didn't have anything to teach me here. Maybe I'm too—good-natured. What if I am? You can be a lot worse things than good-natured. People can act like you'd think they were—Dave! Do you—do you believe in—devils? On earth, I mean, getting inside of people—like in the Bible. Oh, never mind, I guess I am going crazy."

Impressed, I took a flyer. "I can't think of anybody who's got a fiend inside him, around here—of course excepting old Wyck."

She stopped short, breathing quickly, staring with startled eyes.

"Then you know— Oh, then you do— What are you talking about?"

"Things you couldn't possibly know about. Got anything to add to the horrible record?"

She said, "No!" as if in great relief.

"Well, that reminds me. Biddy Connell claims you told her that the amputation wasn't necessary. Maybe it wasn't. But no good can possibly come of saying a thing like that."

"You don't know what you're talking about," she cut in.

"Oh, yes I do. I'm not thinking of Wyck. The hell with him. I'm thinking of the Connells. It's bad enough to be crippled. But it's all the harder to bear if somebody gives you the idea that it wasn't necessary. Don't you understand that?"

"You don't know what you're talking about," she repeated stubbornly. Somewhat nettled, I asked her to explain herself; but she shook her head nervously and walked stiffly along, her mouth twisting, but remaining tightly closed. I fell back on the recurrent philosophical finding that the wheels in women's heads don't spin in the same patterns that men's do, and that there's no use trying to understand females in certain of their moments. No sooner was that attitude established than she turned suddenly toward me and blurted, "Oh, but I've got to tell somebody—something —anything— Even if it's just what happened last night."

"What was that, Muriel?"

"No, never mind."

"Suit yourself," I said with a shrug.

"All right, then, I will!" she cried. "Other people saw that. I wasn't the only one. They can at least make him stop practicing, even if that's all they do. And there was somebody else saw that much, anyway, about half past one this morning."

"Saw what?" I inquired, mystified.

"Saw the way he treated two poor old people at the hospital."

As she hesitated again, I remembered Marjorie Wyck's call to say that her father was wanted at the hospital, after he had stopped in to see Mike.

Finally she got out her incoherent story, in bursts of passionate bitterness. It seemed to me not to be worth all the fuss she was making about it, but I realized that her emotion was being caused by something worse which she dared not speak of. Here is the outline of the incident:

Peter Tompkins, aged fourteen years, had shot himself through the lung while hunting, and had been nearly dead from loss of blood when discovered. I knew this, because Mike had told me "the histhory of the case" a month ago, it having been his blood that saved the boy's life. Peter had progressed fairly well for three weeks or so. Then a lung abscess had developed, and Gideon Wyck had told the poverty-stricken parents that nothing could save their son. At their insistence, however, an oxygen tent had been rigged. At one o'clock on the morning on which my story opens—April 3rd—after the costly cylinders of gas had been hissing for four days and five hours, Nurse Finch failed to distinguish a pulse, and put in a call for Dr. Wyck.

"There they sat, near dead themselves," she said, "the kid's mother and father, I mean, when in comes Dr. Wyck. Four days they'd been watching, with hardly a break, he in his overalls and a patched old army coat. She had on something you couldn't tell what it was, it was so old. Just the way they were when they came down from the farm, when we sent word out about the relapse.

"'Phew,' says Dr. Wyck, coming in, 'what makes this place stink so?' I whispered to him to be careful, and nodded toward them, a little bit. 'Phew,' he says again, 'Why don't you send 'em out for a bath?' A nice thing, with their son dying in the room. I whispered there might not be any use in their coming back.

"'Hey?' he says, 'The boy dead?' just as loud as before. 'Oh, I could have—well, never mind.' The old farmer says, 'We ain't afraid to learn, now, any more, doctor,' and he snaps, 'Why should you be? I told you four days ago it was no use.' He's off his head, Dave, really. Oh, you've got to believe me.

"Well, the kid was dead. But even that wasn't enough for the old devil. He starts right away saying that the hospital couldn't pay for the oxygen. One of the girls told me a few minutes ago he'd really told them that in the first place, but they said they'd get money for it somehow. And there he was, about five seconds after telling them their son was dead, trying to make them say they'd pay forty dollars right away. Forty dollars! They won't see that much actual cash in a year, on the kind of a farm they must have. I know, I was brought up on one, remember.

"And there's old Wyck in his swanky clothes, trying to look like a young dude, telling that ragged old couple to rake up forty dollars. They can't let him go on in the clinic. He's insane. I know he is, I tell you. I know it."

"Got any more reasons than that for thinking so?" I asked, pausing in front of Alling's.

She seemed to shudder. Her hands folded into fists. "No," she said. "No, nothing special."

"Well, have you reported this to anyone yet?"

She gasped suddenly. "No! Oh, no. And you mustn't either. They've got to find some other things about him, that I don't know about. Don't you see? He'd know it was me that told, unless— Those old people! I wish they'd have the nerve to come right to Alling about it."

She stared at me in a strange fashion, turned suddenly, and hurried on.

CHAPTER III

I found that Prexy Alling was waiting for me in his study, and made once more the conscious effort to be at ease which was necessary in the presence of his deformity. You must have seen his picture in the papers; but he usually poses in a fashion to conceal the twisted body that may have more than a little to do with his personal interest in unusual phases of medicine and surgery. All year I had been taking notes for a work, the title of which reveals its author's attitude. Planned to fill at least six sturdy quartos, it pleases him to call it *A Short Sketch for a History of Concomitant Variations in Morphogenesis and Psychogenesis*.[1] The title is not really either frivolous or overly modest, but accurately descriptive of his own work as he himself sees it, in comparison with all that yet remains to be collated.

As I came in, on the morning of which I have been writing, he said, "Hello, Saunders. While it's fresh in mind I want you to take this revision for that introduction to the third part. I at last got it straight in my mind while I was shaving this morning."

I am reproducing this material from my notes, because of the bearing which it has on later events:

"Science," he dictated, "has its own superstitions. Among them is a bewildering tendency to act as if it sees nothing whatever, when confronted by phenomena which it cannot as yet see clearly and fully. Such an attitude, if examined logically, argues that blindness is better than dim sight, or, rather, that nothing is important which is not completely credible because completely lucid. Navigation, on scientific waters, is restricted to hours of perfect visibility.

"This annoys me. If science is to have a true and proper correlation with life, it must give more recognition than it does at present to the fact that the weather is often cloudy, the visibility low. Scientists, like good mariners, must take into account the

1 A history, that is, of deviations from what is normal in the origin and growth of body and of mind.—ED.

28

landfalls imperfectly seen, the stars glimpsed for a moment only, and without certitude. To continue the nautical analogy, the days of the early voyagers are over, in the laboratory as well as on the seven seas. Practically all of the coastlines are accurately charted, by rule-of-thumb methods; the peaks are triangulated; the depths of ocean sounded and set down. Now we must turn from explorers into anthropologists, inspecting not continents but their peoples; and as such we must spend less time measuring skulls, and more time weighing souls.

"The transition, of course, is occurring in spite of us. The bitter resentment felt among general practitioners toward chiropractors and toward the 'healers' of Christian Science is significant; yet these resented categories persist through opposition and grow stronger year by year, for the very reason that they are courageous where orthodox physicians are cautious; they are willing to deal with the fact imperfectly perceived, and to make the most of it, pending its further elucidation. Certainly it is our office, as orthodox physicians, to resist charlatanry, wherever it appears; but when sincere men effect unquestionable results by mysterious agencies it is our duty rather to aid in elucidating the mystery than to suppress it because our own ignorance does not permit us to understand.

"As we advance the science of therapeutics, our methodologies encroach more and more upon realms now loosely described as 'psychic.' Indeed, it has become to my mind a thesis for the most serious consideration that every medicine, every stimulus, of which we make use in the practices of healing, is only a preliminary stage in the coercion of a psychic reaction, and that the result achieved is entirely due to this secondary reaction within the central nervous system. To illustrate: I mean that a person who thoroughly understands all that we now know about the effect of hydrocyanic gas upon the human body could die of the mere mental reaction of implicitly believing that he had swallowed a lethal dose of prussic acid, whereas a person who did not understand the mechanics of its effect would be immune under the same circumstances.[1]

1 "Dr. Alling," if he were as learned as the narrator wishes us to believe, must have known that this thesis is only a restatement, in essence, of the

"Let me cite an experiment which removes the problem from the field of tangible stimuli, and also brings us closer to the specific subject of the following chapters. It has long been known and generally acknowledged that madmen are wont to exhibit superphysical strength. On the 7th of February, 1932, under the supervision of the Director of the Maine State Asylum for the Insane, Dr. A. V. Kernochan, I personally was permitted to measure with a dynamograph the physical reactions of certain inmates of that institution. The most significant case was that of J. T. L., still an inmate, who makes a continual boast of his great strength. Subtracting the nominal quantity of five pounds for the ordinary uniform he was wearing, J. T. L.'s weight is 157 pounds. His proportions are about normal, his muscular development pronounced but not extraordinary. With shoulders strapped into the mechanism shown in plate No. (?) he was able to exert 2600 foot-pounds of contractile effort between shoulders and fists. On the other hand, R. O. M., a professional wrestler who volunteered for the same experiment on the 12th of February, at the Maine State College of Surgery, in the presence of Gideon Wyck, M.D., could exert a maximum of only 1050 foot-pounds in the same apparatus under like conditions. R. O. M. weighed 211 pounds, stripped, and displays abnormal muscular development, but is not muscle-bound. The professional wrestler also permitted me to contract his muscles galvanically to the point of torture, increasing the maximum force by a little more than 10%, which still indicated less than half the strength of his slighter, mad rival.

"What caused the amazing discrepancy? Wise men, in all ages and among all peoples of the earth, have ascribed the strength of madmen to demonic possession. And what is demonic possession? what are demons? The modern alienist does not even inquire. I am not arguing for the acceptance of Christian doctrine[1]

---

central theory of Christian Samuel Hahnemann's *Organum of the Rational Art of Healing.* Unfortunately, Hahnemann's astonishingly prophetic and well-reasoned work has been discredited, in the past century, by the irrational acts of his own disciples.—ED.

1 It is not easy to define "Christian doctrine" on such a point, as various churches, all of which would insist upon a right to use the appellation "Christian", disagree among themselves. Prof. Nathaniel Schmidt, some-

in this matter; but I should like to see the oldest hypothesis—the only one that fully accounts for the phenomenon—examined by the same laws of evidence that are applied to other unproved hypotheses. What, for example, is the relationship between the increased muscular contraction produced galvanically in my wrestler's arms, and that produced by madness in the arms of J. T. L.? Is the demon itself a kind of galvanic manifestation? Could the application of contrary voltaic pressure neutralize the effect of the demon? I do not know, because the overseers of the asylum would not permit me to subject its inmates to any unnatural stimuli or physical pain.

"Listen again to Nevius, the missionary, whom I had occasion to quote at length on spiritualism, in an earlier chapter. 'Is there such a thing,' he inquires in his preface,[1] 'as Demon Possession in the latter part of the Nineteenth Century? The author's apology'

---

time president of the Society of Biblical Literature and Exegesis, has this to say: "Some scholars have maintained that Jesus did not really believe in demoniac possession, but only accommodated himself to the current belief. This is a highly improbable view; and the discussion recorded in Matt. xii. 22 et seq. seems to be decisive against it. . . . In its battle with the demons the Church never struck a heavier blow than when Innocent VIII on Dec. 5, 1484, sent out his bull *Ad futuram rei memoriam*. . . . As Luther and other leading reformers continued to cherish the belief, it maintained its hold upon the Protestant churches and was responsible for much persecution, until, undermined by the attacks of deists and rationalists, it gradually disappeared before the progress of modern science."—*New International Encyclopedia, vol. 6, p. 666.*

However, *The Encyclopedia Britannica* is more cautious in implying that the belief has "gradually disappeared." In the 14th edition, (New York and London, 1929) we find, on page 284 of volume 7, the following conclusion: "The possibility of the existence of evil spirits, organized under one leader Satan to tempt man and oppose God, cannot be denied; the sufficiency of the evidence for such evil agency may, however, be doubted; the necessity of any such belief for Christian thought and life cannot, therefore, be affirmed." As this passage does not occur in earlier editions of the same work, which treat the subject more rationalistically, and as Dr. Schmidt's article was written more than a decade earlier than the other, it may perhaps be assumed that the *Britannica* entry is a cautious recognition of a resurgence in the churches of the older beliefs.—ED.

1 This is accurately quoted from page ix, *Demon Possession and Allied Themes*, by Rev. John L. Nevius, D.D. New York: Fleming H. Revell Co., 1894.

(i.e., for asking at all) 'is, that in the prosecution of his missionary work in China this subject was repeatedly forced upon his attention, so that it became absolutely necessary to examine it, and to form an intelligent opinion respecting it.' As scientists, we cannot improve upon the attitude of this theologian, whether or not we agree, 'that as yet no theory has been advanced which so well accords with the facts as the simple and unquestioning conclusion universally held by the Christians of Shantung, viz: that evil spirits do in many instances possess or control the mind and will of human beings.'"[1]

At the end of each paragraph of dictation, Dr. Alling smacked his lips, as if with relish for the flavor of his own words, and then waited for the nod which showed him that I had caught up. There was more to the new version of the introduction; but the above first part is sufficient for my dual purpose of showing the almost too tolerant quality of Prexy's mind, and of indicating why he alone, of all persons in Altonville, found it convenient to see a great deal of that unpleasant old curmudgeon, Gideon Wyck. In disposition, in tastes, in outlook, they were miles apart. But Wyck, aside from being an excellent surgeon, was deeply, fantastically learned in one of the many fields of historico-medical research to be covered in Dr. Alling's *Short Sketch*. Huge bundles of books arrived every week at the medical school library, on special loan from the Library of Congress and other great repositories of knowledge; but Prexy had told me that every single book he had wanted on the subjects of demonology and witchcraft had proved to be already on hand, in the curious library of Gideon Wyck.

I was next set to copying, from a modern reprint of a work named *Demoniality*,[2] some marked passages arguing that abnormal human beings are products of a love between normal women

---

1 *Ibid.,* p. vii. Quoted from the introduction by F. F. Ellinwood, who adds the perhaps significant postscript: "Since the above was written Dr. Nevius has . . . died peacefully, though without a moment's warning, at his house in Chefoo, Oct. 19, 1893."

2 *Demoniality* by Ludovice Maria Sinistrari, Friar Minor. Tr. by the Rev. Montague Summers. London: The Fortune Press, 1927. (Original edition, Paris, 1875, from Ms. written *c.* 1700).

and men possessed of demons. Midway in the task, I could not help looking up curiously at my employer, wondering what his own inmost feelings must be, when reading such passages—he himself being almost a dwarf. He caught my eye, and smiled half-bitterly, as if understanding the motive of my glance. I blushed, and bent over my work again.

For half an hour we continued in silence, I copying, he browsing through a stack of books which we had borrowed the day before from Dr. Wyck. Presently, looking up to rest my eyes, I saw him take a paper marker from one of the volumes and toss it absent-mindedly into the wastebasket. Then he retrieved it, remarking, "That's a nice way for me to treat another man's property. He probably wants to keep that place. Oh, by the way, Wyck told me last night at the laboratory that he particularly wanted this one back today. I promised I'd bring it over. Besides, I want to see if he's got a copy of a book that Scott's supposed to have written, on this subject.[1] I guess I'll drive us over. Bring this book out, will you, when you're through? I'll go around and get the car."

I smiled at his request that I carry the book out for him. It weighed perhaps eight ounces. But this was typical of one of his foibles: an unwillingness to hold any object whatever, steadily, for longer than was necessary. While driving, his hands continually shifted their grip on the wheel. In the laboratory, his fingers darted quickly and with great precision from adjustment to adjustment. But when any task was under way that required a steady and calm grip, he would ask me to do that part of the job for him.

When my notes were in order I took up the indicated book —a volume of Frazer's *Golden Bough*, and turned curiously to the marked page, wondering what reference it was that Wyck wanted back for immediate consultation. A quick glance at the pages in question revealed nothing that seemed significant. They were about the practice of supplying a "scapegoat," or single individual in no way more guilty than any other, to be sacrificed to appease gods who were supposed to be angry with a whole

[1] *Letters on Demonology and Witchcraft*. Addressed to J. G. Lockhart, Esq., by Walter Scott, Bart.

community. However, as I was closing the book again, a series of notations on the paper marker, made with what seemed to be intentionally faint pencil strokes, caught my eye. Something, perhaps a premonition that he wanted the notations rather than the book itself, prompted me to copy them off. I give them here:

Jl 16 / 300
Sp 3 / 400
Nv 1 / 400
Dc 23 / 500
Jn 29 / 500
Fb 24 / 500

Then I hastened out to the road, called by the horn of Dr. Alling's big old Marmon. We drove directly to Wyck's home, which is situated about half a mile away, diagonally across the road from the northwest corner of the hospital fence. His daughter Marjorie, who kept house for the old widower, answered the bell. Under her somehow ethereal outer calm I sensed nervousness and a resentment of our intrusion into the gloomy building, set off by itself at the town's edge, amid stumpy pines. I never could enter it without thinking of Hansel and Gretel, and the witch's house of gingerbread. Marjorie always had the air of a bewitched princess; and the old place, with intricate scrollwork festooning the verandah and the eaves, was painted a chocolate brown that had faded to the precise color of gingerbread. It must have been built in the late seventies. Some of the townspeople still referred to it as "the Alton place," as it had been the residence of Judge Alton, the father of Wyck's dead wife, for about twenty-five years. Wyck himself had moved in as a result of being unable either to rent or to sell the monstrosity, when he inherited it shortly after his marriage in 1904. Rumor said that the local real estate agent had had it listed, for sale or rent, ever since.

I give this bit of hearsay, whether it be true or false, as the only explanation which occurs to me of the curious fact that an individual so fashionably fussy about the adornment of his own person should be found living in such unlovely surroundings. He was not yet dressed, when we entered. While waiting, Prexy

buzzed around the library like an inquisitive fly, occasionally calling me to take down a book that was above his arm's short reach.
In the intervals, my attention was divided between the spectacle
of Marjorie Wyck, passing and repassing the dining room door
as she cleared up the breakfast dishes, and a general reinspec-
tion of the furniture and decorations of her home. No wonder
she seemed ethereal! How else could so lovely a girl exist, sur-
rounded by stiff furniture upholstered in horsehair, by dull red
wallpaper, mottoes in frames with the corners crossing, wooden
panels painted with representations of dead game? Obviously,
nothing could have been done about the house without razing it
and building it anew. I suppose both Wyck and his daughter had
recognized that minor changes would only make matters worse.
At least it was all of a piece: they had left it just as they found it:
a monument to the most tasteless period of American Victori-
anism. In this setting Marjorie Wyck moved gracefully back and
forth, indifferent to her surroundings. She was clad in a simple
blue morning dress that seemed the height of fashion and good
taste, probably because of its very simplicity.

"Read French?" Prexy asked.

"A little," I admitted, dubiously.

"Good. You'll need it, in our next phase—that is, the next
phase that I plan to take up. It isn't strictly in order, as the Table
of Contents reads, but I want to skip enough to bring us to it
while some laboratory work I've been doing with Dr. Wyck is still
crystal-sharp in my mind. Besides—"

His voice dwindled off, as Marjorie Wyck walked toward the
library. I did not get the rest of that particular sentence until after
we had left the house.

"I think father will be down right away," Marjorie said. "You
should know better than to call so early, Dr. Alling. He's seldom
through shaving before half past ten."

"I know, my dear. But he left my laboratory early, last night.
Early, that is, for him—around half past one."

I mentioned that Dr. Wyck had been called to the Connells',
and thence to the hospital. Prexy said, "Oh?" and Marjorie
seemed to drift out of the room as if on a breeze. She is probably the most graceful, as well as the most preoccupied, person

I have ever known. I have seen her leave other gatherings in the same way, suddenly, with perhaps a vague and slightly apologetic smile, perhaps with no gesture of explanation whatever.

"Ah, here it is. Here's what you'll need your French for," Prexy said, hopping slightly to pluck out an old book from the shelf second below the top. "The Geoffroys[1] were the first to go at the problem of abnormal births with any degree of thoroughness. We still use their awkward and unsystematic system of classification. That is, we have up until now. I'm putting the whole subject on a rational basis in my History."

I looked uneasily at the old books, and confessed that my small acquaintance with French did not include any technical terminology.

"There aren't any technical terms in French," he said. "Look and see for yourself."

We skimmed over a page or two of the work on monstrous births, without coming upon any word that might be classified as an exclusively scientific term. Then a board creaked, and I looked up quickly to see Gideon Wyck lifting from the center table the book we had just returned at his request. "Morning," he said sourly, letting the pages purr under an affectedly careless thumb. As the inserted paper marker flashed by, he snapped the book shut and slipped it into one of the big pockets of his gaudy dressing gown.

"I say, you *are* looking ill, Gideon," Prexy remarked. "You didn't get out of bed to see us, did you? Better go back, if you did."

"Nonsense. Never been sick a day in my life."

Dr. Wyck scowled, and took a cigarette from a box on the table.

Nevertheless, he was pale—paler even than last night. His hand shook as he lit the cigarette. Then, as if in boyish bravado, he took a tremendously deep drag and stood eyeing us insolently as thick smoke streamed outward slowly from his nostrils. I remember noting his almost comical similarity to the theatrical idea of an old roué on a morning after. He wore claret-colored silk pyjamas, open at the neck, and a brocaded dressing gown.

1 Étienne and his son Isidor Geoffroy Saint-Hilaire. The father helped pave the way for Darwin's theories.—ED.

His feet were clad in morocco lounging slippers. His hair, of a suspiciously purple blackness, had just a suggestion of gray at the roots, to indicate that it needed to be re-dyed. The paleness of his features certainly meant that, if he was not ill, he had had far too thorough an acquaintance with the whisky decanter, of late, and far too little sleep.

"Did you get those slides finished, last night?" he inquired.

"The ones from the calf, I did," Prexy answered, "but the moths are no good. We've got to impregnate them in something to stiffen up the cell walls a bit more, Gideon. They crush under the sharpest blade in the shop."

"Forget the moths, Fred. I'll have something better than moths for you before your lecture's due."

"Will you? What?"

"I'll tell you when I've got it. I'm expecting it any day, now."

"Meanwhile, you plan to be cryptic, I gather. Suit yourself. Say, where's the Atlas to this Geoffroy set? May we take the whole thing along?"

"Yes, if you like. The picture-book's in my office, I guess. I'll get it for you this afternoon."

"What else have you got on monsters,[1] that I haven't seen?"

"I don't think there's much. You've got copies of my papers, haven't you? I sent you copies of them all."

"Yes. Well, we'll be going. And you'd better put yourself to bed. You don't look a bit well. Oh, that reminds me—there's

---

1 The author of this narrative perhaps assumes in the general reader a knowledge of the medical significance of the word "monster" that he may have had no occasion to learn. Webster's Collegiate Dictionary gives it concisely, in its third definition of the meaning of the word: *"An animal or plant departing greatly from the usual type; a monstrosity."* The above reference to moths probably comes from the circumstance that the deliberate formation of monsters by external influence in the laboratory is most easily and consistently accomplished with certain forms of insects, notably the *Lepidoptera.* The reference to a calf is significant in that (as every visitor to the side shows of a country fair must know) abnormal births of accidental origin seem to be commoner among cattle than among other domesticated mammals. Dr. Alling, as later events make clear, was preparing microphotographs of sections of tissue taken from various monsters, to be shown in a stereopticon to illustrate a lecture on the causes of such deviations.—ED.

another reason. I don't want you to come to faculty meeting tonight. There was a student in to see me at breakfast time who's going to have you fired by petition to the state legislature. What's his name? P-something."

"Prendergast?" Dr. Wyck asked, chuckling.

"That's it. Prendergast. Prendergast. Now I'll remember. I have enough trouble with the legislature, as it is, without running into things like this, Gideon. You stay away. I want to handle it in my own fashion. It's got to come up tonight, because he filed a formal petition. You'd better tell me about him now, though."

"Nothing much to tell, Fred. I caught him cribbing on his first exam in my course last fall. I was very decent about it, I think. Didn't mention it to anybody, not even to him. We've had a sort of tacit understanding, ever since, Prendergast and I. He knew he'd have to do a little extra work to convince me, after that, and I've given him all the leeway he could want. But he hasn't made much of the opportunity. In fact, he's got steadily worse all year."

"Sure you haven't been leaning down too hard, Gideon? He's been doing excellent work in Anatomy, and he's fair enough in everything else. He claims he's in danger of losing his degree because of your deliberate unfairness."

"Tripe!" said Dr. Wyck, gruffly. "I could have had him fired on the spot. I gave him a chance, instead, but he went right on bluffing."

Prexy must have thought I was out of earshot, carrying books to the car, for he replied in a low voice. "All right. But it's becoming more than just an embarrassment, Gideon, having the rest of the faculty forever voting you down on matters of grades and discipline. When it gets to the point of petitions to the legislature, you're endangering the school itself. I'm not saying you're not right in principle. I'm questioning your teaching methods. Remember, I'd prefer that you absent yourself because of illness, tonight. I can handle the rest of them better if you're not there at all."

A bell sounded, and Marjorie called Prexy to the telephone. He came bustling out, looking remarkably cheerful.

"Here's luck, Saunders. Here's a coincidence for you. There's just been a monster born at the hospital. No calves or moths this time, but a real human. Want to see it while it's still alive? You've just got time before your lecture."

I mastered the smile that tried to take possession of my lips, and then found myself wondering what was the reason for my amusement. What, basically, was funny in the fact that a man of science should seem so pleased at getting wind of a tragic accident, a blunder in the general system of creation? He noticed my inconclusive expression, and his own face sobered.

"Jekyll and Hyde," he murmured. "Doctors have to keep a watch on their emotions, because in real life it's the scientist, it's Jekyll, that plays the brute. I suppose I really ought to weep at such news—and yet, for the last year I've been hankering to get some good slides of tissue from a symmelus.[1] That's what it is, by the way—a symmelus. That bright girl at the switchboard had all the details. I think she knows where I am at any moment all day long. What's her name?"

"Daisy Towers," I said. "She keeps tabs on me, even. She routed a call for me through to the dog cart, the other day. Said she knew I'd be eating there."

"Oh? Well, I'm glad she's not on duty at night. I sense the difference at just about supper time. People stop finding me then, and I have a hunch that it's because that girl must go off duty about then."

"She does. She goes off at seven o'clock. And then for the next hour you always have trouble getting people on the phone, because one of the hospital porters has the board till the night girl comes on at eight."

"So that's the reason, eh? Well, Miss Towers is a remarkably smart girl. They say she used to be the town's worst gossip. But by now, with all the phone conversations to listen in on, she ought to have become the town's best gossip. She said the mother of the monster died. Perhaps that's lucky, the issue being a bastard as well as a monster."

Prexy Alling had delayed starting the car, upon hearing the

1 "The pelvis and lower extremities in the individuals of this group are imperfectly developed, and the two lower limbs are more or less fused. Sometimes this fusion is complete, and the feet are wholly lacking."—*New International Encyclopedia*, 2nd Ed., vol. 16, p. 174.

phone ring a second time. But when no-one appeared at the door-way in the course of a minute or so, he decided that the second call could not have been for him. As the car began to move, he said, "You know, when I was speaking to you in there about why I was taking up the subject of monsters ahead of the proper sequence, and suddenly stopped short when Marjorie came in—? Well, what I was going to say is that another reason for haste is that I want to benefit from Wyck's enormous learning on the subject, and I have my private opinion that he's a very sick man. I didn't want to speak of it before his daughter, but I've seldom seen a man's general appearance change so in a few weeks as his has. Have you?"

I shook my head. The question set me to wondering about more matters than that. My mind seemed to be seething with disconnected portents. Things had been happening too rapidly for comfort, in the ten hours since a little past midnight. What was the demonic understanding, or misunderstanding, between Wyck and Mike Connell? Had the former really received some of the latter's blood, to strengthen him against an ailment which he refused to acknowledge to the world? And why had he demanded the return of a certain book, secretly looking at once to see whether it contained a slip of paper with cryptic nota-tions? What was the horrible information about Dr. Wyck that had driven Muriel Finch to the verge of hysterics, the thing she did not even dare admit that she knew? Why, if his mind was so obviously deranged, did his associates permit him to continue as a practicing doctor and teacher? What had happened that Gideon Wyck, who notoriously was without mercy in cases of classroom delinquency, had failed to report a case of cribbing at once? Was it merely for the pleasure of hazing the culprit slowly, all year?

I resolved to look up Prendergast, whom I knew well, and get his version of the affair as soon as possible.

CHAPTER IV

We were just turning in at the hospital gates when someone behind us on Atlantic Street frantically screamed our names.

"Mr. David! Dr. Alling! You, for the love of God, you come."

The car stopped, spraying gravel at the wheels. Biddy Connell ranged alongside, panting. "'Tis my Mike again," she said, "'tis certain he's dyin'."

"Who's—?" Prexy looked at me. "Oh! she means Mike Connell."

"Himself. And that old divil Dr. Wyck wasn't up, he said, and wouldn't come, says he, if he was up. God have mercy on his black sowl. So I was comin' to drag a doctor meself. Quick, now."

"What's the matter with him?" asked Dr. Alling.

"Oh, the terrible, terrible pain in the arm—you know, where it ain't there. I couldn't stand his screechin'."

"Get in," Prexy said abruptly, eager, as always, to investigate unusual symptoms. As we drove the block or so to the Connells', I got in a few words about the similar occurrence of some time after midnight.

We found Mike in a sleep of exhaustion, from which Biddy promptly awakened him to justify her anxiety. He looked wildly around, as if afraid of the unseen world. "Are you still feeling pain?" Dr. Alling asked kindly.

"No. That is, not enough to spit at. But oh, doctor, I felt the sowl dragged near out of me arm. He was tuggin' at it, but I couldn't see him."

"Please tell me just what happened."

"Wide awake, I was, this time. There's always the little pains. But it started growin', slow, gettin' worse and worse, right here." He put his index finger to a point in the air, three or four inches below the stump of his left arm.

"What did it feel like?"

"Like—like he was tearin' the muscles out o' me. Like his claws was in me muscles, doc. Oh, tuggin'—slow—harder and—"

"His *claws?* Whose claws?"

"The black one. I couldn't see him, only shadowy-like. And when I wouldn't let go to him, he began bangin' me heart, like wit' a big club, right here. And all the while he was tuggin' and tearin'. And then me heart began to burst, doc. Everythin' swimmin', and the room whirlin', and me sowl near torn out. It was the black one, I know. I could just see him hazy."[1]

He turned suddenly on the pillow and sobbed. Dr. Alling looked seriously at Biddy and me.

"Just when did you say this happened before?"

"Early this morning, about one or two o'clock. We called Dr. Wyck a few minutes after it began, but it took perhaps five minutes to locate him."

"I see. Dr. Wyck left my laboratory about then, in response to your call. He'd been helping me with some slides. I didn't note the exact time."

"I saw him plain, that time," Mike cried. "All black and grinnin'."

"Dreamin', he must have been, when it started," Biddy hastily explained.

"No, doc, it was real. And this time I could see him too. Yes, I did see him—the white eyes, wit' black pinpoints in the middle. Doc, if he comes again? I can't stand it again. Next time he'll drag out me sowl. Oh, God, what shall I do?"

"We'll be right back, Mike," Dr. Alling promised. "Saunders, I want to talk to you a minute." I followed out to the doorstep. "You said his heart was behaving strangely, Saunders. Just how strangely?"

I described the symptoms with care. He shook his head.

"Like nothing I've ever heard of. All mental in origin, perhaps, but such terrific physical effects take a physical remedy. He doesn't normally display hyperæsthesia?"[2]

---

1 Although there is no reference to the fact anywhere in the MS. from which this volume was prepared, the reader may be interested in knowing that Guazzo's *Compendium Maleficarum,* a famous handbook used in the Church's persecution of witches, gives it as a common sign of demonic possession to "feel a contraction of the heart, *as if it had been unmercifully beaten.*" See p. 169 of edition tr. by E. A. Ashwin, London, John Rodker, 1929.

2 "A state of exalted or morbidly increased sensibility" (i.e., in this instance, to pain.) —*Webster.*

"I'm sure he doesn't. Charlie Michaud and I were fishing once with Mike and he got a pickerel hook under the quick of his thumbnail. I wanted to take him home and get it out properly, but he made me work it out right there and sterilize it with whisky, so we wouldn't waste a good day's fishing. He did some fine swearing, but that's all."

"We'll have to study this. Remarkably interesting, what you say about the heart. Well, I'll stop back with a hypodermic for the wife to give him, if he has another attack. Risky business, but she probably couldn't get anything in at the mouth, if he was like that. I can't understand why Wyck wasn't interested enough to come in his pyjamas. He really must be ill."

This gave me an opening to speak about what had been nagging my conscience all morning.

"I don't know, of course," I said, "but it may be explained by something else I didn't tell you of. It came out last night that Dr. Wyck had been filling Mike's head with stuff about demons. Well, you've seen the result of it. It may be unethical to say this, but I heard him myself, last night, giving him more nonsense to believe. I think it's a damned outrage."

Dr. Alling cocked his little bird-like head shrewdly. "Thanks for your frankness," he said. "There have been many private matters in which I've had to place confidence in your discretion as my secretary, Saunders. This is another such. Please say nothing about it to anyone. If you need an inducement, I'll admit *sub rosa* that arrangements are being made to have Dr. Wyck unobtrusively retired from actual practice. For years he's handled only emergency and charity cases. He won't have even those, in a short while."

A great burden seemed all at once to be lifted from my conscience. Perhaps it would have been better, in the long run, if I had not been given this early reassurance. In such a case, I might have spoken further, then and there; and my words might have altered the whole course of future events. I am positive now, as I look back upon it, that Dr. Alling at this time could not have suspected that anything was seriously wrong. For years Wyck had acted like an old Tartar, but had had the justification of brilliance in the laboratory, in the classroom, and as a surgeon.

Probably, at the time of which I am writing, Dr. Alling and the rest of the faculty had reached the decision that a temperament unfortunate from the first had merely become a little too much so, with advancing years. They had decided to retire him at 66, rather than at 68. That was all. The step they were quietly preparing to take had not been occasioned by any inkling, on their part, of the gruesome facts which I myself was on the verge of discovering. Had they known, or even suspected, Wyck surely would have been under restraint within a few hours; but it so happened that a little more than half a day of extra freedom gave fate the opportunity to embroil us all in a mystery to which I myself do not as yet see any clear solution—and I think I know more about it than any other living person.

However, I must get back to my story. Dr. Alling and I stepped in again to reassure the Connells, and to caution Biddy to communicate at once with Dr. Alling direct if the symptoms should recur. As only ten minutes remained before my lecture, Prexy drove off without me to see the symmelus, and I walked back toward the school building. I whistled under Prendergast's window, in passing. He roomed in the house next to the Connells', but was not in just then. When I reached the school itself, I discovered why. Prendergast corralled me as soon as I was inside the front door, eagerly waving a paper under my nose.

"Here, Dave, your John Hancock's needed, a trifle, a mere two words I'm asking you to write down. Here's where you sign."

"What's it I'm signing?" I asked.

"Never mind the questions. Take my word for it you'd agree. You haven't got time to read it anyway, before the lecture."

"Show it to me afterward, then," I said, as the hour began striking.

"Oh, don't be an old woman," he urged. "It just says in effect that Wyck's an old son of a bitch, and we all know that."

"Then why sign it, if it's so generally known?" I countered. "Sorry, I probably agree with it, but I won't sign anything without reading it first."

"O. K., O. K.," he said testily. "See you after the lecture. Hey, John, your signature's wanted," and Prendergast began working out on another classmate.

When the lecture was over I became one of a group of doubters who listened while the paper was read aloud by a disinterested third party. It proved to be a perfectly just catalogue of well-known examples of Wyck's arbitrary unfairness, and several malcontents willingly appended their signatures. When it was shoved at me, however, I refused, because it was addressed to the state legislature. Had it been merely a petition to the faculty, I would have signed it at once; but I knew too much about Prexy's troubles with the legislature to put my name on any document that might serve further to embarrass him, in that quarter. By the exercise of an adroit political instinct, he was able to keep a small working majority of liberals on his side, to assure the yearly appropriation; but there was always a bloc of malcontents who thought that all advanced schools should on principle be either endowed privately or else operated on a self-supporting basis; and I well knew that a letter from the anti-vivisectionist societies, objecting to our use of live animals in the laboratory, was enough to send Prexy scooting down to Augusta if the legislature happened to be in session.

I explained my stand briefly, but Prendergast was too fervid to be rational. He had come to think of me as his henchman, because of certain old associations. That I should let him down at such an hour—I of all people—roused his latent choler. He ended by calling me a coward, and some other students had to stop the threatening fight by hauling him away. After that scene I had no occasion or opportunity before the faculty meeting to question him about Wyck's actual behavior.

The whole episode was in character. Prendergast and I had roomed together for a year at the University of Maine, and had hated each other as only roommates can. Then, in the following year, when we both were juniors, we had patched up our differences because of mutual interests; and in our last year we had both engaged in a feat of undergraduate journalism that caused quite a flurry on the campus. Prendergast, who had plenty of money, founded a little crusading weekly that he immodestly called *Prendergast's Pillory*. He was, of course, editor-in-chief. I was literary editor, general proof reader, make-up man, and office dog.

It had been good fun. Prendergast—a brash youth if ever there was one—had got a 500-word leading article every week from some prominent author, cheerfully paying five cents a word. I had the back page, to use as I saw fit—providing of course that the editor also saw fit; and Prendergast filled the two inside pages with excellent militant editorials, naming names and sparing no-one. He put two or three local bootleggers out of business for selling bad liquor, of which *Prendergast's Pillory* published an exact chemical analysis, together with the name of seller, place of purchase, and price. The government took no notice, but the students simply stopped buying. On the other hand, the conscientious bootleggers were never molested. The paper printed frequent attacks upon what were considered unjust administrative procedures. Each issue contained a curt analysis of the teaching qualifications of one member of the faculty. Occasionally there was a really distinguished essay on educational policy in general.

My friend Prendergast, in short, had much of the temperament of Shelley, with the poetic ability absent. He was always crusading for what he believed to be just causes, in a courageous but transient way. On the other hand, he had blind spots of character such as those that caused Shelley to think he was treating his wife with consideration when he offered to take her along on his trip to the Continent with another woman. Despite my period of hating him, he was in general a most likable and magnetic chap. The point was that you had to be careful not to see too much of him at a stretch.

Our relations, all through our senior year at the university, had been quite pleasant. It should be emphasized, however, that the main source of his B.S. degree was the *Pillory,* rather than classwork. Amiable professors, who admired him as a journalist, overlooked his neglect of formal studies. Others, in whose classes he had done very badly indeed, gave him passing grades to keep free of the charge of having flunked him through spite, because of his unfavorable analyses of their teaching abilities. I know for a fact that he got "A" in English all through his senior year merely by handing in copies of his journal, without doing any of the required work.

But the situation at medical school had proved to be decidedly different. No-one would give him a passing grade in Physiological Chemistry on the basis of his worth as a crusader. Glibness and an excellent memory had barely got him by the first two years. We all knew, moreover, that he was a chronic cribber on exams. It had not surprised me in the least to learn that Wyck had caught him at it. The wonder was that no-one had done so before.

No doubt Prendergast was honestly unaware of the implications of all this. Being glib, he mistook himself for a genius. Perhaps he was one, in his way. I have heard him sincerely argue that a medical genius could make as good diagnoses by inspiration as a more careful doctor could arrive at with the aid of infinite exact knowledge of precedent. He was always attentive at lectures, but never took notes. I doubt that he cracked a book all year, outside the school building. His dissections were excellently done, with the aid of a glance or two at the work of tolerant friends; and I must say that he was genuinely gifted with manual dexterity, even if it was of the essentially aimless kind that will lead crackbrained enthusiasts to make huge cathedral models out of match sticks, or to reproduce some ugly and unworthy object in beautiful materials, with the most scrupulous care.

In the *Pillory,* Prendergast had bitterly fought the examination system *per se.* Since he sincerely disbelieved in examinations, as a way of testing knowledge, I suppose he could crib without any loss of self-respect. At any rate, examinations had been the immediate cause of his undoing; and he was certainly displaying journalistic shrewdness in attacking an author for his woes at once so terrifying and so vulnerable as Gideon Wyck. No-one had ever dared attack him openly before, although many, with far better reason than Prendergast's, had passionately wished that they had dared.

When the threatened fight over signing his petition had ended in Prendergast's being hauled away, I loitered in the main corridor of the school building for a minute or two, to let my belligerent classmate get a head start in whatever direction he had chosen. I was about to leave, myself, when a hoarse voice sounded from the basement stairs.

"Hey, doc. Hey, one o' you, give us a hand. Oh, doc. Hey!"

That, I knew, was Charlie Michaud, the diener[1] of the anatomy museum, who indiscriminately addressed all students as "doc" and all members of the faculty as "doctor" except when he wished surreptitiously to imply that one of the latter deserved no better ranking, in his opinion, than that of student.

I descended the basement stairs that led to the preparation room, where bodies for dissection were embalmed, and where some of the infrequently used machines were kept.

"Hello, doc," Charlie said, "want to see my latest invention? It's a whiz. Only trouble is, I invented it so as to make it easier for one guy to do the job, and, by George, it takes two to run it. I got tired o' sawin' all these damn skulls with a handsaw, so I rigged up this little rotary saw—see!—on this extry motor that was kickin' around. Only, it takes both my hands to hold the saw gadget steady, and that damn stiff's head wobbles. Put yer foot on her face, will ya? Hold it steady, so's I can take the top of her head off. I'm scairt I'll dig in too deep, the way my nice new invention's workin' so far."

"How do I know you won't cut my foot off, while you're at it?" I objected, as I climbed up on the preparation bench, beside the corpse on which he was working.

"All you got to do is jump in time, doc," he said, genially. "Here she goes."

He pressed a switch, and the little motor with its rotary saw snarled to full speed. I jammed the instep of my boot down hard on the stiff's face, and said, "Go ahead, but take it easy."

The head shuddered under my foot as if it were alive, as the saw bit into the skull. Charlie moved it slowly and steadily through a half-circle. Then we heaved the corpse over, and he completed the process from the back.

1 The casual use of the term "diener" in this narrative, with no apparent thought of a need for explaining it, is one reason why Mr. Painter feels certain that a genuine medical student is the author. The term does not occur in any of the English dictionaries which I have consulted, and, so far as I have been able to discover, is in use in this country in medical schools exclusively. It apparently comes direct from the German for "servant," and reveals the Germanic training of most of the teachers in such institutions as the one herein described. The author has already stated that Dr. Alling's early researches were done in Germany.—ED.

"There, doc," he said, exultantly, bending the head back a little and taking off the top of the skull as if it were the lid of a box. "How's that? Would 'a' taken half an hour, the old way. Did it in no more 'n a minute, with this new invention."

He stuck his fingers down between the bone and the brain, lifting the frontal lobe free of the temporal.

"Ain't she a beauty?" he said, admiringly. "Inside of her head looks a lot better than the outside, hey? Wouldn't think she'd have such a nice, neat brain, with a mug like that, would you? Well, thanks, doc. I'll give you a yell when I've got another to do."

This little sample episode out of Charlie's routine labors is given to help explain some of the occurrences yet to come. I have already mentioned urban crime, occurring in a back-country setting, as the probable reason why the Altonville mystery remains unsolved at this writing. But all our reactions must also have been to some extent unusual, because of the fact that almost everyone who might have been connected with the mystery was also connected with the medical school. Ordinarily, the very presence of a dead body is a deeply disturbing factor in community life. People in general cannot rest content until they have put a corpse out of the way, underground or in the crematory oven. Our efforts were of an exactly opposite sort. It was difficult for the school to get corpses at all. When we got them, we did all that we could to make them last. Each of us had his own cadaver in the anatomy course, and became exceedingly well acquainted with every wrinkle and secret of it, as Rupert Brooke would say, before the year was over. New students sometimes get sick, on their first day in the dissecting room. I did, I know. But it takes only a week or so to get thoroughly used to working in a room full of mutilated dead bodies; presently you reach a point where you think nothing of holding a dead woman's face steady with your foot, while someone else saws the top of her head off. In such surroundings, the remains of violent crime do not seem quite so appalling as they must among good ordinary citizens.

CHAPTER V

I helped Charlie Michaud load the cadaver on the elevator, and gave him a hand with the ropes. It was really only a very big, very slow dumb-waiter, used exclusively for carrying bodies up to the dissecting room on the ground floor, or to the main recitation hall on the second storey. Dr. Otway, the professor of neurology, wanted this one with the skull sawed but otherwise untouched, for a group demonstration next day. We deposited it on a table in a little arena, built like a football stadium, with tiers of seats rising sharply on three sides, almost from the edge of the table itself.

Jap Ross, a big, squint-eyed classmate of mine, joined me as I was hurrying down once more to leave the building. "Had lunch?" he asked. "Come on over to the dog cart with me."

"I'd like to see that symmelus, up at the hospital, while it's still alive," I said. "If it is still alive, that is."

"That what?"

I explained. There was no reason why a third-year medic should know about the classifications of monsters, a subject that would not be touched upon except in its relation to obstetrics, in the fourth and last year—and perhaps not even then. My own information came from the accident of my job with Prexy Alling.

"Oh, all right," Jap said. "I hear you and Dick Prendergast were going to bust each other in the nose, a little while ago. What was the row? Each of you claiming that you were the true papa of the whatchemecallit—symbolus?"

"No, I'm not a claimant for that singular honor. In fact, I don't even know whether the mother was one of my girl friends. Who was she?"

"Dunno. Hey, Mickey," Ross shouted to a second-year man who was coming down from the hospital on the other side of the street, "congratulations. I hear you're the father of a nice, bouncing, eight-pound, baby symbol-whatchemecallit. Nice going, boy, old boy. Who's the mother?"

Mickey Rehan, a jovial and smart little Irish Canuck from the

St. Croix River country, came prancing over to assure us that if the calendar was to be trusted, he could not possibly have any children in the month of April owing to the fact that he had spent both July and August nursing a lumber freighter from Eastport to Algiers and back, and had been quarantined during his whole stay in the foreign port.

"All right, you're exonerated," Ross agreed. "*Cherchez la femme,* and then we'll have a better idea of who's the proud papa. Who was she?"

"Girl named Mullin, according to Daisy Towers, who ought to know. Ever heard of her?"

The name sounded vaguely familiar, but I could not place it. Neither could Jap, who grunted, "She must have come by way of the Widow."

That remark, which perhaps sounds cryptic, touches upon one of the reasons why Prexy has to be careful about reactions in the state legislature. To say that a woman had come to the hospital "by way of the Widow" meant that she had been resident for a while in a boarding house kept by the Widow Schmidt on the road to South Alton. At one time she had had a place in South Alton village, but had been forced by local sentiment to remove to an old tavern, a relic of stagecoach days, that stands by itself about a mile north of the village limits, and perhaps four miles south of Altonville.

The Widow's was both a practical and a humane institution. However, since it dealt openly and intelligently with a social problem which the nicer element in the community preferred to ignore, it was subjected to continual efforts at suppression. The Widow Schmidt was herself no angel, and she ran her place for profit, making no bones of the fact. It was a boarding house, surreptitiously notorious all over the state as a refuge for pregnant girls and women who wanted both secrecy and intelligent medical care during the latter, more noticeable months of their pregnancy. The opportunity for its existence, at this one place and no other, grew out of the fact that anyone who did not object to an audience could have her child gratis at the Altonville hospital, in consideration of the training thus afforded to students at the College of Surgery. Unless there were complications, such patients were not admitted to the hospital until they were actually in labor. All of them, in consequence, needed a place to stay for at least the last doubtful week or two, and many who could afford it preferred to stay at the Widow's for two or three months, or even longer.

Gossip said that the Widow formerly had been a professional abortionist, and that her establishment had had its origin in this practice. Prexy once told me that she had been convicted on a charge of conspiracy to evade the anti-abortion statute, although not as a principal, and after serving a stiff jail term had come to him with the candid proposition that she set up an establishment along the present lines. He had recognized both the humanity and the scientific advantages of the arrangement, and had offered her some measure of protection in return for the right of medical overseership. He and his appointees were to have free access at any time. An interne from the hospital visited the place daily, accompanied at least once a week by one of the staff physicians. Prexy himself dropped in whenever he felt like it. It was suspected that the Widow occasionally indulged in her old profession, when she got a chance. But no-one had caught her at it. And, so far as the public was concerned, the only difference between her place and a respectable lying-in hospital was the fact that nearly all of her patients happened not to be married, or to be carrying children begotten in the absence of their own husbands.

This, then, was the establishment from which Mickey Rehan said the mother of the newly-born monster had come, which meant that she probably had not been a local resident. As Ross and I neared the hospital, we passed another group of students, among whom the argument over the monster's paternity had not yet palled. Someone was saying, "Hell, you goofs, the proud papa's probably old Gideon himself. She was the Wycks' maid before she got a bit too much of a profile and had to be sent off to the Widow's."

Then I remembered. The girl was one of those who had been discharged from the nursing staff, because of unreliability in the operating room. Her name was Sarah Mullin. She had fetched up as housemaid at the Wyck's, where she had been referred to merely as Sarah. I had forgotten her last name in the interim. As I realized this, and speculated for a moment upon the not unlikely possibility that Wyck had philandered with his own domestic servant, a phrase he had spoken that very morning flashed back into my memory:

"Forget the moths, Fred," he had said, intimating that he would have something better, in the way of monsters, for Dr. Alling to make slides of. And he had added, "I'm expecting it any day."

For a moment my brain spun with the notion, ghastly and fantastic, that Gideon Wyck, by some means of prenatal influence unknown to orthodox morphological science, had deliberately begotten this monster. It was doubly shocking, with such a thought in my mind, to be confronted at the main door of the hospital by Wyck himself. He paused to stare at me for a second or two, in a way hard to describe. There was a bitter smile on his small, handsome mouth. His eyes seemed luminous with a kind of checked passion. His face was still very pale. I felt as if released from an evil spell when he walked slowly past me and down the steps.

Jap and I found the wretched little monstrosity in a room adjoining the free maternity ward. Several other medics were clustered around it, chatting and pridefully displaying to each other their calloused natures. The head and upper body of the creature were well enough formed, but for an abnormally distended belly. Although still breathing faintly, it must soon die; because the lower limbs were completely fused together, leaving no external opening for either the intestinal or the urinary system. I was reminded shockingly of a drawing, which I had seen long ago in a facetious magazine, of babies growing on stalks in a garden; for the creature's single, centrally located leg tapered like the green calyx of a flower to where the knees should have been, and there contracted suddenly to a girth of little more than your thumb, continuing thence for a few more inches and ending in a raw, skinless blob, as if the body had been broken from a stalk at its nodule.

"Not even a semicolon to punctuate his brief career," remarked Ross, who was likely to seize upon unfortunate chances for being witty.

"Yeah," someone else cut in, "Wyck's going to do a post[1] on him, as soon as young symmy cashes in his checks, and find out just what does become of his pipes."

In view of this bit of information, I found it difficult to believe that Wyck could be the father of the monster. We had every cause for thinking the old doctor unbalanced; but even so, it did not seem fair to suppose that he was sufficiently morbid to cut up a child of his own begetting, especially when his co-worker, Dr. Alling, was at least as competent for the special requirements of the job.

A few moments later another incident occurred which seemed for awhile to confirm the assumption that Wyck had not sired the creature. The rest of the students were straggling out of the room. Jap urged me to come too—but I wanted to use a stethoscope on the symmelus, so I told him that I would join him at the dog cart in a few minutes, and went down to borrow one from Jib Tucker, an interne. While I was in the main hallway, downstairs, an old Ford came slurring around the hospital drive with such noisy disregard for the "Quiet" signs that I paused to see what was up. A youth leapt over the door of the flivver without bothering to open it, and dashed up the steps. When he reached the reception window, however, he stopped short and said nothing at all.

Daisy Towers, seated at her switchboard, looked at him with a curt professional air and said, "Yes?"

The youth made no reply; but I noticed that his fists were folding and unfolding in a fashion indicative of extreme agitation. He was rather handsome, of a ruddy complexion, with wavy black hair worn long, and a thin, patrician nose that made all the more incongruous his costume: a faded flannel shirt, grease-stained khaki trousers, army boots, and a floppy felt hat with fishhooks and snells in the band.

When Daisy spoke a second time, he took the hat off, gulped, and asked jerkily, "Is there—was there—did somebody get born here, today?"

"Who's asking?" Daisy inquired. He ignored the question, and she added archly, "Are you a prospective father?"

1 i.e., a post-mortem.

He seemed confused or embarrassed, and again declined to answer. Something buzzed on the switchboard. She attended to the call, and then turned again toward the waiting youth.

"It's Sarah Mullin, I mean," he blurted at last, "You've got to tell me. You've just got to. I heard—"

Daisy spoke more kindly. "What was it you heard?"

"I heard she was—"

"A mother?"

"Oh, yes, but I— Then she's all right? Then she didn't—?"

Daisy looked down and said softly, "She died in childbirth."

He swayed a little, turning to stare toward me with eyes which, I am sure, registered nothing that they saw.

"Is your name—Ted?" Daisy asked.

He nodded.

"Well, they told me to tell you, if you came, that she kept murmuring your name before—the end."

He sobbed, turned quickly, and stumbled out to his car.

"That's one mystery settled," I remarked to Daisy. "But you wouldn't think such a healthy specimen as that would have a deformed child."

"No, you wouldn't—and there isn't any reason for thinking so even now," she answered decisively.

"You mean that maybe he wasn't the father?"

"That's what I mean, Dave, without any maybe."

"You're goofy," I said promptly.

"That's not unlikely," she answered, with a toss of her curls, "but even a goof, if she hangs around a maternity ward much, ought to know that if that fellow was the father you couldn't have dragged him away from the baby with a team of Morgans. He didn't even mention the subject of offspring."

"That's so. Who was he, then, her brother?"

"No. A brother would be interested in the baby, too. It's a jolt to realize all of a sudden that you've become an uncle, without having had any say about it. That guy was just plain in love with her, that's all. Anybody who was as worked up as he was over the situation in general would have clamped all his emotions right onto the kid, if the kid was his relation, Dave."

Her analysis seemed sensible, when I thought it over. "Maybe he was somebody she'd given the gate," I suggested. "Maybe she'd been playing around since then with somebody else, and this lad wouldn't admit to himself that he was still nuts about her —until he suddenly heard that she was dead."

"That sounds a great deal more like it," Daisy agreed. "But they must have had something like a reconciliation, because I'm just as sure as can be that I've seen that pair together, somewhere. Not so very long ago, either. It was six weeks ago yesterday that she went to the Widow's, and—"

"How do you happen to know that?"

She patted the switchboard, by way of reply, and pointed with the other hand to the telephone receiver clamped against one ear. "Six weeks ago yesterday," she repeated, "and it wasn't as long ago as that that I saw them, either. Wait! I remember! A month ago last Saturday I drove down to a dance at South Alton with your friend Jib Tucker. He was driving with his dimmers, and we nearly bumped into a couple walking by the roadside, in the dark. We backed up to be sure of things. I remember them standing there, hand in hand. It couldn't have been very far from the Widow's, because we had to go on a ways before we hit town."

That turned my suspicions about the monster's paternity back again upon the sudden visitor to the hospital. His failure to show interest in the offspring might have been caused by advance news that it was a monster. The affair doubtless was being kept secret from the town at large, at least for the present, but one of the medical students might have made a slip, in public. Daisy was still positive, however, in her disagreement.

"Well, who was the father, then?" I inquired at last, and she came back right away with, "Ask me no questions, and I'll be in no danger of losing my job, Davy."

It was plain enough that she knew more facts about the case than she cared to reveal, so I let it go at that. She was so fond of tossing out bright, startling bits of information as her friends went by that I knew she would not withhold anything except for some very good reason.

CHAPTER VI

I liked Daisy in spite of her tongue. She was pretty, with coppery hair and a kind of golden tan that still lingered in April. Her quick fingers never fumbled over the rows of plugs and switches. Her hearing was so acute that she seldom asked for a number to be repeated.

If my ill-starred affair of the heart, already referred to, had not taken so long to dwindle off into futility, I might have fallen for Daisy. Certainly she was to me the most attractive girl in town, and the only one—barring Marjorie Wyck—who seemed at all civilized. Most of the nurses came from the back country regions. The other girls in town were just small town girls. But Daisy's family really belonged on the faculty side of the town-and-gown division. Her father had been comptroller of the hospital and treasurer of the medical school. His death in an accident, a few years ago, had left his wife and daughter not too well provided for. Daisy in consequence had become a nurse at the age of eighteen, and, three years later, had taken the switchboard job. It paid less, but she liked the work better. She confessed that she never had got thoroughly used to the sight of blood, nor reconciled to the messier intimate jobs which nurses have to perform for patients too sick to take care of themselves.

The medics, in general, ran the nurses ragged when on duty, getting rid of their own inferiority complexes by making the girls dance attendance on trivial jobs, such as inoculations in the free ward. That doubtless was another reason why the high-spirited Miss Towers preferred the switchboard job.

"It's nearly one. Wait a minute, and you can have the joy of walking home with me," she offered magnanimously, as I moved away from the window. I decided not to bother to use a stethoscope on the symmelus, after all. It was the kind of examination that Dr. Alling would certainly have made as soon as he came in. But then I remembered suddenly about the blood transfusions, and thought it would be a good idea to investigate while I was on the spot.

Daisy, when I told her what I wanted, admitted me to the little office behind the reception booth and pulled a drawer from the card index cabinet.

"What's the problem?" she inquired.

"Ask me no questions till I find out whether I'm making a fool of myself," I answered, with a wink; for I as yet had been unable to decide in my own mind whether it was plausible that Wyck could have some ailment which made it possible for him to keep up an appearance of health only with the aid of blood transfusions. The primary anæmias usually take their victims at an age much younger than Wyck's; and the secondary anæmias almost always are complications of other diseases which he could hardly have concealed. Indeed, the only justification for my suspicions lay in Wyck's extraordinary character, which would drive him to bully himself even more than he bullied others, especially after his lifelong boast of perfect health.

If, as my memory of Mike's inadvertent remark indicated, he had been giving blood to Wyck, the process obviously would have terminated at the time of Mike's accident—and that might account for Wyck's recent appearance of extreme pallor. I bent eagerly over the card giving Mike's record as a blood donor. It showed eight transfusions within twenty months. Five of them, all to women, had been accomplished more than a year ago. The sixth, on the 8th day of the preceding October, had failed to save a man who was dying at the time. The seventh was accomplished on February 16th of the current year. The blood had been given to one Joseph Baker—a first-year medic who had gone through the windshield of his roadster and was now at home convalescing. The last entry surprised me. It reads:

7 March 1932 $\left\{\begin{array}{l}\text{to Peter Tompkins, 250 cc.} \\ \text{to Joseph Baker, 250 cc.}\end{array}\right.$

Mike always told me about his cases. I had gathered from what he said that this transfusion had gone entirely to the boy who had shot himself: young Peter. Daisy got me the latter's registry card, which showed that another donor had first been used for a full 500 cc., but that an additional amount had been needed. The explanation seemed therefore to be that, since Mike had been called in to give half the usual amount of blood, at the full minimum price, the physicians in charge had decided to draw off the normal amount and give half of it to Baker, who probably would have been still anæmic. Daisy got me Baker's card, which confirmed this. Mike might not have known anything about the division. All the entries for this operation were marked "citrate" to show that the blood had been drawn off into an intermediary container, and had not been transfused directly. Doubtless it had been done at Peter's bedside, and Mike had not been told that the superfluous 250 cc. had been carried to Baker, preserved from clotting in transit by the addition of a little sodium citrate.

"Well," Daisy asked, "have you made a fool of yourself?"

"I would have," I admitted, realizing that there was nothing to show that Mike had given blood to Wyck, "if I'd told you what I was looking for. But I've found something else to wonder about."

"Which is?"

"I'll trade you this information for yours about the paternity of the symmelus," I offered.

She shook her head. "Rather not, Davy. I'd like to be just a little more sure of it."

"The same goes for mine," I agreed.

What I was wondering about was the coincidence that Mike's awful seizure of pain, a while after midnight, had apparently coincided with the death of a boy into whose veins 250 cc. of Mike's own blood had been introduced not long before. It seemed impossible that similar symptoms could have escaped notice in thousands of other cases when transfusions had failed to save a life; but the tantalizing fact remained that Mike's case was special, because the arm from which the transfusions had been made was now amputated, and the pain had centered in the severed ends of its nerves, giving Mike the impression that the agony which he experienced actually was being suffered in the arm that was no longer there.

Daisy interrupted my reverie by saying, "Hurry up, I'm hungry." When I told her that I wanted to copy Mike's record for reference, she decided not to wait. Nevertheless, the job was done so speedily that she was still in sight on Atlantic Street when I passed out through the hospital gates. There, the noise of a door slamming, some distance away, caused me to look curiously toward the pine grove concealing Wyck's residence. Someone rushed out, and leapt into a parked Ford which backed noisily, turned and came snorting toward me at a furious rate. I saw that it was driven by the same strange boy, who so far was identified only by the name Ted, which he had admitted was his when inquiring about Sarah Mullin. His face now had lost its blank expression. He was frowning. His lips twisted in an almost maniacal way. It occurred to me that, even if my own first suspicion about the monster's paternity was erroneous, as I now believed, the boy might also have thought Wyck guilty; and he could not have known my later reasons for being doubtful. Even if the boy Ted had been only her casual friend, he would have known that Sarah had worked at the Wycks' and would be likely to suspect the old doctor of having seduced her. I thought it might be a good idea to stop in at the gingerbread house to make sure that all was well.

When Dr. Wyck himself answered my knock, I felt rather foolish. There apparently had been no reason for my fears, so I said the first thing that I could think of: "Mike had another of those attacks, this morning, sir. They may be just hallucinations, as you say, but he's terribly hard to handle when they happen. If it's going to keep up this way, I was thinking it might be a good idea to keep him doped for awhile."

For the first time in memory, the old doctor seemed to be without a quick answer. Presently he said, "No, I wouldn't do that. No, not by any means."

It was an unwritten law at the College of Surgery that whenever a student failed to understand the reason in pathology for a given course of treatment, he should sing out and demand an explanation, even at the risk of seeming stupid. I hesitated to do so, this time, because I had a conviction that Gideon Wyck's pause before replying had resulted from the fact that he was unwilling to give the argument behind an unreasonable decision. This was confirmed when he added:

"I warn you, don't do anything like that, at least until tomorrow. Understand?"

There again, as I look back upon it, was a warning I should have heeded, a plain enough indication that something portentous would happen before the night was out. I am now quite sure that Gideon Wyck had his own good reasons for subjecting Mike to a deliberate recurrence of the agonizing seizures; but it was not until long afterward that the reasons were revealed by other discoveries.

As I stood uncomfortably in his doorway, not knowing just how to terminate my call, I surprised myself by bluntly asking the question which had been uppermost in my mind.

"What did Mike mean when he said something about giving blood to you, sir?"

He lit a cigarette with a show of calmness, and countered, "What do you think he could have meant, Saunders?"

"I have no idea, unless he was just delirious."

"Delirious ravings are based on real events," the doctor observed, eyeing me in a malicious fashion, as if to warn me that I might learn more than it would be comfortable to know. Then he laughed sharply and unpleasantly and added, "So far as I can see, he was merely referring to the fact that it was I who drew off blood from him to be injected into various patients—such as your fellow student Joseph Baker, who went through the windshield. Mike must have been brooding on the notion that I make my living by taking blood out of him and putting it into somebody else."

That seemed fair enough, at the time. I dismissed the problem and changed the subject by saying, "How is Joe Baker getting along? Have you heard, sir?"

Again he stared at me queerly, as if wondering whether I was stressing an unpleasant subject with intentional naïveté; and again he answered with a question.

"Have the boys heard anything from him, of late?"

I shook my head, and he added curtly, "Neither have I. Why should I?"

It seemed impossible to talk on any subject without making him touchy, so I took my departure. Once more I had been impressed by the remarkable pallor of his usually ruddy face, by the sagging of his cheeks that had remained so smooth and youthful up to a few weeks before. Something else had struck me, too—an odor such as one gets at the bedsides of invalids who have been subsisting largely on medicines. It was too strong merely to have been the lingering hospital-smell of his clothing. It was his breath that smelt of some chemical which I was at a loss to identify.

As I turned the corner of Atlantic Street, Marjorie Wyck was approaching, with a basket on her arm. I paused to say, "I'm sorry about Sarah. You liked her, didn't you?"

Her throat colored a little. "I did for awhile," she said. Her half-prudish reaction puzzled me. In an ordinary town, no doubt, the subject of a seduced housemaid would never have been spoken of at all, between the sexes, except by persons who knew each other well. But the medical community, bunched at the outskirts of the town, was quite devoid of such inhibitions, and there was hardly any topic that was barred from general conversation. The difference between Altonville and ordinary towns in that respect was impressed upon me at the end of my first year, when Jap Ross and I were invited to dinner at the home of friends of his in South Alton. We were late in arriving, and, when facetiously pressed for an explanation at the dinner table, Jap stated the facts, which were that a woman had died at the hospital of tertiary syphilis and we had both been asked to assist at the post-mortem examination. Our hostess abruptly left the table; her husband maintained a shocked silence through the rest of the meal; and I noticed that he took great care not to shake hands when we departed. No doubt they boiled all the tableware we used, and burnt the chairs we sat in.

But among the men and women of the medical community, no words or facts that pertained to general practice were considered prurient, as such; and that was why I was startled by Marjorie Wyck's reaction to my expression of a perfectly honest solicitude. Once more the weathervane of my suspicions swung around. Did she herself believe that her father had misled the unlucky Sarah? I got no real chance to decide, for her personality seemed suddenly to withdraw into vagueness. It was a frequent trick of hers—a trick or an unconsciously conditioned reflex. She seemed to live in two worlds, and could fade out of the real one without giving offense. I have never known anyone else who could be so utterly preoccupied at times, so oblivious of her surroundings. Doubtless it all came from living with a surly old man, in that hideous old house. The best way to make life bearable, in such a case, certainly would be to withdraw into the imagination and to notice nothing outside.

Marjorie did that. She walked dreamily on past me, without even a glance of farewell; apparently she had quite forgotten, while still looking at me, that anyone named David Saunders existed.

CHAPTER VII

All third-year men at medical school take a course called "Human Anatomy 3 & 4" to become familiar with the body from a specialized surgical point of view. We worked in small groups, at our own pace. As a result, the last day or two of dissection witnessed a grand scramble on the part of less conscientious students to get their cadavers in condition for final inspection. Six P.M. of the day about which I have been writing was the deadline for the year 1932. Consequently, when I drifted down to the dissecting room it was buzzing with prayers and curses. Of those present, only Prendergast seemed at ease.

All year he had kept about one day behind the fastest of us, profiting by our blunders. The oath which meant that someone had cut too deeply always brought Prendergast to the table in question. Next day, when he reached that part of the job himself, he would do it perfectly. He gave me a cool and noncommittal stare, this time, when I noticed that he had uncovered my cadaver to match notes. I was perfectly willing to forget our quarrel; but it seemed to me that the first move toward a return to friendship was up to him; so I merely began to go over my work step by step to make sure that all was in order. Prendergast left before I had finished, without offering to make up. I was preparing to go, myself, when Charlie the diener hailed me for help in getting two freshly embalmed bodies on high shelves in the dank vault.

"Last arrivals for this year," he said. "Tomorrow when the

inspection of them cut up ones out there's all over we'll give these babies their annual bath of chlorine for what ails 'em." The stiff, musty carcasses were sewed up in white gauze shrouds. We heaved them into their stalls and sauntered back into the preparation room. The diener banged the vault door, snapped a solemn-looking system of bolts, and turned the key in the padlock. While I was washing the corpsiness off my hands, Dr. Wyck stalked silently up and laid on the table by the sink a thin book with marbled paper sides and leather back.

"Take that to the President's, when you go," he said. "It belongs with that Geoffroy set. I found it in my office, upstairs."

I nodded and turned to rinse my hands. As I did so his reflection appeared in the mirror, side face. His features, which had been under control when he spoke to me, though still very pale, suddenly were contorted as if by extreme agony. I swung to see what was wrong, and, to my astonishment, found him smiling sourly at me, quite as usual.

Had the mirror played a trick? I looked in it again, but he still appeared normal. Yet I could have sworn that, for a moment when he felt himself to be unobserved, he had betrayed extreme suffering. Was it suffering, though, in the usual sense of the word? Might it not have something to do with the growing mania that apparently was overtaking him? I got out as quickly as possible.

A few minutes later, while walking up Packard Road, I inspected the volume, which contained illustrations to the history of Anomalies[1] which we had taken with us from Dr. Wyck's that morning. The plates showed specific examples of abnormal births, but I found none of the symmelus type born at our hospital that morning. I gave it to Prexy, who placed it with its companion volumes and then dictated a short address for the night's faculty meeting. Presently, while I was typing it out, he picked up the volume of plates and went out on the sun porch to escape the

---

1 *Histoire Générale et Particulière des Anomalies de l'Organisation chez l'Homme et les Animaux; etc. des Monstruosités, des variétés et des vices de conformation, ou Traité de Tératologie,* par M. Isidore Geoffroy Saint-Hilaire. Paris: J. B. Baillière, Libraire de l'Académie Royale de Médécine, 1837. (The volume referred to above is the "Atlas" containing twenty engraved plates and a table of contents.)

noise of the typewriter. When I had finished, and was separating the carbons to be filed away, I looked up to see him standing at the study door, his head cocked on one side in the fashion that betokened curiosity.

"What next, sir?" I asked, to end the tension of his long stare.

"Oh? Nothing. Get Wyck on the phone for me. I want to get all the facts straight about that student's petition."

"He was at the medical school when I left, sir," I said; but when I called the number of his office, Daisy Towers said, "Sorry, Davy. He's home, but he's being pestered with long distance calls today. I'll call you back."

While waiting, I was overcome by a queer mixture of thoughts and emotions. I had the feeling that must come to scientists on the verge of a rare discovery or startling invention. Various causal agents, long unrelated and developing each in its separate way, suddenly were focusing to produce some dramatic result. A whole series of pent-up tensions had started to touch each other off, like a string of firecrackers. I expected some kind of awful revelation, very soon, and yet did not want to witness it.

Daisy's ring broke my reverie, and I called Dr. Alling to the phone. While he argued with the stubborn old Gideon, I looked again at the volume of plates. Quite by accident I noticed, on the contents page, the line:

PLANCHE V. Monstres Syméliens.

"Symélien" ought to be the same as "symmelus"; yet, on going through the book before, I had not noticed the illustration. I turned to the place and found that Plate V had been neatly torn out!

Dr. Alling hung up the receiver. It flashed upon me that his peculiar stare, upon returning from the porch, might mean that he thought I had removed the plate myself. But why should I have done that? Then came the thought that perhaps he had done it while I was typing. But what reason would he have for so doing? I decided at least to be frank, and asked him at once if he had noticed that one of the plates was missing.

"Oh?" He stopped short, and then admitted slowly, "Yes, as a matter of fact, I did."

"I'm sure it didn't drop out en route, sir," I said, leaving it for him to mention if he chose the coincidence that it was a picture of the very kind of monster born that morning. But he merely told me to inform Dr. Wyck of the loss at once, as the book was a rare first edition.

After supper I came early to the medical school, hoping to find in the library a modern edition reproducing the plate; but my curiosity went unrewarded. The work was not indexed at all. Out in the second-floor corridor again, I noticed a strip of light by Dr. Wyck's office door, which proved to be ajar. He answered my knock with a surly, "Come in."

When I told him about the missing plate, he stared suspiciously, and then said, "All right, I can order a photostat from the Library of Congress. Which one was it?"

"Plate five."

"You're sure of that?"

"Positive."

He scribbled a notation, and then said, "I suppose we'd better be getting up to that damned meeting."

Thinking that he perhaps had forgotten Dr. Alling's request, I said, "I thought this was your night off, sir."

"You mean that you thought Jehovah himself lives in this town, don't you?"

Again I wondered whether his mind was becoming deranged, until he explained. "Well, Fred Alling may think he's Jehovah, and he may get away with playing God Almighty to the rest of the town, but he's not going to do it with me. The gathering of nincompoops up there in the faculty room are always changing things behind my back. Well, if anything's to be changed this time, it'll be done to my face, and the responsibility will rest where it belongs."

He rose painfully from his chair. As we climbed slowly to the next floor, I noticed that he was gripping hard at the rail for support. On this cool evening, the building itself was warm enough; yet the old doctor was still wearing a light topcoat indoors. We had reached the top of the stairway when somebody came out of the library on the floor below and called, "Oh, Dr. Wyck."

It was a classmate of mine named Jarvis. The doctor said, "Have you got something to keep busy with?"

"Yes," Jarvis answered, "we both brought our evening's work."

"Keep at it then till I call you," Dr. Wyck said, and stalked into the faculty room.

Dr. Alling, seated behind a kind of lectern on the dais, looked up with surprise; but the flash of annoyance on his face was quickly mastered. Wyck took his seat at the right end of the front row—a place to which he was entitled by seniority on the faculty; he was the only remaining member of the original staff, except Prexy himself. I took my usual place at a small desk at the right of the dais, facing Prexy. A quarter-turn of the head permitted me to see the whole room. The entire faculty was present—ten physicians, eight professors of pre-clinical subjects, as well as three other persons, concerned with administrative affairs in the college and hospital. Also, in the back of the room, I saw Dick Prendergast and a small, rather pompous individual who was unknown to me. They were whispering together, and it occurred to me that my classmate might have gone so far as to hire a lawyer. The man was constantly putting on and taking off his *pince-nez,* with black and silver rims, fastened to his vest by an ostentatious black ribbon.

There was nothing about the preliminary business that needs comment. Prexy read his address; I read the minutes; there were two or three routine motions and votes with no discussion. Prendergast's petition was the last item to come up. Prexy inquired whether he would like it read by the secretary. To my relief, Dick preferred to read it himself. I could reproduce the document from the copy in the files. It is, in its way, a masterpiece; but like most masterpieces, it is much too long—21 typed pages—and does not lend itself readily to quotation. It is enough to describe it as most persuasively worded, vibrant with a sense of injustice that was unquestionably sincere, and studded with shrewd citations of Dr. Wyck's unfairness. These last, I noted, he had chosen exclusively from among those instances in which the old doctor had been voted down by his colleagues, thereby exhibiting an excellent series of precedents for the final eloquent appeal that they vote him, in this instance, not only down, but out of the faculty itself.

I noticed that Prendergast made no reference whatever to the charge of cribbing, which Wyck had given as justification of his own severity toward the student.

Dick finished with a flourish and sat down. Prexy then inquired whether Dr. Wyck would like to have the matter tabled for action at the next meeting, in order to have an opportunity to prepare a formal reply.

"Oh, I don't see any good reason for delaying, Mr. President," Wyck drawled. "Ask Prendergast if he wrote this examination."

Dick seemed surprised, hesitated, and then with a forced show of confidence identified the blue book[1] as his own.

Dr. Wyck then said, "Will the secretary see if Jarvis and Ross are in the library? Any objections, Mr. Prendergast?"

Prendergast shook his head, as if quite puzzled by the problem of deciding why it could be supposed that he would object. I went down to the next floor, and found Jarvis still in the library. Ross was checking up on some specimen or other in the anatomy museum. We hailed him, and ascended the stairs.

"What's it all about, Dave?" Jap wanted to know. I told him that it had something to do with Prendergast's petition, but I didn't know what.

When we entered the faculty room, Dr. Wyck handed Jarvis another blue book, and said, "Where did you sit while writing this exam, Jarvis—if you did write it?"

Jarvis inspected the blue book, admitted that it was his, and said, "I must have been sitting in my regular assigned seat for your lecture, sir, I'm sure."

"Which is where?"

"The left end of the front row."

"Which hand do you write with?"

"My right hand," said the mystified Jarvis, looking quite unhappy.

---

1 A kind of blank notebook, with blue covers, in which formal examinations at most colleges and similar institutions are written. The standard blue book cannot be purchased, and is given out by the proctor at the time of the examination, to reduce the chance for cheating, or smuggling notes into the examination room.—ED.

"Do you remember who sat directly behind you, during that examination, Jarvis?" Dr. Wyck next inquired, and I expected to hear Jarvis say that it was Prendergast; for it was now obvious that the doctor was trying to show that the latter had copied from the former's paper. Jarvis said, however, "I couldn't be sure, sir. Ross usually did."

Ross then replaced Jarvis on the carpet, and admitted that he always had sat behind Jarvis.

"Very well. And at the examination in question, who sat at your right, Ross?"

Before Jap could answer, Dick leapt up to say, "I object."

"Ah, you do at last object?" Dr. Wyck said grimly. "To what, pray?"

Prendergast hesitated, and then said lamely, "To the fact that I'm not given a chance to cross-examine one witness before the next is called."

"This is not a court of law," Prexy said, smiling slightly. "However, we will extend this privilege, if you wish it."

But Prendergast had really had nothing to ask Jarvis. He withdrew the objection, and sat down again.

"What he really objects to, I gather," Dr. Wyck continued, "is to having it known that his assigned seat was so located that he had a good view of the paper Jarvis was writing with his right hand, in the next chair ahead and to the left."

Prendergast whispered with the stout little man beside him, and then said, "I object to the whole procedure, Mr. President. All this is irrelevant to the specific charges of my petition."

"I'm sorry," Prexy answered, "but I must again remind you that this is not a court of law. You will have a full opportunity for rebuttal when Dr. Wyck has finished. And, if you feel that justice has not been done, you have a right then to seek formal redress at law if you care to."

Poor Dick sat down, with the air of a general trying to revise plans in a crisis.

"Ross," Dr. Wyck continued, "do you recall any unusual occurrence during the first exam in my course, last fall?"

Looking most uncomfortable, Ross said, "I don't seem to, offhand."

"Do you recall, then, the fact that I spoke to Prendergast, midway in the exam?"

Jap swung around toward Prexy, and announced, "Sir, I don't know what this is all about, but I think I can smell it. Unless there's a charge of some kind against me personally, I'd like to be excused, and not say anything more. It—well, I'm not a peacher, sir."

"We want no lies," Prexy told him promptly, "but you may refuse to answer any question, according to your conscience."

At once Dr. Wyck turned his attention to Prendergast. "Did I, or did I not, ask you, in the middle of the examination, to finish your paper where there was better light, in a seat alone in the back row?"

"Yes, I remember that you did, now you mention it," Prendergast said, with a show of cordiality. "And I was glad to have the opportunity. The room's abominably lighted. It should have been seen to long ago."

"All I can say is," said the old doctor drily, "that you haven't shown much appreciation, all year, young man, for my solicitous interest in your eyesight, on that occasion."

"My opinion of your solicitous interest, sir, is already expressed at length in my petition," Dick said cuttingly, and sat down again.

"Well, gentlemen," Dr. Wyck concluded, "I leave these two blue books for your comparison. Jarvis got a perfect grade of twenty-five on each of the four questions. Prendergast answered the first two perfectly, when sitting in sight of Jarvis's paper. But he got only three out of a possible twenty-five on the third, and a flat zero on the fourth, while gratefully writing under the better light of the rear windows. I now recommend to your attention the underlined passages of identical wording in the two papers —all occurring in the first two questions—and leave to your discretion the problem of whether Jarvis copied over his shoulder from Prendergast, or whether it was Prendergast who relied upon Jarvis. I may add, although I hope it is not necessary, that Jarvis has stood at the head of his class throughout the last five semesters."

The above is mainly a transcript, with some condensation, from my own shorthand minutes of the meeting, but I shall not attempt to give the rest of it verbatim. The parallel passages from the two blue books were read into the record by Prexy himself. Dick had enough sense to see that the case on its merits so far was all against him; but his basic nature showed up again when he quickly shifted his plans and began to defend himself on an unwritten statute of limitations. He pleaded, ably and even impressively, that since the grade for the examination had been entered originally by Dr. Wyck for full credit of 53 points, and since no accusation had been made at the time, therefore he, Prendergast, had been fraudulently led into wasting time and money ever since, to provide a "sadistic old megalomaniac" with an object to bully. It was an apt point, and might have saved him if he had let it go at that; but the odd quirk which so often made him a sincere defender of preposterous propositions was once more his undoing. He ended by pointing out that, as for the charge of cribbing, it was mathematically possible for such parallel passages to have been written independently, especially in two brief perfect answers to the same question; and he had the quaint crust to ask the members of the faculty to believe that this was the ten-millionth case, and that the parallelism was entirely accidental.

That hardly accounted, however, for the fact that he had done so very, very badly on the last two questions; and it was, moreover, an unfortunate reminder to everyone who had ever graded a blue book by Prendergast that in his exams there always seemed to be some evidence of cribbing. Much as it must have pained them to side with Gideon Wyck on any issue at all, his colleagues voted unanimously by written ballot to expel, from the Maine State College of Surgery, the author of the petition rather than its subject.

As the meeting adjourned, Prendergast was talking quickly and passionately with his companion. Dr. Wyck, still wearing his topcoat, walked up to Prexy and demanded the two blue books. Prexy was obviously more annoyed than he cared to have known, and handed them over without speaking a word. Wyck thrust them into an inside pocket and stalked from the room. I commiserated with Jarvis and Ross, who were waiting around to make the apologies of student ethics to the classmate whose expulsion their testimony had unwittingly helped to bring about.

Presently Prendergast's pompous little companion marched up from the back of the room, and Prexy advanced to meet him, looking cordial and solicitous at once.

"I'm terribly, terribly sorry about this wretched business, senator," he said. "I was altogether sincere in my belief that Dr. Wyck was too ill to be present, as I told you. You must have noticed that he looked unwell? I was sure that no action would be taken at this time."

The little statesman nodded, and snorted something unintelligible. It was only then that I realized the full extent of the calamity, from Prexy's point of view. The stranger was obviously Prendergast's uncle in the state legislature—Senator Tolland—a dilettante in public life who, despite his wealth, had been defeated in a long series of election fights for more considerable offices, and at last had won the pompous title of "senator" in his home state. Later inquiries showed that he had been one of the pivotal group in the legislature, whose allegiance Prexy had gained only through the exercise of much shrewdness and tact. Moreover, Prexy himself had had no idea of the relationship between Senator Tolland and Prendergast until that very evening, a few minutes before the faculty meeting, when they had appeared together.

How badly the fat was in the fire became apparent when the senator expressed himself as utterly dissatisfied with the proceedings, not on any point of law or of procedure, but in that the many grievances in his nephew's petition had been allowed to stand unchallenged.

"Do you mean to say, sir," he asked, "that it is true that on all these seventeen occasions which Dick, here, had cited, the faculty as a group voted unanimously to override this man Wyck, in—in assigning grades, and whatnot?"

Prexy nervously admitted that it was so.

"You should have discharged him on the first repetition of it, sir. Outrageous! Unthinkable, that serious students should be subjected to the cruel whims of such a creature. If he is not cashiered at once—at once, mind you—I shall submit a bill to the legislature, which is now in session, to withhold the carry-over appropriation voted last term, pending an investigation, sir, an investigation by commission, of Dr. Wyck's fitness to teach. The state's good money shall not be perverted in this fashion, I promise you."

Prexy mildly pointed out that Prendergast's record had been continually worse, not only under Wyck, but in all his work except dissections, all year. The nephew at once broke in to say that this was due to the violent prejudice and mental cruelty of Wyck, whose persecution had unsettled him to the verge of a nervous breakdown.

Before he was through, Senator Tolland significantly mentioned a society for protecting animals from cruelty, and a number of religious organizations. It seemed to me that Prexy visibly blanched. It was terrifically hard to get cadavers for dissection, over the prejudices of squeamish folk, and the anti-vivisectionists were continually seeking injunctions against the use of living animals in medical research. If such matters were to come up in the legislature of our state, the lower house of which was overwhelmingly drawn from professional farmers, their vote was sure to be on the side of the angels, against science. I did not blame Prexy for compromising with his conscience, by inviting the senator to confer with him further at his own residence.

The last words I heard, as they went out, were: "—and you will do well to remember, President Alling, that I can talk eye to eye with you on such matters. I hold a degree in medicine myself, although I have always been interested in the legal aspects of medicine—and despite the—ah, fortunate circumstance—that my own income makes it—ah, unnecessary for me to practice."

CHAPTER VIII

Lack of sleep, on the preceding night, had made me feel very tired for awhile before the faculty meeting started; but the extraordinary events of the meeting itself, climaxing a most unusual day, had produced in me a kind of nervous exhilaration. My life of study and secretarial duties had been increasingly more sedentary all year, and I had been troubled with insomnia, perhaps as a result. On this occasion it seemed that the best way to quiet my nerves would be to take a brisk walk for half an hour, and then turn in, skipping for once the usual two- or three-hour session of midnight oil.

I stopped at the dog cart for some cigarettes. The proprietor, a casual friend of mine, greeted me with a bit of news that proved pertinent:

"Wisht you'd 'a' been here 'bout an hour ago, doc. I'd a had a patient for ya. Yeah, faints right into a bowl o' soup."

"Who was she?" I asked.

"Dunno. Some farmer's wife. He was along. Told me she was all done up with watchin' over a kid that died last night. They just planted 'im, and she comes in here and faints into a bowl o' my good soup. They sent an interner over. Yeah. He knew the name, but I forget."

"Wasn't Tompkins, was it?"

"Sure. That's it. Interner said their kid shot himself."

"Well, I'll try to be on hand next time you have a case," I promised, and walked on. Atlantic Street is unlighted on the north side, for the three deserted blocks or so between the lunch wagon and the two big globes over the hospital gates. Consequently, as I swung along the sandy side path, I was able to see two figures standing in the middle of the gateway, and to come rather close to them without being seen myself. Something in their earnest manner interested me. I approached noiselessly, all the more interested when I recognized one of them as Nurse Finch. The other, I soon gathered, was the farmer named Tompkins; he was objecting, "But I can't afford to pay no more to thet place, miss, 'spite of what ye say."

"You leave her for the night," Muriel insisted. "Don't go back. She'll sleep right on through. She's just completely tuckered out, and there's no sense bumping her back to the farm tonight. I'll see to it that you don't have to pay anything. And about the other bill, for the oxygen and all, just you forget it and say you haven't got it. None of the other doctors but him would have billed you with that."

The old fellow growled that he would be glad to hand the money over to Wyck in person for the chance it would give him to do something or other; but he lowered his voice, and just what the threat was I could not hear. Muriel extended her hand. He wiped his apologetically on his thigh before shaking hands with a vigorous, awkward jerk. Then he turned and went back through the gates to get his flivver. Muriel, to my surprise, turned north on the lonely road to Alton Center. There was no house in that direction for miles, except old Gideon's, standing opposite the far corner of the iron fence, a few hundred feet farther along. I had something to ask Muriel, and was about to cross the street to join her when the question of her reason for walking in that direction, at such an hour, made me pause. I decided to follow quietly, a little way, and to intercept her in front of the Wyck residence if she did seem actually to contemplate turning in there.

Sure enough, she crossed the road toward the house. Then, just as I was about to call her name softly, I saw that she had passed the entrance. At once I quickened my pace, only to draw back against the barberry hedge, breathless, as the dapper little figure of Gideon himself, unmistakable even in faint starlight, stepped out and walked slowly after her. With heart pumping, I cautiously followed. Soon they were strolling side by side. I remember my amazement at thinking what an incorrigible old ankle-snatcher the man must be, to go strolling in the darkness with a pretty nurse, at the end of a day when he had seemed pale and shaky with illness; but it was no less puzzling that Muriel, after her hysterical denunciations spoken to me that very morning, should have made this obviously prearranged date with someone she hated so fiercely. The only explanation seemed to be, either that he was able to exercise some tyrannical power over her or that she was deliberately leading him toward some kind of revenge. The fact that both might be true made me all the more wary, as I crept along behind them.

Our route may have a special name on maps, but in town they call it the Bottom Road—I suppose because it follows a stream through a wooded valley for about three miles before rising to the plateau of farm land around Alton Center. Two lanes cross small bridges to the right, over the stream, and disappear uphill. There are no side roads at all to the left, and nothing, really, for a road to lead to. All the area west of the Bottom Road, between Altonville and the Center, had been ravaged by lumbermen fifty years or more ago, and a decade or two later had been unscientifically retimbered, with the result that it now is choked with small pines that interfere with one another's growth, and are as hard to walk through as a hedge.

The first of the little bridges on the other side of the road was familiar to all of us medics as the first landmark cited in directing a stranger to the nearest source of good applejack, which was made by an old man who lived alone at the top of the trail; but he, so far as I knew, was the only person living in the whole area between Wyck's house and Alton Center. The ill-assorted pair of strollers ahead of me might possibly be in quest of applejack, although I thought it far more likely that they were headed for some nearer, secluded spot in which to consummate whatever purpose they had in view. For this reason I followed as closely as I dared, not wanting to lose them in the darkness, if they should suddenly leave the road.

They continued, however, to walk slowly, in complete silence, for nearly an hour, stopping only when they reached the second of the two little bridges. There, as I crept within a few yards on hands and knees, in the moist dust of the roadside, I could see them standing still. The doctor was clinging to the railing of the bridge, as if the walk had exhausted him; it well might have, in the circumstances. My own heart was banging with the excitement of sheer uncertainty, as I crouched near them, half expecting to see Muriel produce a weapon, and wondering what I would do if she did. It was quite apparent now that she was in no danger from him.

"This is the end of it," she said suddenly, in a husky voice that sounded very loud against the utter stillness. "I don't care what becomes of me now. I wasn't going to say anything, till after. But you may as well know now. I said to myself today that this would be the last time, but there isn't going to be another. I can't keep this up any longer, no matter what you do to me. It's all over, do you understand?"

"It was going to end tonight anyway," he said curtly.

"Oh yeah?" she snapped. "Well, anyway, I'm glad I said it first. That much is off my conscience. God's a witness that I said it first. I didn't go on and let it end some other way, because I was too scared. God knows that, now, no matter what you tell people. But if you want me to, I'll go away and keep my own mouth shut, like I promised, when you made me."

"You can go or stay as you please, Muriel. It makes no difference, so far as I'm concerned, after tonight."

"What do you mean, no difference? No difference! Not to you, maybe. It wouldn't. Nothing ever made any difference to you. You never cared what happened to other people, so long as you got what you wanted. But do you think I could go on living here, after—"

The rest of it was lost in the noise made by a car, coming down the bumpy ruts beyond the bridge. I expected the two talkers to scramble, as I did, for shelter; but they merely drew back against the railing. The car turned noisily on the Bottom Road, reversed, and went back to stop on the bridge again, pointing uphill. Luckily for me, the turn had been made with the lights toward the Center, and not toward the side of the bridge where I was crouching. Dr. Wyck climbed painfully into the back seat, followed by Muriel. The driver used his clutch badly in starting, and stalled. As he got out to crank the engine of the battered Ford, I think I gasped audibly; for the face that showed in the headlights was that of the boy named Ted, who had come dashing into the hospital to learn the fate of the Wycks' maid.

"Can't you even keep your engine running, you young fool?" the doctor inquired.

"Go to hell," the boy snapped; "you give me a pain in the neck."

The rebuttal, if any, was drowned in the roar of the motor. As the driver got in again, I had a wild notion that I ought to creep quickly up and hang on the spare tire behind. But I hesitated a bit too long. The car again started with a jerk, and this time did not stall, but went scuttling up the hill in low, making a terrific racket.

Where was it going? At this moment of crisis on a dark deserted road two miles from town, I experienced with full intensity for the first time a sensation of desperate responsibility—of a need to act quickly, with no knowledge of what to do at all. The feeling has recurred often enough, God knows, in the last year; but I think its first coming may have been the worst of all; for that

was the first time I was gripped with an absolute conviction that
something intolerably evil had been occurring in a hidden place
—that Mike's choking terror of "the black one wit' white eyes"
had something real to justify it—that the secret which Muriel
dared not confess was far more sinister than any of the acts which
long ago had made Gideon Wyck the most detested man within
many miles.

With all my heart I wanted to turn and race back to town as
fast as I could go. But I stood frozen by the bridge, watching the
Ford's lights make a weird moving pattern as it climbed higher
and higher between the still leafless trees. Where was it going?
The whole phrase of Mike's rushed through my mind: "a black
one it was, wit' white eyes, like in the hole in the hill."

Whatever the hole in the hill might be, I knew that that was
where the car was going. Dr. Wyck had just said that something
was to end tonight; but would it be for better or for worse that it
should end undiscovered? I had no way of knowing. All I knew
was that what might turn out to be the last clew was disappearing
up the hill. It was less reason than instinct that set my legs suddenly to moving, making on their own account a decision which
the brain refused to face. With cold fear gripping at my viscera, I
started to follow.

The two ruts could hardly be called a road. At several points
the spring thaw had so washed it out that I marveled at the ability
of even a Ford to proceed. For awhile I could almost keep pace
with the receding lights, until the road bent back on itself and my
guide was lost. Thereafter, it was impossible not to keep blundering off into dry bushes. Presently I realized, half-inspirationally,
that I was at a fork. Deep ruts could be felt, leading both ways.
I tried first the right-hand road; but it led promptly into holes
which no car could have passed in that muddy season; so I turned
back. The other way led before long into an open field, with more
woods beyond, but with no spark of light to show where the car
might have gone. Although I could still feel ruts underfoot plainly
enough to follow them, in a short while I realized that they were
lost. It then seemed best to strike for the opposite woods, in the
general direction in which the ruts had at first been leading, with
the hope of finding an opening in the trees.

This was not so easy. The field was far larger than it had appeared, in the starlight, which of course gave no perspective. The usual wire fence was missing from the other edge of it, and there was no stone wall, or other means of tracing the opening for the old road. After blundering into and out of a score of black holes, each time with a cowardly sense of relief at not having found what I was seeking, I realized the ridiculousness of my quest. The car might be a scant ten feet from me. I might have almost brushed it in passing, or have missed its present location by miles. Also, it was obvious that Wyck's secret, whatever it might be, could not have been kept except by close guarding. If he had been up to something that needed concealing, he would have made the place hard to find by daylight. How then could I hope to stumble upon it at night?

Vexed with my own foolishness, and still more frightened than it was pleasant to admit, I started back. But more troubles were awaiting me. The road up which I had come seemed to have vanished entirely. I stared at the constellations, but got no help from that, because I had failed to take any bearings in the first place. I had heard that it was possible to sight the North Star by looking along the two end stars of the Dipper—a bit of half-knowledge that proved a dangerous thing, for I found later that I had chosen the two stars at the wrong end. Finally, in desperation, I started down anywhere through the dark woods.

In the preamble to this narrative, I promised to set down all unusual events of the past year, just as they occurred. But I am going to leave to your imagination the events of the next hour or two, at the end of which time I suddenly found myself on a trail, and sank down in the middle of it, shaking with nervous exhaustion, to remain for many minutes before I recovered enough stamina to go on. When at last able to proceed, I found myself only a few yards above a little bridge which proved to be the first of the two leading up from the Bottom Road. This circumstance saved a mile of the walk back to town; but all the way the muscles of my legs were twitching and shivering.

The Wycks' house, when I passed it with a rousing curse, was as dark as pitch. The first chance to consult my watch came under the twin globes of the hospital gates, for I had not cared to betray my presence by striking a match, even after I had got out of the woods and onto the Bottom Road. It proved to be 1:20 A.M. I had been gone nearly four hours.

This act, of assuring myself of the time, seemed to bring me back into my normal world again. The first thought that occurred to me was that the others might have returned to town before me. I could easily check up, in the case of Muriel; for I knew that she was on the night shift at the hospital, and should have gone on duty at midnight. With Wyck it would be more difficult; but the darkness of his house seemed to indicate either that he had returned safely or that he was not expected back. Aside from its effect upon other persons, I was in no state of mind to care greatly what had happened to him.

I hesitated a moment at the gates, and then decided to call the hospital from the Connells', to find out about Muriel. It would be easier than explaining the purpose of a personal appearance at such an hour. As I approached the house, however, the sight of a lighted bedroom window, downstairs, made me fear that Mike had suffered another of his strange attacks. I quickened the pace of my aching legs, and was all the more alarmed when a closer view revealed Prexy's Marmon, the only one in town, parked in front of the house. There were no lights on the car, a fact which indicated that the call had not been thought of as brief, in prospect, by the driver. I rushed in, but everything was quiet. Through the open door of Mike's bedroom I could see that he was asleep, and that Dr. Alling was seated by the bedside, looking puzzled, holding a watch in his hand. Biddy was nowhere in sight.

"Why, what's happened?" I cried. "Where's Mrs. Connell?"

"What's happened to you?" Prexy asked sharply, ignoring my question and staring at me in amazement.

Only then did I realize the full effect of my encounters with branches, stones and barbed-wire fences. My trousers were ripped. The bureau mirror showed trickles of blood on my hands and face, and a great blue bruise on my forehead. My coat was smeared with pitch from pine trees into which I had blundered, and I was covered with burrs. I was about to explain something of my adventures, if not their cause, when Mike groaned. We both turned toward him. I stepped back in horror from the wholly maniacal expression of fear that contorted his features. He rose to a sitting posture, while a shriek, which I shall never be able to forget, tore at my very heart. As once before, but now far louder, it panted in and out of his throat continuously, as if some fearful power were pumping at his lungs, crushing them mercilessly, only to draw them more forcibly open again.

I could not endure it. I sprang to the bed. Poor Dr. Alling seemed even more affected, for he suddenly lifted the hand that contained his watch and banged it noisily on the bedside table. Mike's right hand seized my left arm in a grip that numbed the muscles—and I realized that he was striving to smash my face with the other, the amputated, fist. Just as Prexy scuttled around the room, making for a hypodermic needle on the bureau, Mike heaved me off the bed and began to slam me against the wall. He was still screaming frightfully. My efforts to get him back on the bed might as well have been addressed to a carthorse. I thought of Dr. Alling's phrase, "superphysical strength"—and, for the moment at least, felt a dreadful suspicion that it was not Mike Connell gripping me, but an iron-thewed fiend who had got possession of Mike's body. In the grip of one hand only, he was actually lifting me from the floor to smash me harder against the door jamb. In that suspended instant, I saw the slight, childish figure of Dr. Alling, maneuvering bravely for a chance to use the hypodermic needle without breaking it. My glance shifted to Mike's eyes, and I went sick with horror upon seeing that the irises had disappeared out of them, leaving nothing but expressionless, inhuman black pupils, expanded as if by the action of belladonna. Then my skull was crashed back pitilessly against the wall, and I can tell you of what happened next by hearsay only, from the testimony of Dr. Alling, corroborated in part by one of the internes.

It seems that the needle did break, in entering Mike's back, before any of the sedative contents of the syringe could be discharged. Conceiving that he was being attacked by Beelzebub again, Mike swung to hurl my limp body at Dr. Alling. This at least had the fortunate effect, from Prexy's viewpoint if not from mine, of shielding him from the chair which was the next thing Mike hurled, before he rushed screaming from the house. Dr. Alling thinks that he himself was only momentarily stunned; and he must have had more strength than I ever credited him with, because when I came to I found that he had stretched me out on a pair of pillows, taken from the bed and laid endwise on the floor. He was seated in a rocker, pressing his side, and groaning softly. When he saw my eyes open, however, he said, "Lie still," and walked swaying to the phone to call for aid.

A couple of internes soon arrived with a stretcher. They wanted to put Prexy on it, but he insisted upon walking to the ambulance, to which I was carried. As they brought me up the hospital steps, I was greatly relieved to see that one of the two nurses who stepped up in attendance was Muriel Finch. Perhaps it was a result of having been knocked so vigorously on the head, but it seemed to me that her face was radiant with happiness. I quelled the temptation to speak with her, deciding that, so long as she was safe, it would be a very good notion to give my aching head a chance to digest the day's bizarre events before saying anything that might betray my own part in them. So I let the two nurses put me to bed without saying anything at all. Muriel kept humming an old jazz tune—called *Hallelujah,* if my memory is correct. At least, I think she did, for I woke up next morning with the tune still singing through my head, which had ceased aching but which bore prodigious bumps both fore and aft. In general I felt well enough, although terribly lame.

It was ten o'clock, and Muriel had gone off duty at eight. Presently another nurse looked in; but she was unable to answer my questions about what had happened to Mike after he left the house. I then demanded my clothes.

"You won't want to wear those things," she said. "He nearly tore 'em to strips, and they're all smeared with blood. Burrs, too. He must have dragged you around in the bushes."

"I don't know," I said. "He must have done it after I was knocked out."

It seemed a good idea, for the time being, to let people think the condition of my clothes was the result of the fracas with Mike. I merely requested that Daisy be asked to locate Jap Ross, so that he could stop off on the way to the hospital and bring me some different clothes.

CHAPTER IX

While waiting for Jap to arrive, I ate breakfast in bed. He came in presently with some clothes of mine over his arm, jeering, "You'll never get a job as keeper in any booby-hutch that I run, Dave, when they've finished making an alienist out of me."

"Why not?" I asked uneasily, half-fearing to phrase a definite question about Mike's mental condition. There was no need; Jap's next sentence told me all I need to know.

"Because in my booby-hutch the keepers have got to be big enough to lick even the guys that think they're big gangsters, or Napoleon or something."

"You mean Mike didn't snap out of it, Jap?"

"Not him. Not that guy. They've got him over in the other wing in a strait-weskit, as the cockneys call 'em, making out he's the archangel Michael, or somebody. Claims he's licked all the toughest devils in hell, and that we'd better let him loose to clean up on the rest, before they grow any bigger."

"Cut out the wisecracks," I ordered. "I liked that guy."

"Well, you haven't got much cause to, after the lathering he gave you last night. They say they found a piece of your pants over in the cemetery, where they got him at last, after an all-night hunt."

"Did they have trouble getting him? Did they have to hurt him, I mean?"

"Nah. They had the jacket on him before he came to. But he's food for the squirrels, all right. What do you think they found he'd been doing? Digging up a grave—looking for blood, he said. Coo! Ghouls, they call 'em, don't they, when they get to that stage?"

I didn't want to hear any more, just then. Jap went out. A little later, when I was getting into my clothes, an interne named Jib Tucker gave me a factual account of what had happened to Mike. The poor fellow (I was about to write "the poor devil," and perhaps I still should) had been found at daylight, lying unconscious on a new grave. The stump of his left arm was thrust into a deep hole which he evidently had clawed with his right hand.

It was lucky that they had had the foresight to clap a strait-jacket on him at once, for he had come to suddenly, screaming and praying for them to put him back with his arm in the hole, so that he could suck up his lost blood through it again. Jib told me that, without drawing any inferences. I don't think that he, or anyone other than myself, saw anything in this but the irrational conduct of a demented person. Yet, as I was hearing the details, an awful, morbid notion took possession of my mind. I knew without needing to be told (and subsequent investigation substantiated the conviction) that the grave to which Mike had gone unerringly in his madness, through the dark night, was that of the boy Peter Tompkins, in whose dead body some of the blood of Mike's own being had so recently incurred the mystery of death.

My head was buzzing, and I felt sick and scared. When Jib went away I lay down in my clothes for a few minutes to regain composure. Two days ago I had been a rational being, directing all the cocksureness of the scientific method upon all phenomena. I had thought Dr. Alling's half-mystical attitude toward many of the problems of medicine a mere technical exaggeration of the principle of being open-minded. Since that time, which now seemed ages ago, I had seen a devil take possession of the eyes of a friend. I had seen the iris of a man's eyes expand into nothingness, leaving only the pupils, hard-rimmed against the white. Like Dr. Alling's missionary, Nevius, I found myself with a problem forced upon me that demanded an answer. It was not enough to ignore the question entirely, not enough even to keep an open mind. I had seen the thing happen to my friend, and by that token it had thrust itself too deeply into my own life to be argued lightly away.

Presently the fit of panic passed. I got a grip on myself when I remembered that Biddy would need to be consoled; but the memory of her plight only deepened the mystery. She had not been at home when I arrived, long after midnight. Where could she have been, and what had brought Dr. Alling to the bedside, while Mike was still quietly sleeping? Was it premonition alone that had brought him, to be on hand when the worst attack of all occurred?

Daisy Towers might have an answer, I thought. It would be out of character for her not to have one, plus a complete history of what had happened, neatly arranged in her extremely efficient, pretty head. I limped downstairs, and stopped at the reception window. She twitted me genially for having been so badly mauled by a one-armed invalid. I found nothing to resent, however, in the way she went about it. Her sense of humor was not callous, like Jap's; and her ability to see the mirthful aspect, in that which to me was all tragedy, brought me back to something like my normal self.

"How's Biddy taking it?" I inquired unaffectedly.

"Don't know, Dave. They've got her upstairs next to Mike's room, pumped full of morphia, just now. They say she was throwing hysterics when they brought her in."

I asked when that was. Daisy looked at a card, and said, "Two-twenty A.M., about fifteen minutes after you and Dr. Alling arrived, feet first."

"Where was she when the fight started?" I asked.

"Out for a walk. She hadn't been out of the house five minutes in ten days, Dr. Alling said. He was bawling you out for that, sweetheart. So it seems he told her to walk around for half an hour or so, even if it was after midnight."

"How did Dr. Alling himself happen to be there just then, Daisy?"

"I suppose she saw what was coming, and called him. He attended Mike yesterday morning, as you know, so he was the logical one for her to call, wasn't he?"

"How did you know he was there yesterday morning?" I asked suspiciously. "He wasn't summoned by phone, that time."

"It's my business to know where doctors are, all the time, my boy, no matter how they're summoned. Want a glimpse of the system? Well, I phoned him at Wyck's that a symmelus had been born, and he said he'd be right over. But when it took him twenty-five minutes to get from Wyck's to here, with a live monster to see, I knew he'd been dragged somewhere in between."

"He's right about one thing," I confessed. "He thinks you're a smart girl, the way you keep track of doctors."

"Oh, I am, you know, very smart," she answered demurely. "That is, I have been till this morning. You don't happen to know where Dr. Gideon Wyck is, do you?"

Perhaps I only imagined that she was watching me narrowly, in spite of her casual tone. I'm afraid I hesitated for a suspicious interval before admitting, "No, I don't. Why?"

"His daughter's been making very innocent-sounding calls around town since breakfast time. Each time she asks a leading question or so, to give anybody who might be looking for the opportunity a chance to explain why her papa didn't come home at all last night."

"Oh, he's an old night-owl anyway," I remarked quickly. "When I was holding down the job of janitor's assistant, my first year, he'd often be still in his office when I came to sweep up at six in the morning."

"Yes, but it's nearly eleven in the morning now," she pointed out.

Dr. Wyck's words, spoken to Muriel on the bridge, flashed back into my mind: "It makes no difference, so far as I'm concerned, after tonight." What had he meant? Had he known that he was at the end of his tether, physically? Had he felt certain that some well-merited revenge, which he had called down upon his own head, was due? Had he deliberately disappeared, because of that, from the scene of some secret crime? Had he— No, that was too weird to be supportable in any mind claiming rationality; but nevertheless, at intervals during the day I was plagued by the insane notion that the soul of Gideon Wyck, having exhausted its proper body, had seized upon the healthy one of poor Mike Connell.

Call me crazy, if you like. I've spent a lot of time, since then, calling myself crazy; but I have promised to set down all the things that may be pertinent; and something happened later to keep me from ever putting that notion wholly out of mind.

One thing seemed certain: Muriel's safe return made it seem altogether unlikely that the old doctor had been kept from returning by a mere accident to the car. I wanted to ponder more upon these matters, however, before saying anything to Muriel;

and I knew that it was good sense to do my pondering elsewhere than under the shrewd eyes of Daisy Towers.

When I got home I found a note from Dr. Alling pinned to the door. It merely said that he would not need my services during the day, and advised that I spend it resting. I was glad enough to do so, thinking it would give me a chance to figure things out. But all day long fellows kept dropping in, singly and in groups, for a first-hand description of the fight. Toward evening they all spoke of Dr. Wyck's disappearance.

Mickey Rehan summed up the prevailing sentiment on the subject when he smiled broadly and said, "Either the crutty old goat's gone off on a beautiful bender, or else he's been quietly knocked on the head—and a good thing too. Wish I'd thought of it first. I'd 'a' had all A's, last semester, if it hadn't 'a' been for that old running sore, Wyck. Hope he died with considerable pain."

Between visits, I made as careful and complete a record as memory permitted of all the events of the preceding day or two that seemed to have any possible bearing upon the mysteries of Mike's symptoms and of Wyck's disappearance. I knew that Muriel and the boy Ted were implicated in some fashion, and that the old farmer, Tompkins, not only had been lurking around town, but had had unusually good reasons for hating an already well-hated man. The curious fate of Prendergast's petition, which had proved such a boomerang, also made it possible to think that Dick might have had something to do with the doctor's disappearance, if only as a prankish kind of revenge.

This last theory was given additional substantiation when Dick's landlady stopped in at noon, to inquire about Biddy, and said that he had not come home at all the night before. Later she called again, to inform me that Prendergast had turned up with his uncle, early in the afternoon, to pack all his belongings, pay his rent for the balance of the year, and leave town. She was a gossipy woman, and of course had tried to find out where her star boarder had been. Dick, she said, had claimed that he and his uncle had driven so far in search of a drink or two that they had decided to spend the night at a hotel in another town.

"Sounds pretty peculiar t' me," she said. "I never heered tell of a student admittin' t' drinkin', before, and his uncle standin' right there too, mind you. Jest as brazen as brass itself, that boy. You'd think his uncle would 'a' boxed his saucy ears. But he didn't say a word about it. I declare t' Betsy. I don't know what the world's comin' to."

I told her that Daisy had phoned, just before going off duty for the day, to say that Biddy was pulling out of it all right and might be home next morning. Mike, she said, had ceased his raving around noontime and had lapsed into a deep sleep.

The last of my visitors was Jarvis, who seemed deeply worried about the disappearance of Wyck, from whom nothing had been heard in twenty-four hours. Jarvis was one of the few thorough-going admirers of the hard-boiled old doctor. He was without question the best student in the medical school, and never had given Wyck any cause to be unpleasant. Jarvis was, of course, a fearfully conscientious bird; and his own frail health had given him a morbid complex, half defiant and half apologetic, when in the presence of normal people. He got a kind of joy out of taking the blame for anything that went wrong in group work, and then demonstrating by subsequent efficiency that it could not have been he who was at fault. I suppose it was exhibitionism; but it had become so much a habit that he had actually come to talk with me about the possibility that his, Jarvis's, own conduct in the matter of Prendergast's cribbing and the petition at faculty meeting might have been the cause of Wyck's vanishing. Of course this was absurd. Probably Jarvis came around with this theory only for the pleasure of getting credit for his conscientiousness, and the added satisfaction of hearing himself exonerated. I doubt that it was deliberately planned. It had simply become his normal way of doing things to blame himself when anything with which he was associated went wrong. I felt rather impatient, but knew that the quickest way to get rid of him was to ladle out the necessary amount of soft soap in big spoonfuls.

When he at last departed, I got out my shorthand diary again and read over the account for the last two days, trying to make more sense out of it; but it was quite as baffling as ever. Only one thing was plain. Obviously, I had to decide at once whether I should confess my knowledge of Gideon Wyck's whereabouts, after he left the faculty meeting. If he had decided to slip away quietly, for awhile or for good—and the remarks I had overheard from his own lips gave some cause for thinking so—then it might be only an embarrassment for all concerned if I did anything to aid in locating him. Perhaps he had belatedly realized the full extent to which his presence was complicating things for Prexy, had repented his insistence upon attending the faculty meeting, and had decided that a prompt job of vanishing would be to everyone's advantage, including his own.

It was not unlikely, either, that a man of his saturnine temperament might reach the point of failing health and faculties whereat suicide would become the logical solution. If he had committed suicide, there was no need for me to reveal what I knew, and the world might be happier if whatever deviltry he had been up to remained undiscovered. If his disappearance was deliberate, I did not honestly feel that I knew enough about it all to risk negating his purpose blindly, by aiding in a search for him or for his body, as the case might prove.

Finally (for it never occurred to me that kidnapping was the answer to the mystery) there was the very reasonable likelihood that he had been murdered. If that was so, Muriel Finch seemed the likeliest suspect. The boy Ted might have had as good an excuse, or better, for hating him; and both had been with him when last he was seen; but I knew from Muriel's own statements that she had both feared and loathed him, for a cause too awful to mention. It was clear that he had victimized her in some way; and mere sexual attentions, in the case of that easy-going young woman, were insufficient to account for the extreme nature of her reaction. Perhaps he had made her an agent to some loathsome kind of perversion; perhaps he was a modern manifestation of the Marquis de Sade, whose works I had seen on his own bookshelves. If that were true, it seemed to me that I had no right whatever to pass judgment upon any means that Muriel might have taken to free herself.

From all aspects of the case it appeared best for me to say nothing for the time being. If anyone in authority had questioned me, I think I would have told what I knew at once. But if the reader censures me for not having reported to the police, I ask him to remember that as yet we had no definite knowledge that anything was seriously amiss. It was two days later before the authorities were officially informed of the doctor's disappearance, and longer than that before we got any definite clew to hint at what had happened to him.

Behind it all, half-consciously, I suppose that I was influenced more than anything else by the difficulty of explaining my sudden entrance, torn and bleeding, long after midnight, at Mike's bedside. Dr. Alling had of course been astonished by my appearance. If Gideon Wyck had been murdered that very night, on the lonely hillside up which I had followed him, how in the world could I clear myself of suspicion? Only by involving Muriel and the boy Ted. And what would my single voice be worth, in testimony, against both of theirs, whether or not either or both of them were guilty? It might so happen that they were possessed of a perfect alibi, and I knew that I had no convincing alibi at all, during those hours on the hillside. In that case I would be defenseless. Subconsciously, I began to hope and at last to believe that Gideon Wyck was still alive. Muriel's expression of happiness, when I saw her in the hospital, had not seemed like that of a murderess, no matter how good a reason she might have had for murder. I decided to wait, and not make a fool of myself. Sooner or later some incident must occur to force the issue, so I settled down to await the event, and at last fell asleep.

Next morning Dr. Alling phoned to say that there was nothing which very urgently needed doing, that day, and advised that I take things easy during the remainder of the week. I reminded him that we had been awaiting a letter from Boston, confirming acceptance of an invitation sent by wireless to a visiting foreign surgeon, whose ship would be docking in a day or two. He said that the answer had not yet been received, but that if it entailed any special arrangements he might call me. Otherwise I could have the week off, so far as his work was concerned. I thanked him and hung up, wondering a little whether he himself might be suspicious of the coincidence that I should have come home so late and so disheveled on the night of Wyck's disappearance. The thought struck me that Dr. Alling might be giving me rope, to see what I would do with it. It surely was odd that he had made no second reference to his surprise at my condition on that occasion. He had demanded an explanation, which I had had no time to give before Mike's seizure. Had he forgotten? It did not seem likely.

I decided that it would not be such a good notion, after all, to attempt to quiz Muriel—at least until something had happened to bring the case definitely into public attention. For all I knew, Dr. Alling might have set people to watch my reactions and to report upon my movements. Just to play safe, I hid my diaries in my mattress, and for several days did nothing whatever outside the usual routine of work in the medical school, study at home, and visits to the hospital. Obviously, I did not want to betray myself by too much of a change of manner, so I continued to stop for a few words with Daisy every day; but I was careful about what I said to her. A good deal of time I spent with poor Biddy, who behaved like an automaton for a long while after her release from the hospital.

At last the awaited event happened, a week after the mysterious night. On the morning of the 11th of April, 1932, Marjorie Wyck received by parcel post a bundle containing every item of clothing worn by her father when he was last seen. Some odds and ends, such as a man would carry in his pockets, were included; and nothing which he might have been supposed to have had on his person at the time seemed on first examination to be missing. But the strange and significant fact about all this was that the linen had been immaculately laundered, the socks washed, the shoes polished. The woolen garments, moreover, smelt so strongly of cleaning fluid that they presumably had been dry-cleaned just before mailing. This left us with two likely assumptions: either Gideon Wyck had been disposed of by a cleverly insolent murderer or else the sending of his clothes was a symbol that for good reasons of his own he was discarding his former identity and disappearing deliberately from among his old acquaintances.

CHAPTER X

There was one curious sidelight on Gideon Wyck's disappearance that ought not to go unremarked. This was the tacit willingness of everyone concerned to do nothing whatever about it. If pushed to it, we all would have said the conventional things, but in our hearts his absence was looked upon as good riddance. Even Marjorie Wyck seemed unaffected, according to Daisy Towers, who said that when other women phoned to offer aid it was refused. She even deprecated the selectmen's insistence that a special watchman be stationed, for the time being, on the Wyck grounds. For my own part, it was a great relief to have cause for believing that he had gone into voluntary exile, in some far place —the farther away, the better.

The delivery of the bundle of clothing of course brought the authorities into action. Hos Creel, the postman, described the beginning of the investigation to a group of us on the school steps. According to Hos, he had known there was something fateful about that bundle as soon as it was shaken out of the sack, and he had loitered for a chat with Marjorie, hoping she would open it in his presence. Hos might have done that anyway, forebodings or no forebodings. He could tell you the contents of most packages he had delivered, and felt a country postman's proprietary right in all continued correspondence.

"Letter from your girl in Biddeford," he would yell from the door. "She the one named Grace? No, that's right, Grace's the Portland one."

Hos, speaking to us within an hour or two of the event, probably had not yet had time to embellish the truth to make a better story.

"Made out like I didn't think it nothin' special," he explained. " 'Hull derned new outfit, here,' I says, 'from the heft of it.' 'Hope so,' she says, just like that, 'but who'd be a-sendin' me one?' So I pertended to sort insurance slips. There's some as don't hanker to let you know what's in their parcels. But she's frank and open.

She cuts the string, and out falls her paw's clothes. Wal, you could have pushed me over with a sassafras leaf, I was that fummed. Took it brave, too. Lots o' starch in that girl. Right away she says, 'Don't ye tetch 'em, Hos. Don't lay even a finger on 'em.' And she calls up Sheriff Palmer. I figgered I'd better wait and give my evidence right in. The sheriff comes and says, 'Ye did right, not to tetch 'em. Fingerprints.' And he wraps the whole bundle, paper and all, in another paper. 'Hos,' he says to me, 'you got an important part in this case.' Them's his very words. Wal, I took him back to help find where the parcel was mailed from. And then the postmaster comes snoopin' in, o' course, and takes the case out o' my hands, he not havin' had a smitch to do with it. Wal, that's how it goes, boys. The higher-ups allus takes the credit."

Next day the *Alton Weekly Clarion* came out with its first scarehead in years, giving all known details of the mystery, which was made more sinister than ever by the finding that whoever had packed the bundle had worn gloves, and had left not a trace of a fingerprint on anything except the inside back cover of the doctor's watch, which bore on its highly burnished gold surface a deliberately placed, perfect impression of a man's thumb. It was so carefully done that it must have been put there either in derision or as a move to put searchers on the wrong track.

This turn of events gave us the comfort of something definite to go on, in place of vague imaginings; but it did not serve altogether to remove my anxiety. Often I rebuked myself for not having spoken at once of my experience on the Bottom Road. But I was still held back by a definite conviction that, even if Gideon Wyck had been murdered, the act was the outcome of some fiendish provocation which he himself had provided. If he had been wholly unashamed to act in my presence as he had acted toward Mike Connell, what might he not have done in secret to someone more in his power? I remembered that Mike himself, while obviously fearing him, had insisted that Biddy summon the old doctor, for the not unplausible reason that he was the only one of whom the devils were afraid.

Now that the case had become an open and generally discussed mystery, however, it seemed the right time to risk a talk with Muriel. She was still on the night shift, and asleep most of the day, which made it necessary to see her in the evening. I did not want to hang around, suspiciously, waiting to catch her by chance. It would be more natural to try phoning at various hours. I purposely confined the calls to hours after seven o'clock, when Daisy went off duty. Each time Muriel was reported as dining at the nurses' dormitory, or simply "Not in." In the former case it was necessary to leave a message for her to call back, which at first I did not care to do. Finally I tried it, and she did not call back. A second attempt made it obvious that she was trying to avoid me.

There was a stringent and doubtless necessary rule to keep medics and internes out of the nurses' dormitory, so I had no way of forcing a meeting except in one of the hospital corridors after midnight. After a few days I decided to leave it to chance. The decision was no sooner made than I found that I had already over-stepped the bounds of circumspection; for the next time I paused to pass the time of day with Daisy, she asked, "How's the love affair coming along?" I inquired what she meant, and she said, "Don't be that way. Tell mamma. I mean the sudden infatuation for Nurse Finch. I thought you were the champion long distance woman-hater."

"I haven't even caught a glimpse of her in days," I had the wit to answer promptly.

"That may be, but you've certainly worked the telephone hard, in her direction."

"Where did you get that idea?" I asked, remembering the care with which I had confined my calls to hours after seven o'clock.

"Thought you were fooling me, did you?" she countered. "Well, sonny, this baby's hard to fool. I'm not going to let any mere slip of a girl slip one over on me. If any of my rivals captures the champion woman-hater, it won't be by way of my switch-board."

"Not much evidence so far that she's trying to," I answered, with a mock sigh. "Good chance for you to chisel in, Daisy."

"Not till you elevate your tastes a bit," she replied, with a toss of her curls.

"No kidding," I said, "how did you get the idea that I had been 'working the telephone'?"

She smiled and shoved a little black desk machine toward me. A long roll of paper in it wound through a kind of little window, and a push of a button shifted it one space.

"New system," she said. "They've got us keeping track of all calls, even the locals, on this."

"Since when?" I asked, full of a sudden alarm at the thought that this might be part of a detective system set up deliberately to aid in solving the mystery of Dr. Wyck's disappearance; but she reassured me by saying, "Since the first of the month." It was on the night between the 3rd and 4th that he had disappeared.

"So that's how you spend your time," I said, "scouting for scandal through the back end of the tape."

"Uh-huh. Lots of fun. Very convenient, too. All the private houses have four-digit numbers, and all the medical school phones have three, and all the hospital ones two."

"What's Connells'?" I asked, quickly.

She came right back with, "One-one-one-eight. You didn't honestly think that I'd fail to keep that number next my heart, did you, David?"

I decided to get out of there, and to be a lot more careful about my phoning in the future. For some time Muriel continued successful in what could not have been anything other than a deliberate attempt to avoid meeting me, even by accident.

Meanwhile, I had been spared through all of the first week the necessity of confronting Dr. Alling in the flesh. The visiting surgeon, it turned out, had been unable or unwilling to accept an invitation to come to Altonville for a lecture, but had asked Prexy to come to Boston for some kind of harangue, which he did. I heard a few caustic remarks about this, because the doctor in question was Vladimir, the Hungarian skin-grafting specialist; and the more orthodox members of our staff thought it beneath Prexy's proper dignity to truckle with a person who made his living by rejuvenating old rakes at $10,000 to $50,000 a throw. He was always careful to describe himself as an expert in skin-grafting and plastic surgery; his main practice, however, had to do with monkey glands.

Some of our doctors, who objected to such associations, would have been still more shocked had they known, as I did, that the monkey gland business was precisely what Prexy was interested in, for a chapter in the *Short Sketch*.

He returned on the 10th, and phoned me in the evening that he would want to resume our usual work the following afternoon. But it was in the morning mail of the 11th that Dr. Wyck's clothes were delivered, and this fact sent Prexy back to Boston again with Dr. Kent, the coroner, on the theory that Dr. Wyck might have been an amnesia victim, who had been picked up by the Boston police.

The theory proved false, and they were back again on the 13th. That afternoon, Dr. Alling phoned to say that he wanted to see me at five o'clock. I was possessed at once by an irrational feeling of panic, by a conviction that he would demand an explanation of my appearance at Mike's bedside, covered with dirt and scratches. The coincidence could not possibly be ignored. Would he, or anyone else, believe that I had scrambled up after that Ford in the darkness out of mere curiosity? Would my cuts and bruises, my torn clothing, be accepted as the result of encounters with trees and fences? It seemed far more likely that I should be suspected of having been in a furious fight—and if so, then what?

While walking up Packard Road from Atlantic Street I changed my mind half a dozen times, and finally entered with a resolve to tell everything I knew for a fact, speaking of Muriel only as someone unidentifiable in the darkness on the crucial night.

Dr. Alling was seated at his desk. "Weird business about Wyck, isn't it?" he remarked, eyeing me quizzically.

I prepared for the worst, nodded, and asked whether he had discovered anything of importance in Boston.

"Not much. The parcel of clothing seems to have been left on one of the public desks in the main post office after closing hours on the evening of the ninth. One of the clerks remembered that a janitor brought it around when they opened up next morning. The clerk remarked it because the person who left it, to make sure of the postage, had put about twice as many stamps on it as were needed. There was a front page item in the papers yesterday, inviting anyone who was in the post office that evening to identify the sender, but nothing's come in yet. There were three speakeasy cards in his wallet, and we went to all of the places with the police. They knew him, all right, but hadn't seen him in nearly a year. Or so they said."

I waited nervously for him to come to the point, and stiffened inwardly when he continued, "What I wanted to talk to you about is something that happened the night Dr. Wyck disappeared."

The blood began to buzz in my ears. I hardly credited what I was hearing when he went on, "At faculty meeting, that evening, Dr. Wyck had two blue books—examinations by Prendergast and Jarvis. What became of them?"

My mind cleared enough to permit me to say, "Why, it was my impression that they were passed around to a few of the doctors, and then back to you. Yes, and then you read parallel passages for me to take down in the minutes, and handed the books back to Dr. Wyck."

"Precisely, and he put them in his pocket. Well, everything else that was in his pockets seems to have been returned with his clothing in that bundle—everything but those blue books." He paused impressively. "I'm telling you this, Saunders, because the matter has got to be cleared up for the good name of the college, apart from all ordinary reasons. I'll need help, and the sheriff's a blundering fool, as you doubtless know. You and I get on well. Do you want to work with me?"

"Why, certainly," I said, thoroughly perplexed by this failure to ask the obvious expected question.

"Good," he answered. "Now, you know all that's been published?" I nodded. "Very well then, we have also this to go on. After faculty meeting Dr. Wyck went to his office. Dr. Kent saw him. I stayed, talking to Mr. Tolland, Prendergast's uncle. When I left the building, Wyck's study window was dark. He must have gone straight home, because his daughter says he came in a little after half past nine. He told her he was going for a walk, and she tried to dissuade him because he seemed ill. He made his usual boast that he had never been ill in his life, which so far as I know is correct, although at the meeting I remember thinking that he was very pale."

"I noticed it too," I agreed.

"Well, Marjorie couldn't dissuade him, but she thinks he waited on the porch a few minutes, because it was some while after he went out that she heard the sound of someone descending the steps. At the time, she had no thought of its being anyone other than her father. What's your idea on that?"

He spoke the last sentence crisply. I hesitated, for it seemed a pointless query. How could I have known? I began to be more wary of this little man's cordial manner. He had failed to ask an absolutely obvious question, which I had come expecting to have to answer. Instead, he asked me about footsteps on the Wycks' porch, heard at a time when I myself had actually been by the barberry hedge, a few yards from the spot. Could he know of my having been there? Was the invitation to aid him merely a trap, in which he wanted me to betray myself? Did he think the footsteps on the porch had been mine? To justify my pause, I said slowly, "Why, I've tried to think of another possibility, but I haven't anything to go on."

He merely nodded. "Very well then, those descending footsteps are our last positive knowledge of the whereabouts of Gideon Wyck. He probably walked toward Alton Center. If he had come back toward town, someone would doubtless have seen him and have reported by now. That is, I assume any one would report to us who saw him after that time, don't you?"

I had got a better grip on myself, and answered, "I can't see why anyone should withhold information—that is, unless he was afraid it might implicate him in something he really had nothing to do with."

"Of course. To continue: I've inquired at the bank. He drew no money for several days preceding his disappearance. On March 26th, however, he made the abnormal withdrawal of $500 in cash. He pays bills by cheque, so that was not in anticipation of the first of the month. Moreover, the tradesmen haven't been paid, and that sum is unaccountably gone. What are we to conclude from that?"

I thought a minute. "It seems to me, sir, that everything points to his deliberate disappearance. I think he was somewhat unbalanced, mentally, and probably knew that he couldn't keep up pretenses any longer. Did he know that he was going to be retired?"

"He had good reason to suspect it, certainly."

"Well, then, things were all closing in on him at once. It seems to me that he may have known he was going insane, and so drew enough money to go far away somewhere—perhaps to fight it, away from old influences. Who knows?"

The discussion went on along such lines. I was almost prepared again to make a clean breast of the facts I knew, since they seemed to corroborate this theory. Then I remembered that even before the disappearance a perhaps trivial incident had occurred to make me wonder whether Dr. Alling really trusted me. It was the occasion of discovering that the *symélien* plate was missing from the Geoffroy Atlas. I had wondered at the time whether he suspected me of taking it, and had wondered still more why he said nothing about the obvious coincidence in the fact that a symmelus had been born that very day.

Here, again, he was definitely avoiding an even more obvious coincidence in asking nothing by way of explanation of my bloodstained appearance on that crucial night. I decided once and for all that my frankness must depend upon his, and that I would do best to keep my secrets until convinced of his sincerity.

THE CADAVER OF GIDEON WYCK

PART II

. . . . WHICH TELLS OF THE BAFFLING
PROBLEMS THAT AROSE DURING THE YEAR
FOLLOWING THE DISAPPEARANCE OF
GIDEON WYCK, M.D.

CHAPTER XI

As I have already noted, the first reaction to the disappearance of Gideon Wyck was undeniably a general feeling of relief. The nurses at the hospital and most of the medical students had breathed more easily. If his daughter was alarmed or grief-stricken, she did nothing to show it. The concern of Prexy and of Wyck's fellow faculty members over their colleague's fate was not so deep as to counterbalance their satisfaction over the fact that an extremely awkward problem had solved itself. Toward the end of the first week, I overheard Dr. Otway telling young Dr. Follansbee, the gynecologist, that if the missing man turned up again his act of dereliction of duties could be made the excuse for retiring him at once; it would be unnecessary to bring up the earlier reasons, which, by their very nature, had caused them all to temporize so long over an unpleasant duty to the school, the hospital, and the community.

This conversation occurred a day or two before the bundle of clothing was delivered. But when news of Hos Creel's surprising burden got around town, a new feeling seemed swiftly to replace the original reaction. A kind of tense calm settled upon Altonville—an aspect of everything going scrupulously right on the surface, the better to hide some brooding catastrophe below. When we lacked even a hint of what had happened to the old doctor, there had been nothing definite to think about; but the mailing of his clothes was a definite act of mystery, provoking all sorts of conjectural solutions. If he had merely gone away, never to be heard from again, our first feeling of relief might have settled slowly into normality; as it now was, however, we were all constrained by the feeling of a mysterious agency, lurking somewhere over the visible horizon.

In my case it had the effect of making me wonder whether the doctor might not still be near at hand, playing dead in order to gain some new advantage. There no longer seemed any question but that he had been demented toward the last. This impression, indeed, had crept into the general gossip of the town and must have been a factor in the common change of attitude. A madman was an unpredictable element. No-one could say what he might be doing, or why. I myself could not help wondering whether the "hole in the hill," to which Mike had referred, might not be the doctor's present refuge. Whatever deviltry he had been up to there, of nights, on the hillside north of town might still be going on, for all I knew.

There had been a consequent temptation to do more exploring, by daylight; but several things stood in the way. It must be remembered, all through the story which I have to tell, that I was (and still am) working my way through medical school—a routine which leaves one with little enough time for sleep, let alone exploring. I still hoped, moreover, to have a talk with Muriel, who obviously knew the secret of the hill. And, finally, I still suspected Dr. Alling's motives. It was likely that he had been more aware of what Wyck had been up to than it was politic to admit. He might have his own reasons for assuming that Wyck's machinations had been conducted somewhere up that lonely road. If so, it was a good place for me to avoid, especially in view of the fact that a grim-faced stranger had been noticed prowling around town, who was reputed to be a special investigator for the county prosecutor.

My freedom of movement was further restricted when Prexy suggested to me a temporary change of employment. Work on the *Short Sketch* had been halted because of his need to give attention to special problems arising out of Wyck's disappearance. Prexy had taken over some of Wyck's work in the school, and also had been called out of town several times to consult with legislative committees and with the county prosecutor. One morning he told me that he did not see any prospect of taking up his historical work for some time to come and asked whether I would care to take a position, at an increased salary, as nurse and "keeper" to Mike.

The hospital authorities were still uncertain whether it would be necessary to commit him to an asylum. They had voted to let him go home for the time being, under observation. After the long sleep which followed his period of violent mania and raving he had been absolutely docile; there had been no repetition of the baffling seizures, all of which had occurred within twenty-four hours. I had been allowed to see him two or three times, under guard, and he had shown no tendency to repeat his rough treatment of me. He was, however, definitely deranged—receptive, but uncommunicative. When a nod or shake of the head would answer a question, he gave it. Otherwise he studiously pretended to hear nothing.

I had not relished the job, by any means; but Biddy's agonized appeal, "Just to give him a chance to get well, Mr. David," had won me over. It was agreed that one or the other of us must be with him constantly. A special phone was installed in my garret, to summon help if he became violent below, and a couple of lengths of two-by-four were arranged in such a fashion that they could instantly be slipped into place to block the top of the stair well.

Nothing very unusual happened during Mike's first few days at home, beyond the fact that once or twice he acted as if listening intently to some inaudible voice. That frightened me, I confess. I could not help imagining Gideon Wyck, or his ghost, speaking words audible to Mike alone. The rest of the time, when awake, he either sat staring out the window or read the newspaper, column by column, with no discrimination whatever, except in an occasional show of annoyance when he came to advertisements covering more than a single column. He seemed to consider these a blunder on the part of the make-up man. I noticed that he was not bothered, however, when stories were continued on another page. He read right on to the bottom of the column, and started at the top of the next one, willy-nilly. He never spoke, and made no progress whatever in accustoming himself to the loss of an arm. When he wanted to turn a page of the paper, it always fell to the floor, because of his automatic attempt to hold it in non-existent fingers. He then would look annoyed and surprised, as if the fingers had slipped, and get down on his knees to rearrange the sheets, still ostensibly using both hands.

On the 18th of April, Dr. Alling asked me to accompany him and Sheriff Palmer as a witness in a complete search through Dr. Wyck's effects. The house had been perfunctorily searched several times, in a general way, without discovering anything pertinent to the case; but no-one as yet had gone carefully through his papers. I thought it rather odd that I should be singled out for this function, and was on my guard; but nothing happened to increase my suspicions. The sheriff spent a lot of time blowing white lead on various articles of furniture, and in this way forced upon himself a most unwelcome conclusion. He had clung, with the proper pride of a small town detective, to the theory that the plain thumbprint in the back of Dr. Wyck's watch had been an insolent murderer's challenge of derision to the majesty of the law; but this painstaking investigation with his pot of white lead only served to clinch a finding which already had been thoroughly substantiated in Dr. Wyck's own office—the finding that the thumbprint was indubitably Dr. Wyck's own.

When I learnt this, the conviction that the doctor was still alive and had mailed the bundle himself became inescapable. I asked Prexy's opinion, and he agreed that it was the only logical inference to be drawn from the facts so far known.

"Do you think he'll turn up again?" I inquired.

He answered with a shrug, and the remark, "It doesn't seem likely, does it?"

I agreed that it did not; but at heart I was less sure. The investigation of Wyck's papers developed no other clew. There was nothing in his desk except the ordinary business records of a householder, a few packages of old letters, lecture notes, and a great many catalogues of booksellers who specialized in psychological, esoteric, and historic titles. Of the missing blue books there was no trace; but I could see nothing remarkable in their disappearance. The essential passages, so far as the testimony against Dick Prendergast was concerned, had been read into the minutes of the faculty meeting by Prexy himself. Considering that fact, it was hard to see why the originals would be important to anyone. It was my own belief that the missing blue books were the kind of clew which could do more to obscure than to elucidate a mystery, by diverting attention from more important aspects of the case, as yet undiscovered.

When I returned to the Connells', I found Mike staring into the corner of his room with an attentive expression, nodding as if to acknowledge phrases no-one else could hear. Immediately I remembered the fingerprint in the watchcase, and its inference that Wyck was still alive. The possibility that he had retained a kind of psychic control over Mike was something I could not get out of my imagination.

This, and a good many other things that have plagued my thoughts during the past year, originated, no doubt, in the strange kind of work in which I had been engaged with Prexy. A horde of possibilities, which the normal mind would never think of, were accessible to me in recent memory, owing to the subject material of the *Short Sketch for a History of Concomitant Variations, etc.,* which was concerned exclusively with abnormalities of body and of mind. One section, for example, had dealt with an appalling series of case histories involving the authentic production, in normal society, of cannibals, rippers, blood drinkers, and ghouls who dug up newly buried bodies for purposes which you can learn, if you care to, when the *Short Sketch* is published. I consider myself a normally callous medic, but this continual emphasis on revolting aberrations probably had done something to my nervous control. Exact clinical descriptions of the conduct of Jack the Ripper are not something to be read at meal times—and Jack was one of the distinctly nicer specimens among the sordid lot whose doings I had transcribed from authentic police reports, coroners' findings, and hospital records, supplied confidentially to Dr. Alling. No-one who has not seen such materials can imagine what incredible degeneracy sometimes lies behind the smug newspaper phrase "a statutory offense" or the equally pussyfooting words "an unnatural crime."

I tried to make allowances for this kind of bias; but there was always the contrary effect of a realization that Wyck himself, as an authority on witchcraft and demonology, had had a chance to become infected from contact with similar material. It was dreadful to think what the effect might be, upon a mind lapsing into insanity, of so much knowledge concerning the darkest phases of the human character. Perhaps you have read descriptions of the Black Mass with a thrill of purely vicarious horror, since it supposedly has passed forever out of the world. But, if enough insane perverts happened to be swayed by a knowledge of its traditions, what was to prevent its celebration on a Maine hill-side, in degenerate farming country? Such ideas plagued me the more because I knew that the entire literature on the subject was preserved in scores of volumes in the curious library of Gideon Wyck.[1]

1 The usual reference given for a description of the Black Mass is *Là-Bas, Par J.-K. Huysmans, Paris: Plon-Nourritet et Cie., N.D.* English translations are procurable, although some of them have been banned from general sale. A good one, by Keene Wallace, was published in Paris in 1928. It is only fair to point out, in this connection, that anthropologists since Frazer have demonstrated that the "horrors" of the Black Mass were really survivals of sincere pre-Christian religions, and that many contemporary reports upon it (most of which were written by attachés of the ecclesiastical courts) can be shown by internal evidence to be exceedingly biased. The sacrifices were no different in kind or in purpose from those described in the Old Testament, and the so-called orgies of licentiousness and promiscuity were a survival of the pagan fertility rites, entered into for the altogether applaudable purposes of assuring healthy offspring to the women of the community as a result of the religious ceremony, and fecundity to the food crops by sympathetic magic. The submission of all of the women to the priest (or, in the ecclesiastical records, to Satan) was not intended or expected to produce offspring. In *The Witch-Cult in Western Europe,* Margaret Alice Murray conclusively demonstrates, by scores of citations from testimony at the witch trials, that in most cases use was made of various disguises and devices, on the part of the priest, to aid him in the performance of rites physically impossible of accomplishment by a single man. On page 63, for example, she says, "The coldness of the Devil's entire person, which is vouched for by several witches, suggests that the ritual disguise was not merely a mask over the face, but included a covering, possibly of leather or some other hard and cold substance, over the whole body and even the hands. Such a disguise was apparently not always worn, for in the great majority of cases there is no record of the Devil's temperature except in the sexual rites, and even then the witch could not always say whether the touch of the Devil was warm or not. In 1565 the Belgian witch, Digna Robert, said the Devil 'etait froid dans tous ses membres.' In 1590, at North Berwick, 'he caused all the company to com and kiss his ers, quhilk they said was cauld lyk yce: his body was hard lyk yrn, as they thocht that handled him.'" The historical change in attitude toward records of the Black Mass is, however, quite recent, as can be seen by comparing the articles on Witchcraft in the 11th and 14th editions, respectively, of the *Encyclopedia Britannica.* The former edition, published in 1911, says "With the rise and development of the belief in the heretics' Sabbath, which first appears early in the 11th Century, another sexual element—the *concubitus dæmonum*—begins to play its part." But two decades

I shall not insist upon arguing, therefore, with anyone who accuses me of avoiding further exploration simply and solely because I was afraid of what I might find. The morbid subjects treated in the *Short Sketch* had been real, but remote, up until the last few days; but Mike's inexplicable madness, Muriel's terror of Wyck, and the new evidence that Wyck might be lurking near by, all combined to bring the possibility of strange and loathsome things to the very edge of town. Let the reason be what you choose, I did hesitate; and when the occasion to go exploring at last arrived it was in the line of duty rather than of voluntary action.

I had been instructed by the alienist to follow Mike without molesting him, if he showed a desire to leave the house while I was on guard. It was thought that he was still too weak to go far. If he did seem to be overdoing it, I was to telephone for aid from some convenient house, or to send a message by a passing automobile.

On the afternoon of the 19th of April, some two weeks after

---

later, we find the new edition of the *Britannica* treating the *concubitus dæmonum*, not as a new element, but as a survival: "The rites with which this god was worshipped are known to all students of primitive or savage religions, ancient and modern. The sacred dances, the feasts, the chants in honour of the god, the liturgical ritual, and above all the ceremonies to promote fertility, occurred at public assemblies as now in the islands of the Pacific or in Africa. The fertility rites attracted the special attention of the recorders of the legal trials. But to the followers of the old god these rites were as holy as the sacred marriage was to the ancient Greeks; to them, as to the Greeks, it was the outward and visible sign of the fertility of crops and herds which should bring comfort and wealth and life itself." It is nevertheless undeniable that a religious belief in human sacrifice and in public exhibitions of sexuality would persist, after several grim centuries of the Inquisition, mainly in persons mentally and sexually deranged: deranged, that is, in the technical sense that they were congenitally unsympathetic to the normal morality of their fellows. The Black Mass, however sincere its religious origins may have been, seems unquestionably to have degenerated into an excuse for sadism by the time of Gilles de Rais. It is difficult to believe at first blush the apparently authenticated records of the scores of children sacrificed by Gilles, until one remembers the recent and unquestionably authentic prowess of the "Butcher of Düsseldorf," who killed even more and lacked only the excuse of an accepted ritual, for self-justification.—ED.

the events with which my narrative opens, I was seated on the little kitchen porch, studying. Biddy was shopping, and Mike could be seen through the bedroom window. From time to time I looked up, only to see him staring dully and changelessly toward the hospital gates. His chair was not more than ten feet from my own, but the intervening wall and window kept me from hearing any minor noise in his room. Once, when I looked, he seemed to be listening intently, for perhaps a minute. Then he decisively nodded his head, as if in obedient approval of an order. I was on my guard, and watched carefully for some minutes, but he lapsed once more into the dull lethargy that characterized him during most of the day. Nothing further happened, so I resumed my work. The next thing I knew Mike was walking slowly down the road toward the hospital.

Thinking a stroll might be good for him, I let him get a start, and then followed. He turned north at the gates. When abreast of the Wycks' house, he paused, listened, nodded, and walked slowly on down the Bottom Road. With woods so near, on each side, I thought it would be best to keep an eye on him, and to send back news by a passing car if necessary. It seemed unlikely that he would go far; but he continued his slow walk all the way to the second little bridge, turned over it, and commenced to climb. I was vexed with myself for not having phoned from the Wycks' house, and scanned the road nervously for a car. Several had passed when we were near town, none since. I waited as long as I dared, and then followed, full of wild imaginings. The deciduous trees were scarcely budding, so it was not difficult to keep him in view, in spite of occasional clumps of pines. Without hesitation he took the left-hand fork, as I had at night, and emerged presently into the upland meadow.

The pasture, at least half a mile across, made it seem necessary to emerge into plain sight, if I was to follow at such a distance as to make sure of not losing him in the dense pine woods beyond. I was thinking of that as a God-sent excuse for turning back to get aid, when Mike obviated the difficulty by turning sharply left along the edge of the woods, as soon as he was in the open. I soon saw that the tracks leading across the field were not the only vestiges of old roads apparent. Others ran at right angles, a few feet from the tree line; so I was able to proceed as before, in the shadow of the trees, four or five hundred feet behind Mike. Something more than a sense of duty urged me onward toward the mystery that was calling the madman: I was appallingly afraid of my own fears, and decided that it was high time to accept any means whatever that promised to substitute facts for imaginings.

I should explain, perhaps, why so lonely a place could exist so near an important town. Altonville might be called the headwater metropolis of a secluded valley. Its eight hundred houses are closely bunched. A strip of reforested state land bends around its northern and eastern edges, the trees growing right up to the hospital fence, the Wycks' grounds, and the Common. Around the town, at distances of a few miles, are four farming centers. The railroad comes up to the main town through South Alton, and a spur proceeds to West Alton. Alton Plain, lying southeast of town, is within easy carting distance. Alton Center is secluded by itself on a rolling plateau in the midst of the state reserve, a little east of north. It has only a score of still inhabited farms, hardly one house being in sight of another.

Throughout the reforested territory there are probably three abandoned farms for every one still being worked. The country lying east of the Bottom Road is especially desolate and hilly. What chance there may have been to farm there in the old days vanished when the railroad came, branching the wrong way. We students knew of only one farmer between town and the Center. He was Tom Hobbs, who lived alone above the first little bridge: an old widower, deaf and half blind, who sold milk and applejack.

Considering turns of the road, I guessed that the pasture along the edge of which I was following Mike was two miles north of Tom Hobbs's farm. The nearest farm out Center way must be four miles off, beyond Lonesome Hill. One could hardly have found a wilder place anywhere, so near a railroad. Twice we passed the cellars of houses burnt long ago. At the corner of the pasture, Mike climbed through a barbed-wire fence, the strands of which, I noticed, were hooked around the nearest post, removable to let a car drive through. Little bushes also had been barked, betraying the passing of some vehicle; and grease had stained the dry grass in the middle of the old vestigial road.

I was going warily now, expecting anything. There was some comfort in having, as it were, an advance guard; but I kept careful watch on both sides of the trail, nevertheless, more than half expecting to see old Wyck, or his ghost, rise up at any moment. As the roadway went deeper into the woods it twisted more and more. I could thus keep nearer Mike. Presently, beyond a thicket, I glimpsed the old Ford with a tarpaulin thrown over it. Mike had gone past it and through another fence. Small trees grew in the middle of the way, thereafter, which dwindled to a pair of parallel paths through the thickets. The trees thinned. I went more cautiously. Mike stepped out into a smaller upland pasture, with nothing remarkable in it but two huge lilac bushes, gone wild, standing against a mound that indicated another burnt farmhouse. I crouched at the edge of the woods, watching, as he walked slowly toward the bushes, a hundred yards away. Then my hair tingled as a voice bade him halt, and asked what he wanted. It was even more frightening to hear him say, "I want me blood back. I ain't been right without me blood."

These were, I think, the first words he had spoken since his madness.

The voice said, "He isn't here now. Go away."

Mike proceeded, nevertheless, till a figure rose up, rifle in hand, between the lilac bushes. For a moment it looked like Wyck. Then I saw that it was the same boy who had come to inquire at the hospital about Sarah Mullin. I crouched lower, my heart thumping painfully. It would now be impossible to hear them, if they spoke in ordinary tones; but there was a depression in the field, farther to the right, along which I could creep nearer, hidden by juniper bushes and the black, tall stalks of masses of last year's mullein. As I wriggled out along it, I was so well hidden that it was necessary to raise my head to glimpse them through the bushes. They were facing each other now, both perplexed.

"How'd you know how to get here?" the boy asked. "You were always blindfolded, before."

Mike seemed unable to comprehend the question. Apparently he had been led by some such inexorable agency as had drawn him to the grave of Peter Tompkins, in the first wild power of his madness. What then? What was there here to draw him? I heard the hiss of my own breath, as my heart labored with excitement.

"Anyway, you've got to go home," the boy said, threatening Mike with his extended rifle.

"I want me blood back. I gave it to the old divil. He can give it back the same way, with the hose and the needles."

"He's not here," the boy screamed. "He's never coming back. It's all done with. There's nobody here now but me." He poked at Mike with the gun barrel, until the poor mad cripple turned and walked slowly toward the path, muttering, "I ain't right, any more, without me blood."

Taking advantage of the fact that the boy was keeping Mike covered, I edged back to the trees unnoticed. There the reaction reached me in a spasm of fright. It was not fear of a country youth and his rifle, but of unknown, horrible things of which the boy might be an insufficient guardian. Was Gideon Wyck hiding there, in the ruined cellar? or was it his corpse, guarded by his murderer, who, to protect himself, would do murder again? As I lay trembling, the boy Ted advanced to the edge of the path, hardly ten yards from where I was crouching in a little hollow. Mike must have disappeared, for Ted went farther, peering, shifting from side to side for a better view. I lay in a cold sweat for fear he would begin to beat the bushes.

Then, to my amazement, Mike reappeared in the path, and walked stealthily toward the lilac bushes again. He must have hidden to let the boy pass by. Seeing him disappear into the ruined cellar, I waited tensely, trying to peer both ways at once.

Then a hollow, agonized scream came faintly, as if out of a deep place. Of course I should have rushed out to see what was happening. Perhaps I would have, in another moment, had not Mike emerged from the cellar, white as a shroud, gripping an axe in his hand. He stared at the blade of it, turned to throw it back into the cellar, and tottered to the edge of the woods. Then I saw him try to support himself against a tree with his missing hand. Of course he fell. The stump struck hard against the tree-roots. It was bandaged and padded, but the shock must have been painful. He did not utter a sound, however, which made me wonder whether it was he who had shrieked in the cellar.

As he lay there, apparently resting, the boy reappeared.

"Trying to get smart, are you?" he said gruffly. "Well, you better not try it again. Go on, now, and don't you ever come back, if you know what's good for you."

Aroused by the prodding gun barrel, Mike wandered dreamily back toward town. The boy followed a little way, then returned and stood by the lilacs, still watching. I carefully crept into the woods, parallel to the path. Mike frequently stopped to rest, so I had time to choose my footing. I expected him to collapse at any moment, and he was tottering as if drunk when we reached the Wycks'. In the deepening dusk I had almost caught up. Once more he paused to listen by the barberry hedge before proceeding.

As we approached the hospital gates Muriel Finch appeared, walking toward them from the other direction. It was my first glimpse of her in two weeks, and I was determined to intercept her, despite Mike; but as I started I heard a queer, strangled noise in his throat. "Ah!" he cried, "'twas ye that helped him take it, the divil." With a ghastly kind of snarl he jumped forward, clutched her shoulder, and tried to sink his teeth in her neck.

I knew his mad strength too well to trust half measures. With a quick leap I knocked them both down, getting his throat in the curve of my right elbow, holding his head back with all the power of both my arms. Again the seeming reality of his missing hand betrayed him. He moved the stump as if to grasp Muriel with the fingers that were not there, and at the same time relaxed his real grip on her to claw over his shoulder at my neck. She rolled free and ran screaming into the hospital. I clung on only just long enough for help to arrive. But, as they were getting him into a strait-jacket, he fainted, and for a long time thereafter was as weak as a child. The devil of his strength seemed to enter his body and to make use of it only in moments when something definite could be accomplished. When the devil was in him, he was more than human, but its going left him an invalid again.[1]

---

[1] The reader perhaps will be interested in checking this account of blood-mania against some of the episodes in *The Werewolf of Paris*, by Guy Endore. New York: Farrar & Rinehart, Inc., 1933.—ED.

CHAPTER XII

The experience I have just described seemed to alter my own position profoundly. Formerly I had been unable to reveal my information concerning the hillside without implicating myself as a suspect, and perhaps Muriel, too. But I had been fulfilling an appointed duty in following Mike up the old road, a fact which gave me adequate excuse for directing others to investigate the ruined farm. There was no question whatever, in my mind, but that the conversation between Mike and Ted gave adequate proof that Wyck had used the tumble-down farmhouse as a scene for illicit practices. Ted had expressed surprise at the fact that Mike had found his way afoot to a place to which he had always been conducted blindfolded. Mike's words indicated that blood transfusions had been performed at that place.

His final conduct with Muriel might have been prompted by a confused memory of legitimate transfusions at which she had assisted, but it could just as easily have referred to events at the ruined farm. Her own ultimatum to Wyck, when they had been standing on the bridge, might be construed several ways; but one of them could easily be that he had forced her to assist, over a considerable period, in experiments which he did not dare to perform in the medical school. Blood transfusions might have been a necessary part of them.

While getting a bite to eat at the lunch wagon by the gas station, I pondered these matters. When the internes had taken Mike away, I had promised to report back to the hospital in an hour or so and tell what had happened. The doctors who formed the committee to pass on Mike's fate had all been at supper at the time of his relapse into homicidal mania; but the internes had said that they would summon them to a meeting at eight-thirty. It was quarter to eight when I glanced at my watch. I munched down a piece of pie, resolved to go at once and report to Prexy before the meeting of alienists was convened. Muriel would no longer have to be brought into my story, nor would I have to mention the night of Wyck's disappearance at all. But it did seem urgently necessary that the place on the hill be investigated at once, perhaps that very night. It was obvious that the boy Ted was guarding something, with his rifle and his truculent language. Mike's appearance might decide him to go elsewhere, and perhaps to destroy or remove whatever it was that he was guarding.

I thought it would be best to confess that I had seen him leaving the Wycks' house in anger, not many hours before the doctor himself disappeared. That fact, and a description of his conduct toward Mike, seemed sufficient reason for a prompt search, and for taking him into custody. He then, of course, might implicate Muriel; but, since I had made every effort to talk with her and to learn her point of view, I was unable to feel much responsibility for the result of her own deliberate avoidance of me. At any rate, promptness was imperative this time. Much of my former worry had been caused by deliberating so long that other things occurred to make it unwise to speak up at all.

The need for haste made itself known all too soon. I was about to pull back the sliding door of the lunch wagon, when someone passed, half-crouching, under its row of windows. As I was suspicious of every even slightly unusual happening, by now, I quickly walked along the counter to the back entrance, which was open, and which led down to a little yard in the rear of the gas station. As I reached the steps, I heard a voice say, "Stalled up the road a piece. Give us a gallon in this can."

The speaker remained in the shadow of the gas station building, and went away as he had come, slouching to keep his face from showing in the light from the row of windows. I had no real reason for suspecting who it was. The voice had not sounded like that I had heard before, either on the hilltop or in the hospital. But both of the previous times he had been excited. Anyway, I could not quite rid myself of a notion that it might be Ted. Just to make sure, I strolled up the street after the dark figure, which turned northward onto the Bottom Road. Soon the stalled car loomed in the darkness, some distance past the Wycks', pointing toward town. I did not want to come too close, but I could half-see, half-hear that he was lifting the front seat to pour in the gas, proving it to be an ancient Ford.

Convinced that it probably was Ted, I turned and hastened back, asking myself how he could best be intercepted. The lights glared before I had reached the Wycks', and I dived into the shrubbery on the other side of the road, by the corner of the hospital fence, in a foolish panic. There was no logic in not having stood still like any other pedestrian; a sense of danger and of intrigue must have betrayed me into this action.

The car stopped in front of the Wycks'. The driver climbed to the porch and tapped, as if by prearranged signal, on one of the porch windows. When the door opened to admit him, I ran quickly across to the car. The tonneau was full of such miscellaneous duffle as a camper might carry: blanket roll, Sterno stove, a large bundle wrapped in a tent. As I wondered with a shiver what might be inside that bundle, the porch door opened and the boy murmured, "Well, I'm not staying any longer. I guess you know what's best for yourself."

As he came quickly down the steps, I shrank into the uncomfortable shelter of the barberry hedge, behind the car. He was carrying his rifle, which he leaned against a fender as he cranked the car. A few moments later he was bowling off southward, and I realized that I had not even had the wit to get his license number. He did not turn into Atlantic Street, but proceeded to the extreme other end of the hospital fence, paused for a few seconds, and went whizzing around a corner that would take him to Alton Plain. My first impulse was to rush in and ask Marjorie if I could use her phone. But that was canceled by the realization that he had spoken to her as if they were familiars. His words made it seem that she also might be implicated, and that I would do well not to let her know what I had witnessed. I moved cautiously across the road, ducked around the hospital gates, and made for home. There, to my consternation, I found Daisy Towers, who had stopped in after supper to console poor Biddy upon the renewal of her misfortunes.

"What are they sayin' now, Mr. David?" Biddy cried, when she saw me. "What are they goin' to do to my Mike?" She rushed up hysterically, grasped my arms in her sturdy washlady hands, and began to shake an answer out of me. It took an appreciable while to get free of the genuinely distracted woman, so that I could go on with the urgent business in hand. I took up the phone and called Prexy's number.

"No use," Daisy said. "He drove out of town about five o'clock."

I was nonplused, for it seemed imperative to relay my information through Prexy. As if reading my thoughts, Daisy said, "Sheriff Palmer went with him. Dan Rouse is deputy, pro tem."

That spelt futility right away. Dan was the nearest thing in town to a political boss. At least half his conversation consisted of phrases such as "Make haste slowly" and "Keep yer shirt on, sonny, the world'll still be here tomorrer." And then, I was startled too by Daisy's assumption that my news was for the police. How could she have known?

The conclusion forced itself upon me that, since my unlucky and characteristic delay for a bite to eat had given Ted a chance to get clear of town, and since I had no concrete charge against him, it would be useless to ask the deputy to apprehend him. I had expected to give the facts to Prexy, letting him take the responsibility for acting upon them. Also, I had been confident that an investigation of Ted's hiding place would reveal good reasons for detaining him.

"When's the boss coming back?" I inquired of Daisy.

"Tomorrow morning."

Knowing that Dan Rouse would subject me to an endless catechism before phoning to have the Ford stopped at another town, I admitted to myself that it would be best to await Prexy's return. The flivver was old enough to be easy to spot even after it was hundreds of miles away. My watch now read 8:20, so I left Daisy with her curiosity unsatisfied and proceeded to the meeting at the hospital. The description which I gave the doctors stressed the climactic attack on Muriel—and omitted any mention of what had happened during the long walk. I left them still deliberating, and paused on my way out to speak to the night operator at the switchboard. She told me that Mike was quiet as a lamb. I then put in a call for Nurse Finch, who, as usual, was reported as being out. On a sudden impulse I asked for an envelope, scribbled a half-threatening note saying I must see her at once for her own good, sealed it, and left it to be given her when she came in. I also asked the phone girl to call me when it was delivered, saying I would be up till midnight. Back at the Connells', I found that Biddy had been put to bed by Daisy, who had gone home shortly before my return.

At midnight precisely my newly installed special phone rang, and a voice said, "This is the head nurse. The switchboard operator says you left a note for Nurse Finch. Did you happen to come across her somewhere else, this evening?"

Somewhat in surprise, I said that I had not, and the suspicious old harridan answered, "Well, she's supposed to be on duty right now, and if she knows what's good for her, she'll be back here inside of five minutes. Good-bye."

I was less worried by the inference that Muriel was suspected of being in my rooms than by a flash of memory of the brief stop made by the boy's car at the far corner of the hospital grounds. I had heard him apparently inviting Marjorie Wyck to go with him. Had he also invited Muriel Finch, and picked her up there by prearrangement?

The thought had such dangerous implications that I found myself manufacturing excuses to prove that it could not be so. But the effort did not sustain itself for long. I had to admit that this would be the crucial rebuke for my blunders and delays. Dr. Alling's absence seemed, however, to paralyze my own freedom of action. At last I snatched up the phone, determined at least to make sure that Muriel's room would be searched at once. Then even that seemed futile. It would obviously be the first thing the head nurse would do, on her own responsibility. Presently I acknowledged to myself that there was nothing left to do but to wait, so I lay down for a night of uneasy and fitful sleep. Suddenly, toward dawn, it occurred to me that if Muriel had disappeared, the fact would surely be ascribed by most people to her terrifying experience with Mike. Everyone knew that she was in a highly nervous condition, and the incident, under the circumstances, could easily explain her flight.

After breakfast I diffidently approached the reception window, and inquired whether a note which I had left the previous evening had been delivered. To my surprise, Daisy Towers drew it from the bosom of her dress, smiled archly, and said, "The head nurse came looking for it ten minutes ago, but I told her I'd already returned it to the writer. What do I get for being so good to you?"

"Loads of affection, collectible after seven any evening."

"Don't I even get a look at the note?"

"Not this one, Daisy."

"Then," she said coolly, "it's lucky I took the precaution of reading it through the envelope against the electric light." Seeing my wordless resentment, she added, "How else would I have known enough not to give it to the head nurse, Davy? Besides, what do you expect me to do with a note addressed to a nurse who's dropped all her baggage out the window with a string, and beat it?"

Muriel must have tossed her bags over the fence into the vacant lot by the cemetery, and probably had walked out herself by the main gate to pick them up. But how could the boy have notified her, in the brief interval between my own return to town and his appearance at the gas station? If he had been so careful to keep out of sight, he would not have gone in person.

"Daisy," I said as if changing the subject, "you know that fellow we thought might have been in love with Sarah Mullin? Have you remembered yet who he was?"

"No. What's that got to do with present cases?"

"Nothing."

"Do you really think so, or are you just saying it?"

That startled me, and I was somewhat more surprised when she added, "I think I'll collect those loads of affection after seven this evening, Davy. Mother's going to a club meeting tonight. Why not drop in for supper, around seven-fifteen?"

"Come clean, Daisy, what's up?"

She looked steadily at me and said, "That's just exactly what we've got to figure out, isn't it? And neither of us knows enough, alone."

I took a long breath, and then a long chance. "All right. Do you still keep a record of all phone calls?"

"Yes, we do."

"Then bring a transcript with you of any calls to the nurses' dormitory for the hour after you left the switchboard, last night. It may help," I said, and set out for Dr. Alling's house.

On the way I tried to assess my reactions and decided that it would be a relief to share the problem with Daisy. Her job at the switchboard gave her a strategic knowledge of the whereabouts and conversations of all the persons connected with the medical school or the hospital. Having grown up in Altonville, she probably knew many old facts that might in some way be significant. Moreover, the abrupt vanishing of Muriel Finch shifted the focus of possible suspicion from me to someone else. I expected Dr. Alling to say something about it, and when he did not, I made a starter by mentioning the facts that were already known at the hospital, about this case of French leave. So far as I could judge, he really had not been notified. This should have seemed reasonable enough, as her disappearance had not been definitely known until well after midnight; and when I told him, he had not been back in town for more than half an hour; but something about his attitude made me decide on the spur of the moment to have my talk with Daisy before saying anything further to him. And that afternoon, to aid toward whatever synthesis the evening might produce, I resolved to revisit the cellar in the hills.

The trip was a kind of reassuring disappointment. There now seemed nothing at all unusual about the place, except traces of someone having camped there. There was a worn oblong under the shelter of the north wall to show where a tent had been pitched. Six little holes betrayed the location of the legs of a folding army cot. The foundations, made of huge field stones, had nothing strange about them. The place was more ruinous than I had supposed; no timbers at all had escaped fire and decay.

Adjoining the cellar I could trace the vestigial remains of a barn. But the grass grew where its floor had been. Only the field stone foundations, and the bushes growing thickly around them in a rectangle, remained. I returned to town relieved, if doubly baffled; and my awful imaginings began to quiet down for a few short hours, before taking on another form.

Daisy Towers herself answered my ring. "Mother had dinner all cooking at seven when she left," she said. "Come on in before it burns up."

She was wearing a black coolie coat with blue designs and loose blue satin trousers. I was pleasantly impressed by the fact that she was considerably more than good-looking. At the switchboard she always had a crisp and business-like air which now was not apparent.

"You heard about Mike?" she asked, and I nodded. He had been sent to the state asylum for an indefinite period.

While eating we talked of trivial things. As I swallowed the last bite of a large piece of Washington pie, she said, "I was waiting for you to get that down before giving you the latest tidbits. We've got another monster on our hands, born at six o'clock this afternoon."

"That's nice. What's queer about it?"

"The thing that's exceedingly queer about it is that it's another symmelus." Her breath was coming quickly, betraying an excitement which she strove not to show in words.

"Good God! Who's the mother?"

"A girl from out Center way. At least she's married."

"Anybody I'd know?"

"Lucy Bennett. She's twenty-two, and her husband's sixty-odd. She spent three years at reform school, fifteen to eighteen, and then was farmed to the Bennetts as a girl of all work. Ma Bennett died about two years later and the old man decided it would be cheaper to marry Lucy than to go on paying her ten dollars a month. A wife doesn't get her hands on half that, on a farm out Center way."

"You seem to have the young woman's case history at your tongue's end," I said. "Does the monster look like the other one?"

"Yes, only more so. You remember how the other one's leg ended in a blob of raw meat? Well, this one has all the toe bones of both feet growing out of the common stump, but about three times as long as they should be, with a web of skin between."

"Sounds as if somebody'd been trying to make a merman."

"Do you think somebody was?"

I scrutinized her to see if she was jesting, which did not appear to be the case. "Do you?" I countered.

"David, I'm not sure what I think—about that. But I'm sure of one thing: that boy who was so interested when Sarah Mullin died reminded me of somebody. Remember? Well, who was it he reminded me of?"

I shook my head. Then the truth came in a flash. The boy was featurally like old Wyck himself. I mentioned it, and she nodded.

"Exactly. Something mother said this morning at breakfast made me remember. I went to school with him, through the fifth grade. His name's Ted Watson. Then there was a scandal about his family and he left town. His mother was shot by her husband. She was pregnant, and he'd been away for a year. The jury wouldn't convict him of murder. It was declared a mistrial twice, and at last they gave him five years for manslaughter. Well, he said at the time that he knew the son wasn't his. He'd forgiven his wife the first time, and owned the boy publicly. But when she did the same thing again, he shot her. And at all three trials, he named Wyck as the father of the boy, and swore that his wife had confessed that Wyck also was the father of the unborn child that died with her. Wyck's own wife was supposed to have died from the shame of the disclosures, but she'd been an invalid anyway, ever since Marjorie was born."

"How much of an invalid?"

"She never left the house."

"I see. That helps to account for Wyck's behavior with other people's wives, perhaps."

"Of course it does. You know that girl who works in the bakery in town? Well, who does she look like?"

"Why—yes, I see. Rather like Marjorie Wyck."

"Almost her double. And there are a few more around town who look a lot more like Wyck than like their mother's husbands. That old rascal certainly did all he could to live up to the popular notion about the conduct of doctors with their female clients."

"Then your idea is that perhaps the boy killed Wyck by way of revenge for what Wyck had made him?"

"Seems likely, doesn't it?"

"Then why did Muriel Finch clear out of town?"

"The answer to that is why I asked you to supper. You haven't been trying to get in touch with her all week for nothing."

"First let me see that transcript of phone calls I asked for."

She got her purse and handed me a slip of paper. Among the calls to the nurses' dormitory was one, at 7:34, from Alton 808, which was the number of Wyck's house.

"Do you know who this was for?" I asked, pointing to the entry.

"Probably for Muriel. The house mother said that the last she saw of her was when she called her to the phone at about half past seven."

"And who put in the call?"

"That question shows why I should be on duty twenty-four hours a day. Jerry, the porter, had the board; and he didn't notice. We called Marjorie Wyck, of course, to see if she'd spoken to Muriel at that time, but she said she'd been out for a stroll, and that the call couldn't have been from her house, which she always locks up, since living alone."

I decided to make the plunge. "That call, Daisy, was from Ted Watson. I saw him stop in at the gas station at about quarter to eight last night with a gallon can. He carried it to his car, which was stalled down the hill past the Wycks'. He drove up to the house, stayed about two minutes, and then drove off toward Alton Plain. But he stopped at the southwest corner of the hospital fence to pick somebody up."

"Then you mean that he called Muriel from the Wycks', on the way *to* the gas station," she said. "But how did he get in to the phone, if Marjorie wasn't there?"

"He might have used Gideon's key."

"Oh! But no, wait a minute." She got a clipping from the *Alton Courier,* giving a precise description of all the articles delivered in the bundle of Gideon Wyck's clothes. Included were keys to both his office and his home. I pointed out that anyone who had had these articles in his possession even transiently could have taken a wax impression, and duplicated the key.

"All right," she admitted. "How did he get in the time you were watching him?"

"He knocked, and Marjorie let him in."

"When was that?"

"A little after eight."

"Then Marjorie's a liar. She said she was out from seven until nearly nine. Which means she probably let him in the first time, too."

"He asked her to go somewhere with him, when I was watching, Daisy, and she refused. But the way he asked made it seem as if he was repeating an offer that he'd probably already made a short while before."

"Listen here," she interrupted, "before we go any further, I want to know why you had your eye on him at all. What happened before that?"

Having gone so far, I decided to go all the way. Therefore, after making her promise to say nothing to anyone without first consulting me, I told Daisy Towers everything I knew concerning the disappearance of Gideon Wyck.

CHAPTER XIII

Out of my talk with Daisy there came a number of changes and one confirmation in my former attitude toward the Wyck case. The changes proceeded from the establishment of a highly logical thesis to account for Wyck's disappearance. If Daisy was correct in her belief that Ted Watson was Wyck's bastard, the conduct of the two toward each other was made more understandable, and a thoroughgoing excuse for murder was unveiled. We decided, from evidence gathered to date, that the boy Ted had been dependent upon Wyck for a livelihood; that Wyck, who apparently had commenced to go definitely insane about a year before, had bullied or wheedled his bastard offspring into doing service as a sort of chauffeur and guard; that Muriel had been forced to become a technical assistant in his experiments; that the mothers of the two monsters had been the immediate victims; that neither Ted nor Muriel had known the ghastly nature of the work in which they were implicated until the monsters were about to be born; that Ted, gradually falling in love with one of the victims, had been enraged to the point of murder when he learnt of her fate; that Muriel might or might not have been his accomplice in the murder, but probably had been at most a passive tool.

The admittedly improbable thesis that human monsters could be deliberately produced, and that they had been in this case, was strengthened by the fact that Daisy had discovered hospital records to show that Wyck had several times been called out to

Alton Center during the past year to attend Lucy Bennett in her pregnancy, and by our former knowledge that Sarah Mullin had been serving as a maid in Wyck's own house up until about ten weeks of the birth of the monster she had carried in her womb. His well-known, devastating glance, moreover, was more than a hint of genuine hypnotic powers, which could have been exercised to aid in getting either woman to the ruined farm, which was located about halfway between their two abodes.

But even if Wyck's secret had nothing whatever to do with the two monsters, there were any number of equivalent possibilities as motives for Ted to murder his father. The rankling fact of bastardy, the memory of a mother killed because of the seducer who had begotten him, the redoubled effect of thinking that a girl he loved had also died as a result of being seduced by his own father —these alone seemed more than ample by way of motivation for the act.

And then there was the obvious understanding between Marjorie and her half-brother, to indicate that they knew of their relationship and that he had thought it his duty to provide her with a means of escape. That she had not taken it, and that he and Muriel had both fled, caused us to conclude that Marjorie might have known of the crime without actually having had any part in it.

The effect of all this was to convince me at least that Wyck was dead, probably killed by his own bastard. But there was also a possibility that Mike, during his few moments in the cellar, had found Wyck hiding and had killed him with the axe which I had seen in his hand when he came out again. I had heard one piercing scream, which I had been inclined to think was a cry of disappointment from Mike himself, upon failing to find what he sought; but if it was he, and not Ted, who had committed the murder, Ted would have had less reason for fleeing so precipitately. Both Daisy and I were of the opinion that Ted's going had been occasioned by the discovery of his hiding place and by the fear that Mike might lead someone else to it.

My talk with Daisy, therefore, resulted in a loss of most of my fears of supernatural occurrences, but strengthened the almost equally appalling suspicion that the insane old doctor had actually been successful in a deliberate attempt to produce monsters in human wombs.

The confirmation, referred to a few paragraphs back, had to do with my recurrent feeling of uneasiness about confiding in Dr. Alling. When I told Daisy that I was going to speak to him the next morning, and put him on the trail of Ted Watson, she replied, "Suit yourself, but you'll live to wish you'd had better sense." I inquired why, and she added, "He's just too, too exceedingly smart, that's all. If you think you can tell him part of what you know, and hold back the rest, you're just living in a fool's paradise. He's the only person alive who's been able to pump things out of me that I didn't want to tell."

"Well," I said, "what of it? Three brains are better than two. It's quite likely that he knows a hell of a lot more about what Wyck was up to than we do. Between us we can probably piece out the whole story."

"Sure," she said. "There isn't a doubt of it. Thanks to the way Mike mauled you, Alling's the only person except little Daisy who knows that you came in with blood all over your face, and your clothes in a mess, the night Wyck disappeared. That's something you don't have to tell him, you know. When you come around with a nice voluntary tale about how somebody else did it, that'll be about all he needs to throw you in jail, sonny. Go ahead, tell him. But if I were you I'd find out where Ted Watson is, first. It smells just a trifle fishy when a murder suspect begins to lay the blame on somebody who doesn't exist, so far as the authorities know."

"What do you mean, murder suspect?" I cried indignantly.

"Just that, deary," she said. "Why do you suppose he's never repeated his request for information about how you got so banged up?"

It did not take any more arguing to convince me that once more I was too tardy to speak at all. If I had phoned the sheriff immediately after Mike's attack on Muriel, we doubtless could have intercepted Ted at the little bridge. My own procrastination now made it too late; and I was confirmed in my former resolve to wait until Dr. Alling himself saw fit to ask for an explanation.

I have said that I told Daisy everything I knew concerning the disappearance of Gideon Wyck; but that does not mean, of course, that I told her everything you have so far read in this narrative. I did not need to describe the town and school to her, and she already knew all the public aspects of the case. However, I did not consciously withhold anything that seemed pertinent, and which she might not be supposed to know already. The reader should also remember that, in separating a number of particular incidents and facts from amid the life of the town in general, I probably have made them seem more meaningful than they did at the time to Daisy and to me. Indeed, I have already recorded much that did not enter into our own discussions until much later on.

That is why I am now going to hurry through a description of the summer vacation, stressing one important episode but sparing you the need to follow all the conversations we had about things which became plainer at a later date.

Institutions in the larger cities draw most of the well-to-do students of medicine whose homes are in outlying regions. Our school is unique in having an enrollment principally from small towns and farms, of boys who go home again to serve as excellent country doctors. Consequently, the second semester ends for us a month earlier than usual, to permit many of the students to aid their families with spring plowing and planting. All except those who are to graduate can leave Altonville soon after May 1st. A few make a point of staying for Prexy's annual lecture, at which he invariably—up to 1932—has presented some genuine and important advance in morphological research.

My own year's schoolwork was over before the close of the first week in May, but I stayed on because of secretarial duties attendant upon the official closing of school. Dr. Alling omitted his celebrated lecture, for good and sufficient reasons. It was to have concerned itself with the tissues of monsters, using chance animal specimens, and monstrous insects developed in the laboratory. But the disappearance of his collaborator left part of the research incomplete; and the altogether bizarre coincidence that two human monsters should have been born at such a time in the local hospital made it prudent to avoid the attendant publicity on such a subject, which the newspapers would be quite sure to garble in fantastic ways.

Meanwhile, Daisy and I continued to meet rather frequently for a comparison of notes; but we succeeded in doing little more than obscure the nicety of our original thesis. Her knowledge of old events in the town made it possible for her to think of a number of other individuals with a grudge against Gideon Wyck. There was Ted's father, who had shot his wife because of her affair with the doctor. He had served his five years for manslaughter, and ostensibly had been at large for as many years more. Daisy knew of several other husbands who might have almost as good cause to hate Gideon, and she remembered a phone call from the Widow Schmidt to Prexy, in which that evil but indispensable harridan had refused to be responsible for Dr. Wyck's safety if he ever showed his face in her establishment again.

And there was Charlie, the diener of the school building, who had lost his job for awhile for going on a fishing binge once too often with Mike Connell and some students, when he should have been on duty. Charlie had stayed drunk for several weeks, buttonholing anyone who would listen to his troubles. He had attributed them all to Wyck, and had vowed that some day he would get even. Daisy pointed out still another possibility which I had not permitted myself to consider—that Biddy, with plenty of provocation, God knows, might have found a way to relieve the world of the author of her troubles. She had acted most queerly since Mike's committal to the asylum; but who, under the circumstances, would not?

For some weeks, Dr. Alling had said nothing at all about the mystery that was making two-faced creatures of us all. I spent more time than ever with him after exams, getting the year's records in order. The *Short Sketch* lay fallow until after commencement, when he asked me to step into his office.

Hunched down into a big overstuffed chair, such as he always preferred, he looked tired and lost. "Well, Saunders," he grunted softly, "there's another year."

In spite of myself, and without warning, I experienced the return of my old feeling of solicitude for this kindly cripple, who in a largely frustrated existence acted so graciously toward a world that could understandably have bred only bitterness in his heart. He inquired about my summer plans. I told him my applications for a job as camp doctor were as yet inconclusive. He turned to stare out the window, and then without looking at me, continued:

"Oh? I should like you to remain here if you will. You can have your meals with me. I presume you can keep your present rooms? There is a great deal to be done on the book. We'll both need two weeks off in August. Your present salary will continue."

Reason told me to refuse, but did not supply me with reasons for doing so. Moreover, as I walked toward the hospital to tell Daisy, and get my bawling out, I realized that I was far less anxious to get out of town than I had been a month ago. Looking at her, I decided it was good fortune that let me remain.

"Looks as if he's still trying to trap you into some kind of admission, Davy," she commented.

"If he is, he damned near succeeded," I confessed. "He looked so worn-out and worried that I was on the verge of doing anything that would ease his mind. Then I remembered I'd promised you I wouldn't."

"I only asked you to promise not to tell my part of it," she reminded me. "The rest is up to you. But I still wouldn't trust him."

"I know, Daisy. I guess if we do any confessing, we'll have to do it hand in hand."

"Suits me," she said, giving my hand a swing.

So we kept our counsel. Once, in July, a police inspector came up from Portland with some teeth found in a burnt body, but the local dentist positively proved that they were not Wyck's. A few days later, Daisy whistled under my windows after the end of her stint, and when we had walked a little way from town toward Alton Plain, she said, "Well, it's happened, kid. Hold your breath, because it's crazy. There's been a third monster born at the hospital, and Alling gave orders to hush the fact up. Nobody's to know, except those in attendance."

"Whew! But I thought your nursing days were over. Then how do you know?"

"For some reason or other, people when they get excited say things over the telephone as if nobody in between could hear. Of course, we're not supposed to hear, but the trick's too easy, if you know how."

"Well, what kind is it, this time?"

She spoke slowly. "It's a third symmelus."

We could not possibly doubt any longer that some external causation was influencing these births. Minor abnormalities of development are frequent enough, but pronounced monsters have always been very rare. It was an amazing coincidence that two monsters of any sort should appear in quick succession at the same hospital. Three of exactly the same class, within three months, could not within reason be ascribed to chance, at least until after all other possible causes had been investigated.

I was thoughtful for awhile, and then asked, "Got any new theories, Daisy?"

"Nothing scientific, except that there isn't a doubt in the world any more that it's Wyck's doing. It would at least be a comfort to know for sure that he's dead, and that this sort of thing therefore can't go on much longer. There's more to it, too, Dave. The percentage of stillbirths from last September to February has been five per cent, and that's twice the normal rate."

I was glad Daisy had been a nurse, as that made it easy for us to discuss from a professional angle such matters as these. But our discussions seemed to get us nowhere in particular, for some time to come.

Early in August I got my two weeks' vacation. As my pay was to continue, I decided to go to Nantucket, which was the most different place I could think of, within a couple of hundred miles. In going over some of Dr. Wyck's effects, with Dr. Alling, I had chanced upon an illustrated folder, glamorously extolling the island. I felt that the boat trip from New Bedford would make it almost like a visit to a foreign country. The room I hired was in sight of the old windmill, and for a luxurious week I did nothing but frog around the outskirts of the town, and take long walks across the lonely heath to swim by myself on the southern beaches, where a heavy surf discouraged the run of tourists. One day I walked the ten miles or so to Onset,[1] on the eastern end

1 This would seem to be Siasconset, or 'Sconset, an actual village on Nantucket.—Ed.

of the island. After changing into a swimming suit in a niche of the sand cliffs, I strolled down the beach. I was a little lonely, and felt like walking among the groups of people near the Onset cottages.

The shortage of men was evident. Several girls gave me something very like the glad eye, but I thought I would I make a choosy inspection of the whole beach before drumming up any acquaintanceships. Presently I came upon a group of five girls, all attractive, in minimum costumes, who were evidently burying a sixth person in the sand.

"Leave his eyes and nose out, but nothing else," one of them squealed. "There!"

I looked down at their victim and had the shock of my life upon seeing half-concealed features that seemed indubitably those of Gideon Wyck! It was like staring upon the immobile face of a corpse, in the midst of gaiety. Trembling, I walked on a little way, and then cast myself down on the beach, with my head half-concealed by my arm. His eyes had been closed to guard against the dribbles of sand, but the lips and nose were unmistakable. I remembered that it was a circular found in Wyck's office that had decided me to come here, and for a moment wondered whether telepathy might have forced the decision.

For awhile I watched, not knowing what to do. Then, in a scattering cloud of sand, the buried one erupted in one great bound, seized the arms of two of the girls, and hauled them, vainly protesting, into the surf. In blank amazement I watched as he ducked them with great agility and came running out to pursue others of the group, who fled up the beach.

Had my eyes deceived me? It was preposterous to think of the old doctor, for all his peccadilloes, acting so like an athlete. He easily corralled two more of the girls farther down the beach, ducked them, and pursued the fifth at top speed for a quarter of a mile. But before he caught her, and just as I was ready to doubt my own sanity, the truth dawned upon me. It was not Wyck, but Wyck's bastard Ted Watson, whose features, half covered by sand, had been indistinguishable from those of his father.

Not far from me on the beach was a typical New England resort patronizer, a testy little man with spectacles and an air of having inherited not quite enough money. He was staring with comically intense disapproval toward the Watson boy. I walked past the little man, assuming to the best of my ability a like expression of distaste, and remarked, "Vulgar clown. Who is he? Do you know?"

"Oh yes. He's always cluttering up the beach. A townie, Ted Gideon."

I swallowed my surprise at the name, which told me all that was needed to confirm my guess, and said, "You mean he lives here all the time?"

"Unfortunately. There he is, still wearing that life-guard emblem. He's not a life-guard at all, this year. If he was, they wouldn't stand for his acting that way with the guests. The vulgar fool. I shall make a complaint."

I questioned the little man further, and learnt that Ted Watson, alias Ted Gideon, was regarded by the summer cottagers as a native of the island. For two years he had served as a life-guard, but had had to be discharged near the end of the preceding season for reasons unexplained, although rumor had it that he had been "acting up" (to use the words of my informer) with the women he was supposed to guard.

I could get no more information of importance from the little man, and so strolled away, being careful to keep out of sight of Ted Watson-Gideon. Before starting back to Nantucket village, I stopped at the Onset post office to ask innocently where a *Mrs.* Gideon lived, and was told that the only Gideon thereabouts was an orphan named Ted. I then inquired whether he had relatives in Nantucket proper. The postmistress said she thought he had once lived with a family named Scruggs. She seemed somewhat reluctant to talk about the boy at all, so I said bluntly, "I'm sorry if I'm bringing up a painful subject. Is the boy a leper or something? Understand, I don't know him from Adam. I'm looking for a Mrs. Gideon, of Marblehead."

"Well, I don't know any Mrs. Gideon, but I do know that boy ain't right in his head," she said, with a sniff, "and fools they all were to make him a life-guard. Now, if they'd of asked *me!*"

I let it go at that, and took the long walk back to the principal village of the island. There I discovered that a man named

Scruggs was proprietor of a small boat yard, and that he had a wife and a son of thirteen. While casting about for an unobtrusive means of quizzing the elder Scruggs, fate helped me beautifully in the person of a fellow from the Harvard Graduate School who had a room in the same house as mine. He was making an anthropological study of the native islanders and for nearly a year had been pestering them to death, measuring their heads and inquiring into their genealogies and occupations. My landlady had warned me against being alarmed by her star boarder, whom she privately considered a harmless lunatic.

Without bothering to consult the Harvard man, who was out, I looked up Scruggs: the shrewd and weatherbeaten proprietor of railroad apparatus to haul small craft out of water and shore them up for the winter. Introducing myself as a student from Columbia University, I told him I was compiling a genealogy of the Scruggs family since William the Conqueror, whose right-hand man Saint-Geraux (according to me) had founded the family.

To my great satisfaction he replied, "Oh, another of you damned fools, hey?"

After listening to a long song and dance about his alleged ancestors, I at last got him down to the present generation. "And how about your other son?" I asked, when he had finished. "They told me you had a grown boy."

"That one? Ted? Naw, he just boarded with us. He's an orphan. We did our best by him, but he was no damn good. Blood tells."

When coaxed, he told how an advertisement had appeared in the local paper, ten years ago, inviting applications from persons willing to bring up an orphan aged ten, for $400 a year. Scruggs and his wife, who had just lost their second child, had been chosen from among the applicants. The contract was to be terminated if the boy revealed that his new guardians had tried to question him about his real parents. At irregular intervals, twice a year, an agent from Boston had dropped in without warning to see whether the boy was being properly cared for. Cheques had been mailed quarterly from the Boston-Phenix Trust Company, and the boy had been privileged to draw personally a small allowance from the local bank.

Scruggs admitted that for a year his ward had been moody and frightened, but after awhile had acted like one of the family. At fifteen he had got in with a "bad crowd," as Scruggs said, of summer tourists, and had worked all summer as a deck hand on their yachts. He ended with, "And four years ago I had to fire him out. I treated him like a son, but he turned out rotten."

And that was all I could get out of Mr. Scruggs. At last I desisted for fear of arousing suspicion.

CHAPTER XIV

Two days later, having pumped every loafer in town to little purpose, I returned disgruntled to my boarding house. The Harvard man invited me to his room for a cocktail, which I was glad to have. It was no use questioning him; when we first met he had told me that he was concerned solely with skull measurements, occupations, and genealogies of genuine residents of the island. We sat and talked shop.

"So you're a medic?" he inquired. "What field?"

"I'm apparently being driven into psychopathology."

"Sorry you don't like it. That's my province, from a different slant. But I picked the wrong place to work in. Confidentially, I'm after indexes of insanity and sexual aberration. You see, these people can't help marrying their own cousins, if they marry on the island. But nobody's ever let in any bad blood, so they can inbreed like Egyptian kings and get away with it. Anybody here could raise the healthiest family you ever saw by his own sister. It's very depressing. The only worth-while case histories I've got, so far, are when scions of fine old Boston families lead Nantucketers astray."

Without hoping for anything, I hazarded the question, "Did you find anything in the Scruggs family? They look shifty-eyed."

"Did I? My only real case, but it's got nothing to do with natives, worse luck. Scruggses are here only two generations, and the young brat's misleader came from the healthy hills of Maine. Look at this, will you?"

I tried to suppress my eagerness as I inspected some index

cards, one almost blank, four closely written. The first, genealogical, simply lacked pertinent information. The boy was from Maine, an orphan, his affairs administered by the Boston-Phenix Trust. That was all. My Harvard friend permitted me to copy the rest of the record, which I give verbatim below:[1]

Ted Gideon at the age of 14/15 had been taught certain perverse practices by the son of a prominent yachtsman, and had in turn corrupted the Scruggs boy. Upon discovery he was committed for juvenile delinquency at a private hearing of the local court, but was paroled in the custody of a retired clergyman living at Onset, who succeeded in imbuing the boy with a desire for normality. It was the investigator's opinion that the subject was not congenitally abnormal. He apparently had lived a normal life at Onset. In the summers of 1930 and 1931 he had been employed as life-guard, in token of renewed confidence of the community. Late in the latter season he had suffered an attack of some unidentified disease. The Boston-Phenix investigator, at his next visit, had taken the boy back to Boston, in September, 1931. Ted had returned to the island in May, 1932, and during the present summer had been guilty of no known reversions to abnormal practices. He had, however, developed a rather morbid attitude toward girls, at times shunning them altogether, with a kind of embittered rudeness, at other times showing-off in their presence like a much younger boy. Outgrowing self-consciousness about the mystery of his own origin, he was now inclined to romanticize it, and continually taunted other young persons of both sexes with the assertion that he knew "more about life with a big L than they would ever know." The investigator had noted that the little finger was missing from his left hand. Since no-one

1 The publishers have asked me to rewrite this information, for two reasons: first, because it is couched in a highly arbitrary psychological vocabulary, comprehensible only to a disciple of Charcot; secondly, because it contains phrases which, while they could be properly printed in any book addressed to the medical profession, would be sure to offend a large part of the general public, and perhaps would be seized upon by self-appointed guardians of public morals as grounds for prosecution under the obscenity statutes. My "translation" omits nothing. It merely presents the facts less technically.—ED.

remembered this before he left for Boston, it was assumed that it had been amputated during the last year.[1]

That night in bed I turned over this information, speculating upon its connection with other events. It was fairly certain that Gideon Wyck had decently acknowledged his obligation toward his own bastard and had attempted to give him a chance to grow up unhandicapped, in a place psychologically remote for all its nearness to the mainland. It also seemed likely that the bank trustees, knowing the father was a famous physician, had turned the boy over to him for direct observation when he was seized by an illness that baffled the island doctors. Such a thesis could perfectly well account for Ted's presence near Altonville during the winter. It could not explain why he had been forced to camp in a hole in the hills. On the other hand, it increased the reasons why old Wyck might have had an uncanny hold of some sort over the boy. I was sure that the doctor himself had become definitely deranged before his disappearance. His old honorable attitude toward the bastard might have undergone any kind of change with the increase of insanity.

And there were ameliorating possibilities, too. If Dr. Wyck had been tending a sick son whom, for the good of both, he had thought best to hide from the town at large, he well might have needed to take a nurse—Muriel—along with him. My speculations as usual ended nowhere in particular. I resolved therefore to take a long chance by confronting the boy and telling him I bore a message from Marjorie Wyck, insisting he must return and confer with her at once. Perhaps I could thus get him into the custody of the sheriff and of Dr. Alling, without having to tell anything else that I knew. If I felt compunctions about doing this, they were rationalized away by the thought that the boy could return to his old life in Nantucket with none the wiser, if he deserved to. If he did not deserve to, other people should not be made to suffer because of his escape.

1 The narrator does not seem to realize the interesting point that such an amputation has been advocated to aid in curing the malady from which "Ted Gideon" is later described as being a sufferer. See the *New International Encyclopedia*, vol. viii, page 25.—ED.

Next day, which was to be my last on the island, I again walked to Onset. The boy was nowhere on the beach, so, with heart beating to the tune of my suppressed excitement, I looked up the retired clergyman and asked to see his ward. He was a kindly old man, but suspicious, and insisted on knowing what I wanted. As I was pondering over what to say, there flashed into my memory a bit of information given me by Dr. Alling. Before his disappearance, old Gideon had withdrawn from his account $500, of which there was no trace. The $500 might be a farewell gift to start the boy in the world. I took a chance on that assumption.

"I'm a friend of the person who's been paying for Ted's maintenance," I said, "and he's asked me to check up on what's being done with the extra five hundred. I'm sorry to intrude, but I promised to do this."

The clergyman looked at me hesitantly, and then said, "You mean the money Ted brought back with him?"

"Of course," I answered, trying to remain calm under the sudden realization that the boy could have murdered his father to possess himself of a sum of money, with no other motive than the sense of disgrace of their relationship.

"You say five hundred? I understood it was four hundred. It's always been four hundred a year from the Trust Company, you know, but that ended this year."

"My friend told me five hundred," I said, looking accusingly at the poor old fellow, who seemed immensely worried, and hastened to say, "I shall have to speak with Ted. You know, we've had—trouble with him—of various sorts. But he's always been honest about money. He's a good boy, at heart."

"I should very much prefer to see him before you say anything," I insisted. "I must do my best to fulfill his benefactor's wishes."

The clergyman nodded and said, "As you think best. He's gone sailing, with friends. He should be coming in at the wharf within an hour, for lunch. But please be careful. He's still—ill. You know, he gave me more than three hundred and sixty dollars, to take care of for him. The rest he said he had had to use for expenses, getting here."

I reassured him and walked down to the wharf. There were

several small craft a few miles out. Presently one of them began to zigzag toward the wharf. Before it arrived I saw the boy in the cockpit, and decided to stroll back a way in the hope of meeting him without his friends. When they had tied the boat up, two of the five walked off down the beach. Ted and the other two approached the spot where I stood at an intersection. His friends said, "Hope you get over your mal de mer," and turned into the intersecting street. I stepped up and confronted the boy, who was walking slowly, as if ill.

An odd look in his eyes may have been what provoked me to say something altogether unintended, on the spur of the moment.

"Ted," I said sternly, "I am bringing you a message from your father, and you know where he is."

He stared at me stupidly and emitted a curious, moaning shriek. Both his arms began to shake. Without warning he pitched forward on the ground, making no effort to ease his fall. His two friends heard the cry, and came running back. As he lay twitching in the road, mouth distorted, teeth snapping, I knew past doubt that I was witnessing the so-called *grand mal* of epilepsy.

"Leave him alone," I ordered. "I'm a medic. Have you got a clean handkerchief?"

One was produced, and I used it, rolled, to separate his foaming jaws, as the only immediate danger in such an attack is that the victim may bite his tongue off. The twitching diminished, and I expected him to go into the series of snores that should end the seizure. Instead, he rolled over suddenly, laughed, and opened eyes with hugely dilated pupils that reminded me of Mike's at the moment of his first violent madness. Ted Gideon's attack had not been bad, as they go. It had lasted less than five minutes. He began to talk in an exultant fashion, disconnectedly; and I knew that he had passed into the state called *epilepsia larvata,* which at times succeeds a minor attack. I motioned his friends away and knelt beside him, listening attentively. Most of what he had to say meant nothing to me; but I felt certain that some of it was significant. His ravings not only confirmed some of our former conjectures explicitly, but also seemed to add new information which we could hardly have surmised.

As he was babbling rapidly for several minutes, and as I was too busy listening to try to take down his words, I shall try to describe rather than to reproduce what he said. At first, between bursts of laughter, he seemed to be making boyish love to a reluctant and inexperienced girl, for he kept repeating the very sort of thing which my Harvard friend had noticed: vague boasts about his experience as a man of the world, chiding the mythical young lady for her prudishness. Then he became angry in tone, as if someone had denied what he had been saying, and began to describe his prowess as a lover with great candor, using the fine old Anglo-Saxon four-letter monosyllables with that peculiar fervor which we sometimes notice in the remarks of patients coming out of ether—an effect which must be the psychological wish-fulfillment atoning for the complete repression of such terms in ordinary speech. Next he was apparently addressing a man—and here again I think he was releasing a speech which he had formulated to himself and never had dared utter; for it extolled the advantages of being a bastard, and climaxed them by pointing out with chuckles and simperings that only if you were a bastard could you expect your father to supply you with mistresses.

Almost before that jolt had sunk home he began laughing in an airy way and announced that his father had not only done that, but had given place to him in the dark. Chuckling with imbecilic glee, he announced that his father had become impotent, and that he himself had inherited his father's mistresses.

All of this came out, of course, as a general impression, garbled with irrelevant words and inaudible whisperings. His ravings next took on a sad tone, and the word "Sarah" was repeated over and over, with promises of marriage and outbursts of invective against his father.

Gradually he quieted, and I questioned his two scared friends. They were positive that he had never had such an attack before; but one of them remembered that while swimming Ted had once fainted at a time when it could not be explained by exhaustion. He had recovered while being brought ashore, had thought that his rescuer was trying to duck him, and had promptly ducked the rescuer. Everyone thought at the time that he had been pretending, but Ted had insisted that he had not played dead, that nothing had happened at all until someone tried to duck him. This confirmed my suspicion that the improperly diagnosed symptoms of a year back had been early phases of the disease of epilepsy. Old Wyck himself surely could not have known what it was, or he would never have allowed the boy to act as his driver.

I had to proceed quickly now, and it seemed wise to take what I had learnt and be satisfied, for the time being. So I told his friends to watch him, and above all things not to let him know that he had done anything other than faint from illness, explaining that an epileptic never realizes that he has had a fit unless told. Then I hastened to the clergyman, described what had happened, and cautioned him that it would be most unwise under the circumstances to mention me or my mission in any way. With a last admonition that the boy's friends must be kept from saying anything to him whatever about the fit, I left for Nantucket. There I gave my Harvard friend all the data except the spoken phrases, confident that he would continue the case history, a fact which might be of use before I was through.

On board the boat, headed back to New Bedford, I had every reason to believe that all these new facts had been collected without the knowledge of Ted Gideon. He perhaps had not even heard my phrase that seemed to incite the attack. If he had heard it, he well might think it a figment of the fainting spell which would have been the explanation of why he found himself lying in the road. Of the things he had said aloud he would have no memory whatever.

CHAPTER XV

Adequate sleep, food, and fresh air—the therapeutic three virtues which all good doctors prescribe for others and skimp for themselves—had worked their usual miracles with me. The chance discovery of Ted Gideon, while it shortened my mental vacation, eased my mind after homecoming. Nantucket physicians hardly would allow him to leave the island. I would know where to find him, and now could turn any accusation against myself more plausibly upon him. If this seems callous, remember that epileptics as such may be homicidal, and—as the boy could have killed his father without even knowing he had done so—it would be almost impossible to convict him of a deliberate crime. Daisy had seen him in a disordered mental state, in the hospital lobby, on the morning before his father's disappearance. This fact would corroborate my story, were I forced to tell it.

When I reached home, at 4 P.M. on August 29th, Biddy seemed genuinely glad to see me. At work over her tubs in the shed behind the kitchen, she still looked hurt and troubled. Her plump, pink Irish face had sagged in less than half a year. But it brightened with a greeting that contrasted hopefully with my memory of her apathetic farewell.

"Hello there, Mr. David. Did ye meet any pretty girls at the beach? I'll bet ye did all yer sleepin' in the mornin'."

"Biddy," I said, "I had trouble fighting them off, but 'tis God's truth that I haven't had a date in two weeks."

"I don't believe ye. But if there's truth in it, then ye must be in love. And that reminds me—Daisy Towers called yesterday to inquire when you'd a be comin' home. She says you told her today, in a letter, and I says why was you writin' letters to her, I'd like to know."

Feeling that my face was reddening, I looked out the doorway as I explained that it was on hospital business. "How's Mike?" I asked, to change the subject. It was nearly three months now since he was committed.

"They say he'll niver be any better"—her voice caught—"oh, and God knows I miss him, Mr. David."

I gave her a squeeze, told her she was a brave colleen, and hurried off to see Daisy, who threw me a kiss through the reception window.

"Well, Romeo, have you been resting or going in for frivolity and riot?" she asked, eyeing me with good-natured suspicion. "Nice letter, but you didn't give me a chance to reply."

My eye was attracted by a slight motion in the back of the half-darkened room. What I had seen move was a reflection in the mirror affixed to a little cabinet over the washbasin. All I could see was a nurse's cap on gray hair, but this was enough to tell me that the house mother of the nurses' dormitory was within hearing distance, in the next cubicle. I stepped out of line with the mirror and reception window, and made an expression of caution for Daisy's benefit. At once she became excessively professional. "I can give you a report at eight-thirty tonight, if you wish, sir," she said. "But I'm sure the telephone company's figures are right." Then she added in a whisper, "Lots has happened."

"You don't know the half of it," I said as softly. "Wait till I tell you who I saw."

With eyes alone she asked the question—*Who?* In the mirror I could now see the face of the house mother, listening intently, unaware of the reflection. I stepped back and silently framed with my lips the name, "Ted Watson." Daisy pursed her lips, said "Number please," and thrust a switchboard plug into the appropriate jack.

I decided to eat at the lunch cart, to avoid the chance of being corralled for the evening by Dr. Alling. Joe, the hash artist, had little to report. "You sawbones must be knockin' 'em off fast, these days," he remarked. "The hearse has been parked at the hospital regular."

"They get careless when I'm away," I said.

"You been away? Never know where you are, these days, doc, now you're eatin' regular with the big shot. Teacher's pet."

Eight-thirty came at last. Daisy was wearing a cool green frock, kind to her coppery hair and to the golden tan of her shoulders. Her mother was seated beside her on the porch, but soon excused herself.

"Thank goodness," Daisy sighed. "I've been burning up since five o'clock. What about"—she lowered her voice,—"Ted Watson?"

"The legal name's Ted Gideon," I corrected her, for an impressive starter, and then gave a full account of the case history, slightly softening the details of juvenile delinquency, and ending with a description of the epileptic seizure.

"Could the epilepsy have been hereditary? That might account for some of the old wretch's conduct," she said.

"It's not likely. But we've got to work on the theory that this trail of monsters and maniacs leads back to a single primary cause. Mike and the son both mad, and three monsters born—"

"It's five now, David. Since you left there was one miscarriage with the baby so macerated that no one could tell what it was. And there was—" She paused impressively.

"Another symmelus?" I asked, grimly.

"Yes, a fourth symmelus, with no arms. The hands were like flippers. Except for the head and the color of it, you could think it was a baby seal."

"You saw it?"

"Yes. It was an emergency case, born in the Widow's old converted Cadillac ambulance. Dr. Kent slammed the porter down in front of the switchboard and hauled me out to help him tie off the umbilical cord, right in front of the hospital doors. But that wasn't the worst of it. The thing that nearly threw me into a fit myself was the way it barked! Instead of a birth cry it lay barking —quick yelps—something like a terrier's. I asked Dr. Kent about it afterward and he said the larynx wasn't human at all."

"Did it live long?" I asked, lighting a cigarette with a match that wobbled in my fingers.

"No. It died right there in the ambulance, and the mother died at the same time."

"Who was she?"

"That's another nice point. It was Mrs. Molyneaux, the Widow's Canuck nurse. And here's something else to think about. Do you know who was the appointed overseer of her place?"

"I didn't know there was one, appointed. I knew they kept pretty close watch over her, to cut down on the abortions. But I thought it took the whole staff, more or less, to keep an eye on her."

"It does, but they shift the principal responsibility every six months. And Gideon Wyck was the official overseer from July 1, 1931, to January 1, 1932. You remember I told you about a call from the Widow to Dr. Alling, saying she wouldn't be responsible for Wyck's safety? Well, that was put through in the middle of December, and Dr. Alling soothed her by saying his term would be up at the end of the month."

"Then do you know how many of these queer cases came from the Widow's?" I asked suddenly.

"I was coming to that. All five of the monsters were born to women living within a few miles of Altonville. But only two of them, the first and last, came by way of the Widow."

"That seems to make hash of a nice theory," I remarked.

"Not a bit of it," she argued. "There's another thing. You know there was an abnormal percentage of stillbirths from September a year ago to last February? Well, all but one of those *did* come by way of the Widow, and the exception was in the case of Mrs. Flanders, who wouldn't have let Wyck come within ten miles of her. She had young Dr. Follansbee all through her confinement."

I whistled. "I see what you're driving at. Girls wouldn't be coming to the Widow's till they were within a couple of months of delivery, so in those cases he started his experiments too late —assuming he did experiment."

"We've got to assume that, David. I don't know much more than a nurse has to know about such matters, but I've been looking things up in a book that couldn't afford to go wrong, and—"

"What book?"

"The *Encyclopaedia Britannica,* and it says there that human monsters take the essentials of their final form during the first three months in embryo."

I nodded. "Sorry to have been so dumb, lady. That means that any woman by the time she got to the Widow's would be beyond the stage where much could be done to influence the form of the fetus."

"Yes, except in the case of the Widow's nurse, Mrs. Molyneaux, who was the last one, and was there all the time—"

"And of Sarah Mullin," I broke in, "who was living at Wyck's own house up to the time she went to the Widow's."

"Exactly, David. In those two cases, and in all three others, Wyck could have exerted some kind of influence—God knows what—over the mothers during the formative stages of the embryos. Lucy Bennett, mother of the second one, lived out Center way, not very far from your famous ruined farm. What's more, her skinflint old husband sent her in to the free ward for treatment, and the records show that Wyck took care of her. The mother of the third symmelus has been living alone in Alton

Plain. Her husband's a lumberjack, and hasn't been home for a year, except a few days at Christmas, so Wyck could have had all the chances in the world to see her."

"And the fourth, the messed-up one?"

"Sylvia Jones was the mother. Remember her?"

I nodded, and felt something of a pang of sadness. She was a gay, considerate little nurse, who had been dismissed from the hospital in February, when she fainted while on attendance upon one of the cases of stillbirth. I had a notion that she had been Daisy's friend, and inquired.

"She was," she said, with a metallic tone of cold, controlled anger creeping into her voice, "and this completes my case. It killed her. When she was dying, she asked for me, the poor sweet little kid. I didn't want to make things hard with questions, her last few minutes on earth. I just let her do all the talking. She wanted to confess something, but talked all around the subject, till it was too late."

"You didn't learn anything?"

"Not much, but enough to know that Wyck himself got her into trouble. Now I come to think of it, she might have meant Ted. Well, when she threatened to have what we so nicely call an illegal operation, Wyck gave her a prescription to take every day for six weeks, but it did no good."

"Anything you'd take daily for six weeks couldn't do any good. Do you suppose he—Daisy, did you get that prescription?"

"No, but she said it's the only one she ever had filled, and it must be on file at the drug store."

"She must have been pretty dumb, not to see through what he was up to. Six weeks!"

"Oh, of course! The poor little youngster. Just tided her along until it was too late to do the usual thing. And the stuff he gave her may itself have been part of his experiment on her, you see."

"Whew! That may be how he worked it with all of them, assuring them they wouldn't have to have their children at all, if they'd follow his treatment—and the treatment itself was calculated to produce a monster. But why on earth should he want to produce monsters?"

"Why should he have wanted to drive Mike Connell mad with

ideas about demons? He was mad himself, David. We must be a bit crazy too, to sit down here trying to talk calmly and professionally about all this. If you'd heard the screaming of those poor women—each time you could hear it all over the hospital. It made me want never to have a child. Poor little Sylvia."

"What's Alling done?" I asked, thinking with a shiver of what might have preceded these tragedies.

"He gave strict orders to hush it up, like the time before, and took all the monsters away to his laboratory."

"Did he say why he wanted it all hushed up?"

"Yes. He called all of us who had witnessed them into a private room and said there was a legislative investigation of the medical school pending, and that it might be extended to the hospital, if the news of all this funny business got out, in which case we all might lose our jobs. He said he and Dr. Kent were making a private investigation, and that we would be protected by the legislature's own laws regarding a doctor's right to keep certain kinds of information confidential."[1]

We had been so absorbed in our discussion that I was startled when the church clock struck eleven. It was a scrupulous tradition among medics that no date should end without at least a good-night kiss. Somehow this climax had never before occurred to me, at the end of my talks with Daisy. I remember feeling rather queer as she called out an awkward, extra farewell phrase as I went out the gate.

CHAPTER XVI

For the next few days Dr. Alling kept me busy at all hours, and was curiously insistent that I bear him company at meals and on walks. It seemed almost as if he feared physical violence, and wanted someone always to be near. But that could hardly be true, as he slept alone in a house in no way guarded. His cook and

[1] In most states, there is little or no information which a doctor may withhold if subpœnaed in criminal proceedings; but there are provisions of law and custom making it legitimate for physicians to refrain from volunteering such information, unasked.—ED.

housekeeper both lived in the village. There was not even one extra bed or cot about for an emergency.

I no longer cared what his motives might be, in keeping me so much under his eye. Morbid and esoteric as he was in many ways, I could not picture him as a cruel schemer, despite Daisy's opinion. His attributes were to me more like those of a da Vinci, merging his private sorrows into the adventure of increasing human knowledge—a feverishly interested observer who could yet remain benignly aloof from fellow individuals. Perhaps it was only a result of the ease of mind that came from knowing about Ted Gideon, but I was able by now to laugh at my own appalling suspicions of the spring.

There was additional reassurance in the change of his own attitude when he said, one morning, "You've doubtless noticed that I deliberately skipped the chapter on fetal deformities in our outline. The reason is of course obvious." When I looked a little puzzled, he added, "I mean that I've got some first-hand speci-mens in my laboratory—in fact, too many for comfort—and I want to finish a complete detailed inspection of them, forget-ting preconceived theories, before writing anything at all on that theme."

The subject of the monsters had not come up between us for some time. Now, in my renewed confidence, I asked, "What's your explanation of them, sir? I mean, having too many for com-fort all at once?"

"Isn't it obvious?" he countered.

"You mean it's linked with Dr. Wyck's disappearance?"

"Of course. When I found out we were likely to be in for this visitation of monstrosities, I was sufficiently perturbed to avoid discussing it with anyone. But I'm beginning to get used to the idea, now."

"You were rather eager about the first one," I said slyly, hoping for more news.

"That was before I knew it was anything but an accident. Well, let's not discuss it now. I feel sure it will soon be over, for a number of reasons that I will tell you, like a wise prophet, after they prove true."

As I strolled back past the school that afternoon, Charlie

the diener hailed me. "I've been hopin' you'd go by, doc," he explained. "'Bout time we pumped some air into that vault, with school openin' in a coupla weeks. I'd just as lief have somebody around in case anything goes flooey with the machinery."

"Don't trust your own invention?" I said, jibingly.

"There's a lot of fine inventors pushin' up daisies, doc, from tryin' to fly with their own brand of wings."

As we descended the stairs, he added, "How's Mike? Gee, it's been a funny summer, with no Mike to go fishin' with."

As I told him of the last hopeless report, he shook his head, but became cheery again as he bent to read the pressure gauge on the chlorine tank. "See that now, Doc Saunders? Take a look at that. Right on the dot where it was last spring. Ask Doc Kent. She was at 70, and he says, let her down to 50 flat. They all told me she'd leak if I left her hooked up. 'Not with them white lead joints, she won't,' I says. And she didn't, did she now?"

"If you want to prove she's at 50 I'll swear to it," I said, after examining the gauge. "I don't know where it was when you finished filling the vault, though."

"Sure I want to prove it, and Doc Kent knows where it was, all right. He bet me a box o' Pittsburgh stogies it'd leak five pounds. You gotta help me collect, doc. That old fool Wyck shot off his mouth about gas leakin', too, and spoilin' things upstairs. 'Chlorine don't walk upstairs,' I says. 'You oughta be enough of a chemist to know that. What'll you bet I don't lose a pound?' I says, but the old tightwad wouldn't bet. Now, doc, you turn that there valve in the exhaust pipe."

I followed directions. It was a two-inch lead pipe running from the sealed vault to a metal tank half the size of an ordinary boiler. This in turn had an outlet running outdoors. Chlorine from the vault would bubble up through water in the bottom of the tank, and then through several copper screens, electrically heated, above which were layers of finely powdered animal charcoal and antimony. Most of the wet chlorine formed $Cu\,Cl_2$ with the copper mesh. Any surplus was adsorbed on the antimony and charcoal. Charlie had not worked out the details, but it was he who had suggested using something like the gas masks he had worn in the war.

When the exhaust valve was open, he snapped a switch. A small centrifugal blower between tank and vault whined to full speed and began drawing out the gas. We could hear it bubbling in the tank. Presently the pump changed its note.

"Gettin' a vacuum in there," Charlie said. "Now we can make a niche or two with no danger of any gas gettin' into the buildin'."

Air whistled through the cracks of the door as he pried at a piece of packing; and when he pulled it free there was a loud sucking noise. "See, doc," he said exultantly, "that vault was *her*metically sealed. That packin' round the door don't leak a mite."

"Well, your machinery seems to work, inventor," I said. "I guess I'll be on my way."

"What's your hurry?" he inquired. "There may be a whiff or two left in there. I don't figger on passing out with nobody around."

I waited ten minutes or so, while Charlie stripped from around the vault door its "packing." This consisted of a piece of cord heavily coated with a tarry preparation and pressed into the crack, with more goo pressed over it for good measure. He opened the padlock and worked hard at the bolts, which had been partly imbedded in the tarry stuff. After some tugging, the heavy door swung out.

"Snap that switch, will you, doc?" he directed. "Yeah, the one highest up."

I turned it, but there was no effect.

"Shoot!" Charlie exclaimed. "Bulb must a gone flooey durin' the summer."

"Maybe it's just loose," I said. He groped for it, gave it a twist, and said, "Now try."

I snapped the switch again and the vault was lighted.

"That's funny," I heard Charlie say.

"What's funny?" I asked, poking my head in and coughing over a whiff of unexhausted chlorine, which did not quite succeed in suppressing the regular vault smell of musty corpses, lying under snow-white shrouds on their tiers of shelves.

"That there," he said. "There wasn't no stiff on the damned go-cart when I sealed this place up."

My stomach took a leap, and then settled down into the

bottom of my abdomen. There was no question of what we would see when we uncovered that body. I resolved in a flash that Charlie, not I, would take off the cloth. I stepped nearer to have a good view of his face when he did it.

"Funny the way you can forget a thing like that," he muttered. "I could a sworn I'd put every one o' them stiffs in bed. Well, let's see how they stood it."

He pulled the cloth from over the feet of the corpse that was lying on the wheeled stretcher in the middle of the room. I expected to see something loathsome, but this body was obviously embalmed, like all the others. I began to doubt the conclusion to which my mind had leapt.

"Fine and dandy," said Charlie. "Now, if this was three years ago, before we figgered out this chlorine stunt, you'd 'a' scraped the mold off'n them feet half an inch thick—an inch, mebbe. Well, gimme a hand heavin' this guy up on the top shelf, and I'll inspect 'em all tomorrow. Let's see if his hair's sheddin'."

He pulled away the head end of the shroud, stretched out a hand to pull at the hair, and then withdrew it slowly. It seemed to me that I could actually see his own hair bristle.

"Holy Gawd, doc!" he whispered. "It ain't— Yeah, it is him. Ain't it?"

If Charlie had actually been aware of what he would find when he lifted that bleached shroud, then he was the finest actor I have ever seen. With eyes popping and fallen jaw, he stood staring at the cadaver of Gideon Wyck.

I stepped forward, with an illogical urge to touch the body and thus satisfy myself of its reality, but Charlie pulled back my hand.

"Nix, doc," he said hoarsely, "nobody's going to do any monkeyin' with this guy till we get hold o' the sheriff. Do you wanna call him, or should I?"

We both stood irresolute, staring at the tallow-colored corpse, showing faint red and purple blotches from extravasated blood and embalming fluid. The face, although somewhat relaxed with time, still was twisted with hideous signs of a convulsive death. I jumped and with difficulty restrained a yell of alarm as one of his arms, which had apparently been disturbed from a precarious equilibrium when the diener pulled at the shroud, suddenly slipped over the edge of the stretcher and dangled rigidly, pointing downward. Far less embalming fluid had been used than is usual. This was indicated by the extreme emaciation of the wrinkled skin, as it hung over the bones like wet cloth. Ordinarily the most wrinkled of bodies is distended to plump smoothness by the embalming fluid. But Gideon Wyck was certainly no pleasanter a man dead than alive.

Charlie was first to regain some sort of composure. "Listen here, young feller," he said, "you go and phone the sheriff. I've been deputy on enough inquests to know that we're in for one fine quizzing, and mebbe a night in the hoosegow. I'm gonna stand in that vault door, and not move for nobody till the sheriff gets here."

Since the school phone is operated from the hospital switchboard, I said, "Daisy, get me the sheriff quick and you'd better listen in on this one." I quickly explained to the sheriff what had happened.

"Have ye called Dr. Kent?" he asked, and when I told him that I had not yet done so, he said, "Well, you do, and save me the trouble."

Dr. Kent was the state pathologist and a professor at the medical school, but he also held the office of county coroner.[1] Daisy had a little trouble finding him for me, but at last she located him at a store in town. As I finished giving him my message a car stopped noisily outside, and a Yankee voice bawled, "Where in hell is this here crime?"

I opened the door for Sheriff Palmer, told him Dr. Kent would be over shortly, and led him down to the vault. The diener was standing in the doorway.

"There he is, sheriff," he said.

"How much have ye yanked him around?" the sheriff snapped, thrusting his head forward shrewdly.

"He ain't been touched," said Charlie, "only to lift the cloth, each end. And that arm fell loose after I pulled the cloth from under it."

---

1 The office of coroner does not exist in the State of Maine. The governor appoints medical examiners, having similar duties. Massachusetts also has abolished the office.—ED.

"Who saw him first?" the sheriff inquired.

"Dunno. Me and Doc Saunders here was both in there. I pulled the shroud off."

"Then you're under arrest," said the sheriff promptly. "And I'm like to want you, too," he added, turning to me.

He did some prowling and sniffing, but nothing else happened until the coroner came, looking extremely worried, and accompanied by a public stenographer. I was thrown into an inner panic by the glance I got from Dr. Kent. He made a quick general inspection, and then asked the diener and me, each with the other absent, to describe what had happened, while the stenographer took down our depositions.

"Very well," he said. "Sheriff Palmer, will you arraign Mr. Michaud and Mr. Saunders before the magistrate, and then return here? As soon as another doctor arrives from the hospital we will proceed with the autopsy."

CHAPTER XVII

As the coroner's court would not be held for a day or two, Charlie and I were arraigned before Judge Cole as material witnesses and paroled in custody of the sheriff. We hung around with him, not quite knowing what to do, as he prowled through the preparation room, asking us questions about the embalming process, and hunting fingerprints on the apparatuses. I observed with some relief that criminology, in Maine, remained doggedly in the romantic stage. We told the sheriff that rubber gloves usually were worn throughout the embalming process, but did not endeavor to dissuade him by further argument. He continued to putter about with a little pot of dry white lead, a device for dusting it evenly, and a magnifying glass. To me it seemed completely absurd that anyone guilty of so well-managed a crime should be suspected of not having worn rubber gloves from start to finish, but I was just as glad to have the sheriff thus harmlessly employed, for the time being.

Presently he said, "Hey, what are you yaps hangin' around here for? Beat it. But if I catch you over the township line, you'll have a hell of a job gettin' out o' jail for the next twenty years."

I stopped for a quick bite at the dog cart, and then hurried across the street to dress for an evening with Daisy.

We were no longer bothering to make dates. Instead, it had become a matter of giving notice once in awhile if the expected nightly meeting could not come about. In front of the Connells', the town clerk served me with a summons to appear for the coroner's investigation, at 9:30 A.M. on the second day following. This would be a trying experience for one who knew so much about the case. I resolved then and there to answer all questions in the simplest possible fashion, and to volunteer nothing.

Daisy met me on the lawn with news that her mother was swamped with callers, in anticipation of the very fact that I, who had first seen Wyck's corpse, surely would drop in to tell about it. I thanked her for the warning, and we began to stroll around the back way toward the hospital, past the cemetery. Quite automatically we joined hands, smiled at each other, and looked ahead again.

While I was describing carefully the afternoon's astonishing occurrences, we passed the hospital and wandered on into the Bottom Road. When I had finished she was silent, all the way to the first little bridge. Then she said, "You don't know how Alling reacted?"

"I haven't seen him since it happened."

"You were there over two hours," she mused aloud, "and he didn't come down to investigate the finding of the body of his own colleague—and he's the head of the school. We've got to figure out some innocent-sounding things for you to ask him in the morning, Davy."

"What for?" I inquired.

"To see whether he did the job himself, or used the diener as a cat's-paw."

I gave a nervous laugh. "Did the job himself? Why, the way he's been trying to protect the school from an investigation—do you suppose he'd pull a bizarre stunt like that? It'll be in headlines all over the country tomorrow morning. As for doing the job himself, as you so quaintly put it, can you imagine that crippled half-pint heaving a stiff around the embalming room? Daisy, I thought I'd been a better influence on your mental growth than that. He won't even carry a book, when I'm around to do it for him."

"At least I'm not letting my emotions play boss to my mental growth—such as it is," she said coolly, and, when I began to protest, she added, "I don't blame you for being loyal to the guy."

"It's not that," I insisted. "You know I was suspicious of him for months, over his not asking me where I'd been when I came in all messed up, that night."

"You only suspected him of suspecting you, Davy. You didn't suspect him of doing it himself. And as for not asking you that question, he doubtless had his own good reasons for keeping the whole business hushed up. Why should he ask you where *you'd* been, if *he* did it himself? More than three hours passed between when you last saw Wyck and the time you came in and found Alling sitting up with Mike. What was he doing there at that hour, anyway? That's suspicious enough, if we had nothing else to go on."

"No, it isn't. It's perfectly obvious: Biddy called him up, because he was the last doctor Mike had had."

"Very good, Watson," she mocked. "Unfortunately, Biddy did nothing of the sort. I've indulged in a little more research, this evening. The record for that night shows only one call from the Connells' line, and that was when Alling called for help after Mike had gone coo-coo. Did you ever ask Biddy?"

"No," I confessed.

"Well, do. The night girl might just possibly have left it off the slip, but it isn't likely. I'd suggest that you ask Alling, just casually, how he happened to be there, too, and see if they tell the same story. Do it the first thing tomorrow morning, and I'll hang on to the line to make sure that the first one you ask doesn't call up the other, so they can get together on an answer."

"You're not meaning that you think Biddy is mixed up in this, Daisy?" I asked, half angry with myself, because I had secretly thought over that possibility more than once.

"Some laundress is," she answered. "And what laundress could have more cause to be than Biddy? Those clothes of his weren't laundered in any commercial establishment or they'd have laundry marks."

"And I suppose she dry-cleaned the suit," I asked, sarcastically.

"Score one for you. I hadn't thought of that. But then, I'm not saying she did it all alone. Obviously, she wouldn't have known how to embalm the body. The diener must have done that. And don't forget that Alling wasn't kept at the hospital, when they brought you two in, after you'd been mauled by Mike. He might have killed Wyck either before or after Mike went mad, and surely would have had time to direct the embalming job between then and daylight, if it wasn't done before."

"How do you even know it was done that night at all?" I asked, still doubtful.

"Because the last call I put through this evening was the coroner calling the county prosecutor, and he mentioned that the vault was sealed on the day of Wyck's disappearance."

A sudden fear gripped me. I clearly remembered having helped Charlie heave two last stiffs into the vault, and could recall his very words—"Last arrivals for this year. Tomorrow when the inspection's all over we'll give these babies their annual bath of chlorine for what ails 'em." Had one of them been Wyck's body? Was I actually an accessory to the crime? Then a thought came to make the fear absurd. I had just finished, and had been washing my hands, when Wyck himself had come to give me the book of plates depicting various kinds of monsters. It was several hours after we had put the last stiffs away that Wyck had started up the hillside, when last I saw him alive. The coroner must have meant the day when Wyck's disappearance became known.

"Well," I remarked, "I'll have to keep on thinking it's silly to accuse Alling while Ted Gideon and Muriel Finch are missing. They're stronger suspects, from all we know. And I have my own private notions about my fine fellow-student Mr. Prendergast, in the light of this new business. We still have to learn what became of those two blue books that were the basis of his getting fired. Don't forget that. And incidentally, mightn't it be a good idea to save our theorizing till we find out what the coroner has to report? We don't even know yet how he was killed."

Daisy murmured something by way of assent, and then said,

"Oh, before I forget, Davy. I saw the prescription Wyck gave to Sylvia Jones."

"How did you get to see that? Those things are supposed to be dark secrets."

"I used my eyes," she said. "I mean this way," and she ogled me shamelessly. "I just wangled it out of the soda clerk. He treated me to a sundae in the bargain."

"Really! Well, what did Wyck prescribe?"

"Of course they wouldn't let me copy it, but I looked at it carefully and all it contained was salt, powdered chalk and oil of wintergreen mixed with water."

"Just a pure fake," I grunted. "She could have taken that for six years and it would only have made her thirsty."

Daisy nodded. "He was just stalling her off, poor youngster."

It was already quite dark. I felt Daisy shiver, as she stood with her shoulder close to mine, and a corresponding tremor went through me too.

"Scared?" I asked, putting an ostentatious, protective, male arm around her waist.

"No, chilly. Winter's on the way. I hate it, don't you? Summer's such a swell time of year."

"That reminds me, Daisy. I'd like one more look at that ruined farm, before it's snowed under. Let's take a picnic up there some Sunday afternoon soon and poke around, providing I'm still at large."

"Good notion," she said. "I'll do it if you'll promise to ask Biddy and Dr. Alling those questions, in the morning."

"All right, if I get a decent chance."

The chance came easily in Biddy's case. I was taking two regular meals a day still at Dr. Alling's, but usually had breakfast with Biddy, partly to try to give her a cheery send-off for each day. Over my third cup of coffee I said, "By the way, Biddy, they'll be trying to account for where some of us were, that night when Wyck disappeared. I want to get my own story straight, and make sure I don't pull any boners. Did you see me when I was lying around unconscious? They'll have to take somebody else's word for what I was doing then."

"No, Mr. David. I come home and found not a sowl in the

house, at all. They'd already taken ye to the hospital. But before all that, before it—happened—Dr. Alling comes in, lookin' funny at me, and asks how Mike is. On the way home, he was, he said. I was still up, doin' a bit of sewin'. I was too upset in me nerves to sleep. He says, 'You go out, Mrs. Connell, and take a walk. I'll watch Mike for ye,' he says. 'What ye need is to get yer mind off him, for a half of an hour, and thin ye'll sleep,' he says. So I did that, and when I come back, there was nobody there. And I run to the hospital, and they—they told me thin."

"What had been the trouble, that you asked Dr. Alling to come?"

"It was himself that came, without askin'. He said he'd been workin' late at the school, like the night before, and thought he'd stop by before goin' to bed."

With that perfectly ingenuous account for a starter, I went on to Dr. Alling's private laboratory. He seemed preoccupied, and scarcely acknowledged my "Good morning." I fiddled around with some notes, cleared my throat a couple of times, and was putting a sheet of paper in the typewriter when he looked up.

"Saunders," he said, his attitude as brisk as it had been preoccupied at first, "I'm called out of town for a day or two, on the most urgent business. Kent tells me you're subpœnaed for tomorrow's inquest. Everybody in town who has a knowledge of embalming is in some degree a suspect in this case. The job was badly done, with insufficient fluid, so even the students who have only a theoretical knowledge of the process are under suspicion. I am going to ask you to keep your eyes and ears open for me, during the public part of the procedure. I have Dr. Kent's permission for you to make a transcript of the report. Please do that as soon as it is prepared, as I am not sure how soon I shall return; but when I do, I shall want it at once.

"This unfortunate affair involves much more than a few individuals. The very existence of this school is threatened. I've given my whole life, Saunders, to the task of making it possible for the country regions of this state to have the best of general practitioners. Last spring, before the legislature adjourned, I went down twice as you probably realize and had the utmost difficulty in killing a bill for investigation, in committee."

He rose, his hands shaking with agitation. I wished Daisy could be there to see and hear him as he continued, "These men don't know what they do! For the sake of a few foolish notions they're willing to risk shutting off the fountainhead of health of this state. Good young doctors won't come here from other schools, to work for less than a pittance in our small towns. We'd get only the dregs, that way. As it now is, we can train men to go back to their home communities, men who couldn't afford to go anywhere else to get their training. Well, the legislature won't meet again till next February, when this may have blown over, unless the governor calls a special session. I'm going down, prepared to do something that is against my deepest moral convictions, Saunders, in the hope that it will keep that man Tolland from calling upon the governor for a special session, which he threatens to do in this telegram."

He picked up the yellow sheet, but it fell at once from his trembling fingers. "I'm prepared to readmit his nephew, Prendergast, over the unanimous negative decision of my own faculty. I asked them privately to do it last spring, after I had had several conferences with Tolland. They refused, on the just grounds that the boy would make a doctor unworthy of our standards. Well, I shall require them to vote favorably, and we shall turn out one bad doctor, if it will save the school."

Having got that out of his system, he quieted, and spoke more normally. "Be very careful what you say at the inquest. Dr. Kent is a superbly upright man. He will do his duties unflinchingly. Their very nature has given him no experience of the fact that meting out exact justice to one may be a bitter injustice to hundreds. Therefore, I must caution you to try to be a perfect witness. Answer his questions in the simplest possible fashion embodying all that he asks for. I advise you to volunteer nothing at this stage.

"Working with me, you have gathered a great many facts about Dr. Wyck that are unknown to others. It would be unwise, for example, for you to tell him what you told me about Dr. Wyck's talk of devils to Mike Connell. If his questions make the answer unavoidable, give it. But there are three reporters up from Boston this morning who would seize upon such a minor, chance factor as that for a most dangerously sensational story. The average newspaper reader simply does not realize that the study of demonology is merely an old-fashioned way of describing necessary researches into a vexing phase of psychiatry. The newspapers would make it into a Roman holiday. Even for the sake of those who are investigating the crime as such, it would be unfortunate if certain false leads were encountered too early. Later on, the time will come when you and I can speak. But I hope you share my sincere conviction that there are features of this crime which cannot possibly be resolved by the usual public methods.

"Ah, and one more thing. Be very sure that Daisy Towers is similarly cautioned. You two have been seen together a lot recently, and if she knows as much as she usually does about what happens in this town, it may be that she already has more facts on hand than the coroner will learn. Have I made myself clear?"

I was thus at last confronted with a perfect excuse, not only to get an answer to Daisy's question of the night before, but also to invite a showdown on the problem that had perplexed me since spring.

"I think so," I answered, resolving to risk it, "but there's one specific thing. I gather that the murder was committed on the night of Wyck's disappearance, and that the suspects will be asked for alibis. If I am technically a suspect, how far should I go in describing my own whereabouts between the faculty meeting and the time I was taken to the hospital?"

"My general remarks hold good for that, as well as everything else. Tell no more than necessary to establish your whereabouts, and only as much as you are asked for."

I went on doggedly. "Should I confess that my clothes were ripped and my face bruised when I came into your presence, and explain why? or should I let it be assumed that my condition, when I arrived at the hospital, was all due to Mike's mauling?"

"I make no special cases at all, Saunders," he said half-impatiently. "Give the briefest possible truthful answer to anything you're asked. If I am called on the stand later on, and asked to describe your appearance upon arrival, I shall tell just what I remember of it, no less, no more." He paused, and added, "But —I do not foresee the likelihood of being asked."

I was so perplexed by this attitude that I quite forgot to press on to the question of whether or not he had come in answer to a call from Biddy. Later it seemed hardly necessary, as her testimony had corroborated the fact that there had been no such phone call recorded, and it was not conceivable that she would have left Mike alone, after midnight, to fetch a physician in any other way, when there was a phone in the house.

Dr. Alling picked up his hat and said, "I'm driving down to Portland. Expect me back any time after tomorrow noon. If my stay is extended, I shall write. You've got several days' work on these slides, to keep you busy."

For the rest of the day I occupied myself by preparing glass mounts or slides of tissues taken from the various monsters born during the summer, to permit the body cells to be studied under a microscope. They were prepared by an elaborate technic for coagulating the proteins, and then differentially staining parts of individual cells. Finally, they had to be rendered transparent by immersion in various oils.

Later I examined carefully the slides of tissues taken from the fused lower extremities of the symmeli. The ordinarily delicate skin was thickened and scaly—and the small, newly formed sweat glands, usually so numerous, were sparse and in many places absent. In a normal newborn infant bone has begun to form, but these creatures showed instead only a curious embryonic type of cartilage, as though something had not only interfered with the usual progression of cell growth, but had actually influenced it to differentiate in a negative direction. The muscular structures were similarly primitive, subhuman. Not knowing the real source, one would have called these tissues from an extinct creature, midway between the lower forms and man, rather than what they probably were—atavistic flesh from a human type modified by obscure and powerful forces.

I no longer wondered that Prexy was so fascinated by the elusive causation of such results. It was that ideal type of investigation which, impractical in itself, might lead toward truly revolutionary consequences. Determination of these factors, and their control, would not only aid in suppressing the birth of monsters, which are rare in any event, but could be used to alter the direction of human evolution, or to quicken its progress toward the utopia of which we dream. By the same token, in unscrupulous hands, such findings could be turned to the most terrifyingly evil uses.

Late in the afternoon my thoughts were running riot with the implications of the theme, and I decided to go out for a short walk to cool off. On the way down I heard a noise in the basement, and investigated. It proved to have been made by the sheriff, who was still poking around for clews and fingerprints in the vault.

"You, hey?" he said, thrusting out his neck and peering shrewdly. "D'ye know any old saws?"

"Some," I said, trying to meet his annoying suspicion with levity.

"Yeah, so do I, Mister—yeah, Mister—Saunders, ain't it? I was just thinkin' of one. Funny, and you comin' right along like that."

He turned and puttered some more, and then said, "Yes, yes. Old saw, but a true one. Murderers haunt the scene o' the crime."

CHAPTER XVIII

Sheriff Palmer's conduct toward me probably had no special significance. He was a typical back-country arm of the law, and his experience came from the nasty types of crime that are committed by back-country people—axe murders and the like—crimes of sudden fury that leave a trail of obvious clews. It was therefore his habit to turn upon everyone a knowing air that might be perfectly successful in frightening some newly-made criminal into a confession, on the spot.

So it was not a fear of the sheriff, but rather of the coroner, that made me sleep uneasily. Dr. Kent was a different kind of person altogether, an officer not only of the county, but of the state. Several times a year he was called from Altonville to make expert analyses of the organs of persons who had died under suspicious circumstances. His experience, therefore, was the opposite of the sheriff's, in kind, and was exactly suited to the discovery of whatever could be found out about this most baffling murder. As I dressed and ate a leisurely breakfast, I was under no illusions that the inquest, set for 9:30 A.M., would be anything other than a tense ordeal.

My agitation was in nowise lessened when, just as I was planning to leave, a deputy came to serve a subpœna upon Biddy, who was thrown at once into a panic of alarm. She pleaded with me to tell "the judge" that she knew nothing about "that old divil," but I had to explain to her that the legal service of papers made it necessary for her to come and say this herself. When finally she agreed, it was only on the condition that she be given time "to put on a daycint rag or two." The tardy service made that reasonable, but the deputy told me I could not be excused for waiting, as it was now 9:25 o'clock.

When I reached the town hall, the sheriff placed me in a small cubicle next to the magistrate's courtroom. Charlie was already there, wearing the first starched collar I had ever seen on him; it was badly wilted from perspiration, although the day did not seem warm. When the door was closed upon us, he began to bewail at length the fact that he had ever settled in Altonville, and before long was wishing that he had never got back from the war alive.

"Don't be a fool, Charlie," I said. "Anyway, I'm in dutch as much as you are, certainly."

"No, you're not, doc," he said. "I'm the only one that could 'a' opened that place, after it was sealed up. The sheriff looked over all that packin' I pulled out o' the door. Covered with fingerprints, and every one of 'em mine. If anybody else had of changed it, after I sealed it up, there'd be some other prints, or at least mine would 'a' been smooched out, if he'd 'a' used gloves. All them nice white lead joints I put on the leaky places in the chlorine pipes, every one o' them had my fingerprints, and nobody else's. The sheriff says I'm gonna hang. Christ, doc, I didn't do it. I didn't do a thing."

"Don't pay any attention to the sheriff, Charlie," I advised. "He tries to scare everybody into a confession, that way. He's done it with me too."

"No kiddin', doc?" He made a great effort to feel comforted.

Just then Marjorie Wyck was shown in. Her conduct was at an opposite extreme from Charlie's—her "Good morning" precise and unemotional. Without further words she sat down and abstracted herself from us and from the situation as completely as if we had all disappeared. I could not detect, on her almost classically molded features, the faintest flicker of emotion. The social code of a town such as Altonville makes the wearing of mourning a formality too sacred for personal choice to oppose. Yet she wore as usual a dress ultra-fashionable in its very simplicity, of russet-brown stuff. As if for deliberate contrast, she carried a string shopping bag, empty except for a book, just as if she had stopped in on the way to the grocery store. I had a weird mental image of her, casually and abstractedly going about the business of embalming her own father, with no more actual attention than she would pay to the preparation of a chicken to roast.

This bizarre vision was broken when a deputy came to summon me before the coroner and his jury. As I was leaving by the inner door, Biddy Connell was shown in at the outer one, mumbling and protesting. "Mr. David," she cried, hurrying up to me, "tell thim I didn't have anything to do with——"

I turned in time to place my finger on her lips and say, "Just answer the questions they ask you, Biddy. Don't spend any time saying what you didn't do. Promise?"

"Oh, all right then," she said, flouncing down in a chair, her new dress bulging sadly in the back, where she had missed a couple of buttons. My last glimpse as I turned again to leave was of Charlie, staring at Biddy with his eyes positively popping.

The door closed behind me. Dr. Kent smiled reassuringly and motioned me to a chair. The jurors were grouped at his left. At his right sat the sheriff and the town clerk. Two of the jurors, a haberdasher's clerk and a fruit seller, I recognized. The other four were strangers.

When I had been sworn, Dr. Kent said, "Mr. Saunders, please tell these gentlemen, simply but fully, the circumstances leading to the discovery of Dr. Wyck's body."

I was annoyed to realize that my voice sounded shrill and unnatural as I told what has already been set down in this narrative, beginning when Charlie hailed me, and omitting, of course, any reference to my thoughts or suspicions. It did not seem to take long. The coroner asked a few questions to clarify points of which I had already spoken. He paused and studied the paper before him, looking toward me once or twice, and then pursed his lips. I steeled myself to meet an embarrassing query, but he only said, "Thank you. You will remain where you are. I may have further questions for you."

As no other witness was permitted to stay after finishing his testimony, I had the choice of thinking either that an exception was being made for me at Dr. Alling's request or that I was the most suspected of all, slated for a final cross-examination in which a knowledge of the other witnesses' depositions might help to embarrass and entangle me.

Marjorie was the second to be called. She was asked to explain what she knew of her father's whereabouts on the day preceding his disappearance, and was also asked to tell in detail about receipt of his clothing, a week later, and to describe the contents of the bundle. She answered with coolness and brevity, concluding that she had last seen her father at about twenty minutes to ten on the evening of April 3rd, and had heard footsteps, which she took for his, descending the porch stairs a few minutes later. Her description of the contents of the bundle, except for one or two trivial omissions, coincided with the official listing made by the sheriff. When Dr. Kent referred to this document to refresh her memory, she agreed with it in its entirety, and gave the opinion that she knew of nothing else which might have been on her father's person just before his death. Incidentally, the two blue books and the missing $500, clews known to Dr. Alling, Daisy and myself, were not referred to at any time during the inquiry, or in any of its documents.

Dr. Kent next asked Marjorie whether she knew of any enemy of her father who might have had reason to kill him. She answered frankly that to the best of her knowledge he had had neither friends nor enemies, but that he never had discussed personal relations with her, nor referred to them in any way. The coroner then requested her to name those who most frequently had visited Dr. Wyck. She replied that, not counting minor calls of a business nature, for years no one at all had come to see her father except Dr. Alling.

"You would not have called them friends, Miss Wyck?"

"No," she said, "I don't think I would. They were merely working on the same medical researches."

"Do you know anything of the nature of these researches?" Dr. Kent asked, and my heart skipped a beat or two as she pondered, before answering. "I don't recall ever having heard them say just what it was all about, but from the books father read most often I'd say they were mainly concerned with mental diseases."

Her words, so carefully phrased to be at once truthful and innocuous, put me on the alert for the next question, which was: "Can you tell us where you were between quarter to ten on the evening of April 3, 1932, and eight o'clock of the following morning?"

She said that she had read for about an hour after her father went out, then had gone to bed, and had slept until about eight o'clock the next morning.

Dr. Kent then cleared his throat, and said in an even, monotonous tone, "It is my duty to inquire whether you have any knowledge, or any suspicion, of sexual relationships between your father and any woman within, say, the last five years."

Again she paused before replying. "I have no knowledge of such relations, and any suspicions that I may have ever had have not been in any way substantiated."

The coroner looked relieved. He nodded to the deputy, and said, "Thank you, Miss Wyck. Will you please wait in the anteroom until officially dismissed?"

The next witness was Hos Creel, who tried to expound his theories of the crime but was held rigidly to matters concerning the bundle he had delivered. Then came Charlie Michaud, scowling at the sheriff as if he were to blame.

Charlie's account of the discovery of the corpse was precisely in accordance with my own—so much so that I feared we would be suspected of having drilled each other. He stated that he had padlocked the vault in the evening, in my presence, and had not opened it again before running in the chlorine next day. The rest of his testimony I shall give from the transcript that I consulted later in Dr. Alling's files.

Q. Mr. Michaud, at what time did you actually seal up the vault, and run chlorine into it?

A. Eight o'clock in the morning.

Q. What date?

A. I don't know. It was the day you gave me orders to do it.

Q. That was April 4, 1932, wasn't it?

A. I guess so.

Q. Was anyone else present?

A. You were.

Q. Tell what you remember of the process, and anything else that seems relevant.

A. I packed the door chinks, and you said, 'Let her down from 70 to 50,' and I turned the valve till that much gas had flowed. Then you said to disconnect the tank, and I said my white lead joints would keep it from leaking, and we might as well leave it hooked up. You bet me a box of Pittsburgh stogies it would leak five pounds, so we left it.

Q. The evidence seems to show that I have lost my bet—that is, unless another tank has been substituted, reading 50. Now, Mr. Michaud, could the vault have been opened without your knowledge after it was sealed?

A. Not unless somebody undid the fittings and ran in some more chlorine afterwards. There wasn't a speck of mold on them stiffs.

Q. Sheriff Palmer, you have thoroughly inspected the vault and the apparatuses. Is there any evidence that the vault was opened after it was sealed in my presence by Mr. Michaud at 8:00 A.M., April 4, 1932?

A. (By Sheriff Palmer) No, your honor. The only person that could have opened it was Michaud. And the only person that could have unhooked the pipes was him. All them white lead joints and the stuff that plugged the door was covered with Michaud's fingerprints, and nobody else's.

Q. And no new gas could have been introduced from another tank, sheriff, except by destroying and replacing at least one of those white lead joints?

A. That's right, your honor.

Q. Is this true, in your opinion, Mr. Michaud?

A. (By Charles Michaud) I guess so.

Q. Did you yourself open the vault, or in any way change the chlorinating apparatus between April 4th at 8:00 A.M., this year, and 5:00 P.M. on September 2nd?

A. No. I didn't open it and I didn't change a thing.

Q. In your six years as diener of the medical school have you done all the embalming?

A. I think so.

Q. Who besides yourself have keys to the vault?

A. You have one, and Dr. Alling, and Dr. Wharton, and Dr. Wyck had.

Then came a series of questions, with answers too devious to reproduce verbatim, which revealed that the diener had once been discharged for drunkenness and for selling liquor to students at a fishing shanty which he had maintained with Mike. The complainant had been Dr. Wyck. The diener had been reëmployed on his good behavior, after a few weeks, and there had been no further complaints against him.

The coroner next asked a question that totally surprised me.

"Mr. Michaud, you were a very good friend of Mike Connell's. Tell us how he saved your life during an engagement in Belleau Woods, in 1918."

Charlie replied that Mike had saved twenty-three lives in all by crawling up under pistol fire to bomb a machine-gun squad which, if it had had a few seconds more to get the gun into action, would have wiped them all out.

A number of shrewd questions also established the facts that Charlie had heard rumors that Mike's arm had been unnecessarily amputated and that the diener believed that his friend's madness was a result of the amputation. I saw that a strong case was being built up against the diener, involving both personal malice and the avenging of his chum Mike. By this time Charlie was fully aware of the bad impression he was making, and was sweating more than ever as he nervously twisted in his chair.

"Mr. Michaud," the coroner asked, changing the subject suddenly, "what kind of instrument was it, in your opinion, that was used to murder Dr. Wyck?"

"How should I know?" Charlie yelled, rising to his feet. "I haven't even had a chance to look at the body!"

"Please be more orderly," the coroner admonished. "You have

a right not to answer any question. I have only one more for you. Please tell us where you were from 9:45 P.M. April 3, 1932, until 8:00 A.M. next day."

"I don't have to answer, you say?" Charlie asked. "Then I won't answer that."

The coroner merely nodded and motioned for the next witness, who proved to be Biddy. I shall not try to give any details whatever of her hopelessly muddled answers. She affirmed the great friendship between Mike and Charlie, admitted defiantly that she did not believe the amputation had been necessary, and answered to a direct question that she was by profession a laundress.

When Kent asked "Do you do dry-cleaning?" she replied in the affirmative, but later changed her testimony to indicate that she had thought the reference was to the use of French chalk for removing grease spots. Curiously, Biddy was not asked to account for her whereabouts during the fateful night. Apparently Kent assumed that she had been with Mike all the time and was trying to implicate her only as an accessory, in the laundering and cleaning of Wyck's clothes. It was an added relief to realize that he probably thought that I too had been at home all through the fateful evening, up to the time when I was sent to the hospital. After a few more questions, to clarify points already made, Kent dismissed Biddy and prepared to read the report of the autopsy which he had personally performed upon the cadaver of Gideon Wyck. After a moment or two of hesitation, he requested me to wait with the others in the anteroom.

We sat there through a tense ten minutes or so. Biddy snuffled continually. Charlie had become torpid. Marjorie was reading the latest muck-raking life of Byron. Presently Charlie was called for further examination, and returned a few minutes later with a surly frown on his face. The deputy told Marjorie she could leave if she liked, and beckoned for me to reënter the courtroom.

CHAPTER XIX

To my vast relief, the jurors were filing out. Dr. Kent said, "Mr. Saunders, Dr. Alling requested that I permit you to make a copy of the post-mortem findings. As it will be filed in the town records, where any accredited citizen can inspect it, I see no reason for opposing the request."

I set to work, under the eye of the sheriff, and made the following transcript:[1]

POST-MORTEM EXAMINATION, of the body of Gideon Wyck, M. D., Æ 66/67 years, found dead and embalmed in vault of the Maine State College of Surgery, on Sept. 2, 1932.

External Peculiarities. 1. An incision in the region of the left groin, leading to the femoral artery. (Made presumably to inject embalming fluid.)

2. An ante-mortem puncture wound in the suboccipital region, penetrating the space between the first and second cervical vertebræ, and transecting the spinal cord at this juncture. This wound was presumably inflicted by means of a sharp, scalpel-like instrument in the hands of a person with a knowledge of anatomy.

3. A group of six minute scars in the left antecubital fossa.

4. An ancient scar, ten centimeters in length, in the lower right rectus region of the abdominal wall.

Internal Peculiarities. 1. A carcinomatous growth of medium malignancy at the neck of the bladder, capable of causing death within a year.

2. Early carcinomatous metastasis to the bones of the skull.

---

1 I have left this in its original, highly technical form, as it may thus have added interest for some readers. Its implications are clearly explained for the layman in an early section of the narrative.—ED.

3. Evidence of pronounced internal hemorrhage in skull cavity and spinal cord.

4. An atrophic and scarred area underlying the rectus scar, with adhesions to the peritoneum but outside of the peritoneal cavity.

Chemical Analyses. 1. Analysis of stomach and intestinal contents demonstrates presence of approximately 8 grams of diethylbarbaturic acid (veronal), enough to have caused death when absorbed.
2. Analysis of other organs shows the presence of the above drug and leads to the presumption of a general distribution of the drug, the quantity probably under 4 grams. Enough to indicate possible chronic poisoning. Probably not enough to have caused death.

Cause of Death. Transection of the spinal cord in the region of the first cervical segment, due to a wound inflicted by a sharp instrument. The nature and position of the wound indicate homicide. The other circumstances lend a strong presumption of truth to the idea that the fatal incision was inflicted while the victim was unconscious from the action of the poison.

Time of Death. Due to the time elapsed, and to the fact that embalming must have occurred within four hours after death, no time of death can be determined by anatomical inspection.

Signed,
HATHAWAY KENT, M. D.
Coroner, Alton County.

Witnesses:
  Eliphalet Smith, M. D.
  J. B. Otis.

Probably anticipating that the jury would take a considerable while to deliberate his charge, which by that token must have been a grave and specific one, the coroner went out while I was copying, remarking to the sheriff that he would be back in twenty minutes. The clerk, deputy, and county prosecutor also left. Sheriff Palmer, the only remaining official, paced up and down the hallway from which both courtroom and anteroom opened. Each time, in passing the door, he shot a glance toward me. Despite my knowledge of his attitude of having the goods on everyone, it made me nervous. Might there be an experiment under way, to see whether I would make a true copy? Could it be that they expected me to betray myself by falsifying some detail in the transcript?

With that in mind, I was doubly careful to be accurate to a letter. Presently the sheriff paused, staring hard at me.

"What's that there stuff they use to embalm a stiff?" he asked abruptly.

"A mixture. Glycerin, water, potassium ac——"

"Leave out your hifalutin words. Supposin' we heated some in a pan till it dried, what'd it look like?"

"Like nothing much, I guess."

"Never mind guessin'. What'd be the color of it?"

"I'm not sure. We can go down and find out, if you like."

"All right. Finish your job and let's git movin'."

A few minutes later the coroner returned; but the jury was still deliberating when I left the town hall and accompanied the sheriff to the cellar of the medical school. I put a few drops of embalming fluid in a pyrex evaporating dish, set it over a Bunsen burner, and let it boil dry. The sheriff stared at the hardly discernible remains, grunted as if displeased, and shoved the dish aside.

"Here," he said, "put yer left hand in that stuff. Come on, now, young feller, no crawfishin'."

I dipped my fingers in embalming fluid. "Shake 'em, now," he added. When I had done so he gripped in turn each of my fingers and the thumb, pressing them on a strip of glass which he took from his pocket. This he passed over the flame until traces of moisture dried, and then stared through it toward the window. I held my breath fearing suddenly that I might have left some fingerprint in the vault, after we opened it, with no way of proving that it had not been put there before.

"Naw, it ain't you, and that ain't it," he decided. "Come in here." He took the vault key from his pocket, opened the place, and told me to switch on the light. Then, with great care, he removed the bulb that was in the vault, replaced it with another, and carried his trophy out into the adjacent room.

"Those ain't yours," he said, "which is too damn bad, 'cause if they *was,* we'd have a nice little party, you and me, down Portland way, 'long about Christmas time: a necktie party."[1]

I looked at the bulb, and even in the dim basement could plainly see four whitish prints on it, of three fingers and a thumb.

"What would you say that was, young feller?"

"Putty?" I suggested.

"Do they plug 'em with putty, anywheres, when they embalm 'em?"

I had to admit that putty was not used at all in the process, and began to thank my stars that it was Charlie, not I, who had turned that bulb when we entered the vault.

As if reading my thoughts, the sheriff continued, "Mister Charlie Michaud turned that bulb before you went in, or so both of you *said,* this morning. So I guess those are his prints, wouldn't you say?"

"I should imagine so. It won't take you long to find out."

He thrust his head forward and stared at me, drawling, "I dunno if you're just dumb, or if you're crawfishin'. You better hope you're just dumb. Tell me all over again, what was it our friend Mister Michaud did just before openin' that door."

"He stripped the packing from around it."

The sheriff took a bit of packing from the waste bin in which it still lay, and rolled it between his fingers.

"Nice and black and oily," he commented. "Had it all over his hands. And then, accordin' to you, Mister—I didn't get the name—"

"Saunders."

"Yes—accordin' to you, Mister—Saunders,—with his nice black oily fingers Charlie leaves some fingerprints that look just like putty. Hmm. We ain't allowed to hang 'em for bein' as dumb as that, but they let us put 'em to makin' baskets. Ever see the baskets they weave, down to the booby-hatch? Not bad, some of 'em, considerin'. Now just take a look here."

1 Here again is evidence that the happenings referred to did not actually take place in Maine, where capital punishment has been abolished.—ED.

He pulled a flashlight from his pocket and turned it upon the bulb. Looking closely, I could see a set of fainter, brownish prints, corresponding with, and partly overlapping, the others.

"Here, Sherlock Holmes," the sheriff mocked, "have the hull works, while you're at it." He proffered a magnifying glass, and I used it in spite of his mockery. It was easy to see that the faint brown lines ran on top of the white ones. It was completely obvious, too, that the prints were made by two different persons.

"Them brown ones are Michaud's and they went on after the vault door was opened, this fall. I was kinda hopin' that the others would be—yours, Mister—Thingumabob, left there in a hurry last spring. The last feller out of that place was in an all-fired hurry t' git out, and he twisted the bulb instead o' takin' time to run back the other way to the switch. Or do you think I'm wrong, perhaps, Mister—ahem—Saunders, isn't it? Yes, Saunders. Got to remember that name."

"No," I said, trying to show neither irritation nor uncertainty, "I think you're right, sheriff. I snapped the switch once, and the light didn't go on. Then Charlie turned the bulb, and it didn't go on. I snapped the switch again, and it did light up. That left the switch back where it was all summer. Therefore it had been in the 'on' position all summer, and the bulb must have been turned off by twisting it, as you say."

"Got it down pretty pat, haven't you? Little bit too pat, mebbe. That is, from a jury's point of view. Well, come on, Sherlock, let's mosey back and see if I have to turn you loose or put you in the hoosegow. Oh, wait a minute, while I git the stencil on the gas tank. Let's see, 01014."

When we returned, the coroner's jury was still deliberating, and it continued to do so for the better part of an hour, during which I had the opportunity to reflect upon unexpected features of the post-mortem findings. At the time they did not make sense at all, and I could not see why the wound in the back of the neck could be definitely called the cause of death if the body contained so much veronal. The likeliest explanation which occurred to me was that whoever had drugged Wyck had wanted to get on quickly with the embalming, and had severed the spinal cord at this vulnerable point in order to make certain that the incision for embalming would not shock a comatose body back into consciousness.

It was well past noon when at last there came a knock, and the jury was readmitted. The deputy then went to the anteroom and returned with Biddy and Charlie. The foreman handed a folded paper to the clerk, who read:

"We find that the cause of death of Gideon Wyck was premeditated murder, since he could not have stabbed himself in the back of his own neck. From verbal evidence given by Marjorie Wyck and Charles Michaud we find that death occurred between the hours of 9:45 P.M., April 3, 1932, and about 6:00 A.M., April 4, 1932, since it would have taken some time to embalm the body afterward, and place it in a vault which was sealed in the presence of a witness at 8:00 A.M. on the 4th. We accept the coroner's recommendation that a bill of indictment be drawn up and presented to a grand jury by the county prosecutor, accusing Charles Michaud of the murder of Gideon Wyck, and accusing Bridget Connell as an accessory before and after the fact."

Charlie blinked, stood up, pulled off his dickey tie and limp collar, pushed both into his coat pocket, and sat down again. Since his compromise with the amenities, in the wearing of these ornaments, had not saved him from a dangerous plight, his mind apparently dictated the only immediate relief possible.

Biddy had huddled down in her chair at the sound of the word murder. Then she turned in bewilderment toward me and asked, "What's that he's sayin' about me, Mr. David? What does it mean?"

The coroner said, "Mrs. Connell, you are accused of helping Charles Michaud to plan the murder of Dr. Wyck, and of helping him to evade justice afterward."

"I didn't. I did no such thing," she screamed, and began to sob.

"Sheriff Palmer," Dr. Kent concluded, as soon as he could make himself heard, "you will hold the accused as material witnesses, pending the filing of the indictments."

I tried to comfort Biddy, and promised to do everything I could to help in proving her innocence. Dr. Kent had come up, and must have heard this declaration; but I was glad that he had, for it provided me at last with a public excuse for being thoroughly interested in the case.

As the sheriff was conducting Biddy and Charlie from the room, toward the two cells that were somewhere downstairs, he turned to me and said, "Well, we've had a pleasant time, ain't we, Mister—let's see—yes, Saunders. Hope we'll be seein' some more of each other. Guess we will, before we're done, hey?"

My head felt like a balloon as I left the town hall. For about five minutes I reveled in mere freedom and thoughtlessness. Then the reaction came from the pressing knowledge that Biddy was under arrest, with no husband or other relative to help her. If her witless way of testifying before the coroner was an indication of what could be expected in an actual trial, the county prosecutor would have no difficulty at all in making Biddy swear that she ate flatirons for breakfast.

Knowing that Daisy would be lunching, I hurried to her house and caught her leaving early for the hospital, where she had hoped to get quicker news of the inquest. We walked the back way, and I had time to tell her of all the important factors during the twenty minutes before she had to go on duty.

After lunching at the dog cart, I crossed to the Connells' and typed out the post-mortem findings. The verdict of the coroner's jury I added from memory, and made duplicate carbons of the combined report for Daisy and for myself. A little later, she herself called me from the hospital to whisper over the phone the news that Charlie and Biddy had been bound over to the Superior Court, which would commence its sessions on the third Tuesday in September. It later turned out that she had learnt this from a phone call by Dr. Kent, from his office in the school building to the attorney-general.

Next I went myself to look up Dr. Kent, who was still at his office, and asked him bluntly what my rights were in arranging for Biddy's defense. He replied that I could apply in her name for a writ of habeas corpus, to free her, but advised me not to do so because a review of her testimony would show multiple assumptions of perjury, whereas the grand jury probably would deal only with the deduced facts. He suggested that my best course would be to retain a competent lawyer for her, and to place all decisions unreservedly in the lawyer's hands.

This was in itself a dilemma, as I had only ten or twelve dollars in the world, and I did not want to be responsible for drawing upon her nest-egg of $1000, which she had finally received from Mike's accident insurance, despite Dr. Wyck's failure to certify the injury. Then I remembered that a fellow named Craig who had been a senior at State when I was a sophomore, had recently hung out his shingle in Phillipston, fifteen miles down the railroad. On the chance that he might be willing to take the case more for glory than for profit, I rang him up, and he agreed to drive to Altonville next morning. The sheriff permitted me to give Biddy this reassurance.

CHAPTER XX

With a whole house on my hands, if a small one, I called Daisy to suggest that we spend the evening in the Connells' gaudy front parlor, studying the findings of the inquest. She arrived before eight o'clock. We pulled down the shades, locked the doors, and spread our documents on a table.

It must be remembered that persons in a small town, in a house somewhat removed from the general group of buildings, are apt to have even less privacy than a city dweller in the middle of an apartment with hundreds of inmates. No-one in the city would think twice about seeing a strange face; but in Altonville you could tell a stranger almost by the manner of his walk, before his features became visible. Once or twice a year a seller of indecent books would drift into town, for example, trying his best to look like a medical student. It couldn't be done. One such fellow told Jap Ross that he had different clothes to wear at every college and school on his itinerary, and yet knew perfectly well that he never quite looked the part. There were subtle matters of local custom that betrayed the stranger in every small town he visited.

That was why we were cautious, and did not set about our business until we were sure that there were no crannies between the shades and the windowsill, and had tried the doors a second time to make sure they were locked.

"Are you still clinging to the idea that it's Alling?" I asked, with just a touch of sarcasm.

"I'm forgetting everything I've thought, Dave, or trying to. Something fresh ought to come out of this cryptogram, if you'll be good enough to explain it to me."

"Here goes," I agreed, taking the post-mortem sheet and considering its paragraphs in order. "Incision number one means nothing special. You've got to cut a body over some artery to embalm it, and that's the handiest place. Incision number two is right here." I showed the spot on the back of her neck with my finger, and she jumped at the touch. "Steady. Now, the head must have been bent well forward to separate those two vertebras sufficiently for the knife to enter between them. Also, there would have to be a straight thrust and then a sidewise movement to sever the spinal cord. Like this, see?"

She nodded with a shiver, and I continued, "Paragraph number three—the six minute scars. The left antecubital fossa is here, just below the bend of the elbow, on the inside surface of the left arm."

"What might they be, Dave?"

"I've still got a hunch that he really did give himself blood transfusions, and that's the precise spot where you do it. Transfusion needles would leave something of a scar. A hypodermic wouldn't, unless he used dope with a dirty needle, but a doctor ought to know better than that. Anyway, the number of scars is significant. I'll tell you why after we get on a bit. Now this abdominal scar——"

"For appendicitis, probably, or gall stones," she interrupted. "Next."

"Hold your horses," I admonished. "What it says farther along makes it seem obvious that the incision didn't go on through the inner membrane, the peritoneum, to get at the internal organs, so it was neither of those. Let it go for the present.

"Now for internals. The first one means he was dying of cancer, in about as painful a spot as it could appear. No wonder he gave himself transfusions, and took dope, and looked so sick toward the end. I remember catching a glimpse of him in a mirror, that last afternoon, and his face was just knotted up with pain. He didn't know I was looking, and, when I spun around, he was actually grinning. He was an old so-and-so, but he had nerve, all right."

"Granted. What about point two of the internals?"

"That substantiates another obvious suspicion. He had cancer of the skull, too, and it probably pressed on the brain, and slowly drove him crazy. Point number three, internal hemorrhage, gives the reason why they claim it was the cut that killed him, rather than the poison."

"I don't understand."

"Well, when the heart's still beating, there's a high pressure of blood in the arteries. In an arterial hemorrhage, blood is actually being *pumped* out of the wound. Blood from a vein just trickles out, but from an artery it spurts. Therefore, if the heart had stopped beating even a few seconds before the big artery in the spinal column was cut, the blood would have seeped slowly for a little way into the surrounding tissues and would have clotted quickly. But the face showed a convulsive death, which means that the heart made a few last violent beats, after the artery was cut, forcing blood into the skull and spinal cord. You see, it was a clean incision, with a very sharp knife, which wouldn't have given the blood much chance to flow out through the wound, especially if the blade remained in it."

"Wouldn't the embalming fluid have washed out the clotted blood?"

"It isn't likely, especially when insufficient fluid was used, as in this case. Now, this fourth paragraph, about what was under the belly scar, I can't understand at all, so let's go on for the present to the analyses."

"I can figure them out," she interposed. "Somebody was wise to the fact that he'd been taking veronal regularly to relieve the pain of the cancer. That must have been the drug you smelled on his breath. The murderer gave him a big dose, with the idea that an autopsy would show traces all through the body, from chronic use, and would therefore make it seem more likely that he took an overdose himself by mistake, or else to commit suicide. Then the murderer got panicky, and used the knife to make sure of things, after Wyck had passed out. He realized too late that the suicide theory was ruined, and then bethought himself of embalming the body and putting it in the vault. I think the last point is our first clew, don't you?"

"You mean we've got to start by considering who might have known that the vault was already locked up, ready for sealing in the morning, and wasn't likely to be inspected again?"

"Of course. Now, who could have known that?"

"Well, Charlie, and Coroner Kent, and D. Saunders, God help him, all knew for certain. Any of the students might have known. They all realize that practically all of the stiffs are taken out in the fall, to be chopped up by the anatomy class, and that it takes till spring to fill it up again with stiffs for next year, arriving one or two at a time. I think it's a tradition that the vault is always sealed up on the day when final inspection of dissections is made, as a symbol of now or never."

"All right. What about the other teachers?"

"They're more likely to have known than the students."

"Well, that doesn't help much. It just narrows it down to the whole school. Now, what about keys to the padlock?"

"Charlie testified that extra keys were in the possession of Kent, and the anatomy prof, and Wyck himself—" I paused uncomfortably.

"And?"

"And—Alling."

"Alling. I thought so."

"But before you make too much of that, Daisy, remember that Wyck had his key on his person, and the murderer returned it with the bundle of clothes. In the meanwhile, he could have used it to put Wyck's carcass in the vault—probably did."

"If he knew what it was a key to," she commented drily. "Well, let that pass for the present. Let's see that other sheet."

I picked up a copy of the sheriff's deposition concerning the bundle returned by mail. We studied it together:

The said bundle was received in a sack made up by mail sorters on a train en route from Boston to Portland at about noon on April 10th, and transferred unopened at Portland to the 4:14 P.M. train for Altonville. The sack was opened at 5:00 A.M., April 11th, at the Altonville post office, and delivered to the Wyck residence at about 10:30 A.M. by Hosea Creel, carrier.

The said bundle was supposedly mailed after closing hours on the evening of the 9th of April, 1932, at the main Boston post office. The postmarks are too smudged to make certain of this, but T. J. Flick, clerk at the said post office, noticed a bundle having twice the right postage, like this one, the next morning. The bundle bore no sender's return address.

The hat and woolen garments in the said bundle smelled strong of cleaning fluid. The shirt, underwear, socks and handkerchiefs had been washed and ironed, but there were no laundry marks on any of them. The shoes had been shined.

The said bundle contained a complete outfit, including a gray tweed suit, blue overcoat, Paris garters, collar buttons, and long necktie, and included the following other articles, viz:

Hamilton watch, serial No. 23,026, with hands stopped at 11:48, and print of Dr. Wyck's right thumb inside back inner case.

Key ring, with pass key to all doors in medical school except offices, key to own office therein, key to own front door, key to padlock of school vault, two keys for Yale locks, both unidentified. Neither fits any door in school or hospital or Wyck's house.

Wallet containing two five-dollar bills, three one-dollar bills, two silver quarters, one silver dime. Also, membership cards to the Joe Zero Club, Romeo's, and the Athlete's Rest, all of which being Boston speakeasies known to police there. Also, a snapshot photograph of Marjorie Wyck in a bathing suit, and a slip of paper with the following numbers on it:

> Jl 16/300
> Sp 3/400
> Nv 1/400
> Dc 23/500
> Jn 29/500
> Fb 24/500

Silver pocket knife, with dull blades.

Fountain pen, made by Moore.

Leather cigarette case containing two Old Golds.

No fingerprints on anything, except the one in the watch-case.

"All right," said Daisy, "who was in Boston on the evening of the ninth?"

"Well, the fact that we know one person was, doesn't mean that others mightn't have been."

"Sir, your logic is irrefutable. But the fact that the one person who was in Boston is named—Alling is hardly to be ignored."

"He went down to see Vladimir because of the failure of an appointment made two weeks before Wyck was killed."

"Who's Vladimir?"

"The monkey gland wizard."

"Oh yes. Well, he could have taken a bundle along even if he was going to see Peggy Hopkins Joyce. What was he doing with Vladimir? I thought he was a high-grade quack."

"Not quite. He has something of a black eye because he spends most of his time keeping a crew of rich old sybarites in working order."

"And what, pray tell, is a sybarite?"

"A guy who burns his candle in the middle, as well as at both ends."

"O. K. Let's get back to work. You haven't said what Alling was doing with Vladimir."

"Just having a conference on the general subject of transplanting glands. Say, I wonder—"

"Yes, yes, go on."

"No, it's in the wrong place, of course. I was just wondering whether that atrophied mess under Wyck's abdominal scar could have been an unsuccessful graft—of some kind."

"You might do a little research into the chances. Now, what about this stopped watch? Does that indicate the time of the murder? It's within the period set by the coroner's jury."

"Yes, but it may be merely the time it ran down, nearly half a day later. We'd have to find out whether the spring was all relaxed, or whether the works were broken."

"All right, Dave. That'll have to wait, and so will the two keys as yet unaccounted for. What about the thirteen dollars and sixty cents? If Ted Gideon did it for the missing five hundred, wouldn't he have taken it all? I think it's still the best explanation that Ted was given the five hundred as a farewell present. Now, how about these other items?"

"I don't see anything significant in them. The speakeasy cards tell us what we already knew, that he was an old rounder and probably did some chippy-chasing when he got down to town. The speakeasy proprietors told Dr. Alling that they hadn't seen him for a year, which isn't so strange, considering the condition of his innards. Maybe they told the truth."

"Maybe they did," she agreed. "Now, what do you make of this slip of paper, with the numbers on it?"

"Well," I said, "that just strengthens the thesis that Mike wasn't raving when he said he'd given blood to keep Wyck alive. That's the same slip of paper I told you about, the one that was in the copy of Frazer. Remember? That book Wyck was so anxious to get right back. When we brought it to him, the morning before he was killed, he looked first thing to see if the paper was still in the book. He probably put it in his wallet as soon as we were out of sight."

"Why?" she asked, when I paused impressively.

"Because he was deliberately hiding the fact that he was in ill health; and that paper was a record of blood transfusions from Mike to him. Notice that there are six entries, one for each of those six minute scars."

"So far so good," she said, approvingly.

"All right. Look here: Jl, Sp, Nv, Dc, Jn, Fb. What do they mean? July, September, November, December, January, February, obviously,—all in the proper order. And look at the dates. Those figures before the slanting bars are obviously the day of the month—all between 1 and 29. See, the interval between each pair of dates is shorter than the last one. He needed blood more and more often. He started out with a modest 300 cc., first time, and increased it to a full 500 cc. before he was through—the most they ever take from one donor."

"Clever lad," she said. "I'm getting to be proud to know you."

"Now look," I added, producing my transcript of Mike's official record card as a donor at the hospital. "October 8th, Mike gave blood to a guy who died right away. That was halfway between the September and November donations to Wyck, roughly speaking. Wyck gave him only three weeks to recuperate, that time. The next official one was February 16th, two weeks and a half after the previous donation to Wyck. Following that, Wyck waited the minimum time required, hardly a week, before taking another pint, on the 24th. It takes about a week for a donor to get back to normal, you see. Then, on March 7th, eleven days later, there was another official transfusion, split between Peter Tompkins and Joe Baker—and Mike hadn't really recovered from that one when he lost his arm, and had to quit the donor racket."

"I see. That cut off Wyck's secret blood supply just about the time he'd be needing another one—and he began to look paler and paler, soon after that—more and more anæmic. Looks like an airtight solution, but where does it get us?"

"Well, for one thing it tells why he resorted to veronal to keep going. I imagine that about that time he must have realized that he was pretty nearly done for, and that it wasn't any use to go on with the transfusions from another donor. The first woman he had been experimenting on was already in the hospital—the wretched Sarah—and he probably knew that Alling would come down on him like a ton of brick as soon as the results of the experiments began to appear in quantity—" I paused again.

"So what?"

"So why wasn't it a clear case of suicide?"

"Fine!" she said derisively, "but even the coroner's jury points out here that he couldn't have stabbed himself in the back of his own neck."

"No," I admitted, "but that's where Muriel comes in—Muriel or Ted. Muriel may not have realized the full meaning of his words on the bridge, when he said it was all over, that night. She probably thought he just meant that the experiments were ended. She or Ted may have thought Wyck was just asleep, when he had taken an overdose of veronal, and one or the other of them seized that opportunity to stick a knife in his neck, when he was nice and quiet."

"And where did all this happen?" she inquired sarcastically.

"Out on this hillside."

"So, instead of leaving him there, where he might not be found for months, they brought him back through the middle of town and lugged him into the school building. Bravo!"

"Yes, they did," I insisted, clinging to my nice theory, "because he wouldn't be found for months in the vault, either, and there'd be a much better chance that somebody else would be suspected."

Daisy shook her head. "I'm willing to wager he was murdered in the school building. Down in the preparation room, no doubt," she said. "Muriel was back in the dormitory before midnight, that night, and there usually are people in the school building up till around midnight. I don't think she had anything to do with it. It might have been Ted. He probably drove both of them back to town, left Wyck at the school building, and then sneaked back later to do the job. That is, if he really did it. I'd be more inclined to think it was your friend Prendergast, or sweet demure little Marjorie Wyck."

I had forgotten about Prendergast's failure to sleep in his own rooms, after the faculty meeting. There had been no reason to suspect him of anything, during the long period when I was half-willing to believe that Wyck must be still alive; but the discovery of the cadaver in the school building, plus the attendant evidence that the murder had been committed on the very night of Prendergast's absence from home, was certainly reason enough for demanding his alibi. As for Marjorie, she was a sufficiently mysterious person to be suspected on general principles, even if there was not a shred of direct evidence against her. It was perhaps for that very reason that I felt an inclination to discount the possibility that it had been she. She might have been the master mind, directing Muriel and Ted; but we had no definite charge against her except that she had lied when she denied being at home at the time of Ted's call to invite her to accompany him in his flight.

When I made this objection, Daisy said, "What about the fact that her picture was in old Gideon's wallet?"

"What's funny about a father carrying a picture of his own daughter around with him?" I objected.

"Nothing whatever. And that's what makes it seem a bit funny for Wyck to do it. You wouldn't expect him to do anything as usual as that."

"Therefore—what?"

"She was reading a life of Byron in the town hall. It may not mean a thing, Dave. But you know what the charge was against Byron when they ran him out of England."

"That's one too many, Daisy. I won't believe that of Marjorie."

"I don't ask you to believe she condoned anything. But look at the situation—a beautiful girl living alone for ten years with a father who's admittedly an old rake. He's at least half mad, and carries her picture—in a bathing suit, mind you—in his wallet, as probably the one and only sentimental gesture of his career."

"I still don't believe it."

"Well, I believe, under the circumstances, that Marjorie Wyck could perfectly well have come to a point where she felt she would be a great deal safer if her father quietly ceased to exist. He could hardly have kept his sickness from her. She could have felt the added justification of easing him of a messy, slow death from cancer."

"Very well, then, do you think she could have known how to sever that spinal cord so neatly?"

"Yes, I do. When we were in high school together, she was the smartest zoology student we had, and she used to claim she was going to study medicine herself. For all we know, she may have gone on studying under her father's direction, or at least in her father's books."

"Yeah, there's somethin' to that," cut in a drawling voice. Daisy and I jumped up and turned to see the sheriff standing in the doorway. "There now, don't disturb yourselves. Go right ahead. Mrs. Connell just asked me to get the stuff that's in her second bureau drawer, second from the top. She said you'd bring it, Mister—yes, yes—Mister Saunders. But I said I wouldn't think o' troublin' you, so she gave me the key to the back door, in case you wasn't in."

Daisy and I looked at each other, wondering how long he had

been standing there and how much he had heard. We were not comforted when he continued, "Yes, yes. Old saws are trustworthy. There's wisdom comes even out o' the mouths of babes. What do ya say, babe?"

CHAPTER XXI

It turned out that the sheriff's errand was perfectly legitimate. By some blessed chance I had the wit to make sure of this by insisting on accompanying him back to the jail to see how Biddy was getting along. We left our documents just where they were, so as to deny him the satisfaction of thinking that we had been intentionally secretive. Nevertheless, I resolved to hide my private papers more securely than before. The ones over which Sheriff Palmer had found us speculating were all essentially public documents anyway. While driving to the town hall, he tried diligently, or pretended to try, to make a date with Daisy, assuring her that his wife could not object to what she never knew.

Some law or other required, sensibly enough, that female prisoners be under the custody of a matron. In consequence, the unusual circumstance of having a female prisoner made it necessary for the sheriff's wife to set up housekeeping outside Biddy's cell. Blankets had been hung across the middle of the corridor, and Mrs. Palmer had established herself with a cot on Biddy's side of the barrier. My landlady, needless to say, was making the most of this bizarre situation.

"I will too have another cup of tay," we heard her bawl, as we entered the magistrate's courtroom, adjoining the two cells.

"You've had four since supper, and that's enough for anybody, land sakes," grumbled the sheriff's wife.

"Then I'll talk and sing all night, and ye'll get no sleep for yer pains," Biddy announced.

Mrs. Palmer, when she heard us, came out looking quite haggard. She was wearing a quilted wrapper, and carrying a teacup. "I declare to Betsy," she complained, "I'll be glad when that there grand jury meets at last, and takes that woman off my hands. I felt sorry for her, up to about the third cup."

We did what we could to quiet Biddy, and told her she must get a good night's sleep in order to be up bright and early for a conference with her lawyer. Then I walked home with Daisy. On the way, we agreed that the best thing to do about the sheriff, hereafter, was to bother him as often as possible with irrelevant questions concerning publicly known facts about the Wyck case. Since he had caught us poring over the record, there would be no point, from now on, in trying to conceal our joint interest. We would do better, we thought, to be shrewdly obvious about it.

My legal friend Craig, when he appeared next morning and studied Biddy's testimony given before Dr. Kent, agreed that it would be best for her to await the action of the grand jury. Privately, in my own rooms, he pointed out to me that the coroner's failure to ask Biddy for an alibi indicated that there was no intention of prosecuting her as a principal; and it was his opinion that the evidence of her complicity as an accessory would not bear much weight with the jurors because of its exclusively circumstantial nature. As he was her counsel, I felt it necessary to warn him that Biddy really had been out of her own house for half an hour, at the approximate time of the murder, and that so far as I knew she had no effective alibi.

He whistled, and asked, "Do you yourself think she's guilty, either as a principal or as an accomplice?"

I answered cautiously that she had had good reason to hate and loathe Wyck, but that I could not bring myself to believe in her actual guilt. Knowing her impulsive and generous nature, I admitted that it was possible that she would have aided Charlie as an accessory after the fact. However, I told the lawyer that I did not believe Charlie was guilty either.

After more study of the record he looked up abruptly and said, "Listen, Saunders, had the coroner any possible way of knowing that Biddy had been out that night, and lacked an alibi? It's damned funny that any suspect, even an accessory, should go unquestioned on that point."

The query put me in a jam. I did not want to reveal anything to the lawyer except phases of the case having to do with Biddy alone. Yet it occurred to me at once that Dr. Alling's influence was revealing itself somewhere in the background. Long before

Wyck's body was discovered, my chief had told me that he and Kent were investigating the disappearance because they thought the sheriff a fool. It was by no means impossible that Alling had cautioned the coroner against asking too much at the initial hearing. Alling and I, presumably, were the only ones who knew about Biddy's walk on the fateful night. Kent, if he had learnt about it from Alling, might be deliberately holding it as a surprise ace with which to disrupt the defense later on.

"What about it?" the lawyer persisted.

"Search me," I said with a shrug.

He then began to fire general questions at me, about Kent, asking presently, "What do you make of this fact, in the testimony, that the coroner himself, who was admittedly present when the vault was sealed, was willing to defer in judgment to this fellow Charlie, on the basis of betting a box of stogies, and at the risk of letting loose a lot of dangerous gas? The coroner let it stand unopposed in the record that it was he himself who proposed the bet."

A wild, new thought arose in my mind. The trend of the lawyer's own thoughts was revealed when he added, "Where was Kent that night, does anybody know?"

"He was at the faculty meeting till nearly half past nine. I don't know where he was between then and eight next morning," I said, realizing that one conflict of opinion between Daisy and myself could be completely explained on this new premise. All my reasons for defending Alling were intimate and personal, and still held good. All Daisy's reasons for suspecting him were concerned with a kind of duplicity that might well be the result of his having worked in good faith with a double-dealer, upon whom these suspicions really should have rested from the first.

"We'd better start finding out where he was," I added, excitedly; but the lawyer said, "No, no. When the criminal action comes up, Kent will be a witness for the prosecution, and I as defense lawyer will, of course, have a chance to cross-examine him. That's the time to find out about his alibi. He won't be expecting any such questions."

When Craig left town, I was quite sure that he carried with him rosy visions of the state's most sensational trial, in which an aggressive young defense attorney would earn everlasting fame by proving that the murderer was the very coroner who had inquired into the nature of the crime.

It was not until Thursday, September 8th, that Dr. Alling drove back to Altonville. The fall term would commence on the 20th, and there were innumerable clerical jobs to dispose of. The first was his dictation of a letter to Prendergast's father, with a copy to his uncle the Honorable Mr. Tolland, announcing that the boy had been officially readmitted, and would be permitted to take in advance the examinations he had missed owing to his expulsion before the end of the spring term.

"Do you think he'll be able to pass them?" I inquired.

"No, but I doubt that he will even take them, Saunders. What they wanted, was, as the Chinese say, to 'save face,' that's all. As a matter of fact, he did have something of a breakdown which might very well have been partly due to Wyck's treatment of him. And his family, who are quite well off by the standards of this state, sent him to Europe with a young psychoanalyst of whom I have heard favorable mention. Just as I started negotiating with the uncle, a radiogram came in from mid-Atlantic saying the boy wanted to enter Harvard to study psychiatry. This notification in effect merely cleans up his record and lets him enter there with advance credits."

It occurred to me, as I thought this over, that his decision was another reason for suspecting that Dick Prendergast might have had something to do with the murder. Certainly he must realize that the affair at faculty meeting made him a suspect, and that it would have been silly of him to dream of coming back to town without bringing with him at least a cast-iron alibi.

I was therefore thoroughly surprised when Dick appeared on the 10th, at the door of Dr. Alling's laboratory. As it was nearing noon I took the hint of a glance from my chief and went out for lunch. When I returned, more than an hour later, they were still talking. Dr. Alling told me he would not need me until three o'clock. As I left, I had a good view of the prodigal, looking florid and very much discomfited. Evidently he had not been welcomed home with music and feasting.

It turned out that haughty Harvard would give him no credit

for courses taken at our humble institution in which he had received a grade of less than A—which meant that he got no credit at all for three years' work, except in one course in anatomy; so he had insolently decided to come back to Altonville and chisel the degree which no-one would dare refuse him now. Prexy must have risked giving him something of a tongue-lashing, however, for he emerged from the conference thoroughly subdued, and maintained that attitude throughout the fall term. He acted as if actually repentant, and certainly gave the appearance of a diligent worker. Perhaps it was all due to the psychoanalyst, who may have straightened out his mental kinks. It was nice to think, anyway, that one psychoanalyst at last had succeeded in doing something useful.

The next week was packed with little jobs, and provided no marked advancement in the Wyck case. I thought it would be good policy to make up my quarrel with Dick. He had got his old rooms back, in the house next to mine; and I was about to walk down to see him one evening when he anticipated the call by coming to see me.

"I guess I acted pretty much like a bloody fool with you, Dave," he said.

"Pretty much," I agreed.

"Sure. Let's shake on that," he suggested, which we did.

I went to bed late on Friday evening, the 16th, and felt extremely resentful when an insistent, prolonged knocking on the front door awakened me at half past seven next morning. I rolled out of bed and vaulted down the stairwell. Hos Creel was visible through the glass pane of the door, waving a special delivery letter.

"Takin' up with a city gal, hey, Davy? What's her name?" he inquired, as I signed for the letter.

"That'd be telling," I countered, wondering who could be sending me such a letter from New York.

"Tellin', hey? What's it worth t' ye fer me not to tell Daisy Towers? He, he, hee!"

He went off sniggering, grinning over his shoulder. The letter, addressed in a feminine scrawl, was postmarked 8:00 P.M., Sept. 15, 1932, and bore no return address. Evidently the writer did not know my exact address, as the envelope bore only the words:

MR. DAVID SAUNDERS,
ALTONVILL, MAIN,
SPECIAL DELIVERY.

As the latter phrase was written out, and the envelope was stamped with five threes, I assumed that it had been mailed intentionally in a corner post box. The message, on a sheet of paper with a spray of violets printed in one corner, lies before me as I write. It reads:

625 E. 22 St.,
New York City,
Sept. 15, 1932.

Dear David:

I have just mailed a letter that I wish I hadnt. But since leaving Altonvill I have had a terrible time and I cant stand it any longer. A fellow named Ted that I went away with promised he would take care of me in Boston. But he acted terrible to me I cant tell you how in a letter, or I guess any other way either. But he kept saying he would kill me if I was to run away from him and I didnt dare. One day he took a boat to the place he used to live called Nantukitt to get some cloths and things and he did not want to take me too for some reason. But he said if I did not stay where I was he would surely find me. Well I did not have a cent but I sold some of my other cloths to a jew and got a train to New York because I wouldnt of dared go back to Main. I tried to get a nursing job but the first place I tried they looked funny at my card and said wait please and I thot all of a sudden they had been told to watch for some girl with that card by the Altonvill hospital, so I ran out while they were looking it up and never came back. A woman I met said she would help me but I wont tell you in a letter what kind of a help it turned out to be. Well I got started that way and I could not get a chanct to stop. I was in jail 30 days on the island and the same woman got me out somehow and I had to start all over again. And today I decided it would be much better to be back with Ted than going on like I am. So I wrote him to come and get me and now I am afraid what will happen when he comes and you are the only one I can call my friend so for God's sake come quick because I have got to tell first about the terrible things I know about Dr. Wick. They are too awful to write in a letter so please come quick because it will take longer I guess for a letter to get to Nantukitt, but not much longer so please hurry. I'm sick and I haven't got a cent.

Yours truly,
M. FINCH.

As I copy the letter now I can remember only too well the unexpected rage it aroused in my heart when first it arrived. The evil that men do certainly was proved to live after them, in this case. Muriel had been no saint in the first place; but there was a world of difference between having lovers and being a prostitute; and it was Wyck's doing that she had been driven to that.

I fairly jumped into my clothes, and, without stopping for a bag, raced for Daisy's house, thinking to intercept her on her way to work. She had gone a little early, however, and when I came breathlessly into the lobby of the hospital, at six minutes to eight, she was already at the switchboard. No-one else was in the office, so I shoved the letter at her, too excited even to say "Good morning."

As she read it, she swore under her breath, and I was glad of it. "Wait a minute, Davy boy," she said, going to a file and taking out a bunch of printed forms. She came back with one of them and held it beside the letter. "Sure enough, it's Muriel's writing," she said. "Here's her application. Besides, the letter has her usual crop of misspellings."

"Daisy, you're a jewel," I said. "I might have gone racing down to New York into some kind of a trap, without even thinking about it."

"You still may," she said. "Watch your step, young fellow. Got any money?"

"About seven dollars in the world. I guess I can write an advance cheque and get somebody to cash it, payable the first of the month."

"You'll need about fifty," she said. "Make me out one for twenty. I'll cash it for you and chuck in twenty-five as my share."

"I can't let you—"

"Then you don't get anything from my cash box," she said. "We're divvying up, Dave, and that includes operating expenses. If this solves the problem, somebody'll pay us back. Besides, you haven't been able to save anything, and I've got half a new Ford in the bank."

It was no time to argue. Two minutes later she gave me the money in an envelope which I put in my inside pocket. I was about to rush off, when she seized my hand.

"Use your head down there, Dave," she whispered, "and, just in case—well, never mind—but, kiss me."

I glanced quickly around, leaned through the reception window, and obeyed orders.

"It's about time," she said. "Now scram. I'll tell your boss you're away sitting up with a sick uncle."

I was making for the 8:28, the second of the two milk trains, as the next one did not leave until noon. I bought a ticket to Boston with $4.64 of my own $7.00, and climbed aboard. We waited twenty minutes extra for a milk truck from the Center, and stopped for more cans at every crossroad all the way down to Portland. The going was better from there to Boston, where I arrived a few minutes past noon, just in time to miss the fast train for New York.

The next one was to leave at 2:00 P.M., and would arrive after dark. As I had never been to New York, the idea was alarming, but I tried to forget my qualms in a copy of *Argosy*. Just before the train left I had a thought that sent my hands frantically into all my pockets, looking for Muriel's letter, which was nowhere to be found.

I stood irresolute in the middle of the big station, wondering just what stray whim had ever convinced me that I was less of a country bumpkin than—say—Hos Creel, let alone my snooping friend the sheriff. I had come 150 of the 400 miles to a strange city, and had left the address of my destination behind. What was worse, I had dropped somewhere a letter that would probably find its way to the sheriff in short order, and thus, if I went back to look for it, would land me in jail.

An announcer bawled, "Two o'clock train for Providence—" and a string of other cities, ending with "New York." I sat down, perspiring, wondering whether to take it, or to get a train back to Altonville. Then the thought struck me that I could phone Daisy, with whom I must have left the letter—for the idea of having been sufficient of an idiot to drop it seemed on second thought absurd.

Perhaps the reader has experienced a similar sensation of absolute loss of memory about some article—money, tickets, or such—the very value of which makes carelessness seem, in retrospect, impossible.

The station clock read seven minutes to two. With the best of good luck I might get a long distance call through in time. As I sprinted for the telephone booths, I searched my pocket for money, having no notion what such a call would cost. I had about $2.00 change from my former ticket, and, to make sure, grabbed for the money Daisy had given me in an envelope.

With a ridiculous feeling of relief, I discovered that she had tucked Muriel's letter in with the bills. Laughing with relief, I turned and ran for the train. With an idea of being able to get off more quickly, I walked to the foremost car and settled down to wonder at leisure whether such a callow idiot as myself had any business on such an errand anyway. The answer, from all angles, was "No"; so I turned my so-called mind over to the literature of escape in *Argosy*.

As we drew into Providence, an hour later, I scanned the platform curiously. The train, grinding to a stop, left my window almost opposite a youth who was lifting his bag and starting toward the foremost car's front entrance. My breath rushed inward in an involuntary gasp as I recognized Ted Gideon. He had probably received Muriel's letter in time to catch the crack-of-dawn boat from Nantucket. I recalled from my own inspection of the schedule that it left around 6:00 A.M.

As the train came to a halt I jumped up and ran back into the next car. Someone was just leaving the rearmost seat, so I took it, keeping a careful watch forward, ready to dart back yet another car if I glimpsed him. As a matter of fact, it was not likely that he would recognize me. I did not think he had noticed anyone but

Daisy the first time we saw him, in the hospital lobby. And he had gone into a fit so rapidly, when I confronted him at Onset, that he might not remember me at all.

However, I had been enough of a chump already, that day, and decided to take no chances. After half an hour of pins and needles and watchfulness, my care was justified when I saw the conductor in the front vestibule, pointing back along the train, for the benefit of someone who proved to be Ted. Quickly I slipped out the rear door, proceeded through the third car, and paused in its farther vestibule to look back through the glass of the door. In a moment or two I saw Ted Gideon enter, still walking rearward.

This time I traversed two cars before pausing in the rear vestibule of the second, and again I had but a few seconds to wait before Ted appeared. I rushed through the next car, wondering where this was going to end, and found myself in the last of all, which was blue with tobacco fumes. That, in a flash, explained what was up. The conductor had been directing Ted to the smoker.

I was now, to put it literally, between the devil and the hard, square ties. The situation made me panicky again. Without a moment's reflection I hurried to the rear of this last car with the idea of shutting myself in the lavatory. I was within two yards of it before I saw that it was labeled WOMEN. This fact, if it increased my discomfort, did not break my stride a whit. I barged right in, somewhat comforted by the facts that most of the people in the car had their backs toward me, and that all of them were men.

And there, for three and a half hours, I stayed. The door remained closed, but unlocked, so that at every station the conductor could open it slightly, cough, and then lock it, without suspecting that anyone was there. Each time I had a terribly uncomfortable moment of fearing that it might not be the conductor; but fate at least gave me that slight break, to compensate for what I hope is the most uncomfortable ride that I shall ever have taken, looking back from any future date you choose.

With terrific labor I propped up the window slightly and occasionally knelt before the crack to watch the towns go by. We stopped at Bridgeport and Stamford, and my time-table told me that we were only three or four minutes late. At last, with indescribable relief, I could see a continually increasing line of lights and billboards, and knew that we were nearing the city. When the train had stopped at 125th Street, and started up again, I very cautiously opened the door and stole a quick glance out. The car was almost empty. Most of the smokers had gone forward to other seats to get their luggage. I did not see Ted Gideon, who must have done likewise.

A fat man, sitting on the arm of a seat, with his feet in the aisle, stared at me and broke into a guffaw as I left my refuge. To have been laughed at in public, at any other time, would have given me acute distress, but this time I did not care. I was intent only upon getting off that train unseen by Ted Gideon, and it seemed best to let him go first, since he was presumably once more in the foremost car.

CHAPTER XXII

I was not ignoring the fact that we were both in for a race. Rather, I was counting on the supposition that Ted would not know it. So I drifted up the ramp from the train platform at the same speed as everyone else, keeping a sharp watch, but feeling fairly sure that he was well ahead of me. Then, once through the gates and in the station proper, I grabbed a porter by the arm, pushed half a dollar in his fist and said, "Get me into the nearest taxi, as fast as you can move."

We went dashing in tandem through a huge crowded room, up a flight of marble steps, and out a door to a platform where taxis were pulling up one after another. My porter swung me into a cab which was just being vacated by someone else, and said, "Where y' goin', boss?"

"625 East 22nd Street," I replied. "Tell him there's an extra dollar for speed."

The porter repeated the address, and slammed the door. My head snapped back as we started. In another few seconds I was learning what a New York taxi ride is like. I don't know yet whether it was the usual thing, or brought about by the promise of an extra dollar, but at any rate it was fearful and wonderful

—not so much for speed, as for agility. The fellow never stopped without a yowl of brakes that seemed to lift the rear seat a foot in the air, and brought his front bumper within a split inch of whatever was ahead. He picked up again with a great roar of the engine, in first, that made the cab jump like a frightened filly. And he went slicing magically through holes in the traffic that just weren't there. After twenty minutes of this crazy progress the car squeaked to the curb, so close to a slowly moving old lady that I shut my eyes and waited for the crunch.

"There y' are, buddy, how's 'at?" the driver queried, grinning back at me.

"Great," I answered, getting out unsteadily. "How much?"

"Be eighty-five cents."

I gave him two dollars, and he was off again as he had come. A quick look up and down the street disclosed no other taxi, and no figure that might be Ted's within at least a block. I resolved to get Muriel out of her room, if she was at home, and into another taxi. A short flight of steps led up to a bell with the number 625 beside it, which I hastily rang, still keeping an eye out, up and down the street. A mustached Italian woman peered out and jabbered at me in a kind of half-English which I had had no experience of before. Finally I understood that she wanted me to use the basement door. This was set behind a grating. I rang there, and to my surprise a sharp-faced man in a tuxedo opened the inner door and inspected me through the grille. I decided that she must be in a fancier establishment than I had imagined, from her letter.

"I want to see Muriel Finch," I said, and added, as he looked dubiously at me, "She's expecting me."

"Hey, Joe," he called, "is there a Miss Finch here?"

I waited nervously, for what seemed like wasted minutes of the precious time that I had gained. Then the reply came, "No. Nobody name-a Finch, Tony."

"You been here before?" the man in the dinner jacket asked, and I shook my head. "Can't let you in then. Sorry. Have to wait for her outside. Do we know her?"

"You ought to. She lives here," I said, angrily.

"Hey, what are you gettin' at, buddy?" he asked. "Nobody of that name lives here."

I then realized that she must be using a different name, and described her carefully. But that got me nowhere either. The man made it known to me with considerable hauteur that they had no hostesses at this speakeasy. I got out her letter again and scanned it for a clew. Even then, it took me another precious minute or two to discover that I was at 625 West (instead of East) 22nd Street. Either the porter had mistaken my words, or the taxi-driver had mistaken the porter's. As I stood there half-dazed by this realization, I wondered how many other people were similarly fooled every day in a city that could be so stupid as to divide itself into halves designated by words as easy to mis-hear and as utterly different in meaning as "east" and "west."

"How far is it to the other number?" I asked, as the man stood grinning at my mistake.

"Must be right on the other river," he answered. "Far as it could be. 'Bout ten blocks."

That did not seem far. Somewhere I had heard that there were twenty city blocks to a mile, which meant that I could walk it in less than ten minutes. I started on the run. Then a voice bawled "Taxi?" and I climbed in, giving the number myself and saying, "There's a two-dollar tip if you make it in five minutes."

"I'll try, buddy," he said, dubiously, and covered the first block in no time. The rest of the way was torture. Last time, the driver had been able to zigzag diagonally across town, turning corners when the lights changed. But now we were going directly east along one street, and my watch soon told me that the crosstown traffic was held two or three minutes at every intersection. Finally, at the fourth of these, with fifteen minutes gone and less than half the distance covered, I hopped out, paid my fare, and ran the rest of the way on foot. Even so, I was nearly three quarters of an hour altogether getting across the city. Later I found the explanation in the fact that crosstown blocks are much longer than the others. If the description of my progress is boring, you will see presently why I feel the need to justify my motives and efforts, if not my good sense.

As the house numbers neared the one I was seeking, the section became more squalid. Unkempt women were sitting on the doorsteps, and masses of ragged children chased each other in the dark street. "Hey, what's yer hurry?" someone said, and I realized I had nearly run into a policeman.

"Just half an hour late to a date," I explained, panting. He grasped me by the shoulder, turned my face toward the nearest street light, and said, "You better lay off the dates in this end o' town, kid, before you git yourself in a mess, see? You better git back where y' came from."

"I'm a medical student," I said, quickly.

"Well, I guess you can take care o' yerself," the cop commented, releasing me. "But I'd be a little more par-tic'lar, if it was me."

I walked on more slowly. A quick glance over my shoulder revealed that the officer had proceeded in the other direction. For a moment I wanted to recall him, and ask him to come with me—for Ted, unless he was as unlucky as I in coping with city conditions, had had every chance to arrive first. The cop turned the corner, and I impulsively decided to continue alone.

A huge woman was sprawled out on the entry step of No. 625, bawling at a couple of kids near by. When I described Muriel and asked if she lived in the house, the woman grinned unpleasantly and said, "Yeah, top floor back, but she's got another guy there now. Yer bigger 'n him, and not so skinny. Why don't you t'row him out?"

"Perhaps I will," I said, starting up the steps.

The first two flights I took three stairs at a bound, and then went on tiptoe. There were three doors, all having cards with strange names on them, but I realized that Muriel would not be using her own name, especially after a jail term.

There was no sound at all on the floor. I stood irresolute for a few seconds, not knowing what to do. Then I heard a labored breathing on the stillness, and a scraping sound, as of a chair or of feet shifted on a bare floor. Suddenly the breathing changed to a horrible gurgling. I turned the knob, and banged my shoulder with all its force against the door. It proved to be unlocked, and the effort landed me in the middle of the room.

What I saw nearly drove me out of my mind. Ted Gideon was seated on the edge of the bed, with Muriel's shoulders resting upon his knees. She was lying on her back. His right hand was beneath her neck, his right elbow pressing her left shoulder against his knees. His left hand was over her mouth and chin, which he had bent completely around behind her own left shoulder.

As he released her and leapt to his feet, her head dangled over the edge of the bed, swaying a little on its broken neck. Ted came toward me, staring with dilated pupils. The lids of his eyes were contracted, showing so much of the white eyeballs that they seemed to be starting from his head. Again I recalled Mike Connell's description of his devil—"White eyes wit' black pinpoints in the middle."

The boy's nostrils quivered. His lips curled in a horrid sneer. I decided that a kick in the stomach would be the safest way to stop him. But like lightning he seized my heel in air and tipped me over backward. Then he was on top of me, and I was struggling in a frenzy of fear against his pulsing strength. My hands were around his wrists, keeping his fingers from my throat. But I had the awful sensation of trying to hold some gyrating part of an engine. It was this irresistible quality of his strength that made me realize that he was not trying to seize my throat. His arms were merely moving in rhythm with the spasms of epilepsy. Froth dripped from his mouth on my cheek. I let go my useless grip on his arms and crawled shuddering from beneath him, leaving him jerking on the floor.

Getting a grip on my first impulse to dash out of the room, I went quickly to Muriel. There was no pulse or respiration. She was quite dead. My glance swept the room, and rested on a cheap tablet of notepaper on the floor near by. Pieces of a smashed pencil lay near it. The sheet of notepaper started in the middle of a sentence. I noticed something about Dr. Wyck. Obviously she had been writing something for me when Ted arrived. With jittery haste I ransacked the room for the other page or pages which she must have written.

The rhythm of Ted's movements altered, and I knew that he might be passing into a third stage which, like the first, could be homicidal. Quickly I knelt to look in his coat pockets and, to my relief, found a crumpled ball of paper in one of them. Without bothering to unfold it I thrust it and the other sheet in my own pocket, closed the door, and hastened down the stairs. The fat harridan greeted me with a guffaw.

"Wouldn't give you no time, eh? Well, try 627. There's a couple doin' business there.'

I walked by without answering and on up to the end of the block, turning up the avenue. I felt dizzy, and feared that I was going to faint. If a policeman had been in view, I would have given myself up then and there, not much caring about the consequences. The horrible memory of Muriel, with her head hanging limp and twisted like that of a dead bird, filled my thoughts. A mere dead body did not affect me. I had seen too many of them. But to witness the brutal murder of someone I had known well proved a very different thing.

A taxi came along. I hailed it. But no sooner had I climbed in than the realization struck me in a rush that if the body was discovered promptly, the passing policeman, the fat woman on the steps, and the taxi driver between them would be able to identify me, and provide a means of tracing me to the station, from which notification could be sent again to have outgoing trains searched for someone of my description. Surely the murder would be discovered before I reached Boston. If so, prompt action on the part of the police in New York might result in my being met by the Boston police when I left the train. Twice the driver inquired, "Where to, chief?"

"What's a good hotel?" I asked, sparring for time.

"What part o' town?"

"Middle."

"How 'bout de Roosevelt?"

"O.K.," I said.

During the ride I was able to pull myself together a bit. But I also realized that I did not dare stay in New York. The murder undoubtedly had been done on the beat of the policeman who had stopped me and studied my face. As soon as the body was discovered, a description of me would be broadcast throughout the city. Therefore, when the taxi left me at the Roosevelt, I walked through and out the rear door. There, on the sidewalk, the thought struck me that my best defense might be to inform the police by telephone, as Ted might still be sleeping in the room. I stepped into a cigar store, shut myself in the soundproof booth, and there had what seemed the additional bright idea of putting the call in roundabout, in case the police should have a way of sending someone quickly to the booth from which the warning came. So I called the lost-and-found bureau at the Pennsylvania Station, and said that I had information that a suitcase containing bonds stolen in that station could be found at 625 East 22nd Street, in the top floor rear, if the police would hurry. Then I walked out, went two blocks westward, hailed another taxi, and was driven to Grand Central, where I got a sleeper for Boston.

It was not until I was lying in my berth, with the curtains fastened, that I dared open out the messy sheet of paper taken from Ted Gideon's pocket.

CHAPTER XXIII

The crumpled piece of paper which I spread out on my knees read as follows:

Dear David,

I am going to write those things down in a letter any way because I am scared you maynt come in time and I have decided to kill myself. How it all started was two years ago almost when Dr. Wick called me in to a room in the hospital and said he was going to have to fire me and I said why and he said because I was too—you know, Dave, good natured with the students. And I was scared first and then I began to coax him like and asked him if it was such a terible thing and he said he did not think so himself but the others were talking.

Well to make a long story short he said he wouldnt let them fire me if I would be nice to him too, and he was good looking then you know and he gave me a new coat and so like a fool I said yes. Well he treated me all right and I helped him in his labratory you know and he was doing some experiments that had to be in a dark kind of a damp place and be secrets from the other doctors. There was a place up a hill where we went. Ill tell you how to get to it at the end of this letter.

He had a two headed calf there and a chicken that was alive with four legs. The calf was dead and embalmed. There were a lot of jars with polywogs that grew funny shapes like two tails on all of them in one jar and three eyes on all of them in another jar. Well I didnt care about that but then he began to act crazy and say he wanted to hipnotize me and I wouldnt let him but I think he did sometimes anyway. And then he began bringing other women out there and doing the crasiest things, like hipnotising them and making them sit to their waists in cold water for hours in a tank that water ran through in front of a fire so the tops of them were hot and the rest cold. And he would paint waxy stuff on them from the waist down and give them things to drink that made them act perfectly crazy, Dave.

Well all that went on from the middle of the summer till it was too cold to go out there—November I guess. And I told him I would not do it any more and he said he would have me fired so I went on. And he scared Mike some other way about keeping quiet about the blood transfusons. And then there began to be a lot of dead children born at the hospital and he told me I was partly to blame and would get put in prison for life or maybe hung if anybody knew. So I was scared not to do just what he said. And then in the spring a boy named Ted came to camp there all the time and he was Dr. Wick's son, you know, and he—

That was all. The letter and Muriel's wretched life had ended at the same temporal point.

There was no sleep for me on that sleeper. I lay awake, reconstructing the whole sickening business. The jars of pollywogs had perhaps climaxed years of research in trying to control forms of incipient life by external influences. I remembered that there were two theories concerning the formation of species which are effective in evolution: one based on the presumption that living organisms adapt themselves to shifting needs by small changes through many generations; the other, that a sudden large mutation may survive and, reproducing its kind, develop a new and hardier group. Occasionally such mutations take the form of monsters which usually die and therefore do not propagate.

Obviously, Dr. Wyck had been attempting to bring about exten-sive mutations producing new types by some kind of external influence. Perhaps he had pursued it for years within the normal limits of scientific inquiry, only to meet success and insanity in the same season. At any rate, out of that combination had come the unconquerable curiosity that could be answered only by experiments upon living humans, carrying human embryos.

One thing I knew now as a certainty, in my own heart. If I could establish the truth of this letter by unearthing Wyck's hidden laboratory, no jury that could ever be impaneled in Maine, would convict Wyck's slayer of murder. But my heart was still full of rage and bitter grief at my own culpable stupidity, that could have averted the death of Muriel.

When I stumbled out of the station in Boston, early on Sunday morning, I got a taxi to take me to the Hotel Lenox. As soon as it left I came out again and got another a block or so away to take me across the river to Cambridge to a hotel there. I slept until about three in the afternoon and then awoke from a horrible dream in which I was being speared by a merman with no skin and huge white eyes with black holes in them, in which worms twisted.

For a long time I lay in bed, not daring to entertain the idea of going back to Altonville. It was hard to believe that I could have escaped from the situation without leaving some sign by which the police could trace me down. For awhile I almost wished that Ted had succeeded in throttling me. Then gradually the despair passed in the realization that nothing had occurred to alter my life passions—the old one, to practice medicine; the new one, to forget my blunders and my fears in Daisy's arms. I could think of no other way to feel safe than to be with her.

I don't know, as I look back over the school year, whether the sudden growth of my love for Daisy was brought about by the fact that she was the only person in whom I could fully confide. That may have had something to do with it, but, from my present viewpoint, it seems an inevitable thing that would have happened anyway.

Late in the afternoon I went out and bought a New York morn-ing paper, half expecting to find headlines about Muriel across the front page. But a diligent search showed no item whatever. As it was Sunday, there would be no evening papers. I decided to stay where I was until Monday's first papers arrived from New York. Their story could decide my next move.

Next morning, as I approached the news stand on the corner outside my hotel, my heart sank as I saw the word MURDER screaming from every tabloid. It proved to be something local, but my fingers were shaking nevertheless as I paid for a New York paper and hastily scanned the front page, fearing there might be a picture of Muriel. If there were, someone in Altonville surely would recognize her features, as several of the doctors subscribed to the metropolitan dailies.

On page five I found the story. It filled hardly three column inches, and referred to Muriel under the alias she had been using. The police, it said, linked the murder to another of a like nature committed in Brooklyn a few days before. I felt reassured, and decided to take the noon train to Portland, which would connect with one arriving at Altonville at 6:35 in the evening. In the station I was able to buy more New York papers while waiting for my train. All carried similar brief accounts, with the exception of a tabloid that did publish a picture under the headline, DEATH ENDS LOVE TIFF. But the photo had been lavishly retouched, turning the sordid little room into a flowery apartment, and the face was scarcely recognizable. Moreover, I was quite sure that this particular sheet had no readers in Altonville. One paper admitted that robbery might have been the motive, as the room had been thoroughly ransacked, and nothing to identify the girl's former associations had been left.

My ride back to Altonville was uneventful, but when I appeared in Daisy's doorway at a little after seven she gave a quick cry and threw her arms around my neck.

"Oh, Davy, I've been hating myself for letting you go," she said, with what sounded like a sob. And with that for provocation I proceeded to go all to pieces, crying like a two-year-old. She conducted me to the porch swing, held my head in her lap, and before long had me in shape again. Then she demanded my story.

"How did things go, here?" I asked, first.

"Nothing new, but I think Alling will need some soothing

words. You'd better call him up, right away. When I phoned for you, he didn't believe that you had a sick uncle."

"What did you really tell him?"

"That."

"You goof. Give me a kiss."

I went in and rang Alling at once. He seemed rather cool over the phone, and hinted that I well might be at the office early, next morning. By the time I returned, Daisy was exploding with curiosity—and what I had to show and tell her proved far more startling than her wildest expectations.

"You have been through plenty," she said, "but forget this idea that your hesitation caused another death. If you'd got there earlier, you'd probably have both been killed when he arrived. I think the god of small boys and drunkards is watching over you, Davy."

"Under which category?" I inquired, and she said, "I hope it'll go on being under both, just to make sure."

Later, with a clear moon sailing up behind the silhouettes of the Altonville pines, we went for a stroll. The night was tangy and vigorous with autumn. It seemed to heal my buffeted spirits in a magical way.

"Listen, kid," I said, pausing and holding her tightly. "Do you know why I dared come back at all?"

"You tell me."

"Because I love you so much that it makes my head ache, thinking about it, when I'm away."

"I've heard similar sentiments more poetically put," she said. "But I don't remember liking the sound of them so well, before, David darling."

Tuesday morning I awoke refreshed and was busy in the office when Dr. Alling arrived at eight o'clock. "Good morning," he said, in a tone so curt, followed by a manner so abstracted that it seemed to give me no chance to commence explanations. The hint that conversation was to be discouraged became even more obvious when he laid a bundle of mail on the desk, with a scribbled note on top reading:

Please give this your immediate attention—

I was really angry for a minute, and then hurt. It was not like Prexy to be officious and petulant. Any employee sometimes has to take an unexpected day off. If he didn't like it, he could say so, instead of sulking. His attitude made it necessary to let him be the one to break the tension.

We both worked in silence for some three hours. Then I looked up to see Dr. Alling studying me with a grave expression. "Saunders," he said, "we're both behaving very childishly, but you have been more childish than you know. Don't you realize that you are under suspicion for murder? Can't you see the implications of leaving town in such a hasty, sudden manner? It wasn't yet noon when Sheriff Palmer phoned me to find out where you were and why. In order to keep him from telephoning your description to the Boston police, I had to take the responsibility of saying I had sent you on a private errand of my own. Wouldn't you say"—his voice became more kindly—"that that entitles me to an explanation?"

My resentment turned to shame for having exposed this man, who had been so kind to me, to an increase of anxiety. In many matters he had to do the thinking for all of us. Perhaps I have overestimated the extent to which he is known in the world at large. Certainly he is the world's foremost authority on "concomitant variations," as famous in his restrictive field as are the Mayo brothers in their more immediately useful work. But aside from all this he was a kind of unofficial mayor of Altonville. The town depended upon the school and hospital for a large part of its trade. Hoover's depression had not spared Altonville any more than any other community. In consequence, the very livelihood of scores of its people, and the well-being of hundreds, came to a center in this one man's executive policies. To this moral burden, great at any time, had been added, for six trying months, the threat of an investigation that might wreck the whole precarious fabric by which we all lived.

These matters flashed shamefully through my mind as I realized the full extent of his kindness and of his confidence in me, as expressed in willingness to shield me with a falsehood that might yet react upon him in an extremely dangerous way. Impelled by remorse and gratitude, I found myself launching into a description of the cause of my departure. And, once started, I found no chance to stop until I had described the whole adventure. Of course, this episode could stand by itself. But it needed only a few logical questions to get my complete story—even including my old fears of his motives when he had come so close to asking an explanation of my appearance at Mike's bedside, only to leave me wondering why he did not do so.

"Why was it?" I asked him.

"Well, Saunders, your belated frankness calls for the same attitude from me—but I can't tell you for a fact what I don't yet know. All I can say is that I had excellent reasons for feeling certain that you and I were together at the precise moment when the murder was committed. As for curiosity about where you actually were, from after the faculty meeting till your appearance at the Connells', I can only say that I preferred not to know. Since you refrained from volunteering an explanation, I assumed—correctly, it now appears—that you lacked a credible alibi. Therefore, if I were to be cross-questioned myself, I much preferred to be able to say truthfully that I did not know where you were at that time. I almost wish I still could say that, because you seem to have got into an extremely dangerous predicament. You yourself can refuse to answer questions that might incriminate you. But I, you see, have no such privilege so far as questions about you are concerned. Knowing what I now do about your part in the case, I should say that a more convincing charge can be drawn up against you than against Michaud and Mrs. Connell. That's another thing. I've been cudgeling myself ever since for having sent that poor woman out for a walk at such a time. I did it deliberately, from the best of motives, because I had reason to suspect that her husband might have another of those attacks within a few minutes, which proved to be the case."

I was feeling so desperately uneasy about my own prospects at this point that it was a kind of relief to transfer some of my anxiety to someone else, so I said, "Then you don't think she had anything to do with it?"

"I'm certain that she didn't, Saunders."

"Then couldn't something have been done to get her out of jail?"

"Yes, if she hadn't made such an idiot of herself in testifying for the coroner."

"Can't we do something now?"

"I rather suspect that by now there's no use. The grand jurors got the bill this morning. I shall be extremely surprised if they indorse it. It contains too little of specific fact."

"Then I don't see why the law has any right to keep a person in jail, under the circumstances," I said, angrily.

"I know," he admitted. "To be quite honest, I could have got her out at once on a writ, despite her foolish testimony. Time was what I wanted. We've got to have time. I wanted nothing further to be done by the state until the start of school tomorrow. You don't know what a load it is off my mind to have the boys register-ing today. For awhile I wondered whether we would ever start another term. Well, the bigots haven't killed us yet. Not yet. And it's harder to kill a thing when it's alive than when it's sleeping." He paused, and looked quickly at me, and went on. "It's the col-lege I'm talking about. They could have put an end to the college without difficulty, before it actually convened. But now, I feel certain that we will finish our year."

"What do you think will be the outcome of the Wyck case, then?" I inquired curiously.

"You can keep this to yourself, Saunders. Up until the last week or so, I've felt sure that the outcome would be a series of increas-ingly less probable charges, dwindling off into an unsolved mys-tery. Time would do it. Time's our friend. But now I'm beginning to believe that the solution may come out, after all. Oh! and of course I shall want to see those letters, Nurse Finch's."

I had been wondering why he had not seemed more eager to see Muriel's confession. "Yes," I said, taking them from my pocket, with the newspaper clippings that told of her death.

"Saunders," he said sharply, "I sometimes do question your sanity. I was going to ask you to let me come and see them. Don't you realize what would happen if you were arrested with those things on your person? Your chance of being connected with the death of the girl is just about nil—except for the fact that you go walking about town with the complete evidence in your pocket!"

Very crestfallen, I produced the damning bits of paper.

"We'll burn these at once," he said, putting the clippings into a little electric oven and turning it on to full. "If they are ever needed, you can get copies from the newspaper's own files. I'd like to read over this confession for myself."

When he had finished, he added, "I'm very glad indeed to have this. It corroborates perfectly my own theories, on a point or two that had become increasingly doubtful. For instance, I was almost driven to believe that the hillside laboratory was a hallucination of Wyck's. No-one knew anything about it until shortly before his death. He spoke to me of it on the last day of his life. The birth of the monsters seemed to prove its existence. But I've had a Pinkerton man scouring that whole region for days, on two separate occasions, without finding a trace of it. Are you satisfied that it isn't somewhere in the vicinity of the old cellar where you say the boy Ted was camping?"

"I'm going back to have another look," I assured him.

"Do," he urged. "As an inducement, if you discover it I'll give you the hundred dollars that it would cost to have the private detective here again. But please wait for a month or so. I'm afraid the sheriff will be shadowing you during the next few weeks. The last thing I want to have happen is for him to get wind of Wyck's connection with the monsters."

"There isn't any question, is there, but that he was to blame?"

"None whatever. Before he was killed he left the complete records of his experiments where only I could discover them, together with an accurate prediction of the birth of these monsters,"—he pointed to the glass cylinders in which the feti were floating—"giving the names of the mothers and the probable sequence of births. Not the least of my worries has been the responsibility of possessing this information. More than once, in bed, I've decided to destroy it next day. But always that thought intervenes—who am I, to destroy a part of human knowledge? I think of the nine lost books of Sappho, burnt by order of a man who had no doubt that he was acting honorably in the services of his God. What wouldn't the world give for those books now! and what might it not be willing to give, at some future date, for these facts that I can let live or die as I choose!"

He paused, reflected, and said, "That was how Wyck himself

started, you know, with the highest motives of a geneticist. He wanted to anticipate curative medicine and throw us all out of our jobs by having the human infant born already vaccinated and inoculated, immune to all known ills, and preconditioned against all known aberrations. Only, he went mad while he was about it, from the very kinds of ailments he most wanted to forestall—the atrophies and malignancies of senile decay."

"I've been wondering about that autopsy report I copied for you," I said. "Was it the cancer of the skull that drove him crazy?"

"Primarily, I guess. That, and the effects of an unwise surgical experiment on his own body. Wait a minute. You have enough to speculate on so that it would be safer for you to know the true facts."

He took from a file which always was kept locked a mimeographed document of some sixty pages, in German. It proved to be confidential case histories of the results of gland-grafting, as performed by the notorious Dr. Vladimir.

"The proper names are all German anagrams, Saunders. Here's Wyck, you see. I spent an amusing Sunday, once, deciphering the names of some of our prominent bankers and statesmen and other celebrities who have paid Dr. Vladimir amounts in five figures for an Indian summer of their youth. Wyck got his youth back for nothing, by the dangerous expedient of submitting for a test of the original method under new conditions, implanting the gland between the peritoneal cavity and the body wall. But, read the report for yourself. It explains a lot."

I never have had a chance to copy this document, and my knowledge of German is nothing to boast of. But the gist of it was that the gland had been successfully ingrafted in July, 1931, and had fulfilled its purpose only too well, inducing satyriasis over a period of about six months. The document apparently had been made up on January 1, 1932. It mentioned in closing that the case was under the direct observation of Dr. Manfred Alling. Below, in Alling's own hand, were written monthly postscripts in German on the first of February, March and April. Number one recorded certain disorders of the nervous system, probably arising from the graft. The second recorded a complete and sudden functional cessation. The third announced that the gland seemed to have become completely atrophied. So that accounted for the anomalous mess of tissue under the incision which Daisy had thought was an appendicitis scar.

"Did Dr. Kent know what it was?" I asked.

"No. But he must have guessed. Well, it's time we were getting out to lunch. Now that I've rebuked you sufficiently, Saunders, I want to perform the other duty and commend you for a piece of intelligently planned research, conscientiously fulfilled. The fact that you have been most unwise at certain junctures in matters of detail does not alter the larger fact. Some time before tomorrow please write me out a minute description of Ted Gideon, as you call him. We can't let a homicidal epileptic go roaming around loose. I shall merely send it to a physician in Nantucket, saying that the boy was seen here last spring at the time of Wyck's murder and is wanted for questioning. From what you say, they must know he is an epileptic, and will be duty bound to forward descriptions of him to the police of principal cities."

I left Muriel's letter and confession with Dr. Alling and went striding homeward feeling a great relief at being released at last from the long period of duplicity with my employer. It was not until I was on my way across the street to the dog cart that my peace of mind was marred by the sudden thought that a man whose motives I had suspected for months was now in possession of my whole secret, without having told me anything of any consequence in return. Moreover, he had in his possession documents that well might be construed to charge me with the second murder arising out of the Wyck case. For a few seconds I felt sick. Then the emotional pendulum swung back again. It was done, for better or for worse. I preferred to think that it was for better. But I kicked myself when I recalled Daisy's prediction that it would be impossible to tell Alling anything without telling him all.

Just as I was turning in at the dog cart, a great yell sounded up the street:

"Mr. David. Yoo hoo! They've turned me loose, Mr. David!"

I hurried to congratulate Biddy, and invited her to dine with me on a revolving stool. She jubilantly accepted. Out of her frenzied monologue I gathered the information, later verified, that the bill of indictment had been turned down by the grand jury, who, had found it "Not a true bill," thus freeing both Biddy and Charlie.

My disgruntled friend, the young lawyer who was to have grown famous because of the trial, came around during the course of the afternoon and tried to collect a fee. From him I learnt that Biddy had not been examined, but that Charlie had been called down to Phillipston for questioning before the grand jury. The questions had concerned his refusal to give an alibi. In the privacy of this gathering he apparently had satisfied their curiosity, and he also had been released. My young friend saw some hope, however, in the fact that the county solicitor was examining witnesses in his own right, preparatory to drawing up further bills of indictment for action by the same jury.

CHAPTER XXIV

Five days went by after the release of Biddy and Charlie, with no factual change in the Wyck case. The only development was an impression which I received indirectly from some of Dr. Alling's remarks: that he himself considered Dick Prendergast the most likely suspect. It seems clear, as I think it over, that Prexy would never have said it in so many words. But the assumption fitted in perfectly with the earlier admission that he had at first expected the crime to remain an unsolved mystery. The factor that made a solution now seem possible was the unexpected return to school of Prendergast.

That this was Dr. Alling's personal opinion seemed confirmed decisively on Sunday morning, when I entered the school building with the idea of finishing the preparation of the last slides of tissue from the symmeli. Dr. Alling's private laboratory connects with his office by an inner door. My key will open the regular entrances of both rooms, but not the door between. I was quietly at work staining the thin sections of protoplasm when Alling's characteristic quick steps sounded in the hall and stopped before the door of the office. I imagined he would look in through the midway door, and so postponed my greeting. Almost immediately, however, a heavier tread sounded on the stairs. Someone knocked at the office door, and was admitted.

"Oh, Prendergast," I heard Alling say. "Yes, sit down. What I wanted to say was this. You remember the unfortunate coincidence that your petition of last spring was presented on the very night of Dr. Wyck's disappearance. Well, as you know, the state has been unable to secure an indictment against the diener and Mrs. Connell, and the county prosecutor has been investigating the case further, with the idea of drawing up new bills of indictment on better evidence; whether against the same suspects, or others, I don't yet know. What I do want to know is, have you been questioned?"

It seemed too late now for me to make my presence known, and I shall not absurdly pretend that any Rollo-book notions of honor kept me from straining my ears to the utmost, and taking down in shorthand all that I could hear.

"Why, no, sir," Prendergast said, with a tone of pained surprise.

"Oh?" said Dr. Alling, as if a little surprised himself. "Well then, I want to warn you that you will be questioned, and probably fingerprinted, very soon. In fact, Dr. Kent has intimated that the sheriff will be empowered to subpœna and fingerprint the entire faculty and student body if necessary. I'm looking up the legality of such a proceeding, but I don't think legalities of method will stop Sheriff Palmer from finding out anything that might later be verified in the usual ways. I'm not making wild guesses, Prendergast. I myself have already been asked how much time you spent with me that evening. Purely for my own satisfaction, and to make sure that what I said was not in error, I should like you to trace for me your own whereabouts between the faculty meeting and the noon of the following day. Do you mind?"

"Not in the least, sir," Dick replied. "That is, to the best of my memory. My uncle and I went home with you. That was between half past nine and ten, I should think. We stayed probably an hour, and then went out and drove to the Inn. We were shown to adjoining rooms, and my uncle ordered highballs for us, but they wouldn't serve any. It made him angry. You know what an ardent Wet he is, politically. So we left the place and drove down to Phillipston. He had the same experience at the Craig, there. Well, that made him furious, and we fetched up in Shoulder Lake, at the Mason Lodge. There's no trouble wetting your whistle there, you know, sir. It was then about midnight, I guess, but we stayed up awhile talking about my—er—dilemma. Then we went to bed, got up about nine next morning, had breakfast at the Lodge, and drove back to Altonville. My uncle conferred with you until about noon, if I remember, and then came to my room to pick me and my luggage up and we drove back to Portland in the afternoon, stopping at the Mason Lodge again for lunch."

"Yes, that seems to dovetail in exactly with what I said, Prendergast. Thank you. And—er—you of course have a right to refuse to be fingerprinted without due process of law."

"I realize that, sir."

"Oh? Well, that will be all, Prendergast."

I heard Dick leave; then came the noise of Dr. Alling using the Hunt & Peck system on the typewriter. After ten or fifteen minutes he also left. Suddenly the phone rang shrilly, and for a few moments I jittered around wondering whether he was out of the building. I heard no evidence of his return, and took up the receiver.

"Learn anything?" said Daisy's voice.

"Why, how did you know I was—"

"Because you weren't in any of the other places where you should have been when I tried to get you."

"What did you want me for?"

"To tell you what you know already, that Alling had phoned Prendergast to come to his office."

"But how did you know they'd left?"

"Oh, just a little device of mine. Listen, you'd better get out of there, because I have a hunch that Alling is going to ask me to find you in about a minute. Yep, here he comes in the drive now. Better scram back to your house."

I obeyed, and was hardly inside the door when the phone rang. It was Alling, sure enough, asking me if I cared to drive to Shoulder Lake with him for dinner. Of course I accepted, and he picked me up a few minutes later. We stopped at the Altonville Inn, where the manager greeted us obsequiously.

"Do you know State Senator Tolland?" Alling asked, and the manager replied that he knew him by sight.

"Has he ever stayed here?"

"Well—er—he engaged rooms once, but I seem to remember that he was called away suddenly."

A few more questions substantiated the first stage of Prendergast's story. We proceeded to Phillipston, where the manager of the Craig produced his night clerk, whose answers fully agreed with Prendergast's statements. The manager volunteered unasked, and with pride, the fact that he had lost two guests rather than break the liquor law. All this while, I had no specific explanation from my chief. At last we drew up at the Mason Lodge, a pretentious hotel catering chiefly to summer tourists. Prexy evidently was an old crony of the manager's. They called each other Tom and Fred, and we had no difficulty in inspecting the ledger. Sure enough, Tolland and Prendergast were the last names entered under the date of the 3rd of April.

"Any way of telling just when they did arrive, Tom?" Dr. Alling asked.

"I can tell you whether it was before or after midnight, by seeing if it's the night clerk's handwriting on the tally slip." After rummaging in a file for a bit he held up a sheet and said, "Before midnight."

"That's useful to know, Tom. May I see it? Here, Saunders, make a copy of this."

The tally slip, marked "Pd. cash," listed a double room and bath at $5.00, $3.40 for room service, and $2.00 for two breakfasts.

"Hmm. I was hoping it would be two single rooms. Any way of telling whether either of them went out again during the night?" Alling asked.

The manager chuckled, and said, "If he did, he went out like a light, or else on all fours. See that room service item? That was just for the ice and ginger ale. The bell boy sold the rye. Tolland had me up for a drink. He always does when he stops here. He puts 'em down in one, two, three order, and the young kid did his share. Heh! I remember he came down next morning with a quart bottle of Corby's empty, and slammed it down on the desk

and said, 'I'll have that legal for you, next year, Tom.' Lobby full
of people, too. He's a card."

We had dinner and motored back to Altonville. I still had
received no actual explanation, but, as we neared the school
building, Prexy said, "Would you mind taking one letter, so that I
can drop by the post office and get it into the night mail?"

I here reproduce the letter from the carbon in the files:

Altonville, Me.,
Sept. 25, 1932.

Hon. Harvey Tolland,
381 East Park Boulevard,
Portland, Maine.

Dear Senator Tolland:

I take pleasure in informing you that your nephew Richard
Prendergast has passed the first two preliminary examinations. His marks, by no means distinguished, were satisfactory
evidence of summer study and of a changed attitude. The
other examinations will come during the Thanksgiving recess.

As you doubtless already know, the grand jurors have found
the indictment against Charles Michaud and Bridget Connell,
in the Wyck case, "not a true bill." The county prosecutor is
in consequence redoubling his effort to secure an indictment.
It is not unlikely that everyone connected with the school,
including your nephew, will be asked for an alibi. I questioned
him in private this morning, and feel sure that his story, if
substantiated, will immediately absolve him from any further
annoyance. His present attitude toward his studies makes me
anxious to remove him from unwarranted anxiety.

It will therefore be helpful to me to have a sworn statement
of the time which he spent in your company from the adjourn-
ment of the faculty meeting, April 3, 1932, until noon of the
day following. The eminence of your own signature to such
a document will unquestionably serve to relieve your nephew
from any further embarrassment.

Very sincerely yours,
MANFRED ALLING.

When I had typed the letter and filed the carbon, Dr. Alling apologized for having usurped so much of my holiday and offered to drive me to my next destination, but I elected to stay and finish checking the cost of new supplies for the coming term —a job which would take only half an hour or so, as I had done most of it on Friday. In the spring each teacher had made out a requisition of what he would need in his course. And, as an element of bargaining entered into buying, to meet budgetary limitations, many of the items had not arrived until late summer. The main chance for error in my check-up had to do with apparatuses for private use, purchased through the school to secure a better price. Such items were marked "Personal" on the requisition sheets, and I had to make out separate bills for them, payable into the school account.

Dr. Alling, who had private means, paid for all his own laboratory supplies, so in his case it was merely necessary to total the bill, and make sure the instruments had actually been received. There was nothing of any special interest, this time, except a newly developed type of kymograph,[1] which made its record upon a ribbon of any desired length, and thus was not limited by the size of the drum as on the older kind. As I was checking up its receipt, I got the pleasant notion of taking a record of my own pulse, ringing up Daisy while the machine was in operation to observe the effect of her voice on my heart. Then I tore off the ribbon to give her as a souvenir—a scientific warrant of my affection.

The requisitions were filed in a kind of loose-leaf ledger that pinched them together with a spring back. As I opened it, and bent the back to slip Alling's requisitions in with his former ones, the first leaf in the book caught my eye with its first item:

Cleaning Machine, Cat. No. 14086 Harley, Fanshaw $9.00 less 25%

The sheet was five years old. As I looked at it, out of my subconscious arose the words of the sheriff's report on the bundle containing Dr. Wyck's clothing, "The hat and woolen garments

1 An instrument for recording wave-like motions, or modulations; especially for recording variations in blood pressure.—ED.

in the said bundle smelled strong of cleaning fluid." I smiled to myself at what seemed the absurd automatic efforts of the mind to make things mutually significant. But the coincidence recurred in memory as I finished my job. Just to ease my conscience, I took down the big catalogue of the Harley, Fanshaw Scientific Supply Company, and looked up item 14086, confidently expecting it to be some device, since discarded, for cleaning laboratory glass-ware. It came as a shock to find the words

"*Harley Home Dry-Cleaner*"

at the top of the page, and an illustration of what looked like an oblong five-gallon can, mounted askew on an axle, so that what-ever was inside it would be slopped and tumbled around in all directions when the crank was turned. Cleaning fluid, not mail-able, was listed at 85 cents a gallon. Fearfully I thumbed through Alling's later requisition slips, and found that on each one, except the last just filed, he had ordered at least two gallons of cleaning fluid.

That, without question, was something to think about. The more I thought, the less comfortable I felt. Alling was precisely the kind of person who would dry-clean and press his own clothes, not because of any considerations of expense, but because of the remarks that he would imagine as passing back and forth among the cleaners about the absurd shape of his twisted coat, and of the trousers with one hip twice as big as the other. Moreover, he had in exaggerated form many of the fussy, fastidious habits of confirmed bachelors. When I had been eating at his house during the summer, I had noticed that he invariably made his own coffee, timed his own eggs, puttered with the pendulums of his clocks if they were more than a few seconds wrong by radio time signals, and without exception paused in the vestibule, when entering the house, to run a buffer over his shoes.

A little later, I was coaxing myself to believe that this too could be merely a coincidence. There were probably thousands of such machines sold. There might be more right here in Altonville. Nevertheless, I knew in my heart that they were uncommon, and that the possession of one was a strong presumption against Alling's innocence, considering the fact that the bundle contain-ing Wyck's dry-cleaned clothes had been mailed in Boston at a

time when Alling himself was in that city. In consequence, I spent
an hour going through the whole book of requisitions, to see
if any other member of the faculty might have ordered such a
machine. But none had.

For the present, I did not dare tell Daisy about this discovery.
Of late, her own suspicions of Alling had been dying down. I do
not think she had actually centered her suspicions upon him for
a longer while than upon anyone else. But he was one of three or
four who best suited her theories. I resolved at least to get some
kind of corroborative evidence before mentioning the matter to
her.

At this point I should mention the fact that bills of indictment had been drawn up separately against Charlie and Biddy,
and that for a second time the grand jury had halted the state's
case by refusing to indorse either one. Rumor had it that Charlie had given a perfectly good alibi when questioned by the jury
in camera. But their oath made it illegal for them to divulge any
such testimony, even to the state's attorney, although they were
entirely privileged to consider it in refusing to find an indictment,

CHAPTER XXV

The whole problem of my relations with Dr. Alling was perplexed by the fact that whenever I worked with him my attitude
was forced to change from what it had been betweenwhiles. After
a night of worry about the dry-cleaning machine, and its significance in the Wyck case, I approached my morning's task in a
most unhappy and distrustful mood. But it took hardly ten words
from Prexy—ordinary words spoken in the ordinary course of
our business together—to convince me that it was absurd to
suspect him of committing a crime. His love for the school was
so genuine, and his passion to improve the curative facilities of
mankind was so sincere, that I decided at this juncture upon a
curiously ambiguous attitude which ever since has stood me in
good stead: I merely fell back upon the old formula "The king
can do no wrong." Like a good soldier and loyal subject, I was
willing for the time being to follow him for his lovable qualities,

and to believe that, even if he really had killed Wyck, the killing must have been an excellent idea in itself or Prexy would not have thought of it.

That was how matters rested between us, through most of the school year. Meanwhile, the state got nowhere with its indictments, and the sheriff was off on fantastic tangents of his own devising. The county prosecutor apparently had been skeptical from the first of the fingerprints which Sheriff Palmer had found on the light bulb in the vault. The bulb itself was of the old transparent tungsten type. It probably had been used not much more than twenty-four hours altogether in the course of each year, and might have been there since before Charlie's time. The diener testified, indeed, that he had never touched it at all until the day Wyck's body was found.

This came out at a second inquest, called to consider new evidence. And thereafter everyone but the sheriff took it for granted that the older, white fingerprints had been left on the bulb by the person who first inserted it, perhaps as much as fifteen years ago. Who that person was nobody knew or cared. But the sheriff stuck to his beliefs, and expended extraordinary amounts of Yankee ingenuity in the obtaining of fingerprints for comparison.

At the time of the second inquest I again asked Dr. Alling whether he wanted me to continue to withhold information which I knew to be pertinent, and he again advised me to construe "the truth, the whole truth, and nothing but the truth" within the limits of the law of evidence—that is, he cautioned me that "the whole truth" meant no more than the full specific answer to any individual question.

"And what," I inquired, "if they ask me to tell everything I know that might in my own honest opinion be an aid in solving the Wyck case?"

He smiled and said, "I doubt that any prosecutor would ask such a question. In general, the law asks nothing of witnesses but facts. To hold opinions about facts is the province of the jury. Legal procedure is too intricate to permit of any such confusion of basic functions. It might help you to remember that the jury gives opinions on questions of fact, and the judge on questions of law."

Another hint of his legal knowledge came out in a special convocation of students and faculty, which replaced, in the fall of 1932, the usual rather meaningless opening exercises. It was held two weeks after the beginning of the term. In it, Prexy spoke without hesitation about the murder of Dr. Wyck, and its effect on the school's fortunes. Five prospective students, he said, had canceled their applications within a few days of the discovery of the body. Six old ones had transferred to other institutions.

"I am only too aware," he went on, "that the question with many of you was not subject to such a solution, and my own pride in this school is curiously bound up with what outsiders might consider a limitation: that for many of you the choice is either to come here, or not to study medicine at all. To me that means only that we are doing something indispensable, irreplaceable, something that no-one else can do. That is why I want to express to you who have returned, my gratitude.

"We have suffered a double misfortune in the loss of a brilliant scientist and in the mystery that beclouds his death. As you know, this school depends for a large part of its sustenance upon appropriations of the state legislature. I must ask each of you to consider it his personal responsibility to guard the school's good name. I ask a full and proper cooperation with the officers of the law who are investigating the death of Dr. Wyck. By the same token, I expect these officers to confine their investigation within strictly legal limits.

"It has come to my attention that efforts are being made by one official to take fingerprints of students, without due process of law. A sense of innocence and curiosity may have caused some of you to acquiesce. But the maintenance of personal liberties is more important than the solution of any one crime. I therefore wish to offer the school's official protection to anyone who feels that he is being imposed upon, during the course of the investigation. I shall be glad to explain to any of you your legal rights. On the point immediately at issue, you have a right to know this: the laws of our state permit the taking of fingerprints only of persons accused of a felony or a more serious crime.[1] The law

1 This provision is true of Maine, Massachusetts, Rhode Island, and of all other states whose laws I have inspected in this connection.—ED.

also provides that the prints must be destroyed if a conviction is not promptly obtained.

"One point more: at the request of the authorities, the vault and preparation room and their contents have to date been kept locked. This has delayed the beginning of laboratory work in Anatomy. A final inspection will be given these rooms tomorrow, and the bodies will be available for dissection on Thursday, October sixth.

"Gentlemen, I wish you the full reward of the endeavor which you bring to your studies."

Hearing this candid speech, and the clapping that followed, I was glad that I had come to a decision about the king and his inability to do wrong. His warning about fingerprints was justified, for the sheriff had been by no means content to confine his print-getting activities to those actually under suspicion. In fact, he was going around with a list of all students of the preceding year, asking if they would like to be fingerprinted, and many had no objections. Jarvis told me that the old rascal compared the prints on the spot with a photograph of those on the light bulb, and then crossed off the name of the "suspect" when they failed to jibe. I saw the sheriff one day in mid-October and asked him how he was getting on. He displayed the list of students, with more than half the names crossed off.

"Why haven't you got mine crossed off?" I objected.

"C'm 'ere and I'll tell ye," he said, beckoning and leaning forward to whisper. "It's because I think you've been crawfishin' with me, see, Mister—Mister—Saunders. I'm goin' t' prove in court o' law ye took off yer shoe and screwed out the bulb with yer toes." Nevertheless, he took the occasion to cross off my name, which he had forgotten to do on the basis of former evidence.

As for myself, I was quite satisfied to have the sheriff's interest in me back at its original level. It meant, among other things, that Daisy and I might safely make our projected search for the hidden laboratory, upon the existence of which the solution of the Wyck murder well might depend. The state, Dr. Alling told me, was deliberately delaying its case now, until the next session of the court, as it was felt that the present grand jury panel would probably stand by its guns and refuse to find a true bill on circum-

stantial evidence of any kind—and as yet, so far as we knew, there
was no other.

We set the expedition for the following Sunday, but a cold rain
pounded down all day, destroying what was left of the colors
of autumn and effectually quieting our explorative tendencies.
Daisy's usual schedule at the switchboard was so long that she
had three half-days off a week, selected by arrangement rather
than being at fixed times. One of the porters took the switchboard while the girls had their meals, and also from 6:00 to 8:00
A.M. But Daisy's freedom to choose an afternoon off was of no
use to me, week-days, as I had laboratory work daily from 2:00 till
5:00 under my new schedule. We had to wait for another Sunday,
the 30th of October, and were not sorry when we discovered the
qualities of the day itself.

It was what we used to call football weather: air with just
enough of an edge on it—say 45° F.—and a high, hard layer of
cloud. I found Daisy helping her mother to tie up shrubs and rose
bushes in wrappers of burlap and straw. She had wheedled the
porter into taking the board at 11:00, and was all ready to go at
high noon with luncheon put up in a small pack basket. As she
slung it from one shoulder, scorning my indignant desire to do the
man's part of the job, I got an entirely new picture of her. Usually
she took no pains to conceal the fact that her ankles were about
as good as they come, and wore dresses distinctly on the peek-
a-boo side, with her hair under a very exacting discipline. But
on this occasion she wore heavy walking boots, twill breeches,
and a short leather jacket. Her coppery-brown hair, moreover,
had been told to shift for itself, and was most pleasantly tousled
even before we set forth. Her—but you get the idea. If I think
too much about Daisy the story will be held up indefinitely. The
subject grows so much more important every hour, and the early
part of this narrative had to be so restrained about it.

The only notable change on the hillside road was a complete
absence of tire tracks. Withering grass had choked even the ruts.
It was doubtful that anyone had passed that way, except perhaps
Prexy's Pinkerton, since the night when Ted Gideon drove off
with poor Muriel. We were famished when we reached the
ruined farm, but Daisy wanted to give her feminine intuition a

chance to discover in a flash what I, on my second trip in an hour of diligent poking around, had failed to find. The flash of intuition stretched into fifteen minutes, with no results, and then she too succumbed to hunger.

We ate on the edge of the cellar-hole, occasionally standing up, still chewing, to survey the surrounding territory and to discuss possibilities. The bottom of the hole was now deep in dry grass, withered asters, and goldenrod. No trace remained to show where the tent had stood.

"Oh, but I'm thirsty," Daisy exclaimed. "Hey, what have you done with the thermos bottle?"

"I haven't even seen a thermos bottle," I protested. "What was in it?"

"Coffee. Don't tell me I forgot it. Oh, Davy, darling, do you know what I did? I didn't even put the percolator on the stove. Remember when you called up? I set it on the ice-box and forgot all about it."

I remembered that Muriel's letter had mentioned a tank with running water; so a brook must be somewhere near by. We went toward opposite ends of the field to find it, keeping a sharp watch meanwhile for pipes. I began to feel like a super-sleuth, until I remembered how few of my clew-hunts had started as acts of my own volition.

Daisy called, and I ran over to join her. The brook looked clean. As it came down the wooded sides of a hill that was quite uninhabited, we forgot about typhoid and drank our fill.

"All right, now to find the pipe," she said.

We started from a point about a hundred yards from the old cellar. I went upstream, she down. Again she was first to call. "Here's one, Dave. Water's running out of it. That's the only way I could have found it."

I joined her, and was glad she had come along, for I don't think I should have noticed it myself. There was a small trickle of water in a niche between two stones, and the pipe from which it came could be seen only by lying on one's stomach with one's head almost at the level of the brook.

"Good girl!" I applauded, and poked around in the woods nearer the cellar until I came upon the pipe-line there. It did not run directly toward the house. But, once we had found it, it was not hard to follow, having been laid flat on the ground and covered with leaf-mold. The pipe ran up the same little gully along which I had crept on my first visit. When it definitely disappeared underground it was pointing about three or four yards above the uphill side of the foundations. We followed along what we supposed was the line of its continuation, stamping to discover any hollowness below. But a hundred feet of closely inspected surface showed nothing. The pipe simply dived into the ground and disappeared.

Next we carefully inspected the adjacent wall of the cellar. It was made of huge granite slabs, doubtless quarried near by in the days when settlers built for the ages. Some of the blocks must have weighed a ton or more. I put my shoulder against each in turn with a faint hope of finding one that "pivoted" in the proper romantic fashion, but Wyck evidently had been a realist. Against the center of the wall stood the enormous base of the chimney —the kind of chimney built to stay hot for hours after the fire was out and act as a heating plant. It was at least eight feet wide and six deep. Looking at it, I even speculated with the idea that the laboratory might be inside it. A little higher than I could reach there was a Dutch oven, the door long since rusted off. I lifted Daisy up to inspect it, but it was only about eighteen inches square and two feet deep, with solid stone all around. There was a cleaning flue on the cellar level. She climbed up to the regular fireplace and thoroughly thumped without results. The top of the chimney had fallen long ago, and she could stand in the main flue and look out over the top.

"There's still a lot of waste space in the bottom of that thing, Davy," she said, when I lifted her down. "Are you sure there isn't any kind of chink below the main fireplace?"

"We can look again," I said. But there apparently was none.

"How about those stones? Hey!" she shouted. "Look!"

On the right, at the base of the chimney, was a shallow pile of stones fallen from the top. They were hardly a foot higher than the general level of the cellar, and gave the impression of lying, as did groups of others, on the solid ground. But Daisy was kneeling, pointing between two of them to a piece of lithographed tin which proved to be a sardine box. Hastily I heaved the stones up, tossing them aside. Beneath them, instead of ground, we came upon more stones, with more tin cans between them. And then as I yanked a big slab loose, part of the chimney itself seemed to crumble, and a neat square hole gaped in the side—about a foot of it above ground and a foot below. The bottom of it probably showed the original level of the cellar. I crawled into it cautiously on hands and knees and looked up. There was just a glimmer of light. My flashlight then showed that it was a regular fireplace with a flue of its own, in the top of which a large stone had been placed, or had fallen.

When I came out, Daisy shouted with laughter. I was covered, it seems, with soot and charcoal. Evidently Ted Watson had used that fireplace for cooking. But why should he have filled it full of stones?

"I'll bet the charcoal was just a blind," Daisy said. "Here, let me look." She bent down and banged at the back of the fireplace with a stick. It clanked metallically.

"Gangway!" I said, and went plunging back into the hole, prying around until I found the edge of the iron plate, which with no great difficulty, came out entire. It was not even hinged. Daisy meanwhile had been pulling more stones from in front of the chimney, making the place easier to get at. When I had hauled out the plate I turned the flashlight into the hole. It showed a dirt tunnel, shored with logs that had not been there very long, and ending in a blank clay wall about ten feet in.

CHAPTER XXVI

Once inside the tunnel, I could almost stand erect. At the clay wall there was a sharp right turn, and the tunnel led about six feet farther, ending surprisingly at a sort of door frame made of granite slabs. There was a recently-made door of unpainted pine boards, hanging slightly ajar from ancient wrought-iron hinges. With hand fast in hand, we pushed it open, and flashed the light into a low room, about eight by twelve feet in extent, made of the same kind of granite slabs that had been used in the foundations of the house. At one end there was another door, round-topped.

"What the devil would a place like this have been here for?" I whispered. "It's old as the hills."

"It's a vegetable cellar, or else a creamery, Dave. Look! look at that tank."

To corroborate Muriel's letter, there was a galvanized tank, of the kind sold by Sears, Roebuck for cattle troughs. Water flowed into it from one pipe, and an overflow pipe carried the surplus away.

The floor, of loose slabs, was comparatively new. The end farthest from where we stood was littered with a pile of smashed glassware and apparatuses, most of the pile kicked under a bench, one end of which sagged unsupported to the floor. I had noticed a peculiar purring noise when I came in. Inspection showed it to be a water-motor in the intake pipe, coupled to a small dynamo, from which broken wires dangled. Near by was a storage battery of light Edison cells, sufficient to set up a tension of about 30-odd volts. I looked around quickly for lighting fixtures, but there were none, and a little acetylene lamp on the débris pile showed what had been used for the purpose.

"He must have done something about ventilation," I observed; and Daisy said, "Try that other door."

It opened upon an irregular dirt wall, not clay, like the tunnel, but of a texture to show that it had been shoveled there. Into the dirt were thrust a dozen 2-inch pipes, through which light glimmered faintly. We marked the spot where the door was, by pacing distances and taking only right-angle turns. Then we went outside and paced in the same fashion until we knew we were standing approximately over the buried door. The ground sloped down before us toward the brook, massed with wild raspberry bushes. To satisfy my curiosity at the expense of scratches, I crawled among them and found some of the vent pipes sticking up through the ground. Originally there must have been a cut, downward and into the bank, to reach the old door. Wyck had filled it in level with the rest of the bank, put in his vent pipes, and transplanted bushes flush with the hundreds that grew wild on either side. It was a neat job.

"That's the way dreams of empire end up, Dave," Daisy said moodily. "Whoever built this place, with a chimney like that, and an underground creamery or cheese factory or whatever it was —well, they must have thought they were founding a dynasty to till the land forever and ever. And instead, it gets used by an old maniac, in the end. My, it's getting dark early."

"Only half past three," I said. "Must be just the clouds. It won't make any difference to us down there. Come on."

We reëntered the dungeon and began to explore the pile of débris under the work bench. I pulled at a piece of wire, and dragged out a sizable induction coil, and then a Tesla coil, and whistled my surprise.

"What are they, Dave?" Daisy inquired.

"I don't know that together they have any real therapeutic uses," I admitted. "But I built the same kind of things on a smaller scale when I was a kid to put on magic exhibitions. That induction coil alone would give enough of a shock to kill you, hooked to that battery. But if you hooked on the Tesla coil too, it would run the voltage up so high and the amperage down so low that you could just do harmless tricks with it. In a dark place like this if you held that brass knob, with the thing running, your hair would stand straight on end with a ripple of blue fire playing around on top of it. Look, if I stood on this rubber mat here, and held the knob, and stretched out my hand to you, there'd be a big brush of thin blue sparks from my hand to the nearest part of your body. Can't you imagine Wyck playing he was Beelzebub? You see, Mike wasn't delirious when he talked about that."

A minute later Daisy said, "Whew! Look here, you're right," and pulled out a kind of mask with sharp brass horns on a metal band to which was attached a binding post. My next find was the business end of an old fashioned X-ray tube, with a pitted cathode. Near it Daisy discovered the anode and target. Connected with the induction coil, this tube could have been almost as powerful as the more modern Coolidge type in general use, but it would have been far more difficult to control and more dangerous. Daisy asked why he would not have used a Coolidge tube, and I explained that it would have required a much more elaborate power plant.

"I wonder what he wanted it for? To see how his experiments were coming out, before the monsters were born?"

"I don't think so," I answered. "This tube wouldn't have been powerful enough to define internal tissues through the whole abdomen. Anyway, it's a more important piece of evidence than that. Last year Dr. Alling had some correspondence with a doctor who had been systematically changing the forms of moths by subjecting cocoons to X-rays. Wyck used this tube in the making of his monsters, that's what.[1] It's also been done in the case of jellyfish by changing the salt content of their water."

"If that's so, look here," Daisy said, triumphantly, hauling from the pile a box full of round cartons of reagents—all metallic salts. "No wonder poor Dr. Alling was scared to death of an investigation. I thought that attitude of his was silly, at first, Davy, or else just a smart blind. It didn't seem that anything that could happen in Altonville could get much publicity. But the other day I ran across a reference in the paper to the Hall-Mills case. Remember, off in the country somewhere in New Jersey? The Pig Woman, and Derussey's Lane, and all that? The metropolitan papers fed on it for months. What wouldn't they do if they got hold of this! Good Lord, it's the best reason in the world why Alling himself would have murdered Wyck, if he thought he could keep this business secret with one neat little knife-cut!"

I had to nod in agreement, but then she added, "However, my suspicions are swinging back to saintly little Marjorie Wyck, these days. She had more personal reasons to be scared than Alling."

"What about Prendergast?" I inquired. "Those blue books have never turned up, you know."

"What about his alibi?" she countered. "You said Tolland wrote back to Prexy a cast-iron verification of it. No, I'm doing a

1 It is a well known fact that monsters are frequently produced among invertebrates by exposing larvæ to abnormal salt solutions. See Morgan, *Experimental Embryology.* New York: Columbia University Press, 1927. Mavor and Muller have both obtained genetic variations in the fruit fly by exposing the female parent to action of X-rays. Little and McPheters have observed genetic abnormalities in descendants of X-rayed mice. See *Genetics,* vol. 17, 1932. More recently in Europe, Goldschmidt and others have produced variations by use of high temperatures.—ED.

little sleuthing in Marjorie's direction, these days. I'm beginning to think Alling would have had too much sense not to know that a murder would be the best way in the world to call attention to the very things he wanted to conceal."

I had never brought myself to the point of telling Daisy about the dry-cleaning machine. Now, once more, I decided to wait for a chance to explore Alling's home, which had not yet come this semester.

"Hey, what's here?" Daisy said, and lifted out to a clear space a box which proved to contain two graduated jars with wide ground-glass stoppers and fused nipples at the top and bottom of the graduations. There were also some lengths of glass and red elastic tubing, part of a hypodermic syringe, and several hollow needles such as are used in vein puncture. One of the graduated glass jars contained a brownish sediment of blood.

"That's his transfusion apparatus," I said. "Things are clearing up, Daisy. Think of the old devil, getting poor Mike up here and performing transfusions of Mike's blood into his own arm. Remember in Muriel's letter she said she had helped with the transfusions? Gee! I can't help admiring that guy, devil or no devil. Living on sheer nerve, with cancer of the skull and his innards going to pieces, and never a yip out of him so that anyone would know he was sick. Cancer anywhere else probably wouldn't have let him go on walking around. As it was, with the help of Mike's blood, he kept going right up to the last, and then took a swallow of veronal deliberately, to polish himself off!"

We continued searching, and found many other bits of apparatus to confirm old clews. There was a large jar of what probably was paraffin oil with some heavier wax in suspension, doubtless used to paint the lower extremities of Wyck's victims when they sat in the water tank. Muriel had referred to a "fire" before which they had sat, half immersed in the tank. We could find no fireplace or stove, but there was a large charcoal brazier, and a shelf in the wall back of the tank where it may have stood when in use. To corroborate this theory, we discovered another vent just above the shelf, leading, like those in the blocked-up doorway, out among the raspberry bushes.

At last we came upon what I had hardly dared hope for—a

locked strongbox which, after twenty minutes of prying, burst open and revealed a ledger with day-by-day reports of Wyck's experiments. Moreover, pasted in the front cover was the missing symmelus plate! It showed signs of having been traced over, and underneath the book itself, in the box, were a dozen drawn copies of it, in various colors, silhouette, outline, showing at the lower end of the fused leg a progressively wider and more developed fish-like tail.

The flashlight was becoming weaker from long use. I glanced at my watch and found that it was already six o'clock. We could not forbear to glance hastily through the ledger, just enough to prove to our own satisfaction that the experiments and their methods were specifically recorded. The invariable preliminary to each was the production of hypnosis in the patient by use of a single candle flame in a dark room, after which a set of thoroughly scientific procedures with acids, alkalis, temperature baths, and suggestion through visual image, were indulged in, while the patient was for all practical purposes unconscious.

Determining to leave everything just where it was, we replaced the book in the strong-box, hid it as thoroughly as possible under the débris, and cast the rapidly dying beam of the flashlight around the chamber for one last inspection before our departure. I pushed the door shut over the vents.

Daisy said, "It's funny that Wyck didn't deliver that strong-box to someone—Alling, maybe—for the inspection of other scientists."

"Perhaps he meant to. It's another reason for believing my old hunch that Ted murdered him up here, and drove down with the body to some accomplice for the embalming job. That would explain why the strong-box was left. It looks as if Ted just wrecked the place deliberately and sealed it up and scrammed. Well, let's scram too. We're a hundred bucks richer than we were this noon, deary."

I stooped to throw the rubber mat over the place where we had hid the strong-box, and then said, "Come on."

Daisy laid a hand on my arm and whispered, "Wait. Did you hear that?"

There was a scraping sound, then a metallic bang in the passageway. I switched off the already very faint light and reached for Daisy's hand in the darkness. It was trembling, but so was mine.

"Davy," she said, faintly, "hold me. Oh, what's hap—"

I clutched in time to save her from falling as she went limp in my arms. What had done it? Horrible suspicions went through my mind. I had let the flashlight fall among the rubbish as I grasped her, and now knelt in the darkness, lowering her gently to the floor. I could hear faint sounds of someone or something creeping near in the passage and had an agonized few moments of wondering whether it could be Mike Connell, escaped, come again to look for his blood. There was no longer any doubt but that this was the place where he had lost it. Even worse, it might be Ted Gideon, returning for the very evidence we had just discovered. These were the likeliest chances, and both were madmen. Hastily, I felt about for the flashlight, resolved to use its last flickers at least to find a weapon with.

Just as I touched it, I was relieved to hear a woman's voice, mumbling, "Can't find it in the dark. I can't find it in the dark. Oh, damn him, why didn't he have some lights? How can I ever find it now? My baby. Oh, my baby."

Now I could hear her creeping across the floor, as if on all fours, toward the trickle of water in the tank. She must have put her hand in the tub, for she gasped and said, "Oh, he drowned him before he was born. A fish. He tried to turn my baby into a fish. Oh, God will punish him. He's dead now. He's being punished. But they told me they put the dead babies in bottles. Baby, my baby."

The woman began to creep toward us, her hands brushing back and forth in front of her on the floor. There was no means of knowing whether or not she was another of Wyck's products —another homicidal maniac to join ranks with Mike and Ted. I had hoped at first that she would go out as she came in, but evidently she was bent on exploring the place, even in pitch darkness. As I felt Daisy stirring against my knee I flashed the light at the woman, growling, "What do you want here?"

She gave a splitting shriek, terrible in the small, stone-walled room. "Oh, he's come back from hell! Don't put me to sleep. Don't do that again."

She arose and rushed for the tunnel. I heard her stumble against the iron plate, and then utter another last awful scream.

Daisy sat up, looking very white even in the scant illumination of the almost exhausted flashlight.

"Fine one, I am," she muttered, "fainting at a time like that. Did you see who she was, Dave? It was Lucy Bennett, mother of that second symmelus. Oh, let's get out of this ghastly place. I'm all trembling."

As we emerged from the tunnel, a blast of snowflakes swirled in our faces. The season's first snow evidently had been falling for some time, as the ground was white under the dark sky. I insisted that Daisy take my coat and remain under the shelter of the north wall while I replaced the iron plate and tumbled stones back into the hole again. I put more in than were there when we found it. Then Daisy made me take my coat back, and we set off briskly through the woods. The snow actually aided us in finding our way through what would otherwise have been inky darkness. The flakes had ceased falling. Several times we got lost, but not for long. When we reached Altonville it was nine o'clock.

"Good land, David Saunders, I thought you had more sense," Mrs. Towers exclaimed cuttingly, "keeping a girl out like that. I was so worried, I've just done phoning the sheriff."

"Oh, mother, you're a jewel!" Daisy cried, collapsing on a sofa. "The sheriff, of all possible people. Don't you know that I'm old enough to take care of David without help from the sheriff?"

"David? David indeed. Take care of David? What you need's somebody to take care of you. And he certainly doesn't seem to be very good at it."

She sniffed at me, and I made an apologetic exit, into the sheriff's very arms.

"Got back, did ye? Hmm. I was jest about to unleash the bloodhounds. Now, we'll jest take a nice little friendly stroll back to the station house and have a little talk about what you two've been up to."

"Why, sheriff," I said, in a tone of extreme incredulity, "how could you possibly be interested in what a young lady and I were doing—on a night as dark as this?"

"Well," said the sheriff, "mebbe you're crawfishin' and mebbe you ain't. I think I'll jest make a date with Miss Daisy myself. And if she's jest as nice to me, as you *say* she was to you, I'll take yer word for it. If she ain't, then I'll be around to see you, Mister— Mister Saunders."

We walked together to Atlantic Street. I then sauntered off toward Connells' unmolested. As soon as the sheriff was out of sight I doubled back to Prexy's to give him a full description of what had happened. But first I asked him to do something to make sure that Lucy Bennett had got home safely. She had no phone, but the operator got him a near-by farmhouse from which a messenger was sent to find out about her.

I had nearly finished my story before the messenger phoned back to say that Mrs. Bennett was at home, sick, and that her husband would not say what was the matter with her, but that the old skinflint apparently did not think it bad enough to war-rant summoning a doctor. Prexy replied that he would send one out anyway, next day, to make sure that all was well. The woman who had acted as messenger then began to pump him about the purpose of the call, and asked what had happened to make him feel anxious about the farmer's young wife. He shot a prompt and politic lie into the mouthpiece, saying that a description had come in of a person unconscious from an auto accident, and that one of the nurses had suggested that it tallied with her memory of Mrs. Bennett.

"Well, I'm certainly glad it wasn't," he said, and hung up the receiver.

CHAPTER XXVII

At this point in my story it should have become apparent to my hypothetical reader why Daisy, Dr. Alling, and I, all have continued to refrain from cooperating fully with the authorities. If any one of us had sensed in advance the structure of duplicity which it would be necessary to maintain, compounding our original reticence, we probably never would have entered into this private and secretive investigation at all. Perhaps I should except Prexy from that statement; for he has made it plain to me, over and over again, that it has been his hope to discover Wyck's murderer in such a fashion as to make it unnecessary to reveal the grim history of the human monsters. It seems to be his thesis that the murderer was driven by motives which had little if anything to do with the worst of the doctor's sins; and he has wanted to keep our part of the investigation private, at least until enough evidence has been gathered to convince him that such an ultimate solution would prove impossible. In that event I believe that he will prefer to let the mystery remain unsolved.

I have not yet been requested personally to join him in keeping our secrets lifelong. That is one reason why I am writing my story down. If he does some day request it, I may destroy this record, for the good of the school. On the other hand, some new revelation may occur at any time to make me glad that I have recorded the whole story in a form which can be turned over, complete, at a moment's notice, to someone else who may be more fit than I to judge the ultimate merit of its suppression.

It should still be borne in mind that for five months after Dr. Wyck's disappearance no-one could say for certain whether he was alive or dead—no-one except the still undiscovered murderer or murderers. During those five months, the three of us who were secretly investigating the matter had committed ourselves to a course of conduct which was not essentially improper so long as the nature, the reality even, of the crime was unknown. The sudden discovery of the cadaver caught us all too deeply imbedded in the consequences of our secrecy to make it possible to withdraw.

If the earlier evidence which I had set down does not substantiate that conclusion, it certainly was validated by the results of my blunders in the adventure that led to the strangling of Muriel. The authorities so far had seen no significance whatever in the disappearance of Muriel (evidently they ascribed it entirely to her fright over being attacked by Mike in one of his moments of blood-madness); they knew nothing of Ted Gideon; but, if we were to make our findings public, the whereabouts of these two would become a matter for immediate investigation; and in that case I myself would be in double jeopardy, under a perfectly reasonable suspicion of having killed both Nurse Finch and Dr. Wyck.

That fear has sealed my lips—and, I assume, it has been a factor in deciding Daisy and Dr. Alling in favor of continued secrecy. We are accepting, of course, a large responsibility, for the reason that certain plain fields of investigation have been left untouched, fields which in themselves might provide the crucial clew. For example, nothing whatever has yet been done to get information from Wyck's female victims. The likelihood that any of these women could have committed such a murder is very remote, considering their condition of advanced pregnancy at the time; but the surviving ones may possess, perhaps unknowingly, the vital link in the chain of evidence. For a while after the discovery of the doctor's body, we all half-expected that one of these women might speak up; but neither has done so; and the reasons for their own silence are apparent enough. In the first place, all the mothers of symmeli probably were guilty of adultery or fornication with Wyck himself, or with his bastard—a disclosure which none of them would care to have publicly revealed in any event, especially after the death of the doctor had removed the only forms of redress: the possibility of getting money from him by legal measures or of having him punished in the event that malpractice or rape could be proven. Secondly, the plain evidence that Wyck resorted to therapeutic hypnosis makes it likely that some of the women did not have any real comprehension of what had been done to them. Finally, they themselves had of course not been told that their offspring had been abnormal. The two who survived had merely been informed that their children were stillborn.

We had all proceeded on these assumptions, up to the time of Lucy Bennett's intrusion into the underground room; but the words which she had mumbled in the darkness proved that she had had at least a partial knowledge of the meaning of Wyck's experiments. I saw that Dr. Alling was worried by this. Although he said nothing, he seemed reproachful and nettled because of my failure to tell him a little more about what Lucy Bennett had said, before asking him to put in the original phone call to see whether she had returned safely. His only remark was, "I think it would have been better, in the circumstances, if I had driven to the Bennett farm myself, at once. An old man with a young wife is a natural target for gossip. The neighbors may have their own opinions about the call, and set her to talking in self-defense. However, the husband seems to be cantankerous enough to discourage local intrusions. It will be just as well for you and me to go out there tomorrow, I think, nevertheless."

Then he brightened, thanking me and asking me to convey his thanks to Daisy for our successful Sunday afternoon of sleuthing.

"She's the one to thank," I said. "She found the pipe that gave us the first clew, and noticed the tin cans under the stones that had blocked the entrance. I'd never have seen either. I looked pretty thoroughly once before without noticing a trace of anything strange."

"Oh? I told you long ago she was a very smart young lady, didn't I?" he observed. "Yes, indeed. I wish though that there were some better job for her than that switchboard. She deserves it. But what would we do without her there? I guess we'll just have to raise her wages. And that reminds me—"

He went to his desk and wrote two cheques, both drawn to "Cash": one covering my expenses on the trip to New York, the other for $100 which he had promised us if we should find the hidden laboratory. It was more money than I had ever had in my possession, all at once, in my life. Having it made me think of something which otherwise I could not have mentioned for some time to come. I resolved to suggest to Daisy that we put it in an account with both our names on the book, as a nest egg. That would be something tangible, something to build on.

And that is what we've done.

Early in November the fall term of the court ended, with no indictments found by the grand jury. The case against Charlie and Biddy collapsed for want of concrete evidence upon which to issue a true bill. None of us could find out what Charlie's alibi had been, but obviously it had satisfied the grand jurors, who had twice refused to indict him. I had never seriously suspected either Biddy or Charlie, but it must be remembered that the state's tenacity in seeking to bring them to trial was based upon a very restricted estimate of the number of persons who might be guilty.

For a while after the grand jury disbanded, the higher officials, if they continued their investigation at all, did so in an entirely secretive way. My friend Craig the lawyer drove up to town two or three times to try to get additional information from me and from several others with whom he was acquainted. I suppose he was reluctant to relinquish his somewhat far-fetched theory that Coroner Kent was himself the murderer; but whether Craig has discovered anything noteworthy I do not know to this day of writing.

Only Sheriff Palmer carried on, confident that the fingerprints on the light bulb would eventually reveal the culprit. His efforts became a standing joke in the school. One day Jap Ross rubbed some putty on the thumb and fingers of the body which a friend of his was dissecting, pressed some excellent prints on another old light bulb, wrapped it in tissue, and mailed it to the sheriff with a typewritten note saying that the woman whose fingerprints were on the bulb would be found dead on the following Wednesday. The note itself was signed with the right thumbprint of Mickey Rehan's stiff, and the sheriff almost broke his heart for a couple of days, trying to decide whether or not he was being kidded. Finally, on Wednesday, Mickey phoned him in great agitation to say a dead woman had been found in the cellar at 86 Atlantic Street, and we gathered outside to watch him come whizzing up from the courthouse, counting house numbers, looking for 86.

When he realized that that was the number of the medical

school, he hesitated, finally got out, and shouldered his way past us without saying a word. In the dissecting room he found a sign gripped in the teeth of the proper stiff, reading:

HERE SHE IS,

SHERIFF

There was another sign on Mickey's cadaver, saying:

I DID IT WITH

MY LITTLE HATCHET

The sheriff was not exactly pleased; but he characteristically made sure of things before leaving by taking the prints of both cadavers, and comparing them with the ones on the bulb and the note, which he had brought with him—much to the delight of Mickey and Jap.

On the way out, the Law regained his majesty and self-possession in the very midst of the students by abruptly yanking out his revolver and firing a shot into the door sill, between his own toes. Of course we all jumped and dodged at the loud bang in the narrow hallway.

"Brain worm," the sheriff commented, poking at the sill with his toe. "Guess I druv him clear through the sill. Don't know what he was figgerin' to feed on around here. Good thing to put him out of his misery, 'fore he died of hunger."

And he stalked solemnly out and drove away.

The incident might have had a more serious result, because on the afternoon of the same day the sheriff received another unexpected communication through the mails; and the nature of this new letter may have made him wonder whether he was being kidded again. Luckily, he did not ignore it; and it turned out to be a startling if not a valuable piece of evidence. Before describing it, I should first explain that one of my early jobs, just after school opened, was to prepare a letter of inquiry about Joe Baker—whom I have already mentioned as the recipient of some of Mike's blood. When last heard from, shortly before Wyck's disappearance, Joe had been convalescing satisfactorily from his accident, but was not planning to reenter school until the fall. When he did not appear, Prexy asked me to inquire about him, but the letter was returned unopened by the post office, with one of those rubber-stamped explanations to the effect that delivery had not been effected for the reason checked below. I had thought that the check mark was opposite the line reading "Present address unknown." But in reality it probably was intended to indicate the line above, which read "Addressee deceased." This is how we found out:

I was taking dictation on another matter, late in the afternoon of the day of the Ross-Rehan hoax, when the sheriff drove up to Prexy's house and delivered a letter.

"Coroner's out o' town," he said. "You better decide whether this thing belongs out o' the waste bin."

As he handed it to Prexy, he looked sourly at me, as if expecting a guffaw. Here is what the letter said:

Little Otter Lake,
Nov. 12, 1932.

Dear Chief of Police:

I have finally decided to tell you that I will give up to the law if you will send someone to the Little Otter House which is where I have been living these past two months. Dr. Wyck committed suicide and it was on account of me, and I want to get it off my conscience and to be at peace with my Savior again.

I didn't dream of what the result of it would be, and I didn't know what the result had been till the middle of the summer. I don't bother much to read the papers. But somebody (a Mr. Bostwick) told me in July about Dr. Wyck disappearing, he remembering that he thought that was the doctor my poor son had been attended by.

I didn't say anything then to Mr. Bostwick, but I kept looking in the Altonville section in the Pine Tree State News, and two months ago when I read the circumstances of the body being discovered I knew only too well what had happened. He wasn't murdered. He committed suicide, and it was all my fault, and I'm happy to confess and clear my conscience. If they can put a person in prison for causing something that she didn't know she was causing, I'll be content to go, to atone for my sin of anger and pride. But it was really only a mother's broken heart that did it.

My boy Joseph, you see, died suddenly on last April third while I was out shopping, in the morning. When I got home I found him there, and I called a doctor, and he said it was heart failure. Well, Joseph never had any heart trouble, and of course I was distracted, and I insisted that it must have been foul play, because he was nearly well, just that morning. So they said an immediate examination was the only way to decide that, and the doctor called up Dr. Wyck in Altonville and asked him questions and got madder and madder and finally hung up and said that the man must be out of his mind, but he wouldn't say anything else to me, why he thought so. I suppose that's what they call professional etiquette.

Well, they made the examination and they said there was a clot of blood that traveled to the heart and stopped it beating. And my son being a medical student I knew something about such things so I asked if it was because the blood transfusion they gave Joseph wasn't done right, and the doctor looked startled as if I'd guessed something he didn't want to talk about. But he wouldn't say. He just said it was impossible to give an opinion.

I was prostrate with grief, and after the doctor went and I could get rid of my friends who came, I called up Dr. Wyck, and I guess I used too strong language, but I was distracted and a bereaved mother and half out of my own mind. And I told him he had murdered my son with his criminal carelessness, and that he would be sorry and that I would have his right to practice medicine revoked.

He spoke very strange over the telephone to me, and didn't seem to care what I was saying at first but only wanted to know the exact time Joseph died. Of course I couldn't tell him, I having been out shopping, and any way I can't see why he wanted to know that. But he kept insisting and I told him I knew it was between ten and eleven o'clock.

Well, then he suddenly began to sound different over the phone and said, "Madam, it won't be necessary for you to do anything. I have performed my last operation. Good bye." As I say I was almost out of my mind with grief, and I forgot all about what I'd said about having his license taken away, and never did anything about that when I came back to my senses and realized that doctors do their best and some accidents can't be helped. But I couldn't bring myself to call up and say I was sorry.

Then I learned he had disappeared, and I think I felt, well, if he did that, he must have felt guilty, so it was all right for me to think it had been his fault. But when I learned he had taken poison and shut himself up in that room full of poison gas, because that's my opinion of what must have happened in spite of what the papers said, why, I felt like a murderer myself. And my lease was up, and I didn't renew it, and I went away without telling anybody where I was going, not even the post office. And I've been living here ever since trying to make peace with my heart and conscience and my Savior, and now I know I can never do it while I carry this secret burden in my breast. So I will give up if you will send for me.

> Yours sincerely,
> MAUDE BAKER.

Prexy read this letter, of course before I had seen it, and immediately he had finished he said to the sheriff, "Mr. Palmer, I should like you to sign and date this, and you, Saunders, I should like you to do the same as a witness of its receipt."

That was what gave me the chance to read it, as I refused to put my signature on it without knowing enough to be able to identify it again. Prexy then handed it back to the sheriff and said, "Please file this as important evidence in the Wyck case. You are of course responsible for the decision of whether you should bring the woman in for questioning."

The sheriff looked relieved, at this indication that Prexy did not consider it another hoax. But he still did not know what to do about it, and asked Prexy's private opinion, which of course was that there could be no possible charge in law against the woman, but that the presumption of attempted suicide was greatly strengthened by her confession.

"Yeah," said Sheriff Palmer, "that's right enough. Mebbe he committed suicide, and there's just a chance he did it by figgerin' out some invention to stab himself in the back of his own neck.

But this woman don't seem to realize he was embalmed—and what we've got to find is the guy that embalmed him."

He stared at me long and suspiciously, and then tramped out to his car. When he had gone I looked at Prexy with growing excitement. "You're thinking—what?" he asked.

"I don't know whether I quite dare think it, sir," I said. "But long ago I had the weird notion that there might be some connection between that first terrible seizure of Mike's and the fact that the Tompkins boy had died at almost the same time, with some of Mike's blood in him."

Prexy nodded slowly, "And so?"

"Well, sir, Mike's second seizure came between ten and eleven o'clock, later that same morning, at about the time that Joe Baker died—with some of Mike's blood in him."

He sank back in his chair, lips pursed. "Yes," he said. "And I remember from some of the records you showed me that each of those two had received only 250 cc. of Mike's blood. What would have happened in the case of someone who had practically been living on the blood of that same donor?"

We both stared at each other, I with the sensation of standing on the sill of some utterly new and perhaps terrible storehouse of knowledge, pausing for a reassuring glance from my guide.

"Now you see, Saunders," he went on, "why it was that I never bothered to question you about your alibi, for the night when you found me at Mike's bedside. At the moment of that third and worst seizure, I had a kind of uncanny but absolute conviction that Gideon Wyck had just died. Before his death he communicated to me the news which you later confirmed by intelligent research—that he had transfused into his own veins, in the course of eight months, several thousand cubic centimeters of Mike's blood. This letter completes the evidence.

"For a long time I have had means of knowing that Wyck himself was aware of the seeming coincidence of the death of young Tompkins with Mike's first seizure. But I did not know that he himself was aware of the second coincidence, and I have remained rather stupidly oblivious of it myself. I shouldn't have. You gave me some time ago the necessary hint for running it down, when you showed me the full record of Mike's blood donations, both the known and the secret ones."

I racked my memory for a few moments, and then asked, "If Wyck was aware of that first coincidence, how do you account for the way he acted when Biddy called him to attend Mike the second time? He just refused to be bothered. Don't you remember?"

"Certainly, and that's what is explained by this letter that just came in. It was the two telephone calls from the Bakers' doctor and from Mrs. Baker herself that made Wyck perceive the significance of the first coincidence by providing him with a second one of like nature."

"And did you mean, sir, what you said to the sheriff about the letter increasing the presumption of attempted suicide?"

"Yes. Don't you agree?"

"Well, what about the knife wound? Could he really a have done that? The coroner said that was the cause of death, and not the poison."

"I think the coroner's right. Moreover, when the knife wound was inflicted, enough veronal had been absorbed to render Wyck unconscious, or at least incapable of defending himself. As a matter of fact, I have reasons, which I prefer not to tell anyone as yet, not even you, for feeling sure that Wyck did commit suicide. That is, he did so far as his own volition was concerned. But someone else, before death actually occurred, inflicted that knife wound."

"If that's so—" I said, and then paused cautiously.

"Yes?"

"If that's so— Well, what makes you so sure that I couldn't have done that part of it myself, just before coming home?"

He smiled. "Don't ask any questions like that of the sheriff, Saunders. I had two good reasons. One I've already mentioned —that Wyck was comatose at the time the knife struck him. He couldn't personally have given you the fight which, to anyone who wasn't aware of the facts, your torn clothes might indicate that he had. And the other reason was the absolute inspirational conviction, which I also have already mentioned, that the knife cut Wyck's spinal cord almost at the precise moment of Mike's third seizure. At that moment, of course, you and I were together at Mike's bedside, so you obviously couldn't have done it. Is that sufficient?"

I nodded, still wishing that he would be as frank about his secret information as I had been about mine.

CHAPTER XXVIII

One cold day after the Christmas recess I saw Daisy walking with Dr. Alling down a little canyon left by the snow plow on the east side of Atlantic Street. I was in my study, and they passed without looking up. That evening, when I dropped in for my usual call, I waited curiously to see whether she had anything new to report. When nothing came voluntarily, I asked her, in a tone of mock jealousy, what she had gone walking with another beau for.

"There's not much use telling you, Dave," she answered. "Let's just say that as long as we're not sure of a solution, I don't trust anybody."

"Including me?"

"Well, I'll make a special exception of you, my lad; but what I said goes for all your friends—and mine."

"Including Jap Ross and Mickey Rehan and Dick Prendergast and—"

"I wasn't thinking so much about them as about Marjorie and —well, one other. Never mind who."

"The same being Dr. Alling, I suppose."

"Let's not talk about it, Dave. You know we can't agree when his name comes up. Just give me the benefit of my own doubts, so far as he's concerned."

"All right. Will you tell me what's new, if I promise not to try to argue about it?"

"I would, but there isn't anything new—yet. Oh, all right. It's just a hunch. It's about what you told me before Christmas, about Mike reacting to the deaths of people with his blood in them. Alling gave you to understand that he was positive that Wyck had died at the moment when Mike went really mad. He was on hand to watch it happen, and so were you. That's why he didn't suspect you, which is fair enough so far as it goes. But he also told you that he had a means of knowing that Wyck himself was aware of the fact that young Tompkins died at about the time of Mike's first seizure. If Alling really has a means of knowing that, it must be in some document that Wyck left for him, or else"—she paused— "or else Wyck told Alling personally, shortly before he died."

"So what?" I remarked, seeing no great light as yet.

"So Alling, who believed all along in this bizarre telepathic business, and in the significance of it, admitted himself that his belief was based solely on the first, and imperfectly established coincidence."

"Yes," I admitted.

"And there was a second attack, about the coincidence element of which he admitted that he was unaware. I mean he didn't know Baker had died too. Now, Dave, he's a scientist, and he claims that in the third instance he was positive Wyck was dead, the moment the attack came. But remember, the past history at that moment concerned two former seizures, on the first of which he had only the doubtful materials for a weird theory, and on the second of which he had no corroborative evidence at that time at all. Well, dear little Daisy just claims that Alling's isn't the kind of mind that would feel certain about such a wildly doubtful point, in a scientific investigation, when the corroborative evidence to start with was less than fifty per cent favorable."

"Point granted, on the merits of materials brought up," I admitted.

"Therefore, when he came to Mike's bedside, he had a better reason than theory alone for thinking that Wyck was about to die. He was sitting there, waiting for the reaction. No wonder he felt sure, convinced, when it happened on schedule. Remember, you said you found him waiting with a watch in his hand? And he'd sent Biddy away for a pretty flimsy reason. Doctors don't usually prescribe walks at half past one in the morning for any ailment. Dave, he came there knowing perfectly well that Wyck was going to die in a few minutes."

I could see the full logic of her argument, which was bolstered by the one thing I had never spoken to her about—the dry-cleaning machine which Alling might have used to clean Wyck's garments—the very garments which had been mailed from Boston on a day when Alling himself was in that city.

"All right," I said, trying not to show that I had been much affected. "I promised I wouldn't argue. Go ahead."

"Well, up to that point it's hardly arguable. The rest is hunch. But it's perfectly possible that Alling came to Mike's bedside to watch for a reaction, after having poisoned Wyck. Veronal doesn't act quickly. We all know Wyck was ill. Alling could have insisted on giving him something for his illness, and loaded it down with veronal. Then he could have left Wyck in a coma, with plenty of time to get to the Connells' before death would actually occur."

"May I make a suggestion, with no intention to argue?" I asked. She laughed and nodded. "What about the fact, then," I continued, "that the knife thrust, and not the poison, caused death? If he was dead before the knife went in, there wouldn't have been an extensive hemorrhage around the cut."

"I know. You told me that before. But, once he had Wyck full of a slow-acting drug, he could have arranged him under some kind of mechanical device that would have inflicted the wound. In fact, he'd want to have something to time it, wouldn't he? Alling's clever enough to rig up something to do that part of it."

I had another sudden shock of memory. At the very time when I had discovered about the dry-cleaning machine, I had also checked the invoice for a new kymograph, an instrument to record varying blood pressure or any other pulsation. The new one had been ordered after Wyck's death. Could Alling have used the old one as a timing device, to check up on the actual moment when Wyck's heart stopped beating? Again I hardly dared to look at Daisy. She seemed to be building up the strongest case yet. There were a dozen reasons why Alling could have wanted to kill Wyck and get him out of the way, at a time when he had become such a terrific embarrassment to the school. And, if Alling had known how near to death from cancer Wyck really was, he could have salved his conscience by calling it an act of mercy.

Daisy was watching my expression, so I said, "Any more to add?"

"Only that Alling told you specifically that he was informed, before Wyck died, of the six transfusions from Mike to the old doctor. Alling's terribly open-minded. He wouldn't let the utterly far-fetched quality of his theory stop him, but he wouldn't believe it too soon, for the same reason. There he had a perfect set-up. A person with 250 cc. of Mike's blood in him had caused a certain reaction. Here was a chance to test the repetition by killing another person who had had two or three thousand cc. of the same blood. The reaction ought to be correspondingly more violent—and it was."

I kept my promise, and did not argue. There was, as a matter of fact, little to argue about. I had two extra items of information to corroborate Daisy's theory—items unknown to her. Nevertheless, I decided to keep them to myself until I had had a chance to look in Prexy's house for the dry-cleaning machine. But I resolved to be far more careful, for the time being, in my own confidences with my employer, and to keep a shrewder lookout for slips on his part.

During the next two weeks or so nothing startling occurred. The sheriff continued (by wiles and subterfuges which I shall describe shortly, all in one place) to add more and more finger-prints to his local rogues' gallery, without, however, getting any nearer a solution of the crime. His main attentions centered on Dick Prendergast, probably owing to the fact that Mr. Palmer only recently had learnt the details of that unfortunate faculty meeting at which Dick had been expelled. At any rate, the sheriff had already got fingerprints of all the other persons who had been publicly questioned or accused, and it was logical that he should concentrate all his attention on someone who was to him a new suspect. Prendergast, however, proved worthy of his opponent's mettle. He knew his rights, and did not propose to be bullied out of them. As soon as he realized that the law was definitely on his trail, Dick took to wearing gloves even in his own room, and at meals.

At last the wily officer got his chance, when he caught Dick doing 46 miles an hour within the town limits and promptly haled him off to the lock-up; but the culprit produced a copy of the state law which forbade fingerprinting except under a felony charge, cheerfully paid a ten-dollar fine for his misdemeanor, and departed again with his fingerprints still strictly private.

For me the two-week period after the talk with Daisy which I have just described was too crowded with other matters to permit any independent sleuthing. The first part of it was crammed with study, and the last was filled with mid-year examinations. Late in January the next important event took place. I myself am inclined to believe that it had nothing to do with the Wyck case, but, since the law has taken a different view of the matter, I shall try to describe what happened, and then will give my own variant interpretation.

Our weekly paper, which had simply fizzed with news and conjectures for a couple of months after Wyck's cadaver was found, had been pursuing through the middle of the winter its usual, and by contrast extremely uninteresting, course. Circulation dropped down to normal again; and the editor, still fired by the memory of those journalistically triumphant two months, began casting about for manufactured excitement. Finally he went to the sheriff and made a proposition. If the sheriff would give him an interview, he guaranteed to print something that not only would bring honor to both of them, but might solve the mystery as well. The sheriff consented, and two days later received his copy of the paper, in which, to his complete surprise, he found a featured story saying that the murderer had been definitely located by Sheriff Palmer, in a brilliant piece of detection, and that his arrest was being delayed for the purely technical reason that a photograph and actual fingerprints had not yet been received from another city. The identity, however, had been absolutely established by telegraph by means of the Bertillon system; the man was under constant surveillance, and would be arrested within twenty-four hours.

Sheriff Palmer went around and read the riot act to the editor, and a retraction was arranged for the next issue. However, six hours after the sheet appeared the telephones of the town jangled and buzzed with the news that a student had committed suicide. It was poor Tommy Jarvis, who had been one of the medics called by Wyck as a witness against Prendergast. He left no note of explanation of any kind, but a copy of the *Alton Weekly Clarion* was lying on the floor beside the bed on which his body was found—a copy of that day's issue, bearing the trumped-up story that the murderer had been located.

Sheriff Palmer immediately let it be known that he and the editor had been in cahoots, and that the hoax had been published for the deliberate purpose of scaring the murderer out of town, thus disclosing his identity. That it had worked better than they intended was perhaps a good thing, because it saved the state the expense of a prosecution.

To me it all seemed entirely preposterous, for two good reasons: first, that Jarvis was one of the very few students who had genuinely admired Dr. Wyck, with all the admiration of a timorous person for a dynamic one; second, that I myself, with a number of others, that very day had witnessed an episode that was a far more likely cause of this latest tragedy.

I have already mentioned the fact that Jarvis was the most brilliant student in the College of Surgery, and have alluded to his ill health. It was about nine o'clock in the evening when Jarvis killed himself by inhaling hydrogen cyanide, but here is what had happened an hour or two before:

On the afternoon in question we all saw a notice on the bulletin board saying that in place of the next pathology lecture there would be a post-mortem examination at the hospital. These "posts" occurred irregularly, whenever we were fortunate enough to get permission from the relatives of the deceased person. Even at our stage of the game we could realize that the P.M.'s were of fundamental importance to the science of medicine, and each one was something of an event. It gave us a chance to correlate organic changes with clinical findings and to complete the picture of a disease—a necessary requirement for accurate diagnosis and treatment.

At the beginning of the course, the class had been divided into sequences of pairs, each pair to assist in turn at an autopsy. My mate for the job was Jarvis; and it was no secret to me or to the school at large that he himself had been cheating us for a long time of our right to perform an autopsy upon his own body. I mean that, even in his first year, the doctors had advised him to give up his dream of being a great surgeon, and go to Arizona or to Saranac. They had told him frankly that the climate of Altonville would be an aggravation of his incipient tuberculosis, and that it was doubtful that he could survive even a year of it.

But Tommy had clung to his dream, principally, I think, for the very reason that he wanted to learn every trick and chance, every special department of pathology that might later aid him in curing himself. A rigorous system of hygienic living, a powerful sun lamp in his own room, (under which he did all of his studying in the nude),[1] and a sheer obstinate unwillingness to succumb to a cruel destiny, had somehow combined to keep Jarvis with us for three and a half years. But each month the red spots in his cheeks grew brighter, and his weight continued to decline. It was only after his suicide that we found a sterilizing cabinet full of mucus bags in his closet. He had done no more coughing in public than the average person would, but he had learned the trick of "raising" phlegm in private.

I mention these facts, because on the day in question it was our turn, and for the further reason that, as I read off the facts of the clinical history of the case for him to copy, I knew that we were in for a grueling session. The corpse had a boyish look, although it was of a man in his middle thirties. He had died after a short recent illness. Tuberculous nephritis was given as the cause. In his youth he had had pulmonary tuberculosis, which had been arrested. The fatal illness was either an exacerbation of the old lesion or a recent infection made worse by his hypersensitive condition.

Tommy tried to conceal from me the extent to which the details of the case struck home to him, but I could not help noticing how wretched it made him feel. Dr. Kent presently entered and went about his preparations. This was a signal for silence and activity. We hurried into our gowns and rubber gloves. I got no chance to offer encouraging remarks to Tommy; anyway, it might have been the worst thing to do.

The autopsy room at the hospital, like most of the classrooms at the school, is built in amphitheater style. During the examination an element of drama was added by the use of one large powerful light bulb, hanging directly over the operating table, its rays focused sharply downward in the center of the otherwise gloomy room. All of us, I think, felt a far different sensa-

1 Medical opinion is in general against the use of such devices for pulmonary tuberculosis.—Ed.

tion toward the body in an autopsy than toward the long-dead stiffs which we carved up in the anatomy course. The color and appearance of life often lingered, in a recently dead body, combining curiously with the faint but sharp odor of the first processes of decay.

Tommy took the initiative in our work; and his hand was steady and deft as we opened the abdomen to show the weight and appearance of the organs, while Dr. Kent lectured extemporaneously to the class on whatever pathological changes were revealed. Presently we discovered the scars of the previous chest infection. They involved an extensive area in the lower lobe of the man's left lung, some parts of which were calcified, one nodule about an inch in diameter resembling bone. There was in addition to this a new focus in the upper lobe, small, but capable of distributing the tubercle bacilli throughout his system. Tubercles, however, were not visible grossly in other organs except his kidneys. Both of these were involved; the left was little more than a dilated sack full of yellow, necrotic tissue. The infection extended even down to his bladder, and adequately explained the diagnosis which had been made on the basis of purely external symptoms.

I had become so absorbed in my work that I had forgotten Jarvis's special interest in such a case. Looking up, by chance, I saw that his lips were bloodless, tightly compressed, and that his eyes were staring downward in a kind of hopeless fascination. The poor chap was really looking at a picture of his own body's interior.

Dr. Kent finished with the facts as noted, and began to speak of their general ramifications. "We might have found no active primary focus in the lungs," he said. "The kidney tubercle may have been slowly progressing for a number of years, and progressing necessarily to this end. For, gentlemen, tuberculosis of the kidneys does not heal."

The bright spots in Tommy's cheeks, which Jap said later had been pulsing hectically all through the operation, became bloodless at these words. I myself chanced to know that Kent was enunciating the theory of a recent worker, in whom he had a special interest and confidence that was not universally shared;

so I took advantage of the assistant's privilege to interrupt with a question.

"Dr. Kent, isn't it true that the idea you've just given as positive fact is actually still questioned by many pathologists? Isn't it also an accepted fact that tuberculous nephritis has been cured by timely surgery?"

The lecturer hesitated, and glanced toward Jarvis. I felt that he realized my motives, for he qualified what he had said by admitting that strong and intelligent opposition to his statements could be expected from certain quarters of the profession. He continued then to explain in detail the possible avenues of infection for the urino-genital tract, without touching again upon the mortality of the disease.

Tommy had apparently heard enough, however, to confirm a suspicion that had been growing upon him. He seemed to me to be on the verge of collapse. I whispered to him to go outside if his stomach was bothering him, but he got a grip on himself and continued doggedly with his scalpel, cutting and weighing organs and tissues while from the instructor he heard a sort of dress rehearsal of his own fate. He was calm when he left the room, but there was a look of determination in his eyes which I wrongly interpreted as a new conquest of his fears. Instead, it must have betokened an irrevocable decision to meet voluntarily and at once the fate which would otherwise come soon enough, but in a messier fashion.

Owing to the presumption that his death was caused by poisoning, an autopsy was performed on Tommy's body, and we found within him an almost exact duplication of the conditions which he had had revealed to him in the organs of another man. The only difference lay in the fact that the pulmonary lesions in Tommy's case were more recent and active, while the infection of the kidneys was less pronounced. The poor fellow had learnt enough, however, in his courageous attempt at continuing in school, to realize from his own symptoms that the infection in his lungs already was spreading to other organs, where there was practically no chance of arresting it—and the autopsy at which he had officiated had confirmed his worst fears.

This tragic event occurred in the last week of January. When the sheriff's preposterous interpretation became known to me, I went at once to Dr. Alling and gave him the explanation I believed to be the true one.

"I've already heard of that from Dr. Kent," he said. "He came in here all cut up about it the very evening it happened. Nevertheless, I think we will do well to let the sheriff cherish his belief. For him, you see, it solves the case. From now on he'll be less trouble to the rest of us."

"What about Tommy's family?" I objected. "It's hard enough on them to have lost a son, without having to hear him accused of being a murderer, on the flimsiest grounds."

"I've thought of that, of course, and have written this letter to them. Please type it off with a carbon."

I shall not bother to reproduce the whole letter, which was an eloquent expression of sympathy, a statement that the murder theory was preposterous, and a promise that Tommy's name would be cleared by the most diligent investigation. Pending that, Prexy asked that the Jarvis family leave to him alone the responsibility for acting. He said it was normal, and to be expected, that they would publish denials of the sheriff's allegations; he even recommended that they do so, merely requesting that they give him a free hand in the duty of clearing the boy's name. I was interested to note that he ended the letter with a definite promise that, if he were himself unable to effect this act of justice by the end of the school year, he would turn over all data in his possession to any agency of investigation which they cared to appoint. As Jarvis's family lived in a small town in the extreme northern part of the state, I did not imagine that they would be able to finance any such investigation and would thus be perfectly willing to leave it in Prexy's hands.

CHAPTER XXIX

I have now brought my story nearly up to date. The last of a late snowfall melted early in March, inaugurating a month of slush and mud that dispelled all outdoor activity, in the Wyck case as well as elsewhere, and removed such excuses as we might otherwise have had for neglecting our work. It made little difference in my own busy routine, but I often heard my friends remarking upon the hidden virtues of a horrible northern spring. We have few traditions at the Maine State College of Surgery. It is too young an institution, as they go, to have many distinctive rites; but the phrase "to throw a March party" is something which has come naturally out of a combination of our work and our climate.

The purpose, like that of many other traditions, is very different from what the words suggest. When a fellow throws a March party at our school he merely invites a few of his friends to his room. They accept with the understanding that each will bring his own snack of grub and that the host will supply a limited quantity of home-brewed small beer. The object of the party is a serious review which may last anywhere from two hours to eight, of some important phase of our studies. The fellows take up unit subjects in turn, rotating the chairmanship round the room. One of us will tell all he knows about a certain phase of a subject. The others hop on any error he makes, and, when he is through, add any details he may have forgotten. Books seldom are opened during a March party; but once in a while the memory of the majority is sufficiently questioned by some maverick to make a reference to the text imperative. Whatever drinking is done does not have any degree of inebriation for its object, but merely a clearing of the throat, for oratorical purposes. Good fighting applejack binges are frequent enough, at the school, but they are not called March parties. The element of tradition enters forcibly, in that one of the latter, so announced in advance, is never permitted to degenerate into a binge.

My special reason for mentioning these parties is that Dick Prendergast, about whose possible complicity in the Wyck case my opinion had fluctuated all winter, seemed to have proved toward the end of the winter that he had got a genuinely new and serious attitude out of his misfortune of the preceding year; and the proof of it was apparent in the fact that he staged the first March party of the spring. He had never thrown one before, and, to the best of our memory, had never attended anyone else's. In fact, the very mention of one, in former years, had been sufficient to make him guffaw. Now, however, he not only inaugurated the season, but also was on hand at more than half of the ones I happened to attend.

All year I had taken it pretty well for granted that his satisfactory grades had been dictated from Prexy's office, and that it was a matter of general policy to get him through the year, give him his degree, and cry good riddance, no matter how badly he did his work. At the March parties, however, we all got the distinct surprise of perceiving that he knew his stuff about as well as anyone else, whether as chairman or as heckler. It was actually a good deal easier for a student to bluff in class, or on an examination, than at a March party. We soon found out that Dick was not bluffing. What seemed to have happened was that he had for the first time in his life actually learnt how to study. It may have been the doing of the psychoanalyst with whom he had gone to Europe after his expulsion from school. But, whatever the explanation, a mind which had always been brilliant and lazy had been applying itself, and in six months had not only kept up with new work, but also had reviewed a vast amount of work in arrears. It seemed apparent that if he only had done this from the beginning, he would have been at the head of his class. As it was, he seemed to have maintained an honest midway position all winter, after having started with a great handicap—even if it was one for which he alone had been responsible.

Since Prexy's trip to check Dick's alibi for the night on which Wyck had been killed, I had been inclined to drop him altogether from consideration as a suspect. With half a dozen hotel managers and clerks, to say nothing of Prexy and a state senator, all accounting for him at various increasingly remote places as the night grew older, it would have been rather preposterous to complicate the solution by continuing to pay any attention to him at all—quite preposterous, indeed, except for two considerations: the first was that he continued most diligent in refusing to allow the sheriff to take his fingerprints, even by accident; and the second was that the missing blue books—the only articles known to have been on Wyck's person when he disappeared that were not returned in the bundle—had never since been discovered.

I had one additional quick shock of suspicion when Tommy

Jarvis was found dead, as I remembered that he had been chief witness for chief inquisitor Wyck, in the proceedings that had led to Prendergast's undoing; but the presumption of suicide in Jarvis's case was so nearly absolute, for the clearest of reasons, that any alternate hypothesis would have to be bolstered by overwhelming evidence. Far from there being any such, it later turned out that Dick had been in attendance as an assistant in the maternity ward during the entire time between the beginning of post-mortem and the finding of Jarvis's body. It had been one of those cases of long-continued labor, after a premature rupture of the bag of water, that make you willing to agree after a few hours that women's work *is* never done.

As soon as I realized that Dick could not possibly have had anything to do with the death of Tommy, my other two reasons for maintaining a lingering suspicion began to look more foolish; and I had quite cast them aside as chimerical after noting how changed he was at the first few March parties. Daisy was not quite so willing to drop him entirely out of consideration. But she had recently been concentrating her attention on a sly job of duplicity that almost made me feel ashamed of her. After our adventure in the old creamery, she had vowed to devote more time to an investigation of the possible double life of Marjorie Wyck; and with this in mind, my sweetheart had slowly and deliberately insinuated herself into that baffling young lady's good graces. By the end of the winter their mutual contact had taken on all the outer earmarks of a real friendship. For a long time Daisy persisted, without finding anything that either increased or decreased her suspicions. But at last, one evening in the middle of March, she called me up in great excitement and asked me to drop around for news.

It proved to be this: she had stopped in to see Marjorie in the afternoon and had found her spring cleaning—and "Flitting" the closets to discourage moths. In the main hall, within two yards of the front door, was a closet which Marjorie herself had never used, but in which her father had always kept his various neatly tailored outer garments—raincoat, overcoat, topcoat, and ulster, together with an incredible variety of rakish hats. The overcoat had been included in the bundle of garments mailed from Boston and still was in the sheriff's office. The other coats, of course, had been examined for clews after his disappearance, and had since been hanging there in the hall closet.

Daisy volunteered to help with the Flitting, and took down the coats. Marjorie turned the pockets inside out and brushed them, and then took each garment out on the porch for a thorough shaking. When she was shaking the topcoat, the two missing blue books suddenly went tumbling down the front steps. Folded longitudinally, they had been in an inside, breast-high pocket, such as is to be found in most coats, but of which no one, to the best of my knowledge, ever makes use except by mistake.

At the time when Daisy was telling me this, I remembered once having lost my own wallet in just such a way, by putting it in the inner, breast pocket of a buttoned topcoat, when I thought I had put it in the corresponding pocket of my jacket.

"He must have realized it wasn't good business to carry them around," I reflected aloud, "and so he tucked them in there while he was in the house, before he went out again with Muriel."

"I don't think that at all," Daisy answered. "He'd have locked them in his desk, or some other safe place, if he was nervous about them. As a matter of fact, I don't think he even cared."

"You mean you think they were planted there? By whom?"

"By Marjorie, of course. Why else would she have them so conveniently tumble out when I was around? She's somewhat slicker than I thought. She realized why I'd suddenly got so friendly, and decided to turn a danger into a defense."

"Say, wait a minute, Daisy," I said. "They called the coat that came back in the mail an *overcoat,* didn't they?"

"Yes. It was a blue Chesterfield overcoat."

"Well, he was wearing a light gray topcoat, a regular ice cream topcoat, at the meeting. I remember perfectly, because he kept it on in the faculty room as if he had a chill. It never occurred to me to suspect that the one in the bundle wasn't that same coat. And now I think of it, he had it on and buttoned when I handed the blue books back to him. I'll bet anything he just put them in the topcoat pocket by mistake, instead of into his jacket pocket. When he went home, he changed to a Chesterfield because he knew he was going up that cold hillside. And the blue books have been there ever since, in a pocket that nobody would ever think to look for."

"Do you want me to believe that men don't use all their pockets? Their clothes certainly bulge out of shape in enough places to make you think they do."

"Well, how many pockets have I got in this suit?" I challenged.

She studied it, and said, "Good gracious, there must be twelve."

"You're three short," I answered. "There are fifteen, which is the usual number; and with two extra outside ones in an overcoat or topcoat, you never have any use for the eighteenth."

"Eighteen pockets? Whew! No wonder men bulge. All right, you win. No doubt the books were there all the time, and maybe they didn't even think to look at the overcoat at all, when they searched the place. Perhaps Marjorie isn't trying to shield her friend Prendergast. Just the same, I still have my suspicions of dear little Marjorie."

"Her friend Prendergast? Are they friends?"

"Not that I know of," Daisy admitted, "but it seemed a swell solution for awhile. All right, Prendergast is out of the picture again, but I'm going to be Marjorie's bosom friend awhile longer, just the same. That young lady interests me a lot."

At about this time the sheriff himself got wind, belatedly, of the real reason for Jarvis's suicide, and showed better sense than one would expect by admitting that it knocked his thesis into a cocked hat. At once he resumed his fingerprinting activities. These, in an early stage, usually had taken some such form as this: He would approach his victim and say, "Hey, young feller, I want to git a list of the home addresses of you birds. Now let's see, your name is—" and he would fumble for a notebook, shifting to the other hand a big steel-backed ledger he was carrying. Then he would half-drop it, while rummaging for a pencil, and finally say, "Here, hold this danged thing for me a minute. Thanks." Unless the victim was on the alert, he would find himself holding the ledger by the polished metal panels that were a part of the spring binding. The sheriff then would coolly take it back, examine the prints the boy's fingers had made, compare them with the photographs of the bulb, and cross another name off his list. The names always got crossed off, and his list of possible suspects had narrowed to a scant half-dozen as the winter deepened. These survivors of course took it as a kind of game, to see who could hold out longest against the sheriff's extra-legal, but not strictly illegal, wiles.

Three of the six were eliminated all in one morning, when the sheriff stood behind a pair of swinging doors with newly polished brass plates on them, leading into the main lecture hall. Before the end of February the list had narrowed down to Prendergast and a chap named Jensen, who forgot himself long enough to leave clear prints on the radiator of his stalled ten-dollar Ford, one morning, when pushing it backwards to the roadside.

Latterly the sheriff and I struck up something peculiarly like a friendship, as in the case of cops and reformed gunmen in the movies. He gave me to understand that I was a natural-born criminal, but that he would be the last fellow in the world to make things hard for me if I lived it down and went straight. By the device of betting him twenty plugs of Apple chewing tobacco that he wouldn't find the right print before the end of the school year, I made myself an excuse for checking up on his progress.

During the Christmas vacation he had extended his attention to the faculty and, before mid-March, could boast that he had checked the prints of every student but Prendergast and every member of the faculty except Coroner Kent. His tally of students, of course, excluded first-year men, who had not been in town when the murder was committed, and did not include such of last year's graduates as had moved any considerable distance from Altonville. Of the latter group, however, a number were serving as internes at our own hospital, and he had corralled all those. He also had had a field day down at the Portland hospitals, and had checked up all the men who were there. In short, on March 16, 1933, Sheriff Palmer had, by his own admission, only five logical suspects left to pursue: Kent, Prendergast, and three of last year's graduates who had moved into other states.

One day I asked him, in a bantering fashion, whether he had fingerprinted all the wives and children of the faculty. Winking shrewdly, he opened the notebook that contained his lists of suspects, and showed me, on the back page, the names of a number of nurses and faculty wives, all crossed off. There also, with lines drawn through them, stood the names of Daisy and Marjorie Wyck.

One reassuring feature of the lessening tension of this period was a resumption of work on the *Short Sketch for a History of Concomitant Variations in Morphogenesis and Psychogenesis*. As I perhaps should have mentioned earlier, Dr. Alling, somewhat to my surprise, had not seemed at all interested in getting the records of Dr. Wyck's experiments from the old creamery—or whatever it had been. When first I offered to guide him there, he declined— which probably was wise. And when I said that I would bring him the book which recorded the experiments, he said that he would prefer to leave it there until spring. The experience of the unfortunate Mrs. Bennett would probably keep her from returning there, and it was not likely that anyone else would attempt to get into it in the wintertime. She, incidentally, had proved completely uncommunicative during our two attempts to get information from her.

One morning in March, however, I got a hint that my boss soon might want all of Wyck's records, when, characteristically, he greeted me with the statement, "I've at last got the right lead for that teratology[1] chapter—or, rather, section it will be now. Please take this before we go on with what we were doing yesterday:

The subject of pre-natal influence, like that of demon possession, has for many years been relegated to the limbo of utter and unmitigated superstitions; but, unlike the case of demon possession, prenatal influence has not been blessed with a new set of names laved clean of the old awful implications; for here again we find the medical scientist playing ostrich, simply refusing to consider the possibility of a fact that has been attested in many instances, from the earliest times to the present, on evidence categorically no worse than that readily accepted to substantiate less embarrassing phenomena. Here again I am not playing Ishmael on a basis of theory alone. In

1 The science of inquiry into the causes of physical abnormalities in growth.—ED.

the last sentence but one, I referred to pre-natal influence as a fact, which, you will remember, I have not made bold to do in the case of demon possession.

The subject of the present chapter was early taken up by those excellent and eager observers, the members of the Royal Society. It was considered a matter worthy of scientific investigation for nearly 150 years. Then something happened which, unless my abundant references (see appendix xxi) are curiously and consistently misleading, has never to my knowledge occurred in any other field of free inquiry. I here make the charge, upon evidence in the appendix above referred to, that a generation of physicians and surgeons, the same generation that taught medicine to the poet Keats, deliberately and concertedly conspired to ridicule a moot scientific point completely out of consideration.

I am by no means attacking the intentions of these men, which were excellent. Indeed, their obviously high intentions are the best proof of their guilt, viz: they themselves knew that the evidence for pre-natal influence was strong; and they knew that it was universally believed in by all classes of society; and, it being a mental causation of a physical effect, they knew that widespread belief in it caused a presumption of maximum occurrence. Therefore they took it upon themselves to deny its right to consideration even as a hypothesis; and it is my charge that they concertedly instituted a campaign of flat denial and of ridicule so markedly successful that not only was public credence in the phenomenon noticeably diminished, but also the next generation of the medical profession itself was deprived of the right to think fairly and freely on a question theretofore honestly listed as possible, and, because of recent researches, now classifiable among the proven facts of science.

There is a lesson to be learnt from this, for I find by direct inquiry through agents in several districts that about 94% of persons in families having an aggregate income below $2,000 still believe in prenatal influence and take all possible precautions to insure good rather than evil consequences from it; 79% of persons of the higher classes believe it, but less fearfully, merely owing to their securer status. Among physicians, only 3 out of 100 admitted that there might be any possibility at all of its reality.

In other words, the medical profession as a whole has been far more credulous than the general public, with that perverse, inverse credulity which refuses to take any notice of an inconvenient fact.

Prexy was going well when he dictated that. He smacked his lips over it, and enjoyed it. But we did not proceed with the chapter at that time.

CHAPTER XXX

It was on the last day of March, when the Wyck case had receded into a state of unreality in our minds, that Daisy and I had the experience which told me that I must make a coherent written account of events of the past year. Otherwise, with two homicidal maniacs at large, Daisy and I might not survive to tell it. I was at home, studying, when I heard the knob of the front door turn. Thinking it was Biddy, who had gone out after supper, I took no notice, until I heard a mumbling voice saying, "The divils. I'll get it back. They killed him, the old divil. But I'll get it out of his daughter. Blood's blood. It'd be the same. Biddy!" He paused, and called again. "Biddy! Ye got to help me. Ye got to hold her still, so I won't spill it."

I remained rigid, trying to think what to do. After a few seconds of waiting, however, Mike went out. I came hastily down the stairs for a quick look to see where he had gone, before phoning the authorities. He must have heard or seen me, or both, for the door came open again and he sprang in, cornering me in the back of the hall before I could get to the kitchen door.

"There," he crooned. "I won't hurt ye. I wouldn't hurt a fly, if I felt right. I ain't been right, Davy. Ye got to help me. I love ye. But I'll kill ye just the same, unless ye help me. Come now."

He grabbed my wrist in his iron fingers and pulled me toward the back door. I tried to cajole him into freeing me, but it did no good. He was used now to the fact that his hand was missing.

"Hey, you're hurting me," I said, when we were outside. "Ow!" and I let out a yell. He had not particularly hurt, but I wanted somehow to attract attention. Instead of help I got for my pains a numbing blow of his stump across my mouth.

"Another sound out o' ye and I drag ye by the neck. Quiet, now," he admonished. "I love ye, Davy, but I'll pinch ye by the neck so ye can't yell."

In desperation, I decided to follow orders and hope someone would come along. But the shrewd madman waited his chance and crossed the road with me when no-one was in sight. He dragged me directly on into the pine grove that extended to the rear of Wyck's property. Fear for myself and of what he might do to Marjorie turned into a different, more intense kind of torment when I saw through the side windows of the living room that Daisy was with her so-called friend.

Mike led me to the back porch, carefully opened the kitchen door, and was about to enter. I could stand it no longer, and quickly cried, "Run, Daisy, Mike's here!" Then I got what was doubtless coming to me. Mike roughly yanked me to a corner of the dark kitchen, pressed me immovably into the niche with his stump, and reached for my throat with his free hand. I grabbed his wrist with both my hands, but it was like trying to bend a base-ball bat. My shriek was cut off when his fingers closed slowly and inexorably on my gullet. The last thing I saw was Daisy, suddenly silhouetted in a doorway. Then my lungs and brain both seemed to be bursting.

When I came to, Daisy was kneeling over me. My throat was so sore I could not speak, but I managed to whisper, "Where'd he go?"

"Out the front way. You'd better lie still a little longer."

"Have you phoned for help?" I asked hoarsely.

"No. He took the phone with him. Tore it off the wall, but we've locked the doors."

"Good God!" I said. "Are we just marooned here with that maniac outside?"

"If he has any sense he's halfway back to the asylum by now," she said.

In the midst of my terror and anxiety I was proud of the way she was taking the situation. I did not bother to hurt my throat with the remark that Mike had no sense at all. Daisy's coolness shamed me into a quick recovery. There was nothing wrong with me but a very sore chest.

"Where's Marjorie?" I whispered.

"She ran upstairs. Come on. Let's go see. We can haul heavy things to the top of the stairs to push down on him, if we have to. That's the safest place."

I picked up a rolling-pin from the kitchen cabinet, and we went softly into the front hall. Mike had evidently swung the telephone at the hall light, for it was shattered, and only a streak of illumination came from the sitting room door, nearly closed. But there was a light in the upper hall. We hastened toward the bottom of the stairs, and were about to ascend when there was a crash of glass immediately above us, and the stained glass window at the turn of the stairs bulged and shivered. Mike was on the porch roof. I tried to herd Daisy back toward the kitchen, but she said, "Wait. See where he goes."

Gripping my rolling-pin, I waited, withdrawn well into the shadows of the hall. The whole frame of the window came out all at once. Mike stepped in, paused, and then slowly ascended the remaining stairs. If I had been alone, I think I would have been an abysmal coward, and not much cared. But, with Daisy beside me, there was nothing to do but whisper, "I've got to try to stop him."

At that moment Marjorie Wyck slipped into view. Mike crouched as if about to spring at her. Then she did something hard to explain. With spread fingers she tossed her hair into a bush on top of her head, which she seemed to shake at him as an animal might its bristling mane. Her face showed neither the horror nor the fear that one would have expected—only fury. I was struck with amazement at its likeness to the remembered face of Ted Gideon, her half-brother, when he was killing Muriel Finch.

"What do you want here, Mike Connell?" she said in a low, hard voice.

"I want me blood," he growled. "Give me back jest as much blood as yer fayther took from me, so I can git well."

"Go away, you fool," she ordered.

He stepped forward, she stepped back. Daisy and I stood tranced, watching.

"I'll take it then," he growled, moving forward.

Her expression changed. "Mike," she said, in a low, solemn voice, "you know my father's dead. But," she cried loudly, "his devils aren't. They're mine to command, now."

A hypnotic look came into her eyes, and she began to trace diagrams in the air. "Go back, Mike Connell," she said sternly, "or I shall call Beelzebub to take you to my father."

Mike shrieked and pitched forward on the floor at the top of the stairs, groveling.

"Oh, for the love of God, not that one. Keep him off. I'll go, I'll go."

He turned and came leaping down the stairs, brushing me aside and making for the front door. It was locked, of course. With a great tug he yanked and twisted the knob off, then turned and threw it through a window, kicked glass out of the corners, plunged through it himself, and was gone.

We turned to see Marjorie walking down the stairs, tucking her hair in order. Her features were composed as if nothing had happened.

"I'm sorry I had to do that," she said, in a matter-of-fact tone, "but I knew it was the only possible way to handle him. Don't worry, he won't be back."

CHAPTER XXXI

I must go on quickly now from where I stopped writing last night, but I hardly care whether I write any more at all. Something has happened today that makes it not seem to matter very much what happens in the future. But I guess it is better to write than to sit around with thoughts such as mine have been in the last few hours.

The story has already been brought up to within less than a month of the day when I now am writing, and practically nothing has happened since, except that I have been busy, making this record, writing ten or fifteen pages in two or three hours every night. Mike went right back to the asylum, and gave himself up, after the event I last wrote about. The realization that he could so easily have killed me is what made me decide to write down this record, in case I should be killed; and the knowledge, which came out soon afterward, that Ted Gideon was once more back in the vicinity, confirmed me in my decision. It is not likely that Mike will escape again. But Daisy saw Ted Gideon two days later, driving up to the Wycks' house, and though she notified Dr. Alling at once, he was not apprehended.

Daisy! Dr. Alling! Well, I must get it told as quickly as possible, and get this into the mails. Yesterday I found that my chance was at last in prospect to inspect Dr. Alling's house on the sly. And if anyone wants to draw a moral, and say I am being paid for my sin of curiosity, well and good. I have at least been put on my guard, at least have learnt what a callow fool I am. At least I know now what I am in for.

Day before yesterday Daisy went out of town, for a week-end visit (so she said) with a cousin who is the kitchen manager or some such thing down at Shoulder Lake. This morning, Dr. Alling drove off for Portland at about 8:30 A.M., saying he would not be back for at least 24 hours. So, late in the afternoon, I took my chance, walked up to the front door nonchalantly, as if expected, and found it locked. So was the back one, but a kitchen window proved to be unlatched. I pried it up, and got in. There was nothing surprising in any of the rooms that were open, but the garret and bathroom were locked.

I thought the latter fact somehow more suspicious than the former. As the bathroom window must, from the room's location, open upon the roof of a kitchen porch, and as trees arched thickly near the house to screen the back of it from passers-by, I took the chance of climbing out an adjacent bedroom window. The one opening into the bathroom was locked fast, and the shade was drawn. But, by squinting through the crack between shade and casement, I could see most of the room. Over the bathtub was a curious apparatus, a rope and pulley arrangement with a little harness like a dog's at the end of the rope. I was at a loss to account for its use.

Next, perceiving that the limb of an oak in the back yard

reached very near the back garret window, I swung up to it, and crawled to a point from which I could see inside. By the rays of the low sun, striking through the window opposite, I could make out, between two trunks, the little dry-cleaning machine I had seen depicted in the scientific supply catalogue.

Even then, I was loath to believe that my supposed friend and benefactor was definitely proved by this coincidence to be guilty of a crime. I swung down to the porch roof again, reëntered the house, locked the bedroom window inside, as I had found it, and spent the remaining daylight fruitlessly poking around in the study for further clews. It seemed safer to wait for darkness before climbing out the kitchen window again, as the tree branches which screened the porch roof did not grow at a lower level.

While I was waiting, a car suddenly paused in front of the house, and then proceeded into the garage. I knew it must be Alling, and that my chance of escape by the kitchen window was now cut off, unless he came around to the front. Just as I was about to risk opening one of the study windows, I heard a foot-fall on the porch steps, and got a glimpse of feminine apparel. Cut off in both directions, there was nothing to do but retreat upstairs, and make my getaway by means of the tree. I worked the bedroom window up and waited, to make sure that Alling was inside. When he came in the back way, and walked directly toward the front door, I waited a little longer, to let him admit the other person before I myself slipped out.

"Sorry to keep you waiting," I heard him say, "but I do like to put the car away when I know I've come in for the night. Just a crabbed bachelor-like foible. Nice drive, wasn't it? I think spring's here at last."

"Gorgeous drive."

It was Daisy's voice answering. At first I thought, and hoped, that they had just chanced to meet at Shoulder Lake, and that he had offered her a ride home. That chivalric idea crumbled promptly when she said, "It was awfully nice of you to go so far out of your way to pick me up."

Alling said, "It was a pleasure. Now, can't we cap a beautiful afternoon by consuming a beautiful Welsh rabbit? They're my specialty, you know."

"Oh, I'd love it," Daisy answered, "but I'd better be getting out before anyone sees me. I shouldn't have stopped at all. It really would have been better to mail it to me. David can be so suspicious."

"You don't think he has any inkling of—" His voice trailed away as they walked into the study. For a minute or two the incomprehensible mumble of their voices was an agony to me. Then I glimpsed them, walking back toward the front door. Alling was waving a cheque in his hand, to dry the wet ink.

"There you are. Well, it's a relief to know that you feel absolutely sure at last."

"I'm so sure," she answered, "that I know I can confront him with a single question, and make him collapse and confess. That's his temperament, you know. He'll carry a bluff to the last minute and then go to pieces. It's taken a long while to make certain-sure, but now we know."

"Thanks to you, my dear. It must have been tedious, at times. You've earned your money ten times over, and you've been ten times smarter than that Pinkerton man I hired. I ought to pay you ten times as much. Well, this little bonus will show you my gratitude, if not its full measure. It's been a wearisome job, holding off the law. I wonder if we've held it off so long that it will have to be up to us now to precipitate the dénouement."

"We can do that too," she said.

"Well, it's certainly been clever of you not to let him suspect anything. It takes a woman. I feel almost sorry for the chap."

She chuckled, in a way that cut my heart in two. This was a fine ending to my idyl. Thinking back, I remembered that it was she who had deliberately suggested that we pool our knowledge. And it was a fine ending after Alling's righteous words, "Tell the exact truth, Saunders, but no more." He must have known well how soon I would incriminate myself, by telling the exact truth, with my hopelessly bad alibi. I wondered why they had let it drag on so long, and what it was that finally had seemed to them to cinch the case.

When Daisy had left, Alling started for the stairs. I slipped quickly out onto the roof, and closed the window. It was dusky now, but I thought it would be wise to remain standing with my back against the outside wall, to find out what Alling was going to do, before risking discovery in a noisy quick descent. The bathroom light went on, and I heard a noise of water in the tub. An irresistible curiosity to see the naked, twisted body of this sanctimonious double-dealer caused me to creep carefully along the slightly sloping shingles, and peer cautiously again past the shade. A minute later I witnessed a curious spectacle, ending in one of the greatest shocks of my life. Manfred Alling, nude, stepped into my line of vision, holding a nude infant in one arm. He fastened the little belt around it, seized the rope of the pulley arrangement, and stepped into the tub, supporting the child by a tension on the rope.

It was only then that I saw what the amazing business was all about, and learnt why this man had elected to live so secretively, and alone. Manfred Alling's interest in monstrosities and abnormalities grew out of the fact that he was himself a monster—in the exact scientific sense of the term. Out of his left thigh was growing another shriveled, half-formed body, with sightless eyes and an imbecilic expression, with mouth sagging open and apt, I suppose, to get full of soapy water during the bathing process if it were not supported by the rope. The thing seemed lifeless, and I felt sure that it did not respire for itself. Otherwise he could hardly have worn it under his clothing, in the kind of corset arrangement which I presently saw him put on.

I am going to mail this now. I dare not wait any longer. It is two o'clock in the morning. I have had a stamped envelope ready all along. Let it go, and let it be read or not, as fate will have it. I don't care what happens to it, or to me either, now.[1]

1 The foregoing portion of the story was received in New York as a unit, on the 6th of May, 1933, postmarked Chicago, May 4th, at 5:00 P.M.—ED.

THE CADAVER OF GIDEON WYCK

PART III

. . . TELLING HOW DAVID SAUNDERS LIVED LONG ENOUGH TO FINISH HIS NARRATIVE, AFTER ALL.

(EDITOR'S NOTE: *The anonymous author, on the next page, claims to have learnt through an intermediary that arrangements to publish the first part of his manuscript had already been made before he commenced to write the second part. It is true that an agreement had been made to publish the work in some form; and it is also true that, before the last part of the manuscript was delivered to Farrar & Rinehart, Inc., I had contracted with them to edit the book at my own discretion and to do whatever seemed necessary to make it publishable. Neither the agency in question nor the publishers, however, were at any time interrogated as to their intentions by the "intermediary" of whom the author writes. If such a person did investigate, it was in a completely secretive fashion; and he erred in reporting that "a prominent writer of mystery stories" was to supply a fictional ending. This is my own first experience of any kind with a mystery story. I was called in only because of my amateur interest in demonology. It was at no time the intention of either the publishers or myself to supply a fictional ending. We originally planned to offer the book with the mystery unsolved, and to post a series of prizes for solutions submitted by its readers. The best of these was then to have been printed and mailed to all registered purchasers of the book. The author's own conclusion arrived in time to cancel this plan. It should also be noted that at no time has an effort been made to suppress publication, or to regain the manuscript. Owing to the peculiar circumstances of its receipt, the publishers from the first were prepared to surrender their rights in this property, at the author's request.—A. L.*)

CHAPTER XXXII

As I take up my narrative again, I wish that I had had the wit to save a copy of the part which I mailed some weeks ago—for I have no clear memory at all of the disordered last pages, written in the most bitterly unhappy moments of my life. A few days ago, through the inquiries of an intermediary whom I think I can trust, I learnt that the agent to whom the first part was sent had already contracted for its publication with a reputable firm, and that, if an end to the story were not forthcoming from me, it would be published as a "stunt book," with the "solution" provided fictionally by a prominent writer of mystery stories.

Such an ending might bring further injustice upon certain persons who were erroneously suspected of wrongdoing at one time or another in the earlier part of my narrative; so I have thought it best to continue with the true solution of the Wyck mystery, which was precipitated shortly after I had mailed, in a fit of misery and despair, the first part of this narrative.

As the truth now is known, it would be silly for me to continue to record incidents which seemed at the time of their occurrence to have a possible significance, but which later proved to be false leads. I am therefore going to pursue a different plan, telling only of the important dramatic events which led up to the final and logical explanation; and I think I shall be able to do this almost exclusively by means of setting down portions of my shorthand diary verbatim, interspersing sections of the official record of the magistrate's court and of the third and final coroner's inquest.[1] However, in order to explain my own conduct a little later on, it will be necessary to give a few excerpts that reveal my state of mind, and the effect upon my conduct of the revelations made in the last part of my story, mailed a few weeks ago.

[1] Throughout this last section of the Ms. I have continued my former practice of editing the quoted speech of various characters, whenever quotations made from memory seemed to be at variance with the speech of the same characters directly recorded at the time of speaking.—ED.

Midnight, Monday Evening,
1st May, 1933.

Nothing new today. Why should there be? Enough happened yesterday to hold me for awhile—almost enough to finish me off for good. I don't suppose I'll take Jarvis's way out, after all. Suicide. When you get to the point of writing the word, and looking at it, there's not much chance that you'll follow through. So the psychologists say. Daisy phoned at ten o'clock and wanted to know why I hadn't come around last night or tonight. I told her I hadn't known she'd be home, last night—that I thought she was going to get back on the late train from Shoulder Lake. She told me Alling had driven her home. I asked her how that had happened, and she said he'd just chanced to be driving back that way, and happened to see her at the hotel. That's a neat mixture of truth and falsehood. If I could count on just plain falsehood, I'd know more of where I am. Well, I think I kept *her* from suspecting that *I* suspect anything of what she's been up to with that little hunchback skunk. Hunchback! That's a compliment, now.

11:30 P.M., Tuesday,
2nd May, 1933.

There's a kind of twisted, abominable, abnormal pleasure in acting with my erstwhile sweetheart as if I suspected nothing. She's playing her part to the hilt, for its own sake. I staged a deliberate little tiff tonight, to see how she would react. If things were normal between us, I'm sure she would have met it in kind, giving me to understand that I wasn't the only duck in the pond. But instead, she acted just a trifle upset, and then became just endearing enough. Not too much so. That would have been suspicious. Just enough to make me feel pretty cheap, if things were normal between us. God, she's clever. She gauged it just right, on the assumption that I really haven't got an inkling of what she and that mucker Alling are cooking up against me. I've got to keep this kind of thing up, too. If their scheme is already worked out, I can't gain anything by provoking a crisis. But if I play my part, and pretend everything's all hunky-dory, she may make some slip, or Alling may, before it's too late for me to checkmate their scheme. Perhaps I should chuck medicine and be an actor. I got a kind of savage satisfaction, tonight, out of kissing the mouth off that little cheat, pretending I meant it.

The sheriff was lucky today, if you can call it luck to discover a blind alley for what it is, and so be able to narrow down the number of important directions left to move in. He's just back from a trip out of town in his car, having located all three of the fellows in last year's class who had moved over the state border to serve their interneships. He said he got the prints of all of them, and none even remotely resembled those on his precious light bulb. That leaves nobody but Muriel Finch (who's dead), Dick Prendergast, and Coroner Kent. The light bulb clew, of course, isn't worth a damn, but the sheriff won't be convinced of it until he has everybody fingerprinted. He has three lists altogether in his book—one of every student who was in school when Wyck was killed—one of every member of the faculty at that time—and one of every interne and nurse and hospital attendant.

There is now only one person left on each of the lists. The rest are all crossed off. And of course Muriel doesn't count anyway. She was on duty at the hospital from midnight to eight A.M., that night. Everything points to the supposition that Wyck was killed after midnight, and it would have taken an hour or so after that to embalm the body. If the prints on the bulb did get put there after the embalming process, they couldn't have been Muriel's. Of course, Prendergast and Alling might just possibly be in cahoots about that period after the faculty meeting when they were supposedly talking things over at Alling's house for an hour. They might have done it then, and the prints might be Prendergast's. But no, that can't be. Wyck started out from his house with Muriel at quarter to ten. They strolled slowly for two miles, and waited awhile for the Ford to appear. It must have been quarter to eleven, nearly, before they even started up the hill. I don't know what they did up there, but the chances are that they got back just about in time to deliver Muriel at the hospital at midnight. And Dick's cast-iron alibi had him all the way down to Shoulder Lake before midnight, with two check-ups on the way. He's certainly out of it. There's nobody really left, out of the sheriff's list, except Kent. Wouldn't it be a beautiful surprise for the populace if the nitwit old sheriff actually proved to have been right, and found that the last man left on his list was the one who had put the prints on that bulb! Nobody even knows whether Kent has an alibi, and he and Charlie are the ones who knew most about the vault. Kent had a key to it of his own. I wonder.

Marjorie Wyck and Ted Gideon are still on my private list. The sheriff doesn't know about Ted, and he already has Marjorie's prints. The fact that she's exonerated on that basis makes me think all the less of the fingerprint clew. I wish I could decide in my own mind whether Alling and Daisy are trying to frame me because they honestly believe my alibi is the bunk, or whether they're doing it to cover their own guilt. I, like a lamb for the shearing, have told them my whole story, and neither of them has confided in me. I didn't really realize, till today, that Daisy has never even pretended to account for her own whereabouts, that night. What a two-year-old I've been! And I gave Alling all the evidence to convict me of murdering Muriel, if he wants to use it. Good God!

I got my marks today. They're nothing to boast of, but I'll graduate all right, if I can stay out of jail long enough to get my sheepskin. I would have done better, if I had spent less time scribbling on this story, night after night, when I should have been studying.

11:50 P.M., Wednesday,
3rd May, 1933.

This has been the sheriff's field day, for fair, and another of my convictions has gone haywire. He's not such a chump after all, perhaps. Here's how it happened. As I have already mentioned, Dick Prendergast had been wearing gloves all year, to assert and protect his right not to be fingerprinted without due process of law. Indoors he's been wearing airy things made out of mesh, crocheted, I suppose. This afternoon, he and I heard a yell of "Oh, doc," from Charlie, and went down to the preparation room. This year the supply of stiffs fell way off, and the vault wasn't filled up on time, but we found Charlie with three of them on his hands, all suddenly arrived that afternoon, and all in somewhat questionable condition. They were three Swedes who had fallen asleep after a binge, all in the same room, with the doors and windows shut and a gas stove roaring under a midnight snack which they hadn't got around to eating before they passed out. The stove used up so much oxygen that they were pretty well asphyxiated, no doubt, even before the flame itself was smothered, and escaping gas finished the job. Charlie said it wasn't a case of "turn-on-the-gas" suicide, because there had been the black remains of some fried eggs in one pan and of some bacon in another, over the two gas burners on the stove. Anyway, the bodies had remained undiscovered for two or three days, and were rather high and gamey before they reached us. One we dunked in the formaldehyde pit, as being too far gone to bother with. The other two we embalmed.

Dick, of course, took off his trick gloves to put on rubber ones while helping in the process. When we had finished, I washed up first, and he followed me to the sink, removing the rubber gloves. These we strip off by seizing them at the cuff and pulling them inside out. Both gloves were damp on the outside from embalming fluid. He pulled off the right one with his left hand, and had placed his fingers of that hand against the other glove, to pull it off too, when I, quite by accident, struck my elbow against a reagent bottle on the shelf beside the sink. Dick caught it in his right hand as it fell, said, "Look out what you're doing, you clumsy dope," and set it back on the shelf. At that moment, like a flash out of nowhere, the sheriff pounced upon it. He must have seen us at work, through the high basement windows at sidewalk level, and had hidden at the turn of the stairway.

Dick grabbed desperately for the bottle, but the sheriff held it at arm's length over his head, and whipped out a gun. "Don't you go assaultin' an officer of the law," he said by way of warning, "or I'll pot ye one through the head, with my friend Saunders here for a witness to self-defense. Save the state a heap o' trouble, gettin' you hung the usual way."

Dick then backed off, with a shrug, and said, "You'll lose your job, Palmer, for this little act. Go ahead, get through with it. I'll have the same witness to prefer charges against you for illegal methods."

"Nothin' illegal about pickin' up a bottle and lookin' at it," the sheriff commented. "Here, Saunders, have a look here."

To my amazement, I noticed a set of prints resembling those on the light bulb, and swung around quickly to see what Dick would be doing. But he was quite nonchalantly washing his hands.

"What'd he have on his hands to make these here white prints?" Sheriff Palmer inquired suspiciously. "Young feller, was you crawfishin' after all, when you showed me what kind o' prints embalmin' fluid would make? Speak up."

I shook my head, and looked again at the prints, which were cloudy white, like the ones on the original bulb. Then the explanation dawned on me. When I had made the test with embalming fluid, for the sheriff, last fall, there had been nothing on my fingers but the fluid itself. But Dick's fingers, before he touched them to the damp left glove, had been covered with talcum powder, which we always dusted inside the rubber gloves to keep them from sticking. The fingers of his right hand, still covered with the fine powder, had touched against the damp surface of the outside of the left glove just long enough to convert the film of dry powder into a thin layer of pasty stuff, which had served to impress on the reagent bottle a set of clear, white, opaque prints.

I explained this to the sheriff, in my own defense. He took some gloves himself from the boxful of them, by the sink, and repeated the whole process, with the same results. Then he grunted, took out his little book, and crossed off Prendergast's name.

"Thought I had ye, at first," he said. "Wasn't you, after all. What the devil did ye put me to all this trouble fer, all year, ye young jackass? Them wasn't your prints on the bulb."

Dick grinned at him cheerfully, and said, "Just to defend the Bill of Rights against illegal usurpation of power by petty officers of the law. Shall we call it quits, sheriff? I won't sic my uncle the senator on you, if you'll quit following me around. It's been something of a bore, the last few months, having you on my trail all day long. Shake?"

The sheriff set down the bottle and shook. Dick picked the bottle up, rinsed it under the faucet, and put it back where it belonged. "Just to protect you from your own impulses, sheriff," he explained. "If you kept those prints, you would be open to prosecution and removal from office. But I guess you're right about there being nothing I can do to you for taking a bottle off a shelf and looking at it."

He slipped on his coat, and was about to leave when an idea occurred to him. "Oh, here, have a souvenir, Mr. Palmer, to remember me by." He handed the crocheted gloves to the sheriff, asked, "Coming, Dave?" and walked up the stairs. The sheriff snorted and threw the gloves into the waste bin. "Hey, you," he said to me, "I got one more question to ask ye. Did ye ever notice Coroner Kent with a strip o' stickin' plaster round his right thumb?"

"Why,—yes. I think there was something the matter with his thumb the last time he performed a post. He usually does most of the cutting for himself, and the assistants just stand around. But he didn't even put on gloves, last time. He just pointed things out with his scalpel, and I remember that his thumb was bandaged."

"Yeah? Now, just when was that?"

"Last Friday evening."

"Ever notice it before that?"

"I don't remember," I admitted.

"When'd he do the last thingummy, before that one?"

"The last post-mortem?"

"Yeah, you know what I mean. Why don't ye answer prompt like?"

"I don't think he's done but that one since Jarvis died."

"Um. And ye never noticed his thumb bandaged but that once?"

"Not to remember it."

"Um. Well, I have. That right thumb o' his has been bandaged for a long time. Ye couldn't possibly figger out any idee why he'd keep it bandaged, could ye? Don't answer, no, don't say a word. Mustn't ever say anythin' ag'in that high an' mighty an' saintly character, around here, young feller."

And the sheriff made for the stairs. I stayed behind to reflect for a few moments. And, the more I reflected, the more startling became the assumption that the sheriff, by his slow, blundering, sly method, might actually have narrowed down his list of suspects in a purely logical way. For it seems natural, certainly, that the one who least wanted to be fingerprinted, and who most feared it, should be the longest to evade Sheriff Palmer's efforts. Prendergast, the runner-up in the game against the sheriff, had been driven as usual by his stubborn, crusading belief in an abstract principle. Anyone who could hold out longer than my maligned friend Dick must have even better reasons. And it is a fact that Coroner Kent is the only person still in town whose fingerprints have not been observed, out of all that list of students, faculty, and hospital attendants. The sheriff himself seems satisfied that Muriel had a good alibi, even though her name is not yet actually crossed off. But no-one knows, at this moment of writing, what Kent's alibi is.

And now, moreover, Dick and I have unwittingly proved, in our little gloves and bottle act, that those fingerprints on the bulb in all probability really were put on in a moment of forgetfulness by the murderer, after he had embalmed the body and was hurrying to leave the scene of his crime. He had been so hasty that he had paused in the process of pulling off his gloves to give that bulb the twist which may yet betray him. I wonder.

At any rate, it's to my advantage to help out the sheriff in any way I can, before Daisy and Alling "precipitate the dénouement," as he so pleasantly put it—the dénouement which they seem to have cooked up to incriminate me. Tomorrow Alling gives his annual lecture. May it choke him. Of course I've had to aid, all along, in the work of preparing his damned slides for him. He's kept up his acting pretty well too.

When I saw Daisy tonight, I couldn't help being a bit sarcastic, no matter how foolish it was of me. But I don't think she suspected anything. She took it the same way as before, instead of flaring up. I wish to hell I didn't still have a lingering idea that I love her, in spite of what she's done. The alluring little bitch.

CHAPTER XXXIII

Well, they've got me. I'm writing this in jail. And as they'll probably take my place apart, brick by brick and board by board, to find evidence against me, I don't see that it makes any difference whether anybody sees me writing here or not. Daisy knows all about my diary. She can lead them to it. Leave it to her, the sweet little— Well, I can't seem to write what I think of her, even now. And besides, so far as I remember, the diary ought to strengthen my presumption of innocence. Perhaps I should tell the sheriff to go get it, before Daisy does. I'd rather trust it to him than to her. It's got stuff in it that would make things look pretty sour for Alling, if they were known. Even she doesn't know what I do about that dry-cleaning machine, and the missing kymograph.

Now let's see if I can remember just what happened, tonight. About noon the town began to be pediculous with doctors from all over the state. Probably there were a great many more than could be expected, owing to the fact that Alling's lecture of the preceding spring had been canceled because of the death of Wyck, who had been collaborating on the researches. Last year, it was Wyck who helped with the slides. This year it was I, and it's been my only important duty, thank God, for some time.

The lecture began at 7:30 in the evening, on this last day of school. Many of the students have gone home. The crowd was composed mainly of visitors from out of town. When I came in, early, to get the projecting machine ready, I found the sheriff there ahead of me, lurking behind the swinging doors, still hoping, apparently, for an unobtrusive chance to get the prints of Coroner Kent. He seems never to have dared to use any of his customary wiles on the coroner. Perhaps he's been almost afraid of what he would find if he did succeed in running the coroner down at last.

Alling's subject was a noncommittal report of researches in direct injection into the blood stream of various chemicals to arrest or ameliorate arteriosclerosis. He himself told me, with his usual smug modesty, that he did not consider that he had developed an acceptable treatment. But his work had reached a positive stage that made it advisable for others to take it up in large numbers, the better to determine percentages of success and of failure. The slides were mainly microphotographs of arterial tissue, stained in various ways to compare the effects of different chemicals. He outlined the problems involved in a speech that took about three quarters of an hour and then signaled for the first slide. Just at this point I noticed Marjorie Wyck coming in. She took a seat in the back row. I didn't notice her again, because of the attention the job required; but I wondered at her interest.

The projector was a standard balopticon, with a double, slotted slide-holder of the kind that permits one slide to be changed while the other is in focus. I was changing them automatically, from long practice, handling them by the extreme edge to keep the illuminated surfaces clean. The lecture was nearing its end, when I noticed that one slide was disfigured in its most significant area, near the center, by the prints, evidently of a thumb on one side and of a forefinger on the other. Thinking for the moment only that Alling would be provoked at my carelessness in permitting a dirty slide in the box, I ran the slide-holder back immediately, permitting the former slide to reappear on the screen, while I hastily pulled out the offending glass oblong to clean it. As I picked the chamois from the box, Sheriff Palmer leaped on the stand, seized my wrist, and took the slide from me.

"Hey, what are you doing?" I asked.

"So I got ye at last, Mr. Crawfisher. Accessory after the fact, and mebbe better charges. Tryin' to destroy state's evidence."

It then dawned on me that the prints had been recognized by the sheriff as those for which he had been hunting all through the school year. But whose were they? The bell in the booth began to ring insistently for another slide. But Palmer was slipping a handcuff on me. The idea flashed into my mind that this must be the trick Daisy and Alling had cooked up against me. Either that, or someone else had made the "plant" and had duped them into suspecting me. Could it have been Marjorie? Did that explain her tardy entrance at the lecture?

"Hey, Dr. Alling," the sheriff yelled. "You better get another feller up here to work this here shebang. I'm arrestin' this gent Saunders."

At once the room was in an uproar. Alling slithered somehow up the crowded aisle and, with a very good pose of genuine agitation, demanded an explanation. He acted as if he had not noticed the disfigured slide at all, which could have been true, as he had faced the audience most of the time while speaking, and turned only occasionally to illustrate his words with a pointer. The sheriff insisted that he would say nothing until he preferred charges formally before a magistrate. Alling then turned and said in a shrill voice, "Gentlemen, the lecture will go on. Please be seated." Turning back to me, he added, "I am unutterably distressed, Saunders. Be assured that I shall come down to confer with you immediately when the lecture is over."

"Don't trouble yourself," I said, unable to suppress a sardonic accent.

"Oh, well, I see. I really am sorry, my boy. Of course, I'll come right away."

But I insisted magnanimously that there was no point in spoiling a good lecture for hundreds of listeners. With a fine show of reluctance, he agreed. A few minutes later the sheriff was grinning at me through a cell door.

"Wal, I allus knew it'd come to this, sooner or later, Mister Crawfish Saunders. Nice little game you been playin', all year. The best thing for you to do is sign a confession, right now. The law's nicer to guys that give it the least trouble."

I turned down this amiable offer, and tried to get him to explain the charge against me. Evidently he considered that the charge itself might be increased or varied by what I might say before it was preferred, so I said nothing. In about twenty minutes Judge Cole, the magistrate, arrived, and I was conducted, handcuffed, into the police courtroom which adjoined the cells. All the way the sheriff tried to bully me into confessing something, but had

to give up in the end and charge me with willfully attempting
to destroy evidence, with full foreknowledge of its significance. I
denied the charge, pointed out that it was my duty as operator of
the machine to clean any dirty slide before showing it, and truthfully declared that I had not particularly noticed anything about
the fingerprints except that they were a blemish on the plate. The
sheriff established, however, what I could hardly deny: that I had
been constantly informed of his efforts to discover a certain fingerprint's original, that I had many times seen photographs of
the prints on the bulb, and that I had evinced sufficient interest
in the matter to make it extremely unlikely that I would not have
recognized the elusive print, wherever found. I said quite honestly that in the machine-like state of mind required for such a
job, you think of nothing at all but the operation. I had not had
time, or a sufficient reason to examine the fingerprints. I just saw
that there were prints, and assumed that they must be my own.
Therefore I immediately commenced to clean them. But that
didn't seem to be a suitable answer, to the magistrate. He examined the original bulb, and the slide, and seemed to be convinced
that they were made by the same person. I was then asked whose
the fingerprints were, and of course said that I did not know.
Judge Cole decided to hold me in $1000 bail for a further hearing.
The sheriff brought me back to my cell, where I am now writing. And here comes Alling now. Hey! I wonder if Alling showed
those slides to Kent—are they Kent's prints?

About Midnight, Same Evening,
(4th May, 1933.)

Here I am back again. There doesn't seem to be anybody with
a thousand dollars in this town who would risk bailing me out.
Just as well, because I wouldn't be accountable for my actions. I
think I'm going coo-coo. I'll try, however, and in spite of that, to
set down just what happened.

Alling came up to my cell, and began to try to reassure me that
I would be released at once—remarks which at the time I took
for what they seemed to be worth. He had been speaking for a
few moments only when the county prosecutor also arrived from

Phillipston, having driven the distance while Alling was finishing his lecture. I was brought back into the courtroom to answer his questions.

(For a while, now, I shall quote the record made by the court stenographer, with such extra descriptions as seem necessary to show what really occurred.)

The county prosecutor said, "Mr. Saunders, do you know the identity of the person whose fingerprints appear on this lantern slide?"

I examined it, and said, "No."

"They are not your own?" he asked.

"No, sir. I think Sheriff Palmer will affirm that they are not."

The sheriff said, "They ain't—they're not his."

"Who else might have handled these slides, except yourself, Mr. Saunders?"

"So far as I know, there was no-one else who handled them, from the time I originally prepared them, except—" I paused, and looked half maliciously at Alling. Somewhat to my surprise, he gave his head a distinct affirmative nod, as if he were expecting me to name him. Something, however, urged me to take a flyer, and I said, "—except that it's possible that they may have been examined by another doctor especially interested in the problems of arteriosclerosis, such as Dr. Kent."

Alling started violently, and the sheriff leapt around and stared at me. My inquisitor also looked distinctly surprised, but he went on firmly. "You have then no knowledge that they actually were handled by another person?"

"No actual knowledge," I said, "except by me, and, of course, Dr. Alling himself."

"Dr. Alling," the prosecutor said, "merely as a formality, will you formally deny that these are your fingerprints?"

"I decline to deny that," Alling replied.

"Do you mean to say that these fingerprints are yours?"

"I don't know, sir. You have given me no opportunity to compare them with my own."

"Oh, I see. Well, as this is a preliminary hearing, would you mind waiving the formality of being charged with a felony? As a matter of routine I must arraign you on that charge in order to obtain your prints for comparison, unless you are willing to give them voluntarily."

"I am willing," said Alling. I noticed that he certainly was living up to the letter of his own prescription for giving evidence; to answer the precise question asked, in the simplest possible way.

Meanwhile, I saw the sheriff staring surreptitiously into his notebook, which contained the record of his search for the elusive fingerprint. "Wal, I'll be damned," he exclaimed. "I'd 'a' sworn I copied this here list right out o' that official register of the faculty, in the yearbook, but your name ain't on it a-tall."

Alling smiled slightly. "I noticed that I was the only person connected with the school or hospital whose name did not appear in your book, when you showed it to me last February, sheriff," he said. "Your error grew out of the fact that you listed only students, members of the hospital staff, and members of the faculty. My own position is listed under none of those categories. You did your copying correctly enough. You merely failed to include the administrative staff, which in all institutions is an entity distinct from the faculty."

I saw in a flash how this could have happened. The administrative staff was listed on the first page of the yearbook, in large ornamental type. All of its other members except Alling were included in one of the other lists, as the treasurer of the school was also comptroller of the hospital, and so on. The sheriff had turned to the solid alphabetical listing of faculty members, and had copied it off, never thinking that the name of anyone connected with the school would be omitted. I hardly dared think, or hope, that the prints on the light bulb were really Alling's. There was still Kent to be accounted for. But the episode shook my recently increased faith in the sheriff's tortoiselike method of chasing down the mystery. He stood scratching his head, then turned to me and made an awkward bow. "I'm downright sorry, Mr. Saunders, fer callin' you dumb. Even if that name wasn't on my list, I might 'a' somehow remembered that there was a man named Alling in town, and eligible. Once I'd started crossin' 'em off, I never thought about anythin' but the names that warn't crossed off yet. And the more I crossed off, I guess, the less chanct there was to remember one I hadn't put on in the fust place. Wal, let's take 'em now, and see what they look like."

He produced his materials, and Alling submitted gravely to the process. As Sheriff Palmer rolled the suspect's fingers one after another on the card, I saw his eyes widen and begin to pop out.

"Hey," he yelled, "you're under arrest!" and excitedly he poked under the nose of the prosecutor the new record of Alling's fingerprints for comparison with those on the bulb. Then, regaining his dignity, Sheriff Palmer drew himself up and announced, "Manfred Alling, I, John Palmer, Sheriff of Alton County, charge you with the murder of Gideon Wyck."

"Wait, wait, Mr. Palmer," the prosecutor interposed. "Dr. Alling, from the first I have considered the matter of the fingerprints of minor importance. Perhaps you will be good enough to explain how they came to be on the bulb."

"Will you please be more specific in your question?" Prexy inquired.

"Very well. We will call this bulb exhibit A, and the slide exhibit B. Do your fingerprints appear on both exhibits?"

"They do."

"Do you know when they were impressed upon the surface of exhibit A?"

"I do."

"When was it?"

"About seven o'clock in the morning of April 4, 1932."

All our jaws sagged, but the prosecutor's dropped wonderfully. He made no objection, this time, when the sheriff placed Dr. Alling formally under arrest. After a long, impressive silence, the prosecutor collected his normal forces and said, "Please tell us, Dr. Alling, the circumstances leading up to the placing of your fingerprints on exhibit A."

"I protest that the question is too general," Dr. Alling replied.

"Very well. Sheriff, swear the accused."

Dr. Alling was sworn in, and at once was asked the blunt question, "Did you, Manfred Alling, with a sharp instrument pierce the skin of the neck and sever the spinal cord of Gideon Wyck, deceased?"

"I did not," said Dr. Alling.

"Did you in any way aid, abet, procure, or conceal the death of Gideon Wyck?"

"I did not aid, abet, or procure it. I did conceal it."

"In what manner did you conceal the death of Gideon Wyck?"

"By embalming his body and placing it in the vault of the Maine State College of Surgery."

"Why did you do this?"

"The answer to that question can best be given if illustrated by the display of certain documents and other exhibits. Until I am permitted to introduce these materials, I stand upon my constitutional privilege."

It was consequently ruled that Dr. Alling be held without bail for the murder of Gideon Wyck, and that I be held, also without bail, as an accomplice after the fact. And here I am, trying to make some sense out of all this. As yet, Alling has not been brought to the adjacent cell, and it is at least an hour since the hearing was concluded. I wonder what they've done with him—

3:20 P.M.
5th May, 1933.

The sheriff has just come in with the pleasant news that somebody got to my place ahead of him, turned it upside down, and left. I asked him what he was looking for, but he wouldn't say, beyond the fact that he didn't find it. Biddy told him, however, that Daisy had gone up around noontime, saying that I had asked her to get some things for me. The sheriff wanted to know what I had told her to get, and why. However, since the damage is done, I decided to keep mum. Daisy's clever enough to have hidden my diaries where the sheriff could never find them. I'd like to feel just a little bit surer about just what her game is, before doing anything about it, so I simply refused to answer his questions at all. That may work out best, in the long run. He now thinks I communicated with Daisy somehow, from the jail, or else by pre-arrangement. Perhaps it's just as well to have him think so, and keep an eye on her.

8:00 P.M. (same day),
5th May, 1933.

I seem to have saved myself some embarrassment by refusing to say anything at all about Daisy, to the sheriff, because he has decided to hold me incommunicado. He says Daisy came around to see me, a little after seven o'clock. She must have just knocked off work. She spent her noon hour looting my rooms, and now she comes around to call. Well, I'm just as glad that he won't let her in. Judge Cole asked me this morning if I wanted to hire an attorney or to have one appointed, but I decided it would be best to refuse to have anything to do with one. The attitude heightens my presumption of innocence. And anyway, I can't decide just how much I'd want to tell a lawyer, if I had one.

The sheriff says they've taken Alling down to Phillipston, which is no skin off my nose. I wouldn't want to be in the cell next to the guy, and evidently they were afraid that we would have a chance to plot together or something. The sheriff also asked me if I knew anybody named Theodore Gideon, alias Watson. I said I wouldn't tell him if I did. That probably means that either Alling or Daisy has spilt the beans about his being in these parts, recently.

I've been doing my best to puzzle out Alling's game. The sheriff, in one of his garrulous one-way conversations, said that the complete hearing will be held by the coroner and the county prosecutor, jointly, as soon as some stuff arrives from Portland— some evidence or other that Alling impounded with his lawyers down there, under bond. It seems funny that the law would allow a lawyer to receive clews and evidence from a criminal, and let him seal them up and say nothing about them, even when it's practically certain that they have something to do with a notorious mystery. But that's apparently what's happened in this case, and the sheriff claims that relations and confidences between a lawyer and his client are protected except when deliberate conspiracy can be proved. But the lawyer is under no obligation to make voluntary revelations of anything whatever that he knows about his client, even when the client is a notorious criminal at large. All of which seems to back up Mr. Dickens's succinct statement that the law is an ass. The lawyer can't refuse to testify if they get him in court as a witness, but there's no penalty in the cast of a lawyer willfully obstructing justice by concealing knowledge of a crime.

I'm beginning to think that I see Alling's grand strategy. He has openly and blandly confessed to the embalming job, but has denied that he committed the act of murder. I think he is confessing to having done part of it, as a bold means of helping to conceal the fact that he did the whole job. Probably he is going to claim that he was at the Connells' when the knife thrust was delivered in Wyck's spine, and that I came in shortly afterward, direct from having inflicted the wound. Well, if Daisy's got my diary, it won't help things any. I remember distinctly that I left a hiatus in the diary itself, and didn't bother to explain all that blundering around in the woods. They'll just take the hiatus to mean that that was the time when I sneaked up on Wyck and killed him. Ho hum, I'm going to turn in on my nice hard little wall cot.

Saturday Evening,
6th May, 1933.

Nothing much happened all day, today, until about six o'clock, when who should turn up but Ted Gideon, handcuffed between the sheriff and a deputy. I haven't yet had any explanation of how they got him, and he hasn't been inclined to talk. Our cells are separated by nothing but a row of good stout bars, with a mesh of thick wire too small to put your hand through. Several times I've caught a glimpse of the sheriff, wandering around in the courtroom next door, as if he were trying to overhear anything Ted and I might be saying to each other. So far, we haven't had anything to say. I honestly don't believe the bird recognizes me from Adam. I asked him what he was in for, and he just grunted and said he didn't know. Maybe he doesn't. Of course, he must remember about all the chicanery up on the hill, but he might have no realization that he killed Muriel. When he came to from that fit, he may or may not have seen her lying there dead; but if he did, from his own point of view it would be perfectly possible for him to think that someone had done it before he came to the room. Doubtless the fit hit him at sight of her, and when he woke up, he might have thought that he found her that way upon first coming into the room. Anyway, it's comfortable to have a few bars between you and a homicidal maniac, when you're cooped up in the same room.

The sheriff says the inquest will be held Monday morning, and that it's going to be a beauty. They'll have in everybody who was at the first one, and all the people who have any part in substantiating anybody's alibi. They've even subpœnaed Senator Tolland, he says, to testify to Alling's whereabouts for the period they were together after the faculty meeting. They aren't taking any chances about the grand jury refusing to indict, this time. They're going to get the state's case all down on paper at the hearing, before the trial even begins.

I suppose what I have most to fear is that Alling will show evidence which appears to prove that I murdered Muriel, perhaps producing Ted to support his claim. Ted may feel himself utterly innocent of the act of murder itself, in her case. If so, he'd make a good witness against me. They'll have no trouble proving that I was there at the time, and Ted no doubt would swear that he entered Muriel's room and found her dead just after I had left. Nice prospect. Of course, I can prove he's an epileptic. But the rub comes in the likelihood that Alling will merely use the Nurse Finch murder to increase the presumption of my guilt with regard to the other one—the murder of Wyck. Oh, hell. This isn't getting me anywhere. I'm going to try to stop speculating, and take a chance that my wits will save me when things come to the testing.

Sunday Evening,
7th May, 1933.

Nothing new. Daisy tried to get a letter to me, but the sheriff wouldn't let me have it. He opened it and read it in full view, finishing up with the remark that that kind of thing would be very acceptable indeed to the prosecuting attorney. He probably was talking through his bonnet, as usual. But Daisy may of course have taken this nice means of making some information known to the authorities which she would rather not give them direct, for some reason or other. It may contain some trumped-up information that's just a deliberate part of the plot to frame me. I wish I knew what it said. One thing I hadn't thought about till today is the possibility that the narrative I mailed off may turn out to be a help to me. Having been sent before this crisis developed, its story would be more likely to be credited than anything I could say now. Well, tomorrow's the day of days. I'm going to get some sleep, and meet it with a look of starry-eyed innocence—which, God help me, is no more than deserved.

CHAPTER XXXIV

(*My story ends with a recording of events that occurred on Monday, the 8th of May, 1933. I find, however, that my diary entries for that day are rather incoherent. It was not until I had a chance to examine the report of the hearing that the full pattern of what had happened became apparent. This time, you see, I was not permitted to hear the testimony of other suspects and witnesses; so my own session before the prosecutor and the coroner was the only part of the official proceedings at which I was present. In consequence, I am abandoning the policy of making direct quotations from my diary, and shall merely use it for reference, telling what happened as directly as possible, with occasional quotations from the stenographer's report of the hearing, which now is public property.*)

A little before nine o'clock on Monday morning, Sheriff Palmer appeared with two deputies. All three were wearing pistol holsters in full view. Ted Gideon was handcuffed between the deputies, and I was escorted by the sheriff, without the formality of bracelets. The magistrate's court was obviously too small for the hearing, which I assumed would be held upstairs in the town meeting hall. However, we were conducted out of the building and up the street to the medical school. Quite a crowd had collected around the doors. I saw Daisy waiting on the sidewalk, half concealed in a group of friends. As I passed, she slipped deftly out to whisper in my ear, "Try not to say anything at all about the monsters. I've got your diaries hidden. Dr. Alling says to stick to his advice about testimony. I'll—" At that point the sheriff noticed her, and yanked me out of hearing distance.

Several state policemen were on guard at the doors of various rooms in the building. I was taken to a small classroom where Biddy, Charlie, and Marjorie Wyck also were seated. I had been there only a moment, when Dick Prendergast and his uncle the senator passed the door, then paused. A state cop barred the way with his arm, as Dick tried to come in.

"Oh, well," he called, "I just wanted to say that uncle and I will get you out on a habeas writ, as soon as this is over, whatever happens. Swell prelude to our graduation, tomorrow, isn't it? Who'll pass out the sheepskins, I wonder?"

The cop objected to the conversation, so Dick went on.

Charlie was the first witness called. The stenographic report of his testimony does not differ in substance from that at the first inquest. Again he refused to give his alibi, but admitted that he had told it to the grand jurors, who could have it again. He was ordered held as a material witness. My turn came next; and, like Charlie's, my answers were about the same as before, in reference to the sealing of the vault and the discovery of the body. But that was not to be all. When the coroner was done, the county prosecutor snapped out:

"Give us a careful and detailed account of your whereabouts, Mr. Saunders, from 9:30 P.M., April 3, 1932, until noon of the following day."

Of course I had realized that the question would be asked, this time; but, up to the very moment of hearing it, I had been undecided as to my answer. That, doubtless, is the reason why I took the plunge without hesitation. Here is what the record shows that I said:

"I am unaware of some of the exact time sequences. I stayed in the faculty room until everyone else was leaving. Dr. Wyck had already left. I went out at about the same time as Dr. Alling, and walked directly to the lunch wagon on Atlantic Street. After pausing there for not more than three or four minutes to purchase cigarettes, I went on to the hospital gates, turned north, walked about two miles to the second of two little bridges, paused there five minutes or so, and then climbed the hill, emerging into a pasture. I lost my way there, stumbled around for hours probably, before finding a trail leading down over the first little bridge. I walked back to town. My watch, when I consulted it under the hospital gates, read about 1:20 A.M. I went at once to the Connells', remained there perhaps half an hour, and was then taken to the hospital, from which I was not released until it was nearly midday."

Q. What was your purpose in setting out on this peregrination?

A. To take a walk.

Q. Do you make a practice of taking long walks in the dark?

A. No, sir.

Q. Why did you do so on this occasion?

A. I was nervous from the strain of a faculty meeting full of unpleasantness, and also from staying up late to attend my sick landlord.

Q. You thought the walk would quiet your nerves?

A. Yes.

Q. Did it?

A. No.

Q. Because getting lost in the dark woods upset them more than ever?

A. Yes, sir.

Q. You wish to put this preposterous story on record to account for your conduct and whereabouts on the night of a murder in which you are suspected of complicity?

A. My wishes have not been consulted in the matter. I have truthfully answered your question.

Q. Very well. When did you last see Gideon Wyck alive, and where?

A. At about quarter to eleven that night, on the second little bridge I have already mentioned.

Q. Oh. Then you accompanied him that far?

A. Only in the sense that I followed him unobserved.

Q. He did not see you?

A. I am sure that he did not.

Q. Why did you follow him?

A. Because he had been acting strangely all day, and I suspected that he was in ill health. When I chanced to see him leave his house and walk into the Bottom Road, I was intrigued by the mystery of such an action on the part of a very sick man.

Q. What caused you to lose sight of him at the bridge?

A. He was carried up the hill in a car, away from me.

Q. Still alive?

A. When last I saw him.

Q. Can you tell us who drove the car? Did you recognize the driver?

A. Yes.

Q. Who?

A. The young man who was detained in the jail with me last night.

Q. Are you positive?

A. Absolutely positive.

Q. You tried to follow the car on foot?

A. Yes.

Q. Why?

A. For the same reasons that I had followed Dr. Wyck in the first place, with more curiosity added.

Here the prosecutor consulted the report of the first inquest and asked, "Why did you withhold these facts before?"

A. Because I was asked no questions to which they would make a relevant answer.

Q. Are you aware that it is an offense against the state to withhold knowledge of a crime?

A. I am.

Q. Then you admit withholding knowledge of a crime?

A. I do not. There was no crime of any kind committed in my presence. No-one knew positively that a crime had been committed until five months later. I myself at this moment have no knowledge of what happened to Dr. Wyck after the car proceeded up the hill.

Q. And it did not occur to you that this information would be of use to the authorities, even though it was not exactly classifiable as knowledge of a crime?

A. It did occur to me, sir.

Q. Then why did you not volunteer it?

A. For three reasons. It was not definitely relevant. It made necessary the volunteering of what I knew to be an unsubstantiable alibi. And I was asked not to reveal it by Dr. Alling.

Q. You told him?

A. Yes.

Q. Then you conspired with Manfred Alling to conceal knowledge of a crime?

A. No, sir. I had no knowledge of the commission of a crime.

Q. Did he have such knowledge?

A. I never knew, until we were both arraigned at the magistrate's court, last Thursday evening. His admission that he embalmed the body seems to indicate that he did have knowledge of the crime all along.

Q. He never told you, or gave you cause to suspect this?

A. He never told me. At times I suspected him, but I also suspected ten or twelve other people, most of them for better reasons.

Q. Who were they?

A. I consider the question improper.

At this point Coroner Kent nodded, and said, "So do I."

The prosecutor did not press the point. I have given the above long sample of testimony as the only convincing means at my command of showing just how it was that Muriel's name never was mentioned in my testimony, despite the fact that I answered all questions directly. It seemed the best policy not to volunteer anything that might lead into the necessity for describing my trip to New York—an almost certain eventuality if the prosecutor then tried to find out what I knew of Muriel's subsequent conduct. As it turned out, he proceeded at once with questions about what had happened after I returned to the Connells'. Several leading questions were asked to try to make me confess that I had seen Wyck at an hour later than 10:45 that evening, and I had to rehearse a number of times my actual progress on the way back to town. But the rest of my testimony brought out nothing that has not already been adequately described to the reader—and all of it concerned only the fatal night.

Biddy was next to be called. She had improved as a witness

in the interim, and her testimony provided the first real surprise of the hearing. She did not tangle herself up nearly so much as before. Her alibi had not been asked for at the original inquest. Now, when she was requested to give it, she merely said that Dr. Alling had told her to go for a walk for half an hour, some time late at night, and that she had done so. She admitted that she had walked up Atlantic Street, past the school building, to the middle of town, and had returned again by the same route. The county prosecutor then inquired:

"Mrs. Connell, did you enter the medical school building either time, coming or going, while you were out for a walk?"

A. No, I did not.

Q. Did you see any lights in the building?

A. Not to notice them.

Q. Did you see any car standing outside the building?

A. I don't think— Yes, I did, that, now I remember.

Q. Please describe the car.

A. It was a big one. The reason I remember was because it had a dog thing on the front end of it.

A long series of questions then established the fact that the "dog thing" was a radiator-cap ornament.

Q. (By the county prosecutor) Do you know who owns the car you describe? Have you seen it frequently?

A. It might be and it might not be that man's car. (Witness indicating Coroner Kent.)

The next page or two of the trial record indicates that Biddy was conducted to a window and identified a car parked in front of the school at the time of the inquest as "maybe the same one. It's got a dog like it." In a series of curt answers, the coroner acknowledged that the car was his own, offered himself in the capacity of an ordinary witness, and suggested that the county prosecutor take over the full conduct of the inquiry. The suggestion was declined.

No other new testimony of significance was introduced until the appearance on the stand of Dr. Alling.

Q. (By Coroner Kent) Dr. Alling, the county prosecutor informs me that you were unwilling to answer a general question about your activities in the early morning of April 4, 1932, until you had an opportunity to display certain pieces of concrete evidence. Are you now prepared to make a general answer, or would you prefer to answer a series of specific queries?

A. If the sheriff will produce a package sent me in his care by my lawyers, I am ready to give a general descriptive answer and to be cross-questioned later.

Q. Thank you, Dr. Alling. Will you please tell us anything which might have a bearing upon the Wyck case, that occurred in your presence during the period from 9:30 P.M. April 3, 1932, to 12:00 noon of April 4, 1932?

As the first part of his answer, Dr. Alling alluded to the baffling nature of Mike's ailment, and described how he and I had been called in by Biddy at the time of Mike's second mysterious attack of pain, on the morning of April 3rd. He referred only casually to the faculty meeting, mentioning that at its conclusion he had walked directly to his home, accompanied by Richard Prendergast, a student, and Senator Tolland.

"I did not notice the exact time when Mr. Prendergast and Senator Tolland left my house," Dr. Alling continued. "Probably it was a little before eleven o'clock. I stayed up, working in my study, until midnight, when Dr. Wyck rang my doorbell. Although he never had spoken to me or to anyone else on the staff about it, I had had good reason to suspect that he was a very sick man. He lowered himself uneasily into a chair, and said, 'Fred, I'm about at the end of my strength, and I'm just on the verge of what may be a tremendously important scientific discovery. You've got to help me with it. I haven't got the strength to go on. Will you help?' Of course I was willing, and asked how. 'You may think me mad,' he said to me. 'You mustn't. This is extremely important—the first wonderful step in a whole new field of inquiry.' He was very earnest. 'Fred,' he said, 'I want you to sit up all night with Mike Connell, and make the most scrupulous scientific report of his conduct from one o'clock till morning.' I reminded him that he himself had seemed very little interested in Mike, that very morning, as Mrs. Connell had said she had phoned him in vain to come to attend her husband. But Dr. Wyck assured me that the significance of Mike's attacks had occurred to him only tardily, late in the afternoon.

"Well, I had had some reasons to think that Wyck's mind was failing, but I also was highly interested in Connell's amazing symptoms. To humor both Wyck and my own curiosity, I agreed to go to the Connells' at one A.M. Dr. Wyck then gave me the key to his office, and told me to stop in there as soon as I came from the Connells', and compare the prediction I would find there with the actual events that had happened. As a final precaution, he synchronized our watches exactly, and urged me to keep a minutely careful record of the beginning and ending of any unusual symptoms. I offered to drive him home, but he insisted that the walk would benefit him.

"When I reached the Connell home, Mrs. Connell was awake, and complained that she had been unable to sleep for two nights. I knew that she needed relief from her vigil as a prelude to sleep, and told her to walk around for half an hour. At 1.23 A.M. Mr. Saunders, who lived at the Connell house, came in. He had been there not more than a minute when Connell began to have the most violent maniacal symptoms. I had little time to inspect a watch to keep track of the time, and impulsively smashed my watch down on the table, to stop it with at least the first important time element on record. Saunders was knocked unconscious by the maniac, and I was physically inadequate to the situation. Connell dashed from the house. I phoned the hospital, and was taken there with Saunders. After reassuring the staff that I was unhurt, I left without an examination of any sort, and had put my car away and locked the garage before I remembered that Dr. Wyck had said an explanation would be found in his office. I felt chilled, and decided to warm myself by walking to the medical school building. The doors proved to be unlocked; a fact which argued that someone was still in the building. As I had seen no light in front, I assumed it must be Dr. Wyck, and hastened my pace, fearing that he had been so ill that he had decided not to try to walk home. The door of his office was ajar, and a light was burning. The light would have been invisible to a passer-by, except from a considerable distance, owing to the solarium on the half-roof of that set-back storey. My suspicions about Dr. Wyck's health seemed confirmed when I found him apparently asleep at his desk, his head resting on his right forearm. A closer look showed that blood was trickling from the back of his neck, and that his left wrist, which was hanging down, was incased in a leather wristlet capable of translating pulse beats into electrical impulses. In a drawer of the desk was the school's kymograph, arranged to register these pulse beats.

"My first reaction, of course, was the thought that my colleague had been murdered. Then I caught sight of a letter on the desk, addressed to me. May I have it, Mr. Palmer?"

The sheriff meanwhile had broken the seals of a large package which had been impounded with Dr. Alling's lawyers. He drew out of it the kymograph, and several documents. Dr. Alling read the letter, which I reproduce in full:

Dear Fred:

I want you to be the recipient of my remains, literary, scientific, corporeal. My daughter is to have my tangible property. Today I have been given the sardonic opportunity to use, as the materials of my last experiment, my own life. As I am slowly dying anyway, I would be a fool not to accept the chance. I cannot live more than a few more months, and they would be sour ones for me and for the immediately contiguous part of the cosmos.

Mike Connell, as you know, has been a regular blood donor. About 24 hours ago, Peter Tompkins died with some of Mike's blood in his veins. A few minutes before the fact of Peter Tompkins's death was ascertained, Mike himself had suffered extraordinary paroxysms. We do not know exactly when the Tompkins boy died, but there is a startling inference that the paroxysms in Mike were a direct reaction to the fact that some of his own blood was at that moment suffering pain of death, so to speak, in another body.

You will think at once of numberless cases when recipients of blood have died without any effect noticeable upon the donor. But Connell's case is separate, because this reaction occurred only after the arm from which the blood had been drawn off was amputated. The nervous system at the point where the arm was severed was the center of the attack.

Now, Fred, we don't know what death is. We don't know

what the relationship is between the life of a supposedly self-sufficient organism in the blood stream and the life of the whole complex community of cells of which it is a part. There probably is an interrelationship extending beyond mere chemical and physical reciprocity. This reaction in the arm of Mike Connell, under unique conditions, is, I believe, the first definite opportunity science has had to make a deliberate experiment in the nature of life and death.

I realized this, alas, only after I had let a second similar phenomenon, this morning, slip by unobserved. Thus it becomes my privilege to give my own life to death, in order that you may observe and record the result. As I told you earlier in the day, I have received more blood from Mike than anyone else has. I have transfused about three liters of his blood into myself. As this is several times as much as in the case of the Tompkins boy, the reaction should be correspondingly more pronounced, should it not?

That we may have a precise record, temporally, I have set your watch and mine in synchronism. The minute hands are in correspondence. The second hand on mine is 17 seconds faster than on yours. At this point, 1:00 A.M. precisely (with my second hand at 60, yours at 43), I have set the school's kymograph in motion. It is adjusted to make one revolution in 15 minutes, and the screw feed is adjusted to permit a continuous spiral record to be taken for 24 revolutions, or six hours. The error in two trial revolutions is—3 seconds in 15 minutes. The needle of the kymograph is actuated by my pulse in the usual way.

Before commencing to write this letter, I swallowed ten grams of veronal, which already is numbing my perceptions, and which should kill me within a few hours at most. The moment of my death will be accurately recorded on the drum of the kymograph. You will be able to observe the time of the consequent reaction (if any) on Connell. The implications, if the experiment results positively, I leave to your scientific acumen as a trust and a legacy.

Farewell then, and one last request. (My brain is swimming, but I shall hold death off to finish my letter, as I have held it off before.) This is a clinical demise, and I desire to go the whole way. It is therefore my well-considered wish that my body be used for dissection in the anatomy course. I charge you to embalm it yourself, immediately, to assure its fitness, and I charge you to supervise its placing in the school vault, in the next vacant stall, to be taken out for dissection in the normal course of events. Play no favorites with it.

My daughter has prepared a typewritten transcript of all my recent notes of scientific labors. These notes are to be yours, and to be held in absolute confidence for disposition at your own discretion. I suggest that you impound them with a trust company if you do not wish to take the responsibility for making them public or for withholding them. Perhaps you will want to order them published at the end of a period of years, the length of which you can judge best. My hand is like cotton. I shall say good bye.

GIDEON WYCK, M. D.

After this amazing letter had been read, Marjorie Wyck, the comptroller of the hospital, and several other persons familiar with Gideon Wyck's handwriting were called in briefly to verify the holograph. They all pronounced it to be genuine, and Marjorie admitted that she had made a full transcript of a book of laboratory notes—probably the same one Daisy and I had found at the ruined farm—and had given the transcript to Dr. Alling in accordance with a wish expressed by her father before he disappeared. When she and Dr. Alling were asked to produce the original or the transcript, in formal corroboration of this part of the dead man's letter, both testified that the original was not in their possession, and Dr. Alling refused in his capacity as trustee of the copy to make it public. Marjorie said that she had taken no note of the highly technical material, while copying, and could say nothing about its specific nature. She left the room, and Dr. Alling continued his story:

"Having read this letter, my first impulse was to refer to my watch, which as I have already told you I had stopped by striking it at the moment of the first symptom of violent reaction on the part of Mike Connell. It read 1:24, with the second hand at 49. I then opened the drawer in which the kymograph had been placed, and noticed that the record of pulsations had made something less than two full revolutions of the smoked drum. As two complete revolutions would have required one-half hour from the moment of starting the machine, which was started at one o'clock, I saw at once that death had probably occurred at very nearly the same moment as that of the reaction noted in the blood donor, Connell. I can plead only my scientific training, and my awe in the presence of an amazing implication, as excuse for having stopped then and there to calculate precisely the length of time which the kymograph had been running.

"Mr. Palmer, will you hand me the sheet of paper covered with figures, from the impounded material? Thank you. As you will see from this original sheet with calculations, the kymograph records the fact that Dr. Wyck's heart ceased beating at 24 minutes and 28 seconds past one o'clock, after corrections have been made for the lag of the kymograph. Since Dr. Wyck's watch, and therefore the kymograph, were 17 seconds faster than mine, it is necessary to add 17 seconds to 28 seconds to show the instant of Wyck's death according to my own watch. Thus—using my watch to time both events, Wyck's heart stopped at 1:24:45 o'clock, precisely, and Mike's maniacal reaction occurred at 1:24:49 o'clock, or four seconds later.

"Assuming that there is a connection between these events, it is to be expected that to any stimulus a sleeping man would react a trifle tardily, and that my consequent reaction in striking my watch was also a trifle delayed. Therefore, so far as a direct scientific analysis of the data available can go, it was inescapably indicated that the death of Gideon Wyck did have a direct and violent effect upon the donor who had given him blood."

The prosecutor interrupted to ask, "Do you yourself, as a sworn witness, believe that the reaction of Connell was caused by Wyck's death?"

"I believe it implicitly," Dr. Alling replied.

The prosecutor then turned to Coroner Kent and asked his opinion of the plausibility of the explanation. The reply of the coroner was:

"Such an explanation is contrary to all known laws of physics and of the science of medicine."

"Do you think it is established, at least as a reasonable hypothesis, by these data?" the prosecutor inquired; and Kent answered, "I should personally want further proof before admitting such a thesis to the dignity of further consideration. Moreover, Dr. Alling has pointed out a coincidence in one case only, out of three seizures suffered by the blood donor. Of the other two, in the first case the coincidence is doubtful, and in the second no cause is given at all."

Dr. Alling at once asked Sheriff Palmer for the letter from Joe Baker's mother and submitted it as evidence that the second seizure had certainly as much claim as the first to be related to the death of a recipient of Mike's blood.

Q. (By prosecutor) Why do you suppose that Dr. Wyck himself did not refer to this second apparent coincidence?

A. I can only suggest that it was because he had swallowed a large quantity of poison, and felt that he did not have time to write about anything not absolutely vital.

Q. Very well. Will you please proceed with an account of your whereabouts and actions on the morning of April 4th?

"When I had read the letter and made these calculations," Dr. Alling continued, "I next happened to notice, and to be impressed by, the fact that the heart action recorded on the kymograph, although progressively weaker through the second revolution, showed at the end a series of slowed, regular, and extremely exaggerated beats, such as one might expect from the sudden inhibition of the accelerator nerves and the complete dominance of the vagus or inhibitor fibers.

"Please give the instrument to Dr. Kent, Mr. Palmer. Thank you. This of course was an indication that death when it came was violent and convulsive, which was not likely to have been the case if the cause of death had been veronal. I then realized that Dr. Wyck, despite his effort to commit suicide, had in reality been murdered, and that I was provided with an absolutely accurate record, on the kymograph, of the moment when the sharp instrument had severed the spinal cord.

"For perhaps ten minutes I pondered the question of what to do. Dr. Kent, as my closest adviser, is fully aware of the intense worry to which I had been put by Dr. Wyck's conduct. It had brought us to the verge of a legislative investigation which might have had the most unfortunate results in rendering it impossible to get cadavers and animals for anatomy courses and laboratory experimentation, to say nothing of the danger of cessation of state funds, without which the school could not exist another month.

"In defense of my subsequent actions, I can say only that this acute worry, sharpened by the lecture which I had just been read by Senator Tolland, must have temporarily unbalanced my judgment. Under the stress of these happenings, it seemed to me that I was justified in following the course of action which Dr. Wyck had adjured me to follow, in the letter that was his last will and testament. I was convinced that a scandal in the school, at that time, would destroy it. This may have been a hallucination of extreme worry, but it happens to be a fact that I had hardly slept at all for several nights preceding the one in question. At any rate, almost mindlessly and automatically I found myself pushing Dr. Wyck's body, still in the swivel chair in which he had been sitting, until I got it to the lift. The chair had castors which made the operation fairly easy. Then I lowered it and myself on the lift, down to the preparation room. There, with the aid of the block and tackle, and an incline plane made from a removable table top, I overcame my physical inadequacy by application of the laws of force, and got the cadaver in place for embalming.

"I then paused and debated again, but it seemed that I had gone too far to retrace my actions. As soon as the incision for introducing the embalming fluid had been made, I knew that I must go on, willy-nilly. When I had supervised the first rapid flow of fluid into the cadaver, I refilled the gravity reservoir, put Dr. Wyck's swivel chair back on the lift, and went up again to remove to my own office all actual traces of the tragedy. The instrument with which the wound was inflicted was nowhere to be found, but I believe it to have been a scalpel which Dr. Wyck always kept on his desk to open letters, and which was also missing. I let the cadaver remain in place on the embalming table for perhaps an hour and a half, and then with a great deal of difficulty transferred it to the cart and pushed it into the vault. I had covered it with a shroud, and was debating the possibility of getting it into a stall, when I saw a pair of legs pass across the high cellar window at street level, which was visible through the vault door. The sight seemed to bring me back to the real world, and to a sense of irrevocable guilt for what I had done. I hastened out and was about to swing the vault door shut. Then I remembered the pile of clothing which I had removed from Dr. Wyck's body. Three things remained to be done, in great haste. One, to get the clothing out of sight; two, to turn out the light in the vault; three, to bolt its door, so that the diener could seal it without having reason for a further inspection.

"As Dr. Kent knows, the switch which controls the vault light is high on the wall, out of my normal reach. I had reached it first by standing on a chair, but afterward had moved the chair to the embalming table, to aid in climbing onto it when I filled the gravity reservoir, near the ceiling. The swivel chair had been too heavy, you see, for me to lift on to the table.

"It seemed to me that the legs I had seen go past the window must be those of a janitor or of the diener; so, rather than waste time by carrying a chair across the room to turn out the light, I climbed on the edge of a stall in the vault, and twisted the light bulb. Even now, I do not remember that I had taken off my rubber gloves, but I must have done so, obviously. It was the slip that the man with a sense of guilt seems bound to make.

"I quickly locked the padlock, gathered up the clothes, and cautiously ascended the stairs. I put the clothes in a case that happened to be in my office. The legs I had seen apparently had not been those of the janitor or of the diener, but, expecting that either or both might come early, I wanted to take no chances. So I left by the back way, carrying the suitcase. I saw nobody on my way to my own house. It was about dawn then, but cloudy. I am not sure of the hour. I slept for some time, and then prepared for a conference with Senator Tolland in the latter part of the morning. That afternoon, I washed and cleaned the clothing myself, and ironed the linen next day."

Such was the significant part of Dr. Alling's testimony, covering phases of the murder about which I have so far been able to give only surmises. His alibi was based upon the fact, attested by the autopsy, that the knife thrust had been the cause of death, and upon the inference that Mike's reaction, while we were at his bedside, substantiated the kymograph's testimony of the exact time of death. Biddy's testimony and mine checked with his, on the matter of his whereabouts at the time when the wound was supposedly inflicted.

The next significant thing in the testimony was the final revelation of Charlie's reason for not wanting to speak about his whereabouts, that night, to anyone except the grand jurors. Jap Ross, when questioned about the faculty meeting, also was formally asked about his conduct for the next few hours, and reluctantly admitted that he had got drunk on applejack with Charlie and Mickey Rehan. It seemed to Jap the only thing to do, after having disgraced himself, according to his own code, by giving testimony that resulted in the expulsion of a fellow student. Therefore he had wheedled a couple of quarts of applejack from Charlie, at a price which made it seem imperative that Charlie help to drink it. They had sat down to it about half past ten, and the two students had put Charlie to bed, very drunk, at three in the morning. His alarm clock, always set for tomorrow immediately after it rang for today, had saved him from oversleeping, and he had been on hand, shaky but almost sober, to seal the vault in the presence of Dr. Kent. However, as he had been discharged once before for drinking with students, he had not wanted to give his alibi to anyone connected officially with the school.

Daisy was called in to testify to the phone calls which had apprised Dr. Wyck of Baker's death, and other minor testimony was given which, at the end of the morning's session, seemed to have established the facts beyond question that Dr. Wyck actually had intended to commit suicide, that he had set up the apparatus and notified Dr. Alling, and that the latter had embalmed the body in the fashion which he described. Both Prendergast and his uncle substantiated Alling's story about events just after the faculty meeting. The only seemingly moot points left were the question whether Wyck had actually called on Alling at about midnight, and, of course, the mystery about who had actually inflicted the knife wound. We then recessed for a noon meal.

Ted Gideon was called in the early part of the afternoon session, and resolutely refused to say anything at all, except that he had been camping in the woods north of town, and that an old doctor had sometimes given him money to drive him out to Alton Center. He would answer no questions about the crucial night, insisting that they might tend to incriminate him. Alling was recalled and asked whether he had noticed the car mentioned by Biddy, parked in front of the medical school building either when he passed it, walking to the Connells' just before one o'clock, or afterward, when he returned from the hospital at some time after two. He denied that he had seen a car at either time, but was peculiarly insistent upon repeating, in each of his answers, a phrase descriptive of the radiator ornament—a leaping dog. The third time he did this, Coroner Kent interrupted the normal course of the proceedings by again suggesting to the county prosecutor that he, Dr. Kent, be relieved of his official part in the inquiry and subjected to questioning as to his own alibi. Again the offer was declined.

And that was about the state of the evidence when the hearing ended, at half past three in the afternoon. The coroner and the prosecutor then consulted together for half an hour, while all the witnesses continued to cool their heels in various classrooms and in the library. Finally the charge was agreed upon, and read to the third coroner's jury to be impaneled in the Wyck case.

I shall not quote the coroner's charge to the jury, which consists of several pages, minutely analyzing Dr. Alling's alibi and making certain recommendations in the light of the deductions to be drawn from this analysis. As formerly, Dr. Kent's recommendations were acceptable to the jury, and were revealed to us shortly in the findings.

It was after five o'clock when the jury finished its deliberations, and we were summoned to hear the result. At this time, of course, I was totally unaware of the testimony of all except myself. I had no inkling of what Dr. Alling had told the coroner or the prosecutor. For seven hours, after my own testimony was given, I had been waiting, waiting, expecting to be called back at any moment for a session of cross-questioning that ought at least to give me some hint of the nature of the frame-up which I had such good reasons for anticipating. From time to time my agitation had slumped into a numb kind of lethargy. Betweenwhiles, the delay had alternately seemed a cause for greater hope and greater fear. Now, standing in the group of material witnesses in the big room, where all eyes were fixed on the jury foreman, I hardly knew what to prepare for.

We all listened tensely as the foreman read the usual preamble, with a section repeating and reaffirming the acceptance of the original post-mortem examination findings. He then paused and cleared his throat, continuing:

"We approve and accept the coroner's recommendation that a bill of indictment be drawn up and presented to a grand jury of Alton County, accusing Manfred Alling of Altonville, Maine, of causing the death of the said Gideon Wyck by piercing the skin of the neck and severing the spinal cord with a sharp instrument. In support of this recommendation we present the accompanying analysis made by Coroner Kent of the testimony of the said Manfred Alling."

The words of this announcement seemed curiously disappointing, and left my own sensations about as they had been before. I had taken it for granted that Dr. Alling would extricate himself by some clever maneuver. There was a kind of relief in the discovery that he had not been able to do so; but it was a relief balanced, for the time being, by a further uncertainty. The speaker was not done with his announcement, and I had yet to find out whether there would still be a charge against me as accessory.

After a bit of fumbling, the foreman produced and read the coroner's analysis of Dr. Alling's testimony—a document which seemed to show by a process of impeccable logic that no positive evidence had been adduced to prove that the kymograph and Dr. Alling's watch had been in synchronism in fact. The kymograph record—a cylinder of smoked paper—had allegedly been signed just before it was started, by Dr. Wyck himself, with a notation agreeing with that in the dead man's letter. The coroner argued, however, that this signature was a forgery. I have since seen it, and it certainly does not agree with Wyck's normal signature, or with the one appended to the letter that very night; but it should be remembered that signing one's name on an upright cylinder, with a metal implement rather than a pen, and on a surface which would be smooched by a touch of any part of the signer's hand, would logically produce a distorted signature anyway.

Be that as it may, the coroner's charge to the jury argued that what really had happened was that Alling had impulsively inflicted the neck wound to make sure that Wyck would really be out of the way, and then had hurried to the Connells' for the specific purpose of establishing an alibi. The letter left by Wyck, admittedly genuine, had suggested to Dr. Alling that all he need do was to induce some kind of violent reaction in Connell, perhaps with the aid of a drug, and then forge a new kymograph record in such a manner that it would seem to have fluctuated violently at the same time as the seizure of supposed madness in Connell.

As I heard this opinion, several objections quickly arose in my mind. If Alling had wanted a witness, why had he deliberately sent Biddy away? Had he taken the chance that I might be upstairs, or might come in just in time? As I wondered about this, it occurred to me that he might have sent Biddy away in order to have an opportunity to administer the alleged drug that had caused the reaction. But again that seemed unnecessary, for a doctor would not have to make excuses for giving a patient something that would be assumed to be medicine. Moreover, there was nothing temporary or fortuitous about Mike's ultimate madness.

The foreman was fumbling with another paper. It proved to be a deposition signed by ten doctors on the hospital staff, all unanimously agreeing that "—there is no basis whatever, either in the history of medicine or in that of psychological hypotheses, for supposing that the death of one person might produce a maniacal seizure in another, in a remote place, under any circumstances, general or special."

The jury's findings then concluded with the recommendation that I, David Saunders, be held as a material witness, or as an accomplice before or after the fact, or both, at the grand jury's discretion, on the specific assumption that I had deliberately aided Manfred Alling in the establishment of his alibi. Thus things remained about where they had been for me, midway between extreme danger and freedom.

But I was not fated to continue much longer in this state of uncertainty. The announcement, made before all witnesses in the main lecture hall, was greeted by a profound and painful silence, into which the voice of the county prosecutor broke harshly.

"This report has been read to all of you," he said, "for the purpose of discovering whether in the opinion of any witness it fails to concur with his own knowledge of the facts from which the findings are adduced."

I started, as I heard from the back of the room the voice of Daisy Towers, saying, "I, for one, have reason to believe that the findings are grossly in error. I have vital evidence that has been entirely ignored."

"Why did you not give it?" the prosecutor asked.

"I was questioned only about certain telephone calls, sir, concerned with a part of the hearing that had no connection with what I refer to. Would you like to have my evidence now?"

The prosecutor looked pointedly at Coroner Kent, who said, "I consider the findings adequate for an indictment. I suggest that any further evidence be taken in a private hearing, or before the grand jury itself."

"I beg your pardon," Daisy said, "but my evidence is visual in part, and is concerned with appurtenances of this building. Moreover, I have personal reasons for refusing to display it at a private hearing. I insist that I be given the protection afforded by numerous witnesses."

With an inquiring look toward Kent, and then at the foreman, who nodded, the prosecutor made his decision:

"With all deference to your prerogative, Dr. Kent, I recommend that the hearing be reopened. If you object, I can hold an additional hearing on my own authority, commencing at once."

"That is quite unnecessary," Dr. Kent said coldly. "The hearing is reopened. Miss Towers, you may give your testimony before all these witnesses, if you so desire."

"I must give it in another part of the building, and in a rather cramped setting," she explained. "I would rather choose six or eight whom I think I can trust to be intelligent and to have accurate memories."

The prosecutor nodded. She pointed quickly to several of the witnesses. I was not included in her choice; but, as an apparent afterthought, she said, "I think it would be well to have the accused also present, in case any questions need to be answered on the spot."

The group filed up the stairs behind her, and stopped opposite the door of Dr. Wyck's office. Dramatically she threw it open. A scream escaped from the throat of Marjorie Wyck, standing next to me, as we saw, slouched down limply on the desk, the figure of a man who seemed to be her father. I realized at second glance that it must be a dummy. The fact that the head was cushioned on one arm, with the face averted, made it however an excellent illusion.

Before anyone had a chance to recover from the first shock of astonishment, Daisy jumped into the room, picked up a scalpel from the desk, and walked toward us, holding it at arm's length. "All right, Prendergast," she said in a tone of complete assurance, "show us how you did it."

I glanced quickly at Dick, who wore an expression of what might have been honest amazement.

"Don't bluff," she said, rapping her words out smartly now, "I know why you got your uncle drunk in such a hurry, down at Shoulder Lake, and left him gassing with the manager while you slipped out on the terrace of room 109. I know that you ran over to the garage and got your uncle's car. It was a duplicate of Dr. Kent's which made it unlikely that anyone would recognize you in it, back here in Altonville. And it was a clever yarn you gave the garage man, with a ten-dollar tip. You told him to keep your secret because you had a rather intimate kind of date with a nurse, going off duty at midnight. That was clever. A good guy wouldn't tell on you, in a case like that—or so you thought, didn't you? That was about quarter to one in the morning. You made the run to Altonville in forty minutes. Fast going, Prendergast. Now, what was it that you really wanted? Do you mind telling us?"

The color had left Dick's face, during this rapid monologue. For several tense seconds Daisy waited, and then continued, "You'd rather not say? Well, I rather think it was because your uncle had promised you that there would be a legislative investigation, and you wanted to get those blue books into your hands.

A transcript wouldn't satisfy the legislators. They'd want the original documents. So you were going to blackmail them out of Wyck, by offering to hold up the investigation. You were headed for his house. But, coming up from the south, you could see the light in his office window, which no-one else could see from nearer the building. So you stopped in here, and found Wyck lying just like that, didn't you?"

She turned and pointed at the dummy.

"And the scalpel was here, where he kept it as a letter opener. And something went pop in your head, Prendergast, and the next thing you knew, you'd cut his spinal cord. You'd murdered Gideon Wyck."

The word "murdered" seemed to shock Dick out of his uncertainty.

"I didn't," he cried. "It's a lie! He'd taken poison. The letter said so. He was dead already."

"The letter you read *after* you'd knifed him? The letter that told you what a fool you'd been?" Daisy asked, almost too cruelly, I thought, until I remembered that Prendergast had so far been willing to let someone else pay for his crime.

He had gone hysterical, standing in the center of the accusing circle of witnesses. "He did leave a letter on his desk," he screamed. "Where is it? Who's got it? It proves I'm innocent. He was dead already."

But the kymograph record and the original post-mortem examination both showed that Gideon Wyck had died of a knife wound, inflicted before sufficient poison had been absorbed to cause death.

POSTSCRIPT

Later, when I asked Daisy why she had never told me about her special job of sleuthing for Dr. Alling, down at Shoulder Lake, she kissed me and said, "Because you're much, much too diligent. You'd probably have trailed Prendergast around, or searched his rooms the way you searched Alling's house, and you'd have ended up by scaring him to Europe again."

Remembering the way I had bungled the trip to New York, I could hardly blame her; so I asked, "What made you still suspect Dick, after we knew his alibi, and had his fingerprints?"

"It was a sheer hunch of Alling's," she said, "from the way Prendergast had behaved next morning, when he drove his uncle back for another short conference. Alling lost faith in his own hunch, after he'd checked up the alibi last fall. But he told me about it reminiscently, and I had another try, and succeeded in vamping the garage man."

I don't believe that an Alton County grand jury will find any indictment against Dr. Alling, if they are as chary as usual with true bills on which to waste the state's funds in a probably useless prosecution. If he does come to trial, a suspended sentence is to be expected. Kent, it has turned out, had an ironclad alibi all the while. He had been called down to Augusta immediately after the faculty meeting to attend an important post-mortem on a body so badly decomposed that no further delay, even of a few hours, was permissible.

Ted Gideon has been sent to join Mike at the asylum; and, as for poor Dick Prendergast, he will plead temporary insanity, with as good reason as anyone ever had for that plea. The episode and its results seem really to have made him into a different and more worthy person; his improved record during this school year, and his obvious belief that the impulsive act had not been the true cause of Wyck's death, ought to aid in procuring for him a lenient verdict.

I have now come to the point of having to decide whether or not I should send this ending to my narrative, to join the main part—and it seems best to do so. I was a fool ever to mail the first part at all. But I did mail it, impulsively, in a moment of terror. Its contents by now most cer-

*tainly are known to some readers, as I am informed that its publication
has already been arranged for. Any effort to stop it probably would bring
only added publicity. For better or for worse, the first part of the story is
out, and it is best for the exact nature of the conclusion also to be known.
If it passes for fiction, I shall be pleased indeed.*

DAVID SAUNDERS